Praise for

Ada to Zembla: The Novels of Vladimir Nabokov

'A superbly lucid account of what Nabokov wrote, how he wrote it, and why it matters; Vernon's critical intelligence always illuminates, and is never sidetracked by the forgotten butterfly of revelation. *Ada to Zembla* can be read by the novice and the more experienced Nabokovian with equal amounts of pleasure. Highly recommended.'

– Prof Rhodri Lewis, Princeton University

'I have long hoped for a book like this to appear … A beautiful work of devotion to the great master.'

– Dr Erik Eklund, Northwestern University

'Vernon writes with as much ebullience and linguistic delight as the novelist does … The sheer scope of topics upon which Vernon touches is remarkable. … He envisages Nabokov as a whole corpus in an excitingly readable way that has not hitherto been accomplished.'

– *Decadent Serpent*

'David Vernon has done an especial service for those who want to try Nabokov but fear his "difficulty". Serious yet accessible, discerning yet appreciative, full of genuine zest and relish, Vernon's *Ada to Zembla* represents what writing for the common aesthetic good must be about. This is a sharp-eyed guidebook that invites, entertains, and challenges readers' preconceptions in the most earnest and sympathetic of ways. The good news of Nabokov's work deserves a wider audience. Vernon is the gifted evangelist to spread that gospel.'

– Ryan Asmussen, University of Illinois

Praise for

Beethoven: The String Quartets

'Authoritative … brings the music vividly to life with colourful scenarios and often amusing turns of phrase … a thoroughly accessible, enlightening, and entertaining guide to these pinnacles of the repertoire … insights that will enhance readers' understanding and enjoyment when listening to, or participating in, their performance.'

– *The Strad*

'Wonderful … driven by deep love and an infectious sense of wonder … a different kind of Beethoven book.'

– *Strings*

'An extraordinary and exciting book.'

– John Simpson, BBC News

'Love for this music shines through on every page – if you or someone you know is a Beethoven fan, this is the book for them.'

– Dr Leah Broad, author of *Quartet: How Four Women Changed the Musical World*

'This is a lively, intelligent, and, above all, *fun* introduction to some of the greatest music ever written, and I very much hope it lures readers into listening to that music who might otherwise have been deterred by its monumental reputation.'

– MusicWeb International

'A fantastic book … easy to read and follow, yet deep enough for experienced music lovers. … Each quartet receives its own chapter, and each starts with a short journey in time to reveal the historical and cultural background of the piece. The music itself is analysed movement by movement, but these are not technical descriptions with musical jargon. Like a guide, rather, these are insightful narrations, often very funny and always properly connecting to the music.'

– *Popular Beethoven*

'Erudite without being pretentious, learned without being dustily academic, philosophical without being obfuscatory, David Vernon's wonderful book *Beethoven: The String Quartets* whirls the reader through Beethoven's sixteen string quartets, locating them in every possible context – social, political, religious, historical, contemporary – as well as rigorously exploring their relationship to the rest of Beethoven's oeuvre. Vernon comes across as a polymath, an intellectual, and a man of culture. That he also demonstrates wit, warmth, and humanity is the icing on the cake. *Beethoven: The String Quartets* is the kind of book that sets the gold standard for non-fiction.'

– Neil Fulwood

Praise for

Beauty and Sadness: Mahler's 11 Symphonies

'A beautiful and important book.'

– Marina Mahler

'Highly recommended.'

– Société Gustav Mahler France

'A book that sends you back to listen again to music you thought you knew, with fresh insight and understanding.'

– Tim Ashley, *Guardian*

'Masterfully paced, just the right balance of continuous narrative and individual essays, all framed in beautiful writing. Can't recommend it highly enough!'

– Brian McCreath, WCRB Classical Radio Boston

'One does not expect a book on music to be this philosophically erudite. [The] use of language is masterful … It's an enormous achievement. An essential book.'

– Jeffrey A. Tucker

'This is an important contribution to the Mahler bibliography. David Vernon has written a perceptive, insightful, and thought-provoking book. Mahler devotees will find much in its pages to enhance their understanding of these ever-fascinating works in which we can always find something new to excite us … Vernon has a deep knowledge of the symphonies – and a great enthusiasm for them. His descriptions of the works are detailed and, clearly, the product of extensive and careful listening – as well as wide reading around his subject. He can bring the music to life through vivid and enthusiastic turns of phrase.'

– MusicWeb International

Praise for

Sun Forest Lake: The Symphonies
& Tone Poems of Jean Sibelius

'[This] book helps everyone, no matter how previously informed, to find their own way into Sibelius's extraordinary world.'

– Sakari Oramo, chief conductor, BBC Symphony Orchestra

'Carefully considered, cogently argued, and elegantly written, this is a study of Finland's great composer which is provocative at times but which presents us with an enlightening and stimulating portrait of the man and his music.'

– MusicWeb International

'Such a pleasure to revisit greater and lesser Sibelius to [this] wise accompaniment … Hans Keller (my old boss at Radio 3) used to argue for wordless musical analysis, but this traditional descriptive approach is the most illuminating for the ordinary listener.'

– John Greening

'David Vernon's range of knowledge is impressive, extending way beyond narrow old-fashioned frames of reference, and he's particularly good at making apposite comparisons right across the arts … His style is refreshing: witty and playful one moment, conveying deepest admiration the next. But what comes over most of all – all too rare in modern books on classical music – is love. If you are familiar with Sibelius, this book will make you want to seek out all the pieces you don't know. If you don't know him, then prepare for an adventure, with *Sun, Forest, Lake* as your enthralling guide and delightful companion.'

– Stephen Johnson, author of *How Shostakovich Changed My Mind* and *The Eighth: Mahler and the World in 1910*

Exquisite Nothingness

The Novels of Yukio Mishima

David Vernon

Endellion Press

Endellion Press

To

Steven Lally

– In friendship, love and admiration

Prince Hal: I do; I will.

Henry IV, Part 1, II.iv.468

Bientôt nous plongerons dans les froides ténèbres;
Adieu, vive clarté de nos étés trop courts!

Baudelaire, 'Chant d'automne' from *Les Fleurs du mal*

Contents

PART ONE: THE EARLY NOVELS

PART TWO: THE MIDDLE WORKS

PART THREE: THE FINAL TETRALOGY

Introduction

THE DARK BUTTERFLY

Yukio Mishima, in his forty-five years on the planet, wrote over thirty novels and fifty plays, almost two hundred short stories, one screenplay, and one libretto – along with innumerable lectures, essays, articles, diaries, travelogues, lyrics, poems, and haiku.[1] It was a quantity of literary material which a small army of authors might have rivalled, and its exceptional quality led to his nomination five times for the Nobel Prize.[2] But this was no intellectual recluse, hidden away in a garret or ivory tower. He also acted, modelled, occasionally sang, played several martial arts to a high standard, and founded a civilian militia. Sexually diverse, he visited gay bars, briefly considered marriage to the woman who would become the country's empress consort, and eventually wed the daughter of the man who designed the carpets for the Imperial Palace, with whom he had two children. He was an active member of the Flying Saucer Research Association

---

1   Published by Shinchōsha between 2000 and 2006, Mishima's complete works require over forty large volumes.

2   In 1963, 1964, 1965, 1967, and 1968. His compatriot and friend Yasunari Kawabata (1899–1972) won in 1968.

of Japan and loved science fiction as much as he loved Greek myth and German philosophy – along with manga, Godzilla, and American animation; at one point he visited Disneyland, in a life of frequent global travel.

And yet for all this extraordinary life, Yukio Mishima is more usually remembered today for his bizarre, almost farcical death, when he attempted a political coup before performing ritual suicide.

We should – perhaps – be wary of moralizing Mishima's death, especially when we come from cultures foreign to his own. Disapproval is easy; understanding is hard. However odd, even darkly comical, Mishima's exit, it sought to match the aesthetic ideals of the traditions he revered. Misguided Mishima might have been, not least in mythologizing Japan's heroic national history and in overestimating the public's appetite for such a skew-whiff perspective – yet he was not insane. He was disciplined, self-controlled, performing an act of artistic rebellion and sociopolitical defiance, something akin to a sacrificial fertility rite, to renew what he saw as a retreating, deteriorating, materialistic Japan. He had grasped the wretched reality of finite existence and, like Socrates with his hemlock, made it his own, shaping the course and conclusion of his own life (while radically determining much of its future interpretation).

But this is to endorse Mishima's own, self-directed, narrative. The reality was rather more complex. Whatever his passion for the past, Mishima nonetheless embodied modernity, and whatever his disapproval of Japan's contemporary westernization, few Asian writers assimilated Western ideas, styles, and techniques quite like he did. He greedily adopted and effortlessly absorbed the lessons of many of the literary architects of the modern world: Baudelaire and Wilde, Nietzsche and Thomas Mann. In addition, as much as he romanticized them, most samurai of earlier centuries would have found his life, work, and death not only absurd but outlandish, even offensive, to their culture of social order, obligation, and communal being, the group above the individual. Suicide was acclaimed, in some circumstances, as a duty but not as an act of self-expression or self-promotion. Aesthetic principles, not self-glamorization, were to attend and complete the requirements of feudal organization.

Over half a century since Mishima's premeditated, stage-managed, and alarming end on 25 November 1970, his suicide still casts a cloud over the immense body of work he created, and remains the only thing many people know about him. This book hopes to change that. Although we will not ignore the peculiar circumstances of his death, or many of the less savoury aspects of his personality, behaviour, and political outlook, these pages will predominantly aim to move out of the shadow of his ostentatious demise and into the (enthralling and mysterious) light of his literary creations. On occasion, of course, the art, death, and politics will crucially meet, but we need to be cautious of such encounters, wary of the flamboyant red herrings that can leap up in the way of literary interpretation, while also allowing them sufficient space to mix, mingle, and mutually enlighten.

Across the passage of his years, Mishima was a sensationalist, a militarist, a self-publicist, a contrarian, a charlatan, a joker, a poser, a paradox, and a hypocrite. But he was also a literary genius – not only one of the Japanese giants of the twentieth century, a figure to rank alongside Natsume Sōseki, Jun'ichirō Tanizaki, Yasunari Kawabata, Yūko Tsushima, Setsuko Tsumura, Kōbō Abe, Michiko Yamamoto, Shūsaku Endō, Kenzaburō Ōe, Mieko Kanai, and Yōko Ogawa, but one of the finest writers of any location or generation.

The gravity and intensity of Mishima's prose astounds. The barbaric opulence of his sumptuous vocabulary, especially in his early work, explores the farthest reaches and depths of the dictionary, creating pleasure and labour for his translators; his troubling aphorisms, exquisite imagery, and dissolute metaphors linger in the imagination for hours, days, weeks, and beyond. Yet Mishima also considered himself heir to a long practice of delicate beauty and meticulous magnificence in Japanese language and literature, and his scrupulous, duteous writing reflects his self-image as beneficiary, successor, and advocate of this tradition. His language can be sensuous, then detached, ice cool or intensely physical. His writing exhibits the minutest attention both to detail and to narratives that transcend time and space, souls apparently migrating across worlds through his pages. Mishima's disconcerting plots, curious characters, rupture of taboos, and unsettling fusion of themes challenge our complacent comfort in routine or security in familiarity, as does his elegant synthesis of Japanese literary customs with external innovations.

Within these mechanics, Mishima's elegance, style, and devastating emotional power work together with his remarkable grasp of time and place and toward some miraculous constructions. In his work he is both a realist, depicting life with frankness and sincerity, as well as a myth maker, able to romanticize past, present, and, on occasion, future, with a disarming charm and persuasiveness. Fluently recreating worlds for us, Mishima can take us back to the fabled lost eras his political ideologies failed to recapture as well as plunge us straight into the cut, thrust, and thrill of modernity. Part of the excitement of his writing is the way familiar worlds become strange, alien ones recognizable – then remarkable, proverbial, unforgettable.

Whether using his literary telescope or his literary microscope, Mishima is alert to the vast tragedy of history – especially Japanese history in the twentieth century – even if he is, on occasion, obstinately oblivious to some of history's less genial nuances or connections. As both a fierce advocate for and severe critic against his country, Mishima was bound to find inconsistency in his threefold role as narrator, supporter, and censor of modern Japan, though in his art this should be seen as a strength where elsewhere it might be deemed a disadvantage. An avid chronicler of catastrophe and misfortune, whether personal or political, public or private, Mishima is almost always simultaneously aware of life's comedy, farce, and caprice. He shows us the quiver and magic, plus the desolation and despair, that lie welded together, shaping our existence. Within his literary inventions, both the ordinary and the unusual can be exotic, and while Mishima sometimes contests an absolute Joycean celebration of the unremarkable, he nearly always shares his older Irish colleague's observance of guarded delight in life and language, knowing that the very act of writing is a positive, triumphant one. Even in his bleaker moments, Mishima retains an ability to convince and transform, to generate significant truths from mere gestures, exquisite possibilities from nothingness, courage from chaos.

As with so many of the colossi of literary history – Aeschylus, Dante, Shakespeare, Milton, Ibsen, Dostoyevsky, Dickinson, Zola, Beckett, Lispector, Achebe, Solzhenitsyn, Morrison, Pinter, Bolaño – the tensions and discoveries in Mishima are frequently to be found in otherness: in overwhelming strangeness, in an unutterable individuality, that always remains just beyond our grasp. Mishima's art – like Goethe's or Proust's – is a locked box in an uncharted realm which we forever want to travel to and break open, even as we know that the greater part of the mystery and magic lies in that very lock itself, in the challenge it represents.

In his novels and stories Mishima performs the delicate trick of making obscurity, ambiguity, and inscrutability tangible and authentic through his consistent verbal fluency, profound gifts of articulation, and an indefatigable sense of life's contrapuntal oddity. He shares these qualities with Yasunari Kawabata and Kenzaburō Ōe, Japan's two recipients of the Nobel Prize to date, along with elements of their intensity and colour. But Mishima's humanity also seems to reside in a special and dangerously unique realm, deep within his ruthlessness, his frequent brutality and sadism, his elaborate feeling for the anomalous burdens that gather next to the delicate splendours of our lives. Not many combine sex, death, beauty, and suffering quite like he does.

Mishima's novels present diverse experiences: there is the challenging realism of his early works and the intriguing miscellany of his middle period before the far-reaching idealism of his closing quartet, *The Sea of Fertility* (1969–71). But, coming as they do from the same pen, all his works share a family heritage, a collective culture: they enjoy gene enjoyment. For all the variety, for all Mishima's evolution and range as a writer, there always seems a glistening golden thread of connection, of an intricate personality exploring love, loss, and identity during a lifelong pilgrimage of discovery.

Aside from some minor excursions abroad, all his novels are set in Japan, and as we move around the island nation, from Kyoto to Tokyo, from its cities to its shores, investigating its complexity and multiplicity, its miracles and failures, we are struck by both its tawdriness and its splendour. The books explore the country as Mishima saw it – often blinkered, often wearing pink-painted spectacles for rosy retrospection, but more often than not staring hard and long, fearless, unflinching.

&

Few writers, and certainly among those from Japan, have generated as much controversy and bitter division as Mishima – in part due to the colourful exhibitionism of his death, in part due to the colourful exhibitionism of his writing. For many in Japan, he is an embarrassment, an awkward family secret, an artificial zombie; for many outside Japan, he is an illness to be recuperated from or a phase to be outgrown. Such intellectual snobbery – for the quality and profundity of Mishima's writing must make it so – is comprehensible, perhaps reasonable, given the provocative, even antagonistic nature of so much of his work, both in fiction and non-fiction.[3] But it is also evidence of insecurity, of fear, of dread at the hard truths Mishima reveals and the uneasy realities he refused to hide – whether about Japan and the Japanese, or humanity in general.

---

3   Of which the neoclassical play entitled *My Friend Hitler* (1968) is only the most barefaced example. It is a more complex and subtle work than its title indicates, exhibited not least through the way it has invited both fascist and anti-fascist interpretations, though its overt romanticization of youthful militaristic ferocity is deeply problematic. For himself, in his article on *Madame de Sade* and *My Friend Hitler*, Mishima stated that though he thought Hitler a political genius, the German Führer was no hero: 'Hitler was a dark figure as the twentieth century was a dark century' (which hardly seems to go far enough).

Like Camus or Hemingway, Mishima can all too often be regarded as merely a young person's writer, feeding the frenzy of adolescent angst and anxiety. Like Plath he is reproached for self-pity and self-indulgence, for jarring poetic effects and an extravagant preoccupation with his own identity. And like Wilde, he is accused of deplorable decadence and cerebral frippery: a shallow, tormented aesthete with nothing to declare but his genius along with his alienation from plebian society. There is an eloquence but emptiness to such charges; they deliberately conceal the audacity, depth, and complexity of these artists' achievements. And no less so than with Mishima. The fixation and magnitude of so many critics' and intellectuals' disgust at Mishima may well expose uncertainty or alarm, but it certainly divulges that this writer, that artificial zombie, has declined to die, and remains an unignorable force in modern literature.

Part of that force, whether positive or negative, lies in his odd relationship to both his homeland and the wider world. For many Westerners, Mishima is the embodiment of Japan; for many Japanese he is the ultimate outsider, almost a traitor, both for embracing Western literary styles and techniques, and for his dangerous, often romanticized and embellished vision of a traditional Japan, one that borders on a naive and grievous orientalism. Add to this the aggressive, performative nature of his death, with its sense of anarchic, archaic angst, and it is clear why Mishima makes so many people uncomfortable.

But the disgust and discomfort engendered by Mishima's work is not a result of mere literary sensationalism. Mishima explores the complex relationship between fantasy and reality, examining the fissures and continuities between childish adolescent spheres and harder adult ones – scrutinizing ideas, emotions, and cultural forces that can seem utopian in their intensity, entirely unpragmatic, and therefore dangerous, in their vivid flourish of images and redemptive possibilities. Mishima is the ultimate mythical realist, reflecting on and responding to the world in ways that are both gladdening and upsetting.

Mishima's sexual predilections and erotic masks, together with his often unpalatable political stances – not least his veneration of the military and deification of the emperor system – have sometimes tended to obscure or overwhelm more rigorous analytical assessments of his work, critics finding it tempting to examine Mishima with only a limited biographical lens. That said, Mishima's sexuality and politics are not irrelevant or inconsequential in considering his work (though nor is either a divine key, a straightforward solution to the many psychological and cultural problems his fiction generates). They form and inform part of the dense composite nexus of his art, as does the crucial catastrophe Mishima came into contact with, both hazily and unambiguously, in his youth: the Second World War.

Just as a comprehensive appraisal of Shakespeare must include the role of the Reformation, or a thorough examination of Wordsworth cannot ignore the impact of the French Revolution, so World War II is a significant spectre haunting Mishima's life and work. In many ways, the war sits at both the literal and symbolic centre of his existence, as both artist and human being, not only as a shattering series of events for a young man to experience, whether directly or indirectly, but also as a lingering presence, throwing a long and often hostile shadow over his career as a writer.

Mishima was judged unfit for service aged twenty in 1945, and his 'missing out' on direct military action doubtless helped foster this curious fixation on the war, militarism, and his body image, creating a complex complex of yearning and anxiety, psychological scars and survivor's guilt. This was then likely amplified by the American occupation: a Freudian father figure on whom Mishima, simultaneously attracted to and revolted by American culture, could project both his desires and revulsions, and which must be extinguished in order to facilitate Oedipal congress with a Mother Japan. The later development of Mishima's emperor worship and obsessive promotion of Japanese traditions would seem a natural, if deferred, outcome of such a mindset, not least when combined with his increasing sense of frustrated romanticism.

In Mishima's work, the ghost of WWII initially occurs as a forbidding post-war wasteland filled with symbolically apathetic and miserable lost souls whose desolation is often circumvented by gaudy allegory and enigma. But in his later work – especially in the *Sea of Fertility* quartet – the war functions as a vast historical-cultural framework within which to develop the creation of romantic heroes and a grander vision of human existence that is both potentially redemptive and merely another manifestation of isolated emptiness. For Mishima, the war was a black hole, a creative and a destructive force, the dark centre of the century, and his sustained engagement with it, however oblique, is a fundamental feature of his art.

Mishima's achievement as a writer lies neither in any uncomplicated glorification of a closed, elitist system, nor in a valiant celebration of diverse sexuality: his work, stimulated by an ironic friction, is far more ambiguous and ambivalent than such sweeping simplifications will allow. Rather, it is in the relentless, alarming collision between Mishima's outsiders – who can be romantic protagonists or dangerous weirdos – and the complacent, self-righteous, conventional, and obedient society in which they find themselves.

His work's dynamic tension resides in his bold exploration of the way psyches, and societies, can be shattered through exclusion and elimination, prohibition and marginalization – whether internally or externally generated. Few societies have placed such an emphasis on normalcy and conformity as Japan, but it is very far from being unique in this regard. Mishima's outsiders are the heir to, continuation of, and negotiation with – from the Western tradition – Dionysus, Medea, Hamlet, Othello, Iago, Shylock, Timon, Caliban, Milton's Satan, Heathcliff, Emma Bovary, Hedda Gabler, Étienne Lantier, Raskolnikov, Roquentin, Meursault, Josef K., Gregor Samsa, Winston Smith, and Holden Caulfield in their respective struggles with Denmark, Big Brother, being an insect, and being an adolescent. Like his literary predecessors, Mishima deliberates how outsiders are exiles, recluses, outcasts, prisoners, freaks, rebels, scapegoats, dupes, oppressed and oppressor, villain and victim, as well as how they can, and perhaps more usually do, exist deep within their own communities, often moving between inside and outside, travelling from acceptance to ostracism, approval to isolation, and vice versa. Mishima's outsiders can be monstrous or humane, threatening or amusing, their creator simultaneously commending ideologies of omission and remonstrating against how outsiders are treated. But what they tend to share is their fluidity and ambiguity, traversing porous boundaries.

In the fiction which accommodates these figures, Mishima's personal biography and national history mix, merge, and extend the miscellaneous literary influences which he admired so much. These include, but are not limited to, myth, romanticism, naturalism, and realism from Europe, along with elements of the confessional first-person fiction to be found both there and in the literary traditions of his own culture. In so doing, Mishima creates his own immense depth and range, taking what appealed to him, assimilating it, and making it his own, so that although there is a definite and deliberate realism to most of his work, many of his motifs, images, metaphors, characters, and plots carry a mythopoeic quality to them, which is fantastical, at times even grotesque or incongruous. The two work together, the oddity a contrast to the realism of the rest of the recreated world.

In part this is a reaction to the dull uniformity of the bleak materialist, populist culture Mishima despised (however much he was also a part of it). Mishima's contemporary Kōbō Abe used the trance-like metaphor of a man's imprisonment in his masterpiece *The Woman in the Dunes* (1962) to emphasize and evaluate the tedium of reality, exploring the claustrophobic and limiting nature of all existence, in a work with ghostly echoes of Camus's equally universal parable *L'Étranger* (1942).[4] Mishima, however, does not merely shrug at the general futility of life: rather, he uses a range of outlandish, misshapen characters and situations to criticize Japan's specific modern wilderness, its sense of lost identity, mislaid souls, absent traditions.

---

4   Mingling the surreal and the absurd, Kōbō Abe (1924–1993) explores with an uncanny, unsettling acuity the nightmares at the heart of modern life – especially the alienation of urban existence (many of his works now seem eerie, prophetic metaphors for our online lives, too, with their hostility, estrangement, and isolation). Along with *The Woman in the Dunes*, *The Face of Another* (1964), *The Ruined Map* (1967), *The Box Man* (1973) – about a man who lives in a cardboard box – and *Secret Rendezvous* (1977) are all excellent exhibitions of Abe's mysterious oddity. So, too, are his hallucinatory SF classic *The Ark Sakura* (1984) and his wonderfully strange blend of post-apocalyptic fiction with a metaphysical detective story, *Inter Ice Age 4* (1959), with its deft, far-sighted probing of genetics, AI, and climate change.

What is more, Mishima goes further than most of his contemporaries by offering a redemptive possibility and emancipating perspective that is often overlooked in the generally unremitting clamour to comment on his politics or self-annihilation. Even in the close of the fourth and final book of *The Sea of Fertility*, *The Decay of the Angel*, when the promises of reincarnation are disclosed to be false, the desolation of this revelation does not entirely negate the hope which preceded it, generated by the tetralogy's structural transmigratory optimism – not to mention the wider sense of positivity all literary creation spawns. In *The Sea of Fertility*, the reincarnation motif acts akin to magical realism in Latin American (and other) fiction: to express emotion and dissect reality, rather than evoke true facts or the supernatural.

Mishima's fiction, composed by an unsatisfied, thwarted romantic, continually offers sites of escape, alternative visions which can transcend dour reality, breaching social and literary boundaries in the process. Outsiders possessing radical or insurgent agendas are one aspect of this end, as they seek to travel from the liminal spaces of the margins toward the centre, where they aim to confront and overturn accepted realities. Such revolutionaries habitually wear the cloak of tradition, literally so in the form of the emperor's robes, confusing our sense of convention, orthodoxy, and progression.

Characters in Mishima can often be terrifying individuals, given to violent and cruel behaviour – eviscerating a kitten in *The Sailor Who Fell from Grace with the Sea*, or committing ecclesiastical arson in *The Temple of the Golden Pavilion* – that go beyond the merely transgressive or unruly. Yet such inclusions are not there simply to colour the narratives, as an appeal to broader, baser, literary instincts. Indeed, much of the tension and interest surrounding Mishima's art lies in the conflict between his active and passive protagonists – violent heroes and solipsistic cynics – and in the complex arbitration between dramatic action and diffident meditation.

Just as with his own seppuku, the ferocious, gory feats of Mishima's novels can be memorable, but they should not blind us to the deeper reflections and brooding possibilities beneath.

As we have seen, Mishima emphasized his dedication to, and inspiration from, a range of literary and cultural traditions. He took in classical Greece, German Romanticism, and fin-de-siècle symbolism as well as the theatrical traditions of both pre-modern Japan and interwar Europe – besides philosophical trends including Buddhism, Nietzsche, and the way of the samurai. Correspondingly, and in a pleasing irony, given that Mishima was an artist who sought to promote a particular sense of 'Japanese-ness', his work, almost uniquely among Japanese writers, has had a widespread and profound global impact.

Film and theatre directors such as Paul Schrader, Ingmar Bergman, Andrzej Wajda, Benoît Jacquot, Kon Ichikawa, and Kinji Fukasaku; opera composers including Hans Werner Henze[5] and Toshirō Mayuzumi;[6] psychoanalysts and cultural critics such as Marguerite Yourcenar, Henry Miller, and Catherine Millot – all have been influenced and inspired by Mishima's work. And even a fractional list of writers of fiction who have directly or indirectly

---

5   *Das verratene Meer*, 'The Betrayed Sea' (1990), a reworking of *The Sailor Who Fell from Grace with the Sea.*

6   *Der Tempelbrand*, 'The Temple Fire' (1976), adapted from *The Temple of the Golden Pavilion.*

continued or reacted against his writing is more impressive still, not only in Japan but across, in particular, contemporary British, American, French, German, Korean, Taiwanese, and Russian literatures, especially those which deliberately and ironically fraternize realism with artificiality, naturalism with surrealism.

His impact and influence on other forms of expression, witnessed in the proliferation of distinctly Mishima-like performative postings on video-sharing sites like YouTube, Twitch, and TikTok, is inherently harder to gauge but seems no less universal, as the imagery and paraphernalia of Mishima's life and work continue to fascinate and permeate popular culture, especially in the spheres of anaerobic exercise and martial arts. The myth of Mishima, inaugurated by the man himself, continues to feed itself, maintaining the global icon and misunderstood character as he is variously claimed, accosted, or hijacked by a peculiar range of wildly different groups, in both popular and intellectual culture, on the left and right, in Japan and far beyond.

As if pre-empting these absorptions and appropriations, in his foremost and most enduring work – the novels which this book explores – Mishima seems both foolishly optimistic and worryingly selective in many of his struggles to overcome both the increasing uniformity of contemporary culture and its rapid and hyper-diverse disintegrations, not least when those struggles involve exciting, dangerously appealing transgressive figures. But his novels, and the defiant expectancy which characterizes them, should not be so easily dismissed as the products of either childish naivete or haughty superiority. Mishima rarely offers an uncomplicated, undemanding vision: he is more interested in the dynamic, illogical, and uncertain complexity which pervades not only Japanese but all human life.

Although Mishima is as much a product of his specific time and place as any artist, his multifaceted work transcends history and soars into the sphere of allegory and archetype. In a perfect Mishimian paradox – resembling his erotic suicides, soldier-poets, or pyromaniac priests – the strength and depth of his exploration of the contemporary experience ironically gives it a universal reach. Mishima is both architect and saboteur of the modern world, and his creative project has an in-built vindictive, destructive, and defeatist element, a desire to self-punish and submit oneself to fate. In part this is because of its intensity, in part because of its complex juxtaposition of cultural forces, but mainly because of its obsessive concern with loss itself – loss of identity, sensuality, spirituality, myth, culture, art, difference.

Consider the title of Mishima's last masterpiece, his four-volume epic that voyages across the twentieth century: *The Sea of Fertility*. It is a beautiful image – sumptuous, evocative, enigmatic. Yet the title is also an ironic paradox, since the sea to which it refers is a lunar one and therefore barren, sterile, infertile. As such, the title perhaps serves as a neat summary of this exceptional writer, a convenient sketch of the way he plays with our expectations while deepening his own sense of mystery and loss, his elusive echoes and sinister shadows.

For all the abandonment, betrayal, and alienation in Mishima, however, there is also a defiance, a desire to not only confront and condemn the world but attempt to offer something in its place, something miraculous beyond the sardonic asylum of materialism or lazy acceptance of conformity. He achieves this through his extraordinary language, which – perhaps even to those for whom he is an unsympathetic figure – is virtuosic, impeccable, sublime. He is a master of not only the Japanese language but language itself, taking the prison house of words and making them a dynamic palace, a challenging ritual, a precarious weapon and life-giving force.

Mishima is the prince of distorted modernity, his art a furious amalgam of genuine paradox, disturbing ambiguities, challenging conundrums, and unpalatable truths. Part of the difficulty in reading (and writing about) his work is distinguishing these features and not mistaking one for the other. Mishima preached the decadent, incongruous creed that beauty is at its most intense at the very moment of its own eradication, and that beauty is always threatened by its own impossible perfection. By reading and rereading his work, we maintain this dangerous conviction, trembling in the exquisite tension between creation and destruction, life and death.

We have been warned to stay away, but we keep returning to Mishima. We revisit *Confessions of a Mask* or *Thirst for Love*, *The Sound of Waves* or *After the Banquet*, *Spring Snow* or *Runaway Horses*, losing ourselves to the dark attraction of his work and finding ourselves again in the exhilarating richness of his vision. And rightly so, for Mishima's art is an inexhaustible realm of temptation, confusion, and imagination, awash with complex dilemmas and intricate, often outrageous, charisma – a profusion of sun and steel, forbidden colours and golden temples.

The Four Rivers

A LIFE OF YUKIO MISHIMA

Tokyo. 14 January 1925. At nine o'clock in the evening, a new human being, weighing just two and a half kilos, entered the world. He was named Kimitake Hiraoka, after a family benefactor – but the world would know him as Yukio Mishima.

His mother, Shizue Hashi, was the daughter of an educator, Kenzō, who was born to hereditary military nobility – the samurai – but adopted[7] by Kendō Hashi, a professor of Chinese classical literature, himself the son of a Chinese scholar and calligrapher who had been granted samurai status.

Mishima's father, Azusa Hiraoka, was a government official in the Ministry of Agriculture and Commerce, who came from a family of regional administrators and politicians. A

---

7   Contrary to practices in many other countries, in Japan the adoption of non-consanguineal adults and older children is a centuries-old custom which was developed as a mechanism for families to extend their family name, estate, and ancestry without an awkward or potentially problematic reliance on bloodlines. This tradition endures: today the vast majority of adoptions in Japan are employers adopting adult employees to safeguard their family business.

great-grand-uncle, Yorinori, had been forced to commit ritual disembowelment (seppuku), along with dozens of his vassals, over a political disagreement concerning foreign interference, while another relative, Yoriyasu, a priest, was banished over his addiction to creating an early form of photographic pornography.

On the maternal side, then, links to martial aristocracy, art, and literature; on the paternal, political strife, personal dishonour, and sexual transgression. All the ingredients for Mishima's life and work were there: certainly, it was a family history that would fascinate and profoundly influence the boy Kimitake as he grew into a man.

๙

For Mishima's paternal grandmother, Natsuko, marrying Mishima's grandfather, Sadatarō, was something of a disappointment. She was a child of shogunate elegance, eminence, and power, entrusted to the prosperous, opulent household of Imperial Prince Arisugawa Taruhito. Sadatarō, essentially from peasant stock but a bright young man, had done exceptionally well academically at the Imperial University, publishing an important book on international law that was of great interest and advantage to the Meiji government as it sought to modernize Japan, turning the country from an isolated, feudal society into an industrialized nation state, learning from and integrating foreign legal, political, scientific, and aesthetic ideas.

Sadatarō went on to become governor of Fukushima Prefecture as well as governor general of Karafuto, and his remuneration and status afforded him and his family a vast house in Tokyo with a striking stone gate, ornamental pond, cherry trees, several guest rooms, and detached quarters for the salaried staff. His elite bureaucratic career came to an abrupt end, however, when he became enmeshed in a political dispute and later financial scandal that necessitated his resignation. He was eventually acquitted of any wrongdoing, but the damage was done. In 1919, the family moved to a less impressive, if still sizeable, house, and Natsuko's hitherto buried ire – kept in check by the fat salary checks and distinguished status of her husband's political career – boiled to the surface. It created a bizarre and often monstrous personality, one that would have a profound impact on Mishima's early life (as well as his first great novel, *Confessions of a Mask*, a work which flirts with the messy discrepancies between memoir, fiction, and fabrication).

Over time, Natsuko grew to be insufferably haughty, neurotic, and cantankerous, given to quick irritation and blazing anger, her long-held sense of frustration and disgruntlement with her husband now erupting and multiplying like a contagious disease. In part it was caused by the understandable ignominy of Sadatarō's enforced resignation, but it was also snobbery, plain and simple, Natsuko believing herself to be a princess and of a class superior to her more humdrum husband. There likewise lingered deep insecurity due to her awareness of the periods of poverty and dishonour her own family had experienced: Natsuko's mother was the younger sister of the disgraced erotica-loving priest Yoriyasu. Ironically, she sought solace in Yoriyasu himself, the old deviant by this time living in a small house on an even smaller stipend; now he would be the frequent solitary audience for his niece's tearful remonstrations.

Mishima's father frequently noted what he saw as his own father's superhuman personality for putting up with the wrath and angst of this conceited, temperamental woman. Nonetheless, it should be said that, far from being possessed of herculean patience, Sadatarō himself simply found refuge from his spouse by occupying himself with several failed business enterprises, including Japan's first zinc manufacturing plant, as well as with drink and other women – none of which, of course, improved matters. Indeed the latter activity likely gave his wife gonorrhoea, which, along with sciatic gout, caused her considerable physical pain and only exacerbated her anxiety, hysteria, and furious irritability.

The 'typhoon' (as she was known in the family) that was Mishima's grandmother would sweep through the household, creating constant quarrel and damage, and the detrimental impact of her behaviour and personality on the young boy was considerable, even if he could later use it for literary ends. Along with his two siblings, a younger sister Mitsuko and younger brother Chiyuki, Mishima lived with his parents, his father's parents, and several servants in a rented two-storey house in Yotsuya, a ward now incorporated into the thriving Shinjuku district of central Tokyo. Four of the six maids were devoted to Natsuko, who occupied the entire first floor with her husband, while the other two, along with a houseboy and older domestic retainer, tended to the rest of the family.

In an action which still shocks, Natsuko separated the child Kimitake from his mother only a few weeks after his birth, on the flimsy pretext that raising a baby on the second floor was dangerous. Grandparents often look after their children's offspring, in Japan and elsewhere, then as now. But this was a deed of an altogether different order. He was locked away in his grandmother's private sanatorium, with its suffocating, malodourous air of illness, age, and resentment, where his little cot was dragged next to her imposing bed so she could watch over, cosset, and begin to indoctrinate her infant grandchild. Incense burned constantly, as did tobacco, the fumes accompanied by Natsuko's low groans, which flared up into spasms of anger and pain, and could continue all day long and into the darkness, night after night after night.

Mishima's mother was powerless, a quiet, unassertive woman happiest when sitting silently with a book; his father and grandfather were unwilling and unable to prevent Natsuko's extraordinary conduct, weary and fearful of the wrath they would incur should they try to intervene. So Mishima remained incarcerated in his grandmother's quarters, punctually delivered up to the second floor every four hours to receive his mother's milk, an intimate act which was cruelly timed by his grandmother's watch as she glowered above them, before snatching the child and re-imprisoning him away from sun, air, and love.

Naturally, under such circumstances Mishima grew into a feeble, sickly child, lucky to escape death on several occasions, and acquiring, as he saw it, an excitable and uncontrollable personality, given to both anger and elation. As the child developed into a boy, his bitter, psychologically damaged grandmother, warped by her aristocratic pretensions and saturnine fear of infant mortality, began filling him with the sense that he was from an illustrious noble family and deserving of greatness, inculcating him with the high-born grace she believed she had both inherited and cultivated. Playmates were limited to a handful of specially selected older girls who were permitted to visit the room at prearranged time slots for origami, doll dressing, or various housekeeping games. His diet was constantly monitored and strictly controlled, and if his mother ever tried to take him outside, the grandmother would swoop and haul the child back into her gloomy lair.

When he was twelve, Mishima was 'returned' to the rest of the family.

For all the damage Natsuko inflicted – repressing many of his instincts, making him haughty, vulnerable, and sometimes easily influenced – she had also given her grandson many gifts, including the emotional and artistic sensitivity which both made and unmade him. As an adult he was both a shy child, a morbid recluse, as well as a gregarious man, an exhibitionist who sought bodily gratification and material success, who made robust choices, as well as one who possessed and cultivated physical strength, willpower, and self-discipline as a crucial facet of his personality.

Although often in curious or even malicious ways, his grandmother had fostered his meticulousness and scrupulousness, his promptness and politeness, from which developed his own personal sense of courtesy and compassion. She had also instilled a respectable, knowledgeable attitude to the rich, varied, and frequently byzantine matters of Japanese etiquette, in both manners and language, which helped advance many aspects of his nascent literary gifts: his awareness of linguistic deviation and potential, his feeling and fondness for phonological, syntactical, and etymological diversity. She had taken him to his first kabuki play – his other grandmother took him to his first Noh drama – inculcating a deep and lifelong interest in traditional Japanese art forms that he himself would both promote and create.[8]

---

8   Poignantly, Natsuko's visits to the theatre with her grandson drained her remaining health, which was already overstretched by her years of physical illness and mental anguish. She died aged sixty-two on 18 January 1939, four days after Mishima's fourteenth birthday.

She also had propagated and nurtured his wider love of reading and writing, activities his mother encouraged but his father considered effeminate and had banned, tearing up the twelve-year-old boy's early manuscripts, though the young Mishima continued to scribble in secret. At school he read far beyond the work that he and his classmates were set and became the youngest member on the editorial board of his school's literary society. He devoured Japanese classics along with more modern writers like Jun'ichirō Tanizaki, as well as the dangerous, colourful, and challenging giants of recent European literature: Charles Baudelaire, Fyodor Dostoyevsky, Oscar Wilde, Marcel Proust, Friedrich Nietzsche, Rainer Maria Rilke, Thomas Mann, and Jean Cocteau. Contemporary Japanese poets, including Itō Shizuo, Tachihara Michizō, and Satō Haruo, captivated Mishima enough to make him want to compose his own verse – which had some remarkable linguistic dexterity and extraordinary, if superficial, imagery – though this was soon ditched in favour of prose, where he felt he could be poetic enough anyway.

At sixteen, he composed a short story, 'Forest in Full Bloom', in which he drew not only on his early life but on the memories and tales of his family, crafting an intriguing story in which the narrator describes how he feels his ancestors somehow live within in him, and employing a range of garish metaphors and striking aphorisms that would become a Mishimian trademark. The story also had a more direct impact on the young man's life. He posted the manuscript to Fumio Shimizu, a teacher he trusted, for constructive criticism. Shimizu was astounded by the technical quality and rich imaginative reach of the text, hurrying to show it to his colleagues on the board of the prestigious literary magazine *Bungei Bunka*. They were equally impressed, printed the story in their next issue, and flamboyantly congratulated themselves on having discovered a new literary genius, a 'heaven-sent child of eternal Japanese history'.

In order to protect their young protégé from the wrath of his military-minded, bibliophobic father, Shimizu and his colleague Zenmei Hasuda – a literary scholar, ardent nationalist, and Shinto fundamentalist – decided that a suitable pseudonym should be arranged for the story's publication. On an otherwise uneventful journey between Tokyo and Shuzenji, on the Izu Peninsula, for an editorial meeting of their literary magazine, their train passed by Mount Fuji capped in snow – for which the Japanese word is 雪, 'yuki'. They also stopped to change lines at an innocuous little railway station: Mishima, Shizuoka. Under such conditions, mixing nature, beauty, and chance, Kimitake Hiraoka was reborn as Yukio Mishima.[9]

In April 1944, aged nineteen, Mishima received a draft notice and was invited to partake in a conscription examination a few weeks later – which he barely passed; he was awarded only an unfavourable 'second-class' category of physical fitness. In the autumn, however, on 9 September, he graduated from high school top of his class in a ceremony attended by no less a figure than Emperor Hirohito himself, who later that day presented the young man with a silver watch at the Imperial Palace.

But then, disaster. At a medical examination the following February, he was (incorrectly) diagnosed with tuberculosis, declared unfit for national service, and sent home. This ignominious turn of events hurt and confused Mishima deeply: on the one hand, it likely contributed, not least in conjunction with his strangely sheltered upbringing, to the inferiority complex over his physical appearance and subsequent obsession over

---

9   The *o* of *Yukio* is a common suffix in Japanese male names.

body image and bodybuilding that he later developed. On the other, there was also an element of personal – as well as familial – relief, something that is sometimes overlooked. There are even indications that he deliberately lied to the doctor about his health, citing prolonged fever and night sweats.

Whatever the truth – and part of the problem is comparing evidence gleaned from the fictional world of *Confessions of a Mask* with factual accounts – it seems clear that not serving in the war romanticized the military for Mishima, allowing him to see all the glory and none of the squalor. For now, though, he felt slightly demeaned and at times disappointed at being left out of being able to serve his country and given the chance to die for his emperor – kamikaze pilots and other members of Special Attack Units particularly preoccupied him at this time.[10] Nevertheless, given that most of the troops in the detachment he had been destined for were killed during action in the Philippines at the end of the war, the literary world at least can be thankful for the young army doctor's inexperience on that chilly February morning when his misdiagnosis kept Mishima out of the way of American bullets and bombs.

As it was, Japan's surrender in the wake of Hiroshima and Nagasaki profoundly affected Mishima, as did Emperor Hirohito's famous radio broadcast at noon on 15 August 1945, which confirmed the defeat. The imperial transmission was delivered in formal classical Japanese with a pronunciation unintelligible to many ordinary citizens, and the blossoming writer and failed

---

10　神風, 'kamikaze', meaning 'divine wind' or 'spirit wind', originally referred to the pair of devastating typhoons which saved Japan from two invasive Mongol fleets under Kublai Khan in 1274 and 1281, but during the war became an informal name for the 'Special Attack Units' of the Imperial Japanese Navy; it gained more universal acceptance after hostilities ceased.

combatant Mishima heard it as a rallying call to revitalize Japanese culture, rebuild its cultural institutions, and preserve and protect its unique, even 'irrational', as he told his diary, traditions.

Four days later, down in Johor, British Malaya, Zenmei Hasuda, the mentor who had christened Mishima with the name under which he would write and become a global icon, shot his superior officer for a slur on the emperor before turning the gun on himself. Hasuda's final words to Mishima before he had left for the war were simple but totemic – 'I have entrusted the future of Japan to you' – and it is perhaps not fanciful to think that this dangerous quasi-guru and literary-political counsellor would beckon to his acolyte from beyond the grave and toward his own death in the autumn of 1970.

The catastrophic global conflict over, Mishima's father semi-sanctioned his son to become a writer, but only on condition he also attend the Faculty of Law at Tokyo University – which he did, dutifully attending dour legal lectures in the day and then writing in the small hours. He graduated in 1947, swiftly obtained a position in the Ministry of Finance, and looked set for a promising if ultimately uninteresting bureaucratic career, following in his father's and grandfather's footsteps. Mishima continued to write so much at night, however, exhibiting the kind of ferocious literary outpouring for which he became famous, that he exhausted himself at his departmental desk. Just a year after Mishima took the office job, his father allowed him to quit, in order to devote himself full-time to his art.

中

In the aftermath of Japan's defeat in World War II, and the reckonings which followed, numerous right-wing nationalists were purged from political high office as well as several cultural institutions, including the media and publishing industries; these incorporated a number of prominent literary figures. Many writers turned to the left, reacting against the nationalism of the war years and placing an emphasis on stark social realism in their work.

Mishima feared that his own more romantic and traditional (at least on the surface) kind of literature would become outmoded and obsolescent before he had even had the chance to perfect and expand it into something more challenging. Hearing that the celebrated writer Yasunari Kawabata, later the first Japanese recipient of the Nobel Prize, had praised some of his writing during the war, Mishima set off to visit his older colleague in January 1946, with the manuscripts for a couple of short stories, 'The Middle Ages' (中世, 'Chūsei') and 'The Cigarette' (煙草, 'Tabako'), in his satchel. The meeting went well, the two became friends, and both stories were published later in the year. Elegant, elevated, with an eye for image and detail, both stories were positively Mishimian in style, but 'The Middle Ages' is especially fascinating since it also carries the themes of homosexuality and suicide, as well as a vast historical backdrop, the latter of which would structure Mishima's immense final masterpiece, the *Sea of Fertility* tetralogy.

Suicide, too, was a motif he carried over into his next major work, and first novel, *Thieves* (1948), which, although not a huge commercial success, was deemed interesting and noteworthy enough to place Mishima on an influential list of significant young post-war writers (which included Kōbō Abe, future author of the great twentieth-century classic *The Woman in the Dunes*). The following year, however, came the Mishima thunderbolt:

Confessions of a Mask (1949), a precocious work of brilliance, insight, and invention concerning a young homosexual man who hides his true nature from society, and which catapulted its author to literary renown at just twenty-four.

The following years saw several plays and more novels, including but not limited to *Pure White Nights*, *The Age of Blue*, *Thirst for Love* (all 1950), *Natsuko's Adventure* (1951), *Made in Japan* and *Forbidden Colours* (both 1953), and the key short story 'Death in Midsummer' (1952), as well as several works of non-fiction, such as an extended essay in praise of his mentor and benefactor Kawabata. They all confirmed Mishima's status as a leading figure on the contemporary Japanese literary scene, with his innovative fusion of traditional Japanese and modern Western styles, and exhibited an extraordinary talent for merging beauty, sensuality, violence, and death.

Now that he was a celebrity intellectual, global travel accompanied his bourgeoning literary eminence. Although technically problematical to obtain due to post-war restrictions, a travel permit allowed Mishima to visit Europe and the Americas between December 1951 and May 1952, when he took in San Francisco, Los Angeles, New York, Miami, Rio de Janeiro, São Paulo, Paris, London, Athens, and Rome.[11] In London, he shopped on Oxford Street, strolled in Hyde Park, and saw several plays, including *Much Ado About Nothing*. He also watched a new opera at Covent Garden with a strong homoerotic undercurrent (for those who chose to see it): Benjamin Britten's *Billy Budd*, with a libretto by E. M. Forster from Herman Melville's novella,

---

11 Amid these glamorous global cities, Mishima's trip also included a very brief excursion to Guildford, an innocuous midsize town in Surrey, some thirty miles south-west of London – and the pretty if humdrum place where the present author grew up.

aspects of which would find their way into a future novel, *The Temple of the Golden Pavilion* (1956).

In New York, he saw musicals such as *South Pacific* and *Call Me Madam*; new movies such as *A Streetcar Named Desire*, starring Marlon Brando as Stanley Kowalski and Vivien Leigh as Blanche DuBois; and his countryman Akira Kurosawa's groundbreaking recent masterpiece *Rashōmon*, a film which had enthralled the American intelligentsia. There was also time for more opera: Puccini's *Gianni Schicchi* and Richard Strauss's *Salome*, the latter which he found especially fascinating musically ('Strauss is the direct heir to the scorpion Wagner') and longed for there to be discovered a lost Strauss setting of Thomas Mann's *Death in Venice* (Britten, of course, would write this opera in 1973, though Mishima did not live to see it). The recalcitrant Mishima slightly bemoaned the bland, conventional staging of *Salome*, which he thought lacked a stimulating fin-de-siècle atmosphere, though he found this did have the advantage of both giving discipline and focus to the secondary roles and heightening the dramatic weight of the leading actors – all of which he felt gave a pleasing kabukian ambiance to the opera.[12]

In South America, he lamented the lack of a gay scene – which he had flirted with in New York, via a couple of 'adventures', as he put it, during his ten days in the metropolis (though he did not tend to find Americans attractive). He had also visited gay bars in Japan, in part as a feature of his research for *Forbidden Colours*, but also because they were a crucial aspect of his diverse sexual identity, as we will discover. Mishima's global tour also

---

12   Eight years later, Mishima would himself direct a stage production of Strauss's source material, Oscar Wilde's one-act tragedy *Salomé*, incorporating elements from this New York opera performance that are not included in Wilde's original play.

included a week in Greece that would inspire one of his next novels, *The Sound of Waves* (1954). A huge popular hit, it sent Mishima's status rising further into the stratosphere, even if it also attracted criticism from those who perceived its author an advocate for dangerously conservative values and customs. (In fact, as we shall see, the novel is more speculative and complex than such a reading allows.)

New stories and theatre works continued to stream from Mishima's pen, including the extraordinary, weird, and haunting *Five Modern Noh Plays* (1956), which won him the Kishida Prize for Drama. Several more novels also followed in the second half of the decade, of which the most significant were *The Temple of the Golden Pavilion* (1956), a fictionalized account of the famous 1950 arson attack on a Kyoto landmark, and *Kyoko's House* (1959), a key work, though it has yet to be fully translated into English.[13]

Kyoko's House is a huge, dark, ambitious, beautifully constructed, and exquisitely uncompromising novel weaving together four interconnected stories of young men who represented different sides to Mishima's character – a boxer, a

---

13 When he intended to employ *Kyoko's House* as part of his biopic *Mishima: A Life in Four Chapters* (1985), permission for using *Forbidden Colours* having been denied by Mishima's widow, American filmmaker and screenwriter Paul Schrader had an English version of *Kyoko's House* specially translated. The film itself has a wonderfully constructed screenplay, and the overall production design is stunning, though it is a little let down by some under-par performances and rather uneven direction. One of the most interesting aspects of the film is its score by Philip Glass (1937–). It has three distinct layers: a symphony orchestra employed for those scenes portraying Mishima's works; a string orchestra for those parts showing Mishima's final day; a by turns pensive and jubilant string quartet for those black-and-white sections of the film presenting his childhood in flashback. Glass later adapted these latter parts of the score for his Third String Quartet (1985), now nicknamed 'Mishima'.

painter, an actor, and a businessman – and was a self-confessed reflection of his growing sense of nihilism at the time, a pessimism that would continue, largely unchecked, for the rest of his life. *Kyoko's House* itself sold very well, Mishima's fame guaranteed that, but was probably left unfinished by many of its readers on account of its length and complex structure. Besides this, it was generally panned by the critics, which affected its author badly: ten years after the phenomenal success of *Confessions of a Mask*, it was his first serious public failure as a writer.[14]

During his youth and early manhood, Mishima had pursued a number of romantic liaisons – primarily with women, but occasionally with men. He was clearly attracted to both, though he cultivated a particular passion for the aesthetics of the male body, especially when in combination with death or suffering, which he pursued both in person and through art and photography, most famously with Guido Reni's oil on canvas *Saint Sebastian* (c.1615), which would be immortalized in *Confessions of a Mask*. In the 1960s, he would also frequently recreate the image of the Christian martyr as a sadomasochistic fantasy, with varying degrees of malice and caprice visible from the many posed photographs.

With women, Mishima told friends, he could develop powerful crushes, adore them, kiss them, relish the chase and games of courtship – but did not always enjoy the physical act of

---

14 Since it is not yet available for English readers, I have not included a separate chapter on *Kyoko's House*, though it is discussed at some length in the chapter on *After the Banquet*.

love or extended periods of intimacy. Certainly the sensation of his earlier successes meant there were no shortage of offers from rich and/or desirable women, as Mishima flattered the echoes of his dead grandmother's desires by mingling amid Japanese high society, including one notable occasion during the summer season of 1951 where he mixed cheese, wine, and song with actresses, models, and future TV presenters. Mishima might express frequent contempt for Japan's increasingly consumerist, materialist society; yet, in his all too common acts of self-promotion and self-indulgence, he was an active, enthusiastic participant in that culture. It was all part of the Mishima myth: the paradox, the complexity, and the hypocrisy that lay at the dark heart of him.

When he was thirty, in 1954, Mishima fell in love with Sadako Toyoda. The relationship didn't work out, though elements of her character were incorporated in his novel *The Sunken Waterfall* (1955) and short story 'Building Bridges' (1956). It was also at this time that Mishima was introduced to Michiko Shōda, a cultured young woman from a successful Tokyo family. Marriage was considered, but again nothing became of the relationship – and in 1959 she went on to marry Crown Prince Akihito, becoming Empress Michiko upon her husband's accession to the Chrysanthemum Throne in 1989.

In 1958 Mishima married Yōko Sugiyama, the daughter of a prominent painter, Yasushi Sugiyama, who had designed the carpets for the Imperial Palace in Tokyo (his stylized clouds for the Grand Hall and formalized, schematic grass for a banquet hall are two of his most dazzling creations). The couple had two children: Ichirō, born in 1962, a businessman, and Noriko, born in 1959, a theatre director who would eventually marry Koji Tomita, the Japanese ambassador to the United States (2020–23) under President Biden.

It was also during the 1950s that Mishima, the sickly youth, began to take a more direct interest in physical activities and the promotion of his own body. Yet it was more than surface masculinity, shallow machismo (however much it was often just that); it was an attempt to control himself and his destiny. He took up weight training – a strict regime of three weekly sessions he pursued for the rest of his life – in order to, as he saw it, overcome his weak constitution and develop self-discipline. It also became a precarious obsession, in due course ironically resulting in a paranoid dread of bodily decline that, in some measure, hastened his own demise. Boxing, military drills, and martial arts also became a passion, and he achieved a high level of skill in kendo, karate, and battōjutsu, while also – for he was a good-looking man – pursuing minor modelling and acting interests.[15]

By the 1960s, his fame had made him an international star and Japanese icon, as well-known as the actor Toshiro Mifune, who Mishima once pipped to the title of 'Mr. Dandy', awarded by a popular men's magazine.[16] (Mifune had also starred in the first film adaptation of Mishima's *The Sound of Waves*, made soon after the novel was published in 1954.) It was also during this decade that Mishima developed a more overt interest in politics,

---

15 He starred in Yasuzō Masumura's 1960 yakuza drama *Afraid to Die* – while also taking the time to sing the movie's theme song, for which he had also provided the lyrics.

16 Mifune (1920–1997), one of the greatest actors in screen history, was an exceptionally gifted lead for most of Akira Kurosawa's masterpieces, including the outstanding *Drunken Angel* (1948), *Stray Dog* (1949), *Rashōmon* (1950), *Seven Samurai* (1954), *I Live in Fear* (1955), *Throne of Blood* (1957), *The Hidden Fortress* (1958), *The Bad Sleep Well* (1960), *Yojimbo* (1961), *Sanjuro* (1962), *High and Low* (1963), and *Red Beard* (1965).

writing newspaper pieces criticizing the government's pursuit of closer military ties with the United States and penning one of his most famous short stories – 'Patriotism' (1960) – which he later made into a film that he himself directed and starred in.[17]

This lyrical, violent story, which concerns a young man's growing militarism and subsequent ritual suicide, was the clearest indication of Mishima's more radical shift toward right-wing politics. He had always been of a conservative and traditional leaning, but his disillusionment with the westernization (which others might call industrialization) of Japan in the period after World War II was growing stronger. The story's title, 'Yūkoku' (憂国), is usually translated as 'Patriotism', though a more literal rendition might be 'Concern for One's Country', reflecting Mishima's apprehension about the direction Japan was taking – which was, of course, little more than a pursuit of democracy, reconstruction, and modernization. Ultimately, this more deep-seated, far-reaching, and drastic development in Mishima would lead to both a literary masterpiece, the four-volume *Sea of Fertility* (1969–71), and his death.

Before then, his literary life continued, with new novels, stories, and plays appearing all the time. *After the Banquet* (1960) was a more overtly political novel than he had hitherto written. Though it maintained Mishima's familiar motifs surrounding loneliness and death, it seems to chime with neither the challenging frankness of his earlier work nor the idealism of *The*

---

17 A strange and hypnotic wonder in monochrome black and white, with music from Wagner's *Tristan und Isolde*, it is full of long expository intertitles explaining at length the story and its historical background. Visually powerful, *Patriotism* was shot in a single room, with inert wide shots and lingering close-ups, and has the aura of Mishima's beloved Noh theatre.

Sea of Fertility. Other novels of the 1960s were similarly less easy to place in his output: *The Frolic of the Beasts* (1961) is a parody of a classical Noh drama; *Life for Sale* (1968) a magnificently camp and surreal satire on modern life; while *Beautiful Star* (1962) is truly avant-garde, breaking with literary taboos and stale, constrictive genres, and coming close to contemporary modes of experimental science fiction.

Science fiction itself had long been a Mishima passion – Arthur C. Clarke in particular he revered – and he felt the genre to contain important human truths behind the sometimes puerile or ridiculous exterior. He also enjoyed manga ('whimsical pictures') and gekiga ('dramatic pictures') comics and graphic novels, plus kaiju ('strange beast') fantasies like Godzilla, all these less directly serious forms of literature both feeding his imagination for fiction and allowing it a little time off from the intensity of his own writing. (Mishima and his wife had even visited Disneyland in California, not long after their marriage, and they had promised themselves another visit to celebrate the completion of *The Sea of Fertility.*)

Mishima's other major novels from the 1960s included *The Sailor Who Fell from Grace with the Sea* (1963), in many ways a return to the hard honesty of his earlier works, but with a slightly more astringent bite; *Silk and Insight* (1964), concerning a textile workers' strike, which was a commercial flop but won the Mainichi Prize; and *Music* (1964), a peculiar but entertaining work which investigates the dark and spectral connections between sound, sexuality, and psychoanalysis.

There were also two radical plays: the historical all-female *Madame de Sade* (1965), an exceptional drama exploring the life of the notorious marquis, and the unfortunately, provocatively, perhaps foolishly titled neoclassical all-male *My Friend Hitler*

('Waga Tomo Hittorā', 1968), which investigated the political skill and limitations of the German tyrant and gave vent to the darker side of Mishima's supercharged but all too often naive views on history, right-wing politics, and national engagement. In June 1966 there was also a short story, 'Voices of the Fallen Heroes', which denounced Emperor Hirohito's relinquishing of his divine status at the end of World War II, arguing that the Japanese army had died for their living god and that to de-deify himself in this manner was an insult to their memory. Mishima, as so often in his life, chose to largely ignore both the wider context and pragmatic necessity of Hirohito's actions.

Despite, or indeed in part because of, his nationalism, in which he sought to preserve, promote, and protect his particular image of Japan, Mishima continued to travel abroad widely and take an interest in global affairs. In February 1967, together with fellow writers Yasunari Kawabata, Kōbō Abe, and Jun Ishikawa, he wrote a newspaper editorial condemning China's Cultural Revolution and its suppression of intellectual, academic, and artistic liberty, while later in the year he visited India and Southeast Asia with his wife.

The Indian leg of the trip had been part of an invitation by the country's government and included meetings with Prime Minister Indira Gandhi. Mishima greatly enjoyed India, impressed by the people's desire to preserve their traditions and national identity, repelling westernization. As was so often the case by this time, Mishima habitually saw only what he wanted to see, overlooking or downplaying those aspects that jarred with his increasingly narrow outlook. (What he sometimes regarded as a resistance to materialism was in fact bald, ugly poverty, which he did, at least, accept as a major problem India faced, along with drought and a pugnaciously expanding population.)

On the way home from India, Mishima also travelled to Laos and Thailand, and the culture, religions, and landscapes of all three countries would strongly influence the third volume of his *Sea of Fertility* tetralogy, *The Temple of Dawn*. Work on this huge four-part closing work – a grand, varied, but superbly integrated final statement – had begun in the mid-1960s, with some of the material appearing in a serialized monthly format. The tetralogy, a masterpiece exploring the apparent transmigration of a human soul across the decades, and offering a richly detailed, beguilingly intricate vision of twentieth-century Japan, occupied most of Mishima's few remaining years, as he sought to overcome the critical disappointment of *Kyoko's House*, which still pestered and plagued him a decade on.

Beyond fiction, there were also several more political, critical, and autobiographical works, including *Aesthetics of Ending* (1966), *The Way of the Samurai* (1967), and *Sun and Steel: Art, Action and Ritual Death* (1968), this last of which presented nothing less than an autobiography of Mishima's relationship with his own physical being. An extraordinary book, an unusual model of self-revelation and personal discovery, it is an intimate, harrowing journey into a man's soul via his body – and an alarming vision of what was to come.

On 25 November 1970, Mishima completed the final volume of *The Sea of Fertility*, *The Decay of the Angel*. Although much of the text had been finished some weeks before, the manuscript he left stated, on the top sheet, '*The Decay of the Angel* (Final Instalment)', and on the last page, in his immaculate hand, '*The*

Sea of Fertility: *Finis*. 25 November, the Forty-Fifth Year of Shōwa.'[18] Later that day, Mishima attempted a military coup, then committed suicide, disembowelling himself before an acolyte cut off his head.

Despite their familiarity and the passage of years, actions like this do not significantly lose their power to shock, as we learn again about what happened to Mishima at the end of his life. Although plenty of warning signs were there, in both his actions and his writings, especially in the 1960s, little prepared Japan – and the world – for the very public demise of such a renowned, respected, and revered cultural figure.

In 1967 Mishima had undertaken several weeks' training with the Japanese Self-Defense Force and promoted his desire to form a Japanese National Guard, ten thousand strong and made up of civilian soldiers. When this ambition was largely ignored by the media, politicians, and general populace, in October 1968 he formed the Shield Society (楯の会, 'Tatenokai'), a private militia composed mainly of right-wing university students and various other disaffected parties, which swore undying loyalty to the emperor – 'shielding' him. Mishima personally oversaw the group's military training, practice in physical fitness, and devotion to several martial arts. Membership barely reached three figures.

At 9:00 a.m. on Wednesday 25 November 1970, his literary work completed,[19] Mishima travelled in a white sedan car, purchased for the purpose, with four members of the Shield Society to the headquarters of the Self-Defense Force in Tokyo.

---

18   The Shōwa era (昭和時代, 'Shōwa jidai') was the period of Japanese history corresponding to the reign of Emperor Shōwa, usually known in English as Hirohito, from 25 December 1926 to his death on 7 January 1989.

19   The last thing he ever wrote, in a note penned and left on his desk that morning, was 'Human life is limited, but I would like to live forever.'

On the way, Mishima joked that if this were a gangster film, music would be playing at this point, and wondered what kind, before breaking into song.

Having arrived at their destination at 10:50 a.m., in full uniform, they forced their way into the commandant's office, took him hostage, and barricaded the doors. With a prepared manifesto, Mishima stepped onto a balcony and gave an impassioned, somewhat deranged speech to the assembled soldiers on the parade ground below, who were at first bemused, then both angry and amused at the situation. Rebuking the soldiers for their apathy and passive acceptance, like the rest of Japan, of a constitution that undermined tradition and integrity, Mishima rambled on, hardly making himself heard over the news and police helicopters that had gathered above. He demanded that full power be restored to the imperial throne and with three cries of 'Long live the emperor!'[20] returned inside.

Polite to the end, his grandmother's morals and manners lingering on, Mishima apologized to the commandant before performing seppuku, a ritualized form of disembowelment practiced by the samurai (among others). After he stabbed himself in the abdomen with one of his short swords, an adherent attempted to sever his master's head with the long one but was unable to complete his task, so another follower stepped in to finish the messy job. It was 12:20 p.m.

Whatever the shambolic, confused, and slightly ludicrous local aspects to Mishima's demise, in aesthetic and technical terms, it was a 'good' seppuku, realizing the customs Mishima upheld and revered. Moreover, it was a ceremonial termination to his life which the author had long planned. He was well aware the

---

20   'Tennō Heika banzai!'

coup would likely fail, so this was, to all intents and purposes, a premeditated and deliberate act of suicide: observed, avowed, and fashioning a rite of a body still in relative youth (as he had wanted, even dreamed).

He left a wife and two children, and was survived by both his parents.

⁂

Throughout his life, but especially in its final decade, Mishima made a romantic, irresponsible, and self-centred cult of misplaced martial grandeur and austere warrior masculinity. Theoretically attempting to restore Japanese society to its mythical pre-war glory days, with deference to a divine emperor and defiance of rampant commercialism, in fact both the failed coup and Mishima's suicide were theatrical performances, a final embellishment of his swashbuckling, vivacious art. Putting it like this can sound flippant, even wilfully incongruous, though it will only be through an examination of Mishima's writing – especially *The Sea of Fertility* – that the truth of his death, such as it is, can be more sincerely pinpointed.

Mishima's death was an expression of optimism and nihilism, articulating both the perfection and the transience of beauty, its purpose and pointlessness, ideas writhing in desperate splendour at the heart of his work. It was a melodramatic closing act, full of Mishima's hysterical dread and disgust of ageing, but intended as well to give meaning and some kind of sense to a dark, dejected, manic self-annihilation that had been a year in the planning and a lifetime in the making. To some extent it did; but in reality it threatened, and still threatens, to outshine and eclipse all the wonderful creativity, all the astonishing invention, Mishima had achieved in his life.

Between 12 and 19 November 1970, just days before his death, an exhibition of Mishima's life and work had been arranged, with his permission, by the Tōbu department store in Tokyo. It was immensely popular, attended by over one hundred thousand visitors, including Mishima's beloved mother, Shizue. Hung with morbidly prophetic black curtains, the hall presented a range of photographs and memorabilia – including the very sword, a metre long, with which his own head would be detached on 25 November.

In his introduction to the show's catalogue, itself edged in black, Mishima acknowledged that his was a life full of contradictions, and that it would be best to see it divided into four rivers: writing, theatre, the body, and action, all of which, he claimed, finally flowed into *The Sea of Fertility*. He went on to say that he hoped people would be interested in all four of the rivers of his life but conceded this might not be possible, though people should not get swept away by any particular river they disliked.

This book endeavours to step into and explore the extraordinary, challenging, and magnificent waterway for which Yukio Mishima should be most remembered: the great river of his writing.

Note on Texts and Translations

Mishima's collected works – published by Shinchōsha between 2000 and 2006 – require over forty fat volumes. They incorporate literary fiction and literary criticism, modern drama and traditional theatre, civic satire and science fiction, poetry and romance, plus writings on philosophy, politics, photography, martial arts, film, ballet, and music. There are pieces for highbrow periodicals in addition to frequent excursions into popular culture and mainstream entertainment. Every genre, style, theme, and audience seems to have been covered.

Most of Mishima's works, however, including the bulk of his stories and plays, and – most glaringly of all – the great 1959 novel *Kyoko's House*, remain out of reach to those who do not read Japanese. This book has selected just fourteen of his novels for exploration and analysis, partly because they represent the pinnacle and most enduring aspect of his literary achievement, as well as much of its remarkable range, including the more avant-garde and experimental works of the 1960s. But it is also for the more mundane, pragmatic reason that they are the only ones that are widely available for readers in English.

By reading Mishima in translation, we simultaneously bolster and undermine his intentions, making his work and vision better known while also taking it further from its cultural core. Nonetheless, although we always undeniably lose something in translation, we lose far more by not reading his books at all.

Editions Cited

Novels:

Confessions of a Mask (Penguin Classics, trans. Meredith Weatherby)
Thirst for Love (Penguin Classics, trans. Alfred H. Marks)
Forbidden Colours (Penguin Classics, trans. Alfred H. Marks)
The Sound of Waves (Vintage Classics, trans. Meredith Weatherby)
The Temple of the Golden Pavilion (Vintage Classics, trans. Ivan Morris)
After the Banquet (Vintage Classics, trans. Donald Keene)
The Frolic of the Beasts (Penguin Classics, trans. Andrew Clare)
Beautiful Star (Penguin Classics, trans. Stephen Dodd)
The Sailor Who Fell from Grace with the Sea (Vintage Classics, trans. John Nathan)
Life for Sale (Penguin Classics, trans. Stephen Dodd)

The Sea of Fertility:

Spring Snow (Vintage Classics, trans. Michael Gallagher)
Runaway Horses (Vintage Classics, trans. Michael Gallagher)

The Temple of Dawn (Vintage Classics, trans. E. Dale Saunders & Cecilia Segawa Seigle)
The Decay of the Angel (Vintage Classics, trans. Edward G. Seidensticker)

Other Works:

Death in Midsummer and Other Stories (Penguin Classics, trans. Edward G. Seidensticker, Ivan Morris, Donald Keene & Geoffrey W. Sargent)
Voices of the Fallen Heroes and Other Stories (Penguin Classics, trans. Jeffrey Angles, Sam Bett, Stephen Dodd, Paul McCarthy, John Nathan, Hannah Osborne, Aoyama Tomoko, Juliet Winters Carpenter & Oliver White)
Five Modern Noh Plays (Europa Editions, trans. Donald Keene)
My Friend Hitler and Other Plays (Columbia University Press, trans. Hiroaki Sato)
Madame de Sade (Peter Owen, trans. Donald Keene)
Sun and Steel: Art, Action and Ritual Death (Grove Press, trans. John Bester)
The Way of the Samurai (Basic Books, trans. Kathryn Sparling)

Note on Naming Customs

In Japanese, surnames are usually written first, followed by given name: Mishima Yukio. However, to avoid confusion and maintain consistency, in this book names are given Western-style, with forename first, followed by family name: Yukio Mishima.

PART ONE

THE EARLY NOVELS

Chapter One

Confessions of a Mask
PERSONALITY & PERFORMANCE

When the twenty-four-year-old Yukio Mishima's second novel, *Confessions of a Mask* (仮面の告白, 'Kamen no Kokuhaku', 1949), became a literary sensation in the dour wasteland of post-war Japan, observers may have been excused for expecting this to be merely a single firework, a bright young star set to immediately fade. Many authors – Harper Lee, J. D. Salinger, Djuna Barnes, John Kennedy Toole? – have only one (great) novel in them, and the attempts to find another are often painful, embarrassing, traumatic; others literally and metaphorically dine out on the success of their triumph, finding neither time nor interest to develop their ability into successive works.

That Mishima bucked the trend of one-off youthful literary accomplishment and went on to write a substantial wealth of wonders is fortunate – but it was not fortuitous. In 1948, the year before *Confessions*, Mishima's first novel, *Thieves* (盗賊,

'Tōzoku'), had generated quiet curiosity among the literary classes, enough to place its author on the well-regarded list of 'Second Generation Post-War Writers' (which included Kōbō Abe, Shōhei Ōoka, and Toshio Shimao). Even before this, the celebrated writer, and future Nobel winner, Yasunari Kawabata had shown considerable interest in the young Mishima's early short stories, especially 'The Middle Ages' (中世, 'Chūsei', 1945) and 'The Cigarette' (煙草, 'Tabako', 1946).

So Mishima had form. But in *Confessions* he took that talent to a new level of erudition, sophistication, and transgressive candour, employing a mixture of gaudy and astringent styles within a web of playful games. In a world of overt courage, virility, and one-dimensional wartime masculinity, the hero of *Confessions* is compelled to wear a mask to hide his true nature, which is physically feeble and sexually unorthodox, and the novel exquisitely explores the violent tension between his inner life and the catastrophic realities of the Second World War. We visit his dark fantasies of valiant warriors and their gallant, blood-spattered ends and the frightening truths concerning his dread of conscription.

No one-hit wonder, *Confessions of a Mask* is a crucial text in laying the foundations for Mishima's later work. The thrilling, dangerous extremities of his life and art, especially around violence and beauty, are delved into, pulled apart, meticulously inspected, as are his complex relationship with his own sexual identity and his intense, quasi-erotic attraction to the concept of heroism, particularly in a military context. It is a blistering, fearless scrutiny of the shadows within Mishima's psyche, as well as the bright lights of his soul. And it contains the vital ingredients which he would revise and rework in a network of intricate new ways during the course of his career, toying with and speculating on the blurred margins between art and life, fiction and non-fiction, personality and performance.

❧

The act of writing is the intellectual equivalent of biological propagation, a means of promulgating thoughts and ideas across generations, a process of immortality to match the dissemination of organic offspring. The fruits of a writer's pen are the textual equivalent of their loins' produce, in some cases a direct substitute for perceived or actual, literal or metaphorical, impotence. In *Confessions of a Mask*, with its fictional/autobiographical sport, its layers of camouflage, concealment, and performance, as well as its sexual subject matter, such substitutions become uncanny, disconcerting – but ultimately intriguing.

Sex has always been at the heart of literature. Where pre-modern works tended to see sex as a positive, celebratory act, by the early modern period, and as time and society wore on, a more tortured, darker vision took hold, as sex became an aspect (and symbol) of wider corruption. By the time of the nineteenth-century European novel, especially in the naturalist school of writers like Émile Zola,[21] the connection between sex and socio-economic forces was more blatant. The squalor and disgrace of sex, in which the true desire and pleasure were removed, was closely related to the progress of industrial civilizations and the degradation of humanity. Modern Japanese literature, too, frequently explored the tormented nature of sexual obsession, incest and adultery

---

21 Not least in novels like *Thérèse Raquin* (1868) and those from the great Rougon-Macquart cycle, such as *Germinal* (1885) or *La Terre* (1887).

common themes as writers such as Tayama, Shimazaki, and Shiga consciously sought to explore the confrontational battlefield of existence in which sex is both metaphor and fact. All this would be crucial to the formation of *Confessions*.

Among these influences, Katai Tayama (1872–1930) was instrumental in not only cultivating a local form of naturalism to match Zola's but developing a particular kind of Japanese confessional narrative: the so-called 'I-novel'.[22] Here a typically first-person perspective is restricted to its own author's lived experience, along with their inner reality, all of which is presented in a natural fashion to the reader. Compared with memoir, this looser relationship with reality makes a deeper personal and emotional exploration possible. Tayama's great masterpiece *Futon* (蒲団, 1907), arguably the first I-novel,[23] recounts how the stale marriage of a middle-aged novelist leads to his obsessive fantasies about younger women, and then one younger woman in particular – all of which was directly based on Tayama's experiences with his pupil Michiyo Okada.

Accordingly, within the I-novel form, the reader is invited to consider the narrator and the author as in some sense identical, but never entirely so. With a delicious irony, the fictional elements of the I-novel allow for greater truths of the author to be disclosed, especially in matters of sex. Negative or antisocial sexuality, outside the convenient, compartmentalized world of social prejudices, norms, and hypocrisies, could here be neutralized, liberated, explored. Confessions could become celebration, then assimilation.

---

22   私小説, 'Shishōsetsu'.

23   Which, even as the first instance of the form, breaks the custom by having a third-person narration.

By the time of the Second World War and its aftermath, trends had shifted, and even established writers like Jun'ichirō Tanizaki (1886–1965) and Yasunari Kawabata (1899–1972) took their hitherto fairly normal – albeit exquisitely rendered – erotic fiction into more explicitly antisocial territory. Whatever the sexual transgressions they explored, however – such as voyeurism, in Tanizaki's *The Key* (1956) and Kawabata's *House of the Sleeping Beauties* (1961) – they tended to remain within tightly controlled private spaces, worlds not so far from the socio-sexual partitions of the earlier Edo society (1603–1868).

However, a new and more deliberately daring generation of writers wanted to take their antisocial sexuality *into* society. Thus, Kenzaburō Ōe's 'The Sexual Human' (性的人間, 'Seitekiningen', 1963) features perverts on a train; Kōbō Abe's magnificently alarming, sometimes surreal or even grotesque, novels investigate the role of an antagonistic sexuality within quasi-public zones such as infirmaries or research laboratories; late Mishima has the central character of his *Sea of Fertility* novels, Honda, behave as a grubby voyeur watching couples canoodling in the park.

In *Confessions of a Mask*, elements of both the I-novel (which Mishima often dismissed with a derisive grin) and semi-public revelation, along with classic features of the Bildungsroman, coexist: Mishima sought to use a composite, lively, and convoluted literary form of his own development to explore various layers and meanings. He also employs an aggressive, scandalous sexuality not just as a means of personal proclamation, but as a sociopolitical statement too. Fragmented sex, and fragmented images of sex – akin to T. S. Eliot's broken heap in his own earlier post-war wasteland of 1922 – destabilize the wholeness his narrator apparently pursues, echoing the wider broken society the global conflict had both created and reflected.

Mishima's novel is self-consciously, confrontationally sexual. Amid the triple fogs of war, sexuality, and autobiographical fiction, *Confessions of a Mask* both mirrors and critiques a repressive, controlling society desperate to evade confrontation with itself. Illicit sexual behaviour becomes a powerful metaphor for a shattered culture – while also simultaneously pulling off the trick of celebrating difference, and even offering hope. Frustrated desire dominates the page, and 'unnatural' desires (onanism, homosexuality) ultimately prove to be the only fulfilment in an empty, broken world. But, as so often in Mishima, more than a hint of redemption and salvation exists in this apparently negative vision than many of his literary contemporaries were prepared to offer.

ॐ

Mishima's *Confessions* constantly invites us to question its status as a literary artefact, less in the sense that we read it as autobiography – it's too clever for such a cheap trick – but rather that we quiz why we read, what we look for, how we interpret texts, and how literary satisfaction is derived. Plot and character do exist in *Confessions*, with a clear trajectory and narrative journey, but they mask deeper truths about both identity and storytelling. As we voyage with the narrator and his perplexed, gloriously epiphanic world, his recollections move like waves, reaching the shore of insight only to retreat into the vast ocean of anxiety and incomprehension.

Confessions of a Mask falls into two distinct halves. In the first, we witness the narrator retrospectively describe his childhood and adolescence and his burgeoning awareness not only of his weak, inadequate body, but of his attraction to men, especially those with more masculine torsos than his own. During the course of his narration, the 'I' tries to isolate signs of his homosexuality, creating a 'rhetoric of confession'. This exploration of his sense of self adds to his sense of seclusion from the repressive, tightly controlled society around him – all of which is aggravated and intensified by the arrival of WWII with its national demand for strong, healthy male bodies. The second half of the novel charts I's strategic attempts to mask his true nature by courting a young woman, Sonoko, which only exacerbates his attraction to men.

The novel opens with the narrator's explanation that he can remember his own first, postnatal bath. We are given the earliest of what will be many colourful and convincing descriptions, including the glittering reflections of light on water, anticipating the closing line of the book – and helping reveal the self-consciously artificial nature of the entire narrative. A novel which claims to be an eyewitness account offers up a barefaced and obvious fiction in its opening moments, with even its narrator acknowledging the falsehood and recollecting how adults would respond awkwardly or with justifiable misgiving when, as a child, he repeated the untruthful memory. Already the strata of masks and masquerades are being laid down.

The made-up/misremembered glittering light will, as we have said, recur in the novel's final image, closing the circle of fiction and allowing a new, more honest kind of birth than the one recalled, but glistening fluids play other roles in the text as well. The narrator's now rather famous masturbatory/ejaculation scenes in *Confessions* are no mere salacious inclusion (however much they also helped shift copies of the novel), but integral aspects of the liquid literary journey of the tale. In the first of them, the narrator recalls his arousal at seeing a picture of the

Christian martyr Saint Sebastian in an art book. The messy aftermath of his excitement sees the narrator's homosexual desire literally mark the objects of words and writing: his ink bottle, schoolbook, notes, dictionary, all of which gleam in the light.

In this passage, words themselves operate as masks. Following both convention and aesthetic choice, Mishima (rather than the narrator) avoids explicit language, employing euphemism, loan words, and erudite verbiage. Although our self-indulgent narrator is a studious, pretentious schoolboy, his language knowingly exceeds his grasp, covering his mixture of shame and exhilaration with an exaggeratedly academic jargon and intellectualization (citing psychological literature) just as his erotic discharge covered the paraphernalia of writing. It is a mischievous game of sexual-textual teasing.

Glittering baths, glittering semen, glittering beverages – these sparkling liquids course through the narrative, uniting it in a shimmering, twinkling, playful humour that is also scandalous and provocative. The strategic – i.e., artificial – placement of such images at the beginning and end of the text, and then tactically throughout, highlights the narrator's writerly mannerisms as well as his desire for authorship – his yearning for a pen and ink beyond that of his *pen*is and personal fluid (which will, by the novel's end, *come*).

❧

Although it tends to be overlooked, even overshadowed, by the gaudy goriness of the first, the second half of the novel illuminates many of the complexities of its predecessor. The more obvious sense of heterosexual performance in part two highlights the true theatrical nature of the earlier reminiscences, so that the narrator is revealed to be neither repentant nor interested in repressing his homosexuality. His apparent confession, along with his apparent mask, is merely a means to assert control over the dictatorial social forces which swirl around him. The mode of confession sanctions, indeed encourages, a series of opportunities to stage-manage or outfox society. All of this, of course, takes place in the context of a society held within the heightened strictures and structures of war.

Within this wartime context, just as the narrator's homosexuality merges into the mask of his heterosexual performance, so happiness and dejection, bravery and cowardice, honesty and artifice merge and interact. No longer the property of the nation, the narrator – and his body – can evade both the Japanese war machine and its weapons of war, refocusing his interest in the workings of complex machines closer to home: the mechanics of liquid pressure and pumped fluids (the intimate/ expansive hydraulics of an erection) and the contraction and expulsion of other liquids (the agreeable/appalling release of his ejaculation). These bodily machines themselves are the complex apparatuses of the narrator's own grander appliance, the theatre of his imagination and the performance of his personality: a falsehood device, a contrivance of contrivance, a machination machine.

The confession of the mask does not purge the narrator, cleansing him of sin and allowing him to re-enter society. Rather, it isolates him further, displaying his contempt for society, now with a sense of personal fulfilment and defiance. The autobiographical elements to *Confessions*, and the games Mishima plays with them, add fuel to the fire, the author and narrator taunting the very society which seeks to control and condemn them. That the life the narrator is coerced to repress – his homosexual one – is colourful, intense, gruesome, and grisly, while the normal, socially sanctioned one is sufficient, insipid, unexciting, only heightens the provocative, truculent attitude.

This void of bourgeois society is most obviously seen in the second half of the novel – so far from the gory passions of the first – yet it is only the 'failure' of the narrator's attempt to enter conventional society which gives truth to the first part of *Confessions*. The clandestine visions of blood, ink, and ecstasy – a dying soldier and the image of Saint Sebastian – carry immense power when considered in retrospect from the perspective of the bland courtship of Sonoko (which, of course, has occurred before the narrator sets down the entire confession). Ensnared in the flat wilderness of heterosexual wooing and kept from the thrilling theatre of war, the narrator recommends 'sugary novels' to Sonoko, while imagining his own surreptitious 'murder theatre', a phantasmagoric playhouse of blood and butchery, death and decadence, cannibalism and chaos.

This visionary coliseum of pain represents a desire, of course, to escape not only society, with its bland conventions and rules, but the prison of the self, the tormented mind of a desperately intellectualized young man. Even the arrival of the Americans in Japan is to be welcomed, an invading army that will invite the narrator finally to his own macabre demise, his martyrdom fantasy fulfilled. Like Hamlet or Humbert Humbert, the narrator is an archetypal intellectual self-publicist who shares both the Dane's and the poet-pervert's desire for external revolution to clear up internal difficulties. Unable to take action to free themselves from their condition, all three suffer a prolonged, often passive, wait (which gives us their texts) for exterior forces they hope – consciously or otherwise – will save or destroy them.

For Hamlet, this is Norway or Claudius; for Humbert, Quilty or the authorities; for Mishima's narrator, Uncle Sam's army. Each of these three male figures has their internal, psychological inaction further deferred into sexual impotence, frustration, or unfeasibility: Hamlet in his failed affiliation with Polonius's daughter, Ophelia; Humbert in his criminal relationship with and kidnap of his stepdaughter, Lolita; for Mishima's protagonist, his unsatisfactory courtship with a woman, Sonoko.

The war itself is a disturbing phantom in *Confessions of a Mask*, its relative textual absence an ominous indication of its fundamental significance. This was a novel written in 1949 and set during the war, yet we experience its presence only as a feature of the narrator's self-centred preoccupations. It might be easy to suggest this is because of the narrator's / Mishima's guilt at missing the war. A more complex condemnation of war and a simultaneous anguish at its repercussions is at work here, however. The narrator's private fantasies of sacrifice and murder are only the internal manifestation of the much wider Japanese journey toward destruction and the devastation of its own societal structures, a loss of traditions that, in time, will come to invade and dominate Mishima's fiction. The fact that Mishima did not serve in the war allows him the space (and imagination) to fantasize on the whole notion of glory and sacrifice. *Confessions* contains the germ of this idea, though here the calamity of potential obliteration has emancipated the mask to acknowledge his sense of shame more of his society than his self.

Although the novel concludes with a suggestion of despondent self-realization, it is not ultimately pessimistic. Rather, it carries that strange, ironic note of redemptive possibility and stimulation which pervades so much of Mishima's work, but which can so easily be missed. It is akin to the hint of 'otherworld' which characterizes the dark ecstasies of Nabokov's fiction or the comforting catharsis of Shakespearean tragedy. Hamlet and Humbert were destroyed not by internal or external forces, but through something curiously in between: Hamlet by the self-willed poison of Laertes's (Claudius-derived) sword; Humbert by heart disease while in prison. In a similarly intriguing fashion, for Mishima's protagonist, part of him must die, but it will not be the end of him – quite the opposite.

In (apparent) despair because of his ineffectual, helpless failure to make love to a woman, the narrator offers up a performative gesture, an additional mask: his own self-destruction. Yet this is a mask the narrator cannot wear, and so another is taken up: a different man is located to metaphorically serve as a sacrifice that will generate a personal rebirth. At a dance hall with Sonoko, the narrator's ex-girlfriend now safely married and therefore unattainable and as such a much more interesting character, our protagonist finally tears off his multiple masks and is able to more fully acknowledge his unavoidable, indisputable attraction toward men. Observing a handsome young tough and coarse figure in the dance hall, he forgets about Sonoko's existence and fixes upon this half-naked ruffian, fantasizing about witnessing him fight some imagined rival gang, observing his body cut open and bleeding.

This figure is not only the object of the narrator's desire; it is the mask he wants to wear but knows he cannot. This tears him in two – and yet it does not destroy him. On the contrary, it creates him whole, allowing him to finally, genuinely and authentically, be, revealing all the preceding text as neither apology nor escape nor confession but a journey toward true identity, performance dissolving into personality. Knowing he can never become a figure like the beautiful lout, seeing the 'glittering, threatening reflections' of a spilled beverage which close the book (and which point back both to the opening of the novel, with its falsely remembered postnatal bath, and the splattered subjective fluids of the I's onanistic episodes), the narrator realizes who he is. By imaginatively sacrificing the young man, the narrator can be born again, acknowledging himself in an act of 'reverse suicide' – Mishima's own description of *Confessions of a Mask* – which is incongruous, paradoxical, peculiar, but ultimately satisfying and optimistic.

In killing the young lout in his imagination, the narrator discovers his true being through the negative process of knowing what he can never be, while at the same time Mishima, author, in the act of writing the book we have been reading, becomes a new being born into the life of language. No longer the puny weakling closeted by his grandmother or avoiding war, the masks of fiction finally removed, the narrator is now transformed: into Yukio Mishima. Only via this deliciously sly process do we realize the true mask of *Confessions*, as the narrator and its author merge into one.

And, of course, there is the further slice of irony that it would be this book's success which made Mishima's name, allowing him to truly exist as a full-time writer, not bound to an unadventurous job in a conventional office. But the games don't stop there, since the name 'Yukio Mishima' is itself, naturally, a literary mask, a pseudonym, a nom de plume: Mishima's real name was Kimitake

Hiraoka. And the diminutive version of 'Kimitake'? 'Kochan' – the name of the narrator of *Confessions of a Mask*.

Less a box of facades and disguises, *Confessions of a Mask* is a set of Russian dolls trapped in a hall of mirrors, whose layers and reflections are a magnificent means to display the truth. It is a brilliantly (and literally) self-indulgent literary exercise, which arouses our interest, rises to the occasion, and discharges its delights with a mischievous complexity and the playful pleasure of personality and performance.

Chapter Two

Thirst for Love

EMBRACING OBLIVION

Many of the great heroines of European fiction – Emma Bovary, Hedda Gabler, Anna Karenina, Molly Bloom, Constance Reid (that is, Lady Chatterley) – share a comfortable, educated, middle-class, but frustrated existence, craving something more in their lives than the dull routine of a stable marriage. And all these women, we note, are penned by men. With sinister veracity and tantalizing intimacy, these male authors devoted their imaginations to liberating women's consciousnesses (and bodies) in their experimental art, transgressing neat divisions, disobeying social, moral, gender, and literary boundaries. But the women were not always entirely free, of course, and most of the intellectually and sexually unshackled feminine creations of masculine writers ended up penalized – sometimes to serve a work's aesthetics; sometimes to satisfy an ethical requirement (or manly insecurity).

In Japan, shortly after the Second World War, Yukio Mishima set about creating his own native version of these foreign tales, with a story inspired by his mother's sister, who had worked as a gardener near Osaka. With *Thirst for Love* (愛の渇き, 'Ai no Kawaki', 1950), Mishima produced a classically structured and deceptively restrained novel that resonates like a contemporary parable, a Greek tragedy set in modern Japan. Its richly imagined and delicately nuanced protagonist, Etsuko, begins as an incurable romantic and becomes a voracious, parched lunatic, bent on self-destruction and abject misery, weaving complex webs of mental torture and emotional anguish around herself and her (admittedly ghastly) in-laws.

To some extent we might have Mishima say 'Madame Etsuko, c'est moi' – and she certainly shares many of her author's emotional patterns and passions, not least a death wish and a violent, unchecked compulsion to hurt the object of her love. But, like Flaubert in his relationship with Madame Bovary, Mishima also had the ice-cool objectivity of the architect, knowing his construction well enough to both love and mock it, displaying its flaws and foibles for all his readers to see.

Etsuko is a superb creation, convincingly assembled and exhilaratingly executed. She inhabits an intricate, non-linear narrative awash with exactly the kind of violent vocabulary and delectable metaphors Mishima is celebrated for: a wall clock 'chopped heavy, melancholy seconds, one by one' through guilty air; jealousy and desire are likened to 'craving for carrion'. Via flashbacks and occasional stream-of-consciousness techniques, Etsuko's inner world is thrillingly realized for us, and her actions – extreme, impractical, or plain foolish – carry the harsh conviction of reality while always retaining the whiff of myth and fable, a tension at the heart of the novel's power.

There is a dangerous, distressing intensity to *Thirst for Love*, for all its elegant design and often unruffled exterior. We witness a damaged character simultaneously hollowed out and electrified by her own desolation in a novel illustrating the festering, simmering desires and complex range of traumas that lay beneath the surface of post-war Japan. For although focused on one particular unfulfilled need, this novel also suggests a much wider longing for affection and tenderness. In the aftermath of global conflict and amid the uncertainty of nuclear Armageddon – which Japan, of course, was uniquely placed to fear – the late 1940s and early 1950s were an age characterized by the thirst for love, by the often unsatisfied yearning to bring life and hope to a time of widespread sterility and despair.[24]

Thirst for Love is a relatively short novel, told via five long chapters,[25] and its basic plot is simple to relate. Widowed from

---

24 Not so for Mishima. By this time a fashionable novelist, *Thirst for Love* received extensive critical praise and was a popular triumph, selling some seventy thousand copies in a few months and enabling its author to buy his first home, a spacious two-storey house in a residential Tokyo district – into which he moved most of his immediate family (he was now the sole breadwinner). Mishima's father, so long the bibliophobe and general sceptic regarding his son's literary vocation, was compelled to concede it had been a success, living as he was literally amid the proceeds of that career. They would all live there for eight years, until Mishima married and moved everyone on into a new house, one which he designed and built himself.

25 Almost the five acts of a Shakespeare drama, with Mishima both incorporating and destabilizing elements of the playwright's familiar plot formula that divides the action into exposition, rising action, climax, falling action, and resolution.

her philandering husband, Etsuko goes to live on a farm near Osaka with her dead spouse's family, a hodgepodge assortment of generations thrown together through the chaos of war and circumstance. Etsuko effectively becomes mistress/wife/cook to her ageing father-in-law, Yakichi, while herself harbouring an unrequited passion for their muscular young gardener, Saburo – whom she eventually murders with an agricultural tool, her lust/love thwarted and turned to violence by her own infatuation and confusion, along with the duplicitous social mores of her time and culture.

Etsuko is thrust into a new life with these relations, one mirroring the fragmented nature of post-war Japan. The household she finds herself in is disjointed, uneven, a strange fusion of employees and extended family, all living and quarrelling in close proximity and within carefully defined social strata (the respective size of their rooms, given in the Japanese fashion as a number of tatami mats, is an especially telling early indication of relative station and worth). Money, chores, work, and politics (sexual, domestic, or farther afield) dominate their lives, the subjects overlapping and intersecting as post-war hardships and upheavals endure, even for a reasonably well-to-do family.

The modern world, and the transition from being a rural society to a city-centred one, which Japan was facing as keenly as any other nation in the twentieth century,[26] to some extent infects and embodies *Thirst for Love*. Osaka and its suburban influence, we are frequently reminded, are never far away (and,

---

26 In 1920, approximately 18 percent of Japanese lived in cities. By 1950, when *Thirst for Love* was written, this had grown to 38 percent. In 2023, over 92 percent of Japan's population were urbanized, comparable to Israel or Argentina, and ahead of Britain (85 percent), America (83 percent), Germany (78 percent), and China (64 percent).

indeed, the novel opens with Etsuko disconcertedly buying a gift for her love interest in the often bewildering contemporary city that hovers both close to and remote from the village). Crucially, however, the rural farm is no bucolic haven from the barrenness of metropolitan existence, either: physically beautiful, it nonetheless forms its own inhospitable wilderness, despite the material bounties its land produces. The country is cradle of both freedom and restriction, just as the city is source of both misery and opportunity.

Yet this rural/urban tension, so common a conflict around which to build a story, is only one struggle among many contrasting energies – a favourite Mishimian stratagem – which the novel explores: life and death, nature and art, mind and body, beauty and ugliness, love and lust. Each of these dynamics, however, investigates only a false opposite, just as town and country are rarely as diametrically opposed or as different as we imagine. Still less are they contradictions: they need and invigorate each other, motivating and revitalizing the forces which shape and surround them, both empowering and emasculating.

We first encounter Etsuko in her present situation, already bound by love/lust to Saburo, and it is only gradually that her backstory is revealed to us, an enticing technique which parallels the masked nature of society and the need to remove layers to uncover its secreted torments and truths. Here, on the surface, we see Etsuko as a passive, even submissive, figure: first orphaned, then widowed, then turned to a mistress, a series of fates not uncommon given the place of women in Japanese life (and elsewhere).

Yet Etsuko has an ominous preoccupation with control and a remarkable capacity for survival: no intellectual or overly rational thinker, she is nevertheless fierce in her need to manage and manipulate events both around and within herself. This is something we see textually via her mix of diary entries – many of which are simply a false trail to confuse Yakichi – and her stream-of-consciousness thoughts, as well as, of course, sexually in her ardent but ultimately useless desire for the rough and primitive Saburo. (Who is as much an ideal as a tangible bodily appetite, a desire based on admiration, one evidently shared to an extent by Mishima.)

During her marriage to a womanizer and wilful tormentor – Ryōsuke – who played with the flames of his wife's understandable suspicion and resentment, Etsuko was enslaved to a jealousy which fed her need for control (and is regenerated in her spiteful envy for Saburo's lover, the maid Miyo). She wore the mask of a passive, acquiescent wife, but beneath she began to dominate her husband with a masochist's desire for pain and degradation and a narcissist's desire for the nutritious purity of self-love, both sustaining and humiliating herself in the process.

Then, when Ryōsuke contracted typhoid, the situation was reversed, and a peculiar kind of orgasmic happiness filled Etsuko: he was forced to be her object, she compelled to control him utterly, moving into his hospital room, ostensibly tending him and delighting in the fearful absence of his lovers. Amid death and disease, blood and filth, Etsuko created a prison island for two, a place not unlike Thomas Mann's Venice, where life can exist in an enigmatically ideal form, with no outside interference, fringed and defined by mortality.[27]

---

27   *Death in Venice* ('Der Tod in Venedig', 1912) obsessed Mishima for many
     years, and he fantasized about turning the work into an opera (long before
     Benjamin Britten realized it with his astringent masterpiece of 1973).

This place is also intensely, weirdly, sensual: tense, sharing the fleeting pleasures and inevitable transience of sexual gratification. Indeed, at one point Etsuko explicitly compares these dying days with her husband to the tireless unquenchable agony and desire of their honeymoon. Sex and death in this novel, as in so much Mishima (and beyond), are linked not only as cause and effect but as mirrors, echoes, or shadows of one other.

＊

This strange union of sex and death is reborn in Etsuko's ravenous longing for Saburo, whose energy, youth, and beauty disturb the widow from her lassitude and back into a desire for control that will, in due course, undo her and confirm her new love object's dreadful destiny. So too is renewed, and intensified, her sense of mortification, incarceration, and self-destruction, traits so many of Mishima's characters – and their author – share. In Etsuko's sexual torment and corrosive resentment, there are also some clear parallels, hinted at in the introduction to this chapter, to one of the great protagonists of French fiction: Flaubert's Emma (in *Madame Bovary*, 1857).

Like Emma, Etsuko is a sexually unsatisfied housewife caught in a sterile union – in Etsuko's case with her father-in-law, adding a certain incestuous frisson to the proceedings, which magnifies the intense boredom she feels. Confined by tedium, ennui, and communal vexation, Etsuko's longing for social and sexual freedom fixes upon the desirable Saburo as the object key for her flight.

In *Thirst for Love* we witness again the immediacy and vibrancy of *Madame Bovary*, the astonishing intensity of its sights, smells, and sensations, the exquisite detail in its rendering of the material and everyday world (and Emma's/Etsuko's desire to escape from them both, into the realm of the rare). Etsuko's various bloody cuts and nasty burns – along with her more damaging and deeper wounds – are rendered in often excruciating detail to match Flaubert's evocative descriptions of Emma's habits and routines, obsessions and desires. The particulars of Etsuko's appearance and expressions are as exquisitely rendered by the Japanese as the Frenchman for his heroine. (Mishima had complained that most American novels he had read offered little by way of pleasure in minute detail, especially when it came to women. He loved describing the pattern of crinkles and creases in a dress when a woman spins round in anger; the sight of the inside of a woman's throat when she laughed; the tension in a woman's face just before tears.)

We also see Emma's voluptuousness and shapely sexuality in Etsuko's leisurely, 'pregnant' walk, with its feline sensuousness and languorous charm: these are vigorous, sensual women, unwilling to be mere passive sexual fodder but yearning for sexual and romantic sovereignty. As Rodolphe says of Emma, intriguingly anticipating Mishima's novel's title, 'Poor little thing! Gasping for love, just like a carp on the kitchen table gasping for water.'[28]

For all these resemblances, however, Mishima clearly wanted to also create a character very distinct from Flaubert's heroine, someone particularly and peculiarly Japanese in their manner. Etsuko presents a numb facade of apathy and unconcern with her situation, feigning a personality that is resistant to misery, grief, or ill will. As such, Etsuko faces her desolation with a reflexive, almost robotic determination and calm exterior that

---

28 *Madame Bovary*: part 2, chapter 7.

cuts her off from those around her (ironically including, perhaps, Saburo himself, until their great final confrontation at the end of the novel).

Where Emma chooses suicide as the only means of escape from her mixture of amorous turmoil and pecuniary ruin (she has, we remember, accumulated a mountain of debts with various creditors to sustain her numerous obsessions), Etsuko's curious death wish is more affirmative and authentic, however appalling. Emma seeks a breakout from her dreary existence and then an escape from the calamitous results of that diversion into her true self – into death. Etsuko pursues something more complex, a self-styled departure linked to her husband's death. It is a widow's atoning expiration, a Wagnerian demise akin to Isolde's or Brünnhilde's,[29] or those in historical Hindu societies, a long-drawn-out quasi-suicide offered not in mourning but in envy, yearning for the exquisite freedom of nothingness. Eventually, she finds a way to embrace oblivion via death. But that death is not to be her own.

After her husband's passing, Etsuko seeks to rebuild her life, hunting less for independence than for a renewal of her true being, which she glimpsed during the strange days of her husband's illness and death. Evidently this renovation will require another death, another attempt to relocate herself after being spurned by the world. And this death will not be a passive passing via a common disease but an actively pursued loss of life, a lethal act of revenge, retaliation for Etsuko's various forms of rejection: by her husband, by Saburo, by the world.

It is keenly sought, this death, yet it is also curiously unconscious: both planned and unplanned – a perfect Mishimian

---

29   In *Tristan und Isolde* (1865) and *Götterdämmerung* (1874) respectively.

paradox. Etsuko's 'relationship', such as it is, with her father-in-law is a humiliation, but it is also a necessary part of her intricate death wish, part of her falling into – and drowning within – the insipid emptiness of her dreams of Saburo, the sacrificial figure who must be killed to satisfy her obsessions.

❧

This key image of drowning will – in a fine juxtaposition of the elements – powerfully recur in the celebrated central chapter of the novel: at the autumn fire festival. Carnivals and holidays are a key motif in Mishima's fiction (as they are in Flaubert's), not only expedient settings for some colourful set pieces but crucial metaphors for unrestrained passion, scarcely masked sexual activity, and the threat of impending violence (though in *Thirst for Love*, its festival scene obscures the boundaries between the literal and the symbolic with malignant glee).

Saburo's death is clearly and keenly anticipated from the outset of the novel, not least in the links Mishima makes (often using the imagery of graves and flowers, sun and light) between Etsuko's yearned-for lover and her now dead husband, and in the organization of stages Etsuko must proceed through on her journey toward murderous fulfilment (almost perverse stations of the cross). Most of these stages occur within the claustrophobic reality and Apollonian atmosphere of the house, with its hierarchies and hegemony, but the dazzling autumn festival chapter is a surreal and alfresco Dionysian episode that ominously and evocatively portends the homicidal activities to come.

Amid the constraints and tensions of the household, the festival is Etsuko's only opportunity – apart from some snatched/

orchestrated occasions to talk with him – to be physically close, and potentially attractive, to Saburo after months of yearning. She dresses exquisitely in her finest chrysanthemum-patterned silk kimono, and wearing expensive French perfume, as if attending a fashionable party in Osaka or Tokyo rather than an open-air gathering in the provinces. It might all be dangerously absurd, and the tearing of her haori[30] on the way there indicates trouble ahead, but such is Etsuko's single-mindedness and assurance that we are swept along with her own desires, her own imprudence.

With Etsuko, the whole household go down to the local village to watch the manic and frantic exhibition of a hundred near-naked young men taking part in an intriguing blend of religious rite and dancing gala. Wearing only loincloths ('fundoshi'), the youths rush about in front of the village's temple shrine, feverishly pursuing a lion's head displayed on a standard. Fires and flames are everywhere, adding to the tumult and craziness of the scene. Bamboo firecrackers are set off at uncomfortably regular intervals, a frenzy of noise and light, the pyrotechnics unmistakeably matching Etsuko's passion, at this, the emotional apex of the novel.

As Saburo plunges into the frenzied pit of naked male bodies, a homoerotic manifestation unlikely to be far from Mishima's own desires, Etsuko remains – with the rest of her family – a mere spectator to the spectacle. A masculine symbol of life and living, Saburo is appropriately writhing like a virile serpent among the other phallic forms and flickering flames of the festival. Yet the fierce infernos of the bonfires are also connected, for Etsuko,

---

30 A traditional hip-length jacket, resembling a shortened mini kimono (though with no overlapping front panels).

with the bright November sunshine that greeted her husband's coffin: a portentous association that bodes ill for Saburo.

Drawn by the power of her infatuation, Etsuko descends the stone steps of the temple sanctuary and seeks out Saburo – or, more specifically, Saburo's body. Engrossed by and then absorbed into the animalistic orgy of energy the men are generating, Etsuko becomes enraptured by its vitality – the vim and vigour so absent from her own dreary life. Yet she is also a deity seeking the blood of a sacrificial victim to both sate her thirst and generate almost superhuman powers of momentum. Her control now feels invincible and divinely ordained, capable of achieving anything, not least because she, a goddess, has sublimated masculine capacities into her feminine being.

Amid the waves of the unreadable, expressionless human throng, with their rhythmic, recurrent thrusts of strength and the phantasmagoria of colours in the night air, Saburo's vast naked back confronts Etsuko and all her obsessive whims, and gives us perhaps the novel's key passage:

> Metaphorically that back was a bottomless ocean depth to her; she longed to throw herself into it. Her desire was close to that of a person who drowns himself; he does not necessarily covet death so much as what comes after the drowning – something different from what he had before, at least a different world.

Not content with merely observing Saburo's body, however, Etsuko plunges forward amid the propellant anonymity of the orgiastic human confederation and savours the touch of his majestic warm flesh. Then, in what is clearly a form of sexual assault, she gouges her fingernails into his back: he feels not a thing in the midst of the uncontrolled jostling and shoving as his blood trickles between Etsuko's fingers – an image of disturbing macabre magic worthy of Zola's Thérèse Raquin or Shakespeare's Lady Macbeth.

From here the gruesome caprice turns into hallucination and mirage as the shouting men elbow and shoulder each other around a burning bamboo pole, their bare feet dancing amid the embers. The branches of an old cypress tree are lit by the flames of the bamboo shaft, which explodes and then topples like the mast of an ancient ship. Etsuko watches it all in a bacchanalian daze of delight, her prey's blood dripping to the floor. She thinks she sees a woman with her hair on fire, laughing manically, the sky filled with sparks and arcs of fire – but we are now in the realm of dream and delusion. Etsuko remembers nothing else, somehow stealing away back to the stone steps, toward a semblance of sanity and transformed reality.

For now, she has enjoyed and controlled Saburo's body – but only partially. Soon she will possess ultimate control over it: as a corpse.

Mishima's metaphysics of the flesh and philosophy of the heart converge in the spectacular scene of the fire festival, a prose panorama which generates some of his greatest writing. Lucid, evocative, and formidable, the chapter is a brimming cornucopia of literary and psychoanalytical insinuations. Love, lust, death, gender, power, station, status, mind, body, and the seductive glamor of violence inextricably collide in its sexual-textual delirium.[31]

At the very end of the fire festival chapter, the announcement of Saburo's girlfriend's pregnancy – the result of a relationship that is both natural and enjoyable – simultaneously cuts him off from Etsuko and inseparably ties him and his fate to her by fuelling her desire for revenge and distorting her sexual desires into deadly ones. But this is only the confirmation of what the previous passages have implied to us. Etsuko is unable to achieve sexual congress and ecstasy with Saburo via conventional means, and her fanciful, illusory, and group communion with the object of her desires is a blatant metaphor. Helpless reality gives way to controlling fantasy. Yet this fiction is more than a slim reward for her frustrated cravings: the festival 'intercourse' seems as powerful and satisfying as sex itself, more so since it gratifies much deeper ontological, emotional, and spiritual needs.

Etsuko here is intriguingly close to both the unthinking, unexceptional, unintellectual Saburo and one of her author's own ideals: she is able to shift easily between impulse and action, a being not pulled apart by the mind/body difference but relishing the porous (or non-existent) boundaries between them. But instinct and intoxication, those Dionysian paradigms, will have consequences, destroying order, for the fire festival is a ferociously written section of *Thirst for Love*, one which plainly intimates Saburo's imminent demise at Etsuko's hands. There, the rapacious wrath of her fingernails will be replaced by the infinitely more injurious rage of a mattock, the gardener's tool for digging the earth turned upon its owner in an act of ghoulish allure.

---

31 Mishima later admitted that *Thirst for Love* owed a great deal to his reading of Sigmund Freud's *Studies on Hysteria* ('Studien über Hysterie', 1895).

The actual murder of Saburo can feel curiously disappointing, even unsatisfying. After the saturnalia of images and passionate concentration of the festival, which is clearly the sensual and emotive culmination of the novel, the consciously more generic 'murder theatre' scene of the killing might seem a let-down. But, significantly, it is a return to the real world after the hostile commotion of the temple revels, inhabiting the grim actuality of existence – though, this being Mishima, it is hardly devoid of suspense, tension, and some deliciously grisly writing.

Saburo meets Etsuko at her request at 1:00 a.m. in the grape orchard (perhaps a sly reference to Dionysian wine). Their confrontation is awkward, embarrassing, as she tries to intimidate the farm boy into telling her he loves her (which he eventually does merely to extricate himself from the uncomfortable situation). Less angry than disgruntled by his obviously false declaration, Etsuko then kills him to fulfil her deranged lust, her death wish, and her desire for revenge. The whole scene seems a deliberately muted echo of the festival violation, its more subtle colours a terrifying glimpse into the shadows of Etsuko's dark, twisted, but ultimately defiant soul.

Repeatedly during the tryst/murder scene it is stated that words are not enough, that only actions will bring them together. This reflection is at once glaringly obvious (given the inability of any of this novel's characters to sufficiently communicate via language), and filled with a delectable double irony (given both the potency of Mishima's words to convey the scene to us and his growing later belief in the superiority of action over words – a view that would, of course, ultimately lead to his own death).

Words stand between Etsuko and Saburo like stubborn spirits, at once oppressor and saviour, enemy and friend. Saburo fails to understand Etsuko's web of words, her mix of sentences that are both confused and controlled (as well as controlling). For his part, he can only blunder and bundle fabrications across to her, which make her feel neither especially irritated nor outraged but, in an unusually malicious manner, justified. It is this combination of unaffected, authentic feelings – anger, disappointment, fulfilment – that echoes the environment of the fire festival, thereby apparently sanctioning Etsuko to commit her act of unpremeditated, intuitive, and profoundly gratifying erotic violence.

Just as she passed into a wordless, eerie (and evidently ecstatic, even orgasmic) trance after her pseudo-ravishment of Saburo at the fire festival (perhaps in part the 'outside' or 'different' world she longed for), in the aftermath of his murder and burial of his corpse in the garden, Etsuko slips into a deep, unflustered, silent sleep (while her sole earthly witness and semi-accomplice Yakichi is a squirming mess of insomnia and agitation). The narrator suggests her untroubled slumbers are a 'divine favour', confirming her eminence as a goddess figure: sated, satisfied, and having achieved her state of euphoric repose.

The eternally crowing roosters that squawk in the distance when Etsuko wakes in the murky early morning, when the novel closes, further indicate heavenly good will: their chant is associated in Japanese culture and mythology with the gods, especially Amaterasu, the celestial sun goddess in the Shinto pantheon, who brings an end to human darkness, lured out of her cave by the rooster's cry. Within Buddhism, too, the rooster is a symbol of dawn, new life, and non-material desires and is, along with the snake and pig, one of three animals which accompany humanity in the cycle of birth and death. As such, the rooster's crow is clearly a fitting, if somewhat unnerving, sound with which to end *Thirst for Love* and audaciously mark Etsuko's perverse, pertinacious attainment of a nihilistic grace.[32]

❧

Mishima's extraordinary art persuades us that Etsuko's behaviour is both right and wrong, terrifying and reassuring. He disturbs us with both the pleasure of her misery and the exhilaration of her ennui.

The sublime and immersive nothingness Etsuko yearns for, and which she finds amid murder and morning roosters, will find an even greater literary expression in the closing pages of Mishima's remarkable final quartet of novels, *The Sea of Fertility*, not to mention a biographical manifestation in their author's self-annihilation in November 1970. Nothingness is woven into the very texture of all these works, as well as into Mishima's life, through his extreme employment of a redemptive negation that embraces oblivion – which is at once impudent, scintillating, and deeply disconcerting.

Too often the puzzles and paradoxes of Mishima are written off as insanity, disregarded as the unhinged ravings of a right-wing idealogue or lunatic with a death wish. Yet to do so is to miss the profound awareness of human nature Mishima communicated through his fiction, the mysterious insights into our troubled psyches which he perceived with his novelist's inquisitive eye as precisely as any psychoanalyst's probing inquiries.

---

32 Roosters are considered to be sacred birds even in contemporary Japan, and often strut freely around Buddhist temples and Shinto shrines. During harvest festivals or New Year celebrations they are occasionally released as a means of expressing hope for good fortune and prosperity in the coming year or as a way to ward off evil.

Chapter Three

Forbidden Colours
FIFTY SHADES OF GAY

In the early 1950s, Mishima's favourite gay bar in Tokyo was the Brunswick.

Situated in the fashionable Ginza district, it was one of a number of new openly homosexual hang-outs that had arisen after the war. This was partly due to the domestic social changes the conflict had wrought, but it was also thanks to the influx of a sizeable gay community from overseas, especially American GIs who congregated in the capital during the US occupation. A popular coffee house and drinking spot that apparently employed exclusively good-looking young waiters, the Brunswick attracted a cosmopolitan clientele of businessmen, diplomats, soldiers, artists, writers, wheeler-dealers, and assorted ne'er-do-wells looking for a good time.

During the day it was a fairly respectable café – albeit one featuring a tropical aquarium, as well as bullfighting posters and Mexican sombreros on the walls. But as the afternoon wore on, beer, then hard liquor, increasingly began to flow so that, by night, it was a riotous venue, the bar swarming with young men alternately primly and provocatively dressed. In the evenings, table staff doubled as performers in the (in)famous Brunswick floor show, which mixed conventional cabaret with rather more risqué drag acts.[33]

To some extent, Mishima frequented the Brunswick for research into his new novel, *Forbidden Colours* (禁色, 'Kinjiki',[34] published in two volumes in 1951 and 1953[35]). But this line of research was personal as well as professional: at the time Mishima was embarking on a series of both hetero- and homosexual relationships, of varying degrees of intimacy and importance. To a degree, he was more comfortable with men, with some of these lovers marvelling at his ability to enjoy sex and alcohol during the evening before serenely settling down to write all night. Alongside these liaisons, however, Mishima was dating

---

33 One of their number, Akihiro Maruyama, would go on to become a famous transvestite actor-singer – as well as a close friend and associate of Mishima, starring as the lead in his play *The Black Lizard* ('Kuro-tokage', 1961), in addition to a film based on his novel *The Too-Long Spring* ('Nagasugita haru', 1956).

34 The Japanese title 'Kinjiki' (禁色) can be understood as a euphemism for same-sex relationships: the second kanji character (色) can refer to erotic love as well as colour. 'Kinjiki' carries wider socio-historical implications as well, since the term also refers to the colours prohibited to be worn by people of lower ranks at the Japanese court. In a hierarchical and symbolic system developed since the eighth century, certain shades of traditional clothing were reserved for the upper echelons of officialdom, with the emperor exclusively permitted to use the colour sumac (a gorgeous golden chocolate brown) for their outer garments, in particular the ceremonial robes worn at their enthronement: the stunning imperial sokutai.

35 Volume 1, *Forbidden Colours* ('Kinjiki', 1951), chapters 1–18; volume 2, *Secret Pleasures / Secret Drugs* ('Higyō', 1953), chapters 19–32. (Both volumes are now usually published as one properly unified whole.)

an array of attractive and affluent women who were far more
to him than either social springboards or mere beards used to
conceal his sexual oscillations.

Without doubt this assortment of relationships helped feed
the complex sexual politics of *Forbidden Colours*, his longest novel
and one of his finest: a furious, decadent delight which explores
the problems of youth and old age as much as it does those of
gender, vengeance, and erotic personality. On the one hand
Forbidden Colours is a radical exploration of the new homosexual
demi-monde in Tokyo, a lewd, licentious adventure of beauty,
temptation, guilt, envy, and revenge. Yet it is also a poignant
consideration of the passing of the years, of ugliness and ageing
– two of Mishima's paramount and persistent neuroses. Indeed,
the novel combines the themes of sex, identity, art, ageing, and
time as powerfully as Oscar Wilde did in *Picture of Dorian Gray*
(1890), Thomas Mann in *Death in Venice* (1912), and Marcel
Proust in *À la recherche du temps perdu* (1913–27) – three writers
and a trio of works which were already a powerful influence on
the young Mishima.[36]

Forbidden Colours is an exquisite book, a treasure house
of gaudy prose and sumptuous ideas, as we observe an ageing,
manipulative protagonist and the beautiful young man who
eventually comes to control him – a subtle and devastating shift
in power which strategically structures the work (though with
a twist). The dualities – especially concerning gender and age
– which lie at the heart of *Forbidden Colours* can be angry and

---

36 The Mann and Proust in particular, Mishima claimed around the time of
    Forbidden Colours, showed that old age was a time when 'despondency'
    and 'empty hope' could only deteriorate further (and which, of course, in
    part explains his self-annihilation at the age of forty-five).

indignant, even offensive, but they are a vital part of the novel's elaborate textures and extraordinary design.

These oppositions reflect many of the divergences Mishima felt in his own life, not just personally, as he fluctuated between same-sex and (so-called) straight relationships, but in professional terms. In some measure, as a young writer he naturally wanted to be an accepted member of the Japanese literati, a successful and respected novelist; but he also despised the literary establishment, with its posturing and parochial air, and longed to be a spirit free of such formal boundaries and institutional ideals.

What was hard in life is rich in art, however, and in *Forbidden Colours* these private conflicts give way to creative complexity as we witness the depth and splendour of an intricate artistic vision, brilliantly constructed and boldly told. Like so much of Mishima's work, this is not a book for the faint of heart or easily distracted, but those who can stay the course are rewarded by revelation after revelation, a dark psychological wonder in which sexual cruelty and aesthetic debate consort in a vibrant display of the novelist's art.

Early on in his career, Mishima was keen to present to the world a persona very much in the tradition of Oscar Wilde and the aesthetes: a purveyor of wit and connoisseur of beauty, a dandy and flâneur, an acute observer of modern life (an act of witness which would take on a much darker tone later on, as Mishima came to more actively despise contemporary trends and the damage being wrought on tradition).[37] Alongside his more significant literary fiction and stage drama, Mishima wrote flippant lifestyle articles for inconsequential magazines; penned light-hearted novels aimed at housewives; and authored a number of plays that might be best regarded as being very much in the style of Wilde's *Importance of Being Earnest* and *An Ideal Husband* (both 1895): social comedies of manners with deeper truths lurking behind their witty wordplay and frivolous facades. Mishima's art criticism was more directly serious, seeking to make a true literary form out of the genre, raising prose about paint and porcelain, as he put it, to the level of poetry – something he largely succeeded in doing, and his extensive work in this arena remains widely read, at least in Japan.

With Wildean aplomb, Mishima made a fantasy and fetish of interior design and objets d'art: a beautiful home, he claimed, was as important as a beautiful body. The house which he built for himself and his family in the 1950s was featured, at Mishima's insistence, in various newspapers and glossy magazines at all stages of its design, construction, and habitation. TV crews came to chart its progress and connotations. The recent acquisition of some new Spanish table or Indian ornament would feature in whatever article Mishima was writing, and might even be

---

37 The year before the first serialization of *Forbidden Colours*, Mishima's essay 'On Oscar Wilde' (1950) had appeared in the magazine *Gunzo*. In the article Mishima uses the word 'dōrui' for himself and Wilde, literally meaning 'fellow' or 'comrade' and emphasizing their shared aesthetic, their love of Greece, their complex sexuality, their foppishness and self-absorption (though in *Forbidden Colours*, 'dōrui' carries deeper connotations of a specific same-sex relationship). For all that, Mishima would be immensely critical of Wilde: courteously condemning most facets of his persona, before serenely dissecting his legendary paradoxes and finding them wanting.

the subject of that article itself. Filling his home with a range of both Japanese and international paraphernalia, he created a monument to taste and extravagance, an ironic and exquisite heterogeneity that matched his writing.

Especially in his youth, Mishima was a keen consumer of the European aesthetic movement(s) of the nineteenth century. Art, music, literature, philosophy – he devoured them all in vast quantities and let their influence sweep over his work, infecting it with their delicious cocktail of sex, death, beauty, and corruption (though he was by no means blindly uncritical of their limitations and many perceived failures). Wilde, Huysmans, Wagner, Nietzsche, and Baudelaire in particular frequently appear in Mishima's early writings as he sought not only to be their Japanese heir but to go beyond them, to find an artistic, even erotic, resolution to the anxious crises of aestheticism and decadence, and in so doing to truly unite mind and body, beauty and annihilation, life and art.

This was something his highly choreographed death, in a sense, ultimately achieved, and the last image we have of the writer has a curiously Wildean connection, one which links back to Mishima's earliest literary pursuits and his lifelong preoccupations. Moments after his ritual suicide (involving disembowelment and decapitation), his detached head was photographed next to his body: an object of erotic horror and morbid fascination just as Jokanaan's severed head was to Salomé in Wilde's eponymous 1893 play. It was this work, *Salomé*, which had been the very first book Mishima, as a boy, had bought with his own money. Reading it in a Japanese translation (from Wilde's original French), he was urgently obsessed by its mixture of sex and death, the worship of beauty and the need to destroy it, subjects that would dominate his work, not least in the novels *Forbidden Colours* and *The Temple of the Golden Pavilion*.

Salomé would go on to play an important role in Mishima's theatrical career, the writer directing a performance of the drama in Tokyo in 1960, while his controversial short story 'Patriotism', begun soon after, parallels many of Wilde's themes of the body and the gaze, of lust and fate, of violence and ceremonial (self-) destruction (and was subsequently turned into a strange avant-garde film written and directed by Mishima himself). Only days before his suicide, he was supervising another production of the play. It was a work that haunted and stalked his whole life, his art, his whole view of the nature of existence: he rewrote its story and reworked its motifs into much of his own oeuvre, a lugubriously obsessive theme and variations.

Yet it was another Wilde work which perhaps even more closely paralleled Mishima's gothic fixation with beauty and violence and with the permeable borders between the truth of art and the fiction of reality, especially as witnessed in *Forbidden Colours: The Picture of Dorian Gray*.[38] The novels share common themes and a similar structure, along with an analogous old man / young man dynamic and a plot that turns on its head the initial enterprise. Mishima's novel concerns a successful ageing novelist, Shunsuké, whose virulent contempt and nauseating animosity toward women

---

38   Since, in the second paragraph of his first chapter, Wilde sumptuously describes the artist's studio where the eponymous picture was painted as being Japanese in effect, we might see Mishima's novel as both returning the compliment and closing the circle.

(following a series of failed marriages and tumultuous affairs) belies the immaculate perfection of the female characters in his fiction. After chance meeting a gay man, Yuichi, Shunsuké decides to use this beautiful youth as an instrument through which to exact his nasty misogynist revenge on the opposite sex.[39]

Sight, seeing, and the male gaze (whether outward or inward) are crucial elements of both Mishima's novel and its Wildean source material, with the Japanese hero, Yuichi, like his Victorian counterpart, Dorian, learning to recognize and utilize his own beauty in the manipulation of others. Pursuing yet another young woman to seduce, in the opening chapter of *Forbidden Colours*, Shunsuké first sees Yuichi emerging from the sea, near naked and with obvious parallels to and precedents in everything from Botticelli's Venus and Thomas Mann's Tadzio to Ursula Andress's Honey Ryder.[40] Enforced voyeurs, through Mishima's striking, post-Wildean prose we are compelled to stare at the beautiful object, to contemplate in wonder and admiration (and envy?) as Yuichi is born from the waves and into our hopeful hearts and lustful loins.

---

39   Lest we automatically presume Mishima shared the vehemence and cruelty of Shunsuké's prejudices, we should remember that Nabokov never craved nymphets, Jules Verne never went to the bottom of the sea – nor the centre of the earth – and Shakespeare, so far as we know, was never duped by a subordinate into murdering his wife. In *Forbidden Colours* especially, the connection between Mishima and his protagonists is an extraordinarily complex one, approaching the multi-floored and many-mirrored world of Nabokov's last completed novel, *Look at the Harlequins!* (1974).

40   In 1961 the Japanese photographer and filmmaker Eikoh Hosoe (1933–2024) collaborated with Mishima on his series *Ordeal by Roses*, placing the author in a succession of exquisitely dark and surreal positions, many of which intentionally mirrored classical poses and artworks, including Botticelli's *Birth of Venus*.

During this seaside scene, Mishima employs a brilliant narrative technique which blurs the boundaries between narrator and character so that we are never quite sure how far Shunsuké is musing on the parallels between the boy's body and Greek sculpture or if this is a gloss provided by the storyteller. It is a subtle literary game, toying with human psychology and aesthetic discussion, which will inform many aspects of the novel to come (though a refinement regrettably made less apparent in English translation from the Japanese).

Mirrors, those key tools (and symbols) of both beauty and narcissism, naturally enter into matters too. When Shunsuké initially meets Yuichi, following his marine ur-sighting, a mirror transfixes the youth into comprehending his own beauty for the first time, just at the point when both this characteristic and its recognition will be misused to the full, when the older man enters into his grand plan of exploiting the boy in order to manipulate and humiliate women. Just as Lord Henry awakened Dorian Gray to the power of his youthful magnificence while the infamous picture was being created, Shunsuké develops his dishonourable scheme via the magical, degenerate power of words as Yuichi gazes on and on at himself, the boy becoming trapped in the snares of vanity and corruption. Mirrors here are both verbal and visual, Yuichi hearing about his beauty as he contemplates it via the image of himself in the looking glass. It is a devastating synthesis.

Mirrors had a curious role in Mishima's own life as well as his work. The study on the second floor of his house was a sacred space, at once a temple of art and torture chamber of the mind, eventually filled with some fifteen thousand volumes (including everything from hardcore German philosophy and classical Japanese literature to fragile French poetry and transient

American periodicals). It was the place where he could retreat at midnight to write, after a day of sleeping followed by playful, vigorous social activities far from the demanding, lonely graft of his trade. His desk faced the room's door, upon which hung a mirror meaning he could scrutinize himself in the act of writing, something which spoke not only of his aesthetics and narcissism, but also his occasional self-disgust – with himself and the whole grisly egotism of literary creation.

There was also the fear and revulsion of ageing, of the end to beauty and the beginning of ugliness, themes of both *Forbidden Colours* and *The Picture of Dorian Gray*. In the latter, the eponymous portrait acts as the true mirror, as the 'most magical of mirrors', reflecting soul as well as flesh – and it will, of course, soon reflect Dorian's internal corruption, recording the various iniquities as his Faustian pact spills out into chaos. In both novels, Wilde's and Mishima's, awareness of personal beauty soon leads to egotism and self-absorption and thence, with appalling certainty and swiftness, to malice and aggression.

In Yuichi, Shunsuké creates a living work of art, an organic doll, one over whom he believes he has total aesthetic and ethical control. Indeed, evil and beauty become interlinked in *Forbidden Colours*, not least in the notion of Wilde's euphemistic 'love that dare not speak its name', which is both the love of an older man for a younger and homosexuality more generally. If homosexuality is only implied – albeit rather intensely – in *Dorian Gray*, in the Mishima it is explicit: a vital structural tool for, and thematic motif of, the novel as well as a key aspect of both Yuichi's and Shunsuké's characters. In *Forbidden Colours*, homosexuality is vice and victim, design and destiny.

Turned into an instrument upon which Shunsuké can play his abhorrent misogynistic tunes, Yuichi contrapuntally develops his natural homosexuality alongside becoming a serial womanizer, indifferently ravishing women (he is not attracted to them) and either abandoning them or abusing them at the behest of his virtuoso tyrant. In the gay world he frequents, too, men are demeaned and degraded, the noxious, even radioactive power of Yuichi's good looks and charm an indiscriminate weapon of brutality and oppression.

Against Yuichi's physical beauty and strength, Shunsuké is physically weak and visually ugly, while his true potency lies in words (as we might expect of a distinguished novelist). At their initial meeting it is crucial, as *Dorian Gray* also recognized, that words could work their poisonous charm upon the beautiful but innocent and vain youth, in order that language could then exploit all three characteristics in a whirlpool of manoeuvring. Crafty and persuasive, the older man uses his capacities of verbal control to first awaken his creature's self-awareness, then allay the youth's guilty conscience, before repeatedly enacting their chilling potential to maintain the manipulative scenario.

Even at the end of the novel, when Yuichi tries to fulfil his aim of refuting Shunsuké's domination (by returning his money), the youth is swept into the cyclone of the novelist's oratorical storm. Lost in the tempest of words, which eerily echo those of Lord Henry to Dorian in the second chapter of Wilde's book, Yuichi forgets the purpose of his visit, which allows Shunsuké a malicious final victory at the last moment: the old schemer dies by his own hand before the money can be given back. In authoring his own death Shunsuké makes an aesthetic sacrifice which fuses his art and life (and, as such, is a premonition of Mishima's own demise).

And even then he's not done. It transpires that in his will he has bequeathed the youth a fortune, sanctioning the curious and remarkable final page of *Forbidden Colours* where Yuichi weirdly ponders – in a resonance with the flower-infested opening paragraph of *Dorian Gray* – how many blooms he can buy for ten million yen. Yuichi strides forth into the world knowing the financial (and therefore multifaceted) clout he himself now wields, yet he feels depressed as well as liberated. On the one hand he is blithely indifferent to Shunsuké's martyrdom for art and merely glad of his own good fortune. But, on the other, he is quietly aware that the cycle of exploitation has not been evaded. It is set to continue in his own new life, one built on and bound to his own cynical manipulation by Shunsuké, in whose financial and spiritual debt he will forever remain.

The conniving maestro has enacted a final, posthumous, control of his creation.

Clearly Mishima put elements of himself, plus his fantasies and his phobias, into both Shunsuké and Yuichi. In the latter, the author could admire the Adonis body, its beauty in addition to the innocence of its owner. In the former, fearful of growing old, with its implications for both his body and his art, Mishima could project notions of his future self into his characterization of elderly corruption. Mishima never acquired the truly vile misogyny of Shunsuké, but for a mixture of comic, serious, and artistic reasons, he could extend some of his personality – and fears of what he might become – into the spite and vindictiveness of a deliciously sour old man.

Casual readers tend to prefer straightforward biographical readings of novels/characters: they are uncomplicated and undemanding. But whatever elements of his own personality Mishima distributed into his characters, he was not simply Shunsuké, woman-hater and devious rogue, any more than he was simply Yuichi, naive and conventionally gorgeous youth (even if he shared the one's profession, and the other's narcissism, and had the egotistical energy of them both).

For the most part, Mishima presents women positively and in significant depth, though they are, it is true, sometimes reduced to ridiculousness or erected as targets for his satirical venom (as, of course, are many of his men). The malicious attitudes they face in this novel (their 'piglike smell' and the infamous birth scene[41]) are directly connected to the personality and behaviour of Shunsuké, the repulsive individual Mishima wished to depict – and the ageing bitter writer Mishima wished never to become. A nasty man needed nasty views. Ultimately women as either sensual or supportive beings become both abhorrent and alien to Shunsuké's experiences and true desires, rendering them easy subjects for his vile invective.

The homoerotic atmosphere and homosexual characters of many Mishima works have led to almost reflex accusations of misogyny, as if homosexuality is a routine guarantor of an anti-female predisposition. In fact, women in Mishima not only tend to be constructively described but are frequently granted roles wherein they are not reduced to mere sexual functionaries or maternal minions. Though their very existence can often appear as a threat to art and creativity, there is also an important, and surely positive, sense that women offer a way of quashing ostentatious

---

41   But which, we might suggest, are somewhat balanced out by the exquisitely gentle – if Oedipally complex – scene in *Temple of the Golden Pavilion* where a women offers milk from her breast to a soldier heading to war.

artists or energizing inert intellectuals. They tend to embrace qualities Mishima, especially in his later work, commended: physically eye-catching, impulsive, somewhat egotistical, active, and gracefully un- or anti-intellectual (though rarely attaining the kind of distinguished nobility Mishima reserved for his men of action).

Whatever we might claim about how Mishima presents his women, we can hardly maintain that men fare well in his fiction, indicating either a misandry or general misanthropy more than any committed misogyny. For all their superficially attractive qualities, Shunsuké's linguistic dexterity and Yuichi's visual prowess, both principal characters of *Forbidden Colours* are depicted in an essentially detrimental light – as are countless other Mishimian males who appear as adulterers, arsonists, and animal abusers. Yuichi is, beyond his physical perfection and straightforwardness, easily manipulated and then a ruthless, repugnant exploiter of both men and women. For all his seductive brilliance with words, Shunsuké is shown to be ugly in mind, body, and action, the distorted depth and caricature of his sexism its own self-indictment.

The misogyny in *Forbidden Colours* is another of Mishima's masks, and the novel's principal female characters – Yasuko, Kyoko, Mrs Kaburagi – endear themselves to our affections not only because of the mistreatment they suffer (at the hands of Shunsuké, Yuichi, and the narrator), but because of their goodness and inner strength, their sense of mystery and renewal and the particular kind of aesthetic harmony their creator cherished. Their struggles to find a purpose in life, given both the social constraints of the time and the abuse they receive, are something Mishima is evidently immensely sympathetic toward. Yasuko continues to love her husband, Yuichi, despite months of neglect and justified suspicions of adultery. The maternal Mrs Kaburagi falls for Yuichi's good looks, then discovers her husband has gone further with this pretty youth than she could, before sacrificing herself in order to prevent a vain and empty playboy's homosexuality – his forbidden colours – from being revealed, a selfless act that encourages Yuichi to become a better husband.

As he wrote the book, the aesthetic discussions within *Forbidden Colours* – Walter Pater and Aubrey Beardsley litter both Shunsuké's study and his diatribes – seemed to interest Mishima less than the profound psychological appeal and presentation of his fictional individuals. Although the internal debates with Wilde et al. over art/nature/beauty remain a necessary and intriguing layer of the text, *Forbidden Colours* was not simply to be a vehicle for verbose and witty chat, his characters mere mouthpieces for essays on art and aesthetics that he had created better elsewhere. Mishima's doubts about both his own art and literature in general were conflated with his sincere belief that this novel was to be a mature realization of his advancing artistic vision of what the novel was capable of. It was a double attitude both ironically distant from and uncomfortably close to Shunsuké's contention toward the end of *Forbidden Colours* that the novel is a cheap and vulgar art form compared, say, to the marble perfection of Greek sculpture.

Sculpture is – of course – exactly what he compares Yuichi to hundreds of pages before in the first chapter of the tale. Certainly Shunsuké's sordid transformation of Yuichi from 'Greek statue' into what he calls a novelist's artistic project reflects the tawdry nature of his own warped perception of literature, the debasement to which he will subject it. When Shunsuké first formulates his plan to use Yuichi to get back at women, the narrator remarks that the writer is 'outlining the plot of a novel he had not yet written.'[42]

To an extent, the fin-de-siècle decadence of *Forbidden Colours* is a misleading, if crucial, mask in a novel of mid-century, post-war gravity, one which can be modestly restrained in its language and in its expenditure of sharp literary devices such as Wildean epigrams (indeed, their controlled deployment in many ways makes them far more effective darts in striking their targets). Given its frequent flamboyance in both words and action, however, many readers of *Forbidden Colours* have been taken in by Mishima's/Shunsuké's challenging and sometimes offensive games, manipulated by both author and protagonist into ignoring the psychological profundity at work, as the young actual novelist and his elderly fictional counterpart plan with great attention to detail, evaluating and gauging the mental states of their artistic creations.

Mishima wanted to explore in depth Shunsuké's relentless animosity and its connection to both his sexual relationships and his role as a complex creative figure, one portrayed with just the right fusion of comedy, satire, and credibility to produce a truly disturbing fictional supervillain: a Japanese Joker. Though Yuichi

---

42   Mishima himself famously visited Greece, as part of a world tour, in between writing the two volumes of *Forbidden Colours*, and the experience of his beloved Hellenic world – albeit several centuries too late – helped foster his novel's fusion of both the Apollonian and Dionysian, its mixture of grace and chaos, self-control and self-indulgence. For Mishima, the novel's two halves had a more personal meaning, the second representing a break from his Romantic youth and into a new phase of externality and outward forms, with a simpler, more classical style (discernible in his next major novels, *The Sound of Waves* and *The Temple of the Golden Pavilion*).

is a not-quite-equal co-protagonist with Shunsuké, Mishima wished to investigate the fascination of his fluctuations between victim and manipulator, as he learns to use his fleshly appeal toward evil ends. Beyond Shunsuké's appealing and appalling acts of coercion, much of the allure of the novel comes in our eyewitness to the young man's combination of sexual-emotional development and spiritual stasis – so that he is, by the novel's close, and in a fine Mishimian paradox, simultaneously set free and forever bound to the old man. In some ways, Yuichi has become Shunsuké.

Closely connected to this is the exquisite way the book not only shows us Shunsuké falling victim to his own plan, as he takes a shine to Yuichi himself, but also discloses Yuichi's increasing, if fickle, awareness of his own independence and manipulative power. Two characters so often regarded as opposites, as contrasting caricatures/archetypes, take on an unsettling interchangeability: as on an artist's palette, bright paints are mixed to create subtler shades. Each becomes a more intricate, even more natural, version of the other's parody – with profound implications for our perception of sexuality and psychology, and all the socio-cultural baggage that goes with them (while also confirming their origin in the same source: Mishima's complex personality).

The gaudy exposé of gay bars and homosexual culture was interesting enough, on its own terms, as were lurid, loquacious discussions of Art and Beauty. But neither was sufficient for Mishima the master novelist, who also wished to create an unnervingly persuasive psychosexual world.

For all this alarming, convincing reality, *Forbidden Colours* also has a delectable neo-Gothic quality to it. We witness this not only in the *Dorian* negotiations but as Shunsuké/Frankenstein creates his monster before becoming manipulated by it, unable to control it and distorting the lines between creator and creation, father and son, master and pupil. By the end of Mary Shelley's masterpiece, Victor Frankenstein is dead, while his creature roams on into the unknown; so, too, in Mishima, Shunsuké is no more, but his creative project is left to drift into an enigmatic future.

Just as there are liquid margins between Shunsuké and Yuichi, by making Yuichi aware of his own beauty and sexuality, both an object of desire and desiring subject, Shunsuké creates a split personality, a sinister binary force familiar from Stevenson, Dostoyevsky, and Nabokov. Now awakened to his identity as a homosexual man, Yuichi becomes active in the Tokyo nightspots, the cream of the gay community, while living as a 'respectable' husband/student during the day. It is a dangerous, almost aberrantly inverted Jekyll-and-Hyde double act which plays on our accepted notions of propriety while also exploring repression, guilt, and bourgeois hypocrisy. Given the manipulative game Yuichi is playing in order to persecute and punish women via his sham marriage, and his identity as a gay man, Mishima's text destabilizes conventional perceptions regarding sex, gender, and marriage, inviting us to ask ourselves what is natural or criminal, artistic or iniquitous.

Such questions, as well as the networks *Forbidden Colours* concocts with both the Greek world and the Nietzschean notion of death as the giver of meaning to life, also invite comparison with Thomas Mann's *Death in Venice*.[43] Like Gustav von Aschenbach, Shunsuké is an eminent novelist of maturing years who abandons one artistic life for another in the contemplation of a youthful male beauty. As Tadzio was to Aschenbach, Yuichi is to Shunsuké: an embodiment of classical ideals as well as a source of sensual destiny. But this embrace of life also leads to death, which is either ironic or paradoxical depending on your point of view, and is a death electrified by intense erotic overtones, a Wagnerian Liebestod.[44]

Yet there are instructive differences: Aschenbach has put all his life into his art and created masterpieces, a consolidation and repression which then finally explodes into his passion for a Polish boy in Venice. Shunsuké, on the other hand, has written a wealth of what he perceives as futile material, and has plenty of artistic energy left to manipulate classical beauty for his own ends. Where Aschenbach has put life into art, Shunsuké puts art into life, making himself author of and character in a new creative work. Where Aschenbach's previously Apollonian

---

43 A writer for whom Mishima expressed intense admiration on several occasions. It was not only the seriousness of the works themselves but the assiduousness with which Mann went about the task of writing, treating it with the fastidiousness of the bank clerk. Far from the decadence and languid indulgence of Wilde, Mann erased the borders between art and life, treating both as serious tasks – something with acute consequences for Mishima's own life and work.

44 Literally 'love-death', the German term has particular significance in Wagner's groundbreaking music drama *Tristan und Isolde* (1865), where, at its close, the eponymous heroine sinks into lifeless union with her beloved, singing music now usually referred to as 'Isolde's Liebestod'. Mishima would employ the music in the short film he wrote and directed, *Patriotism, or The Rite of Love and Death* ('Yūkoku', 1966), based on his own short story of the same name. Wagner himself, of course, underwent his own 'death in Venice' on 13 February 1883.

willpower gives way to Dionysian pandemonium (and can only do so in the luxuriantly decaying decadence of the lagoon city), Shunsuké is continually conflicted in a more complex way, a strange combustible alloy of the two forces: precariously enthralled by but ostensibly more in control of his passions.

Such manipulation is enacted in Shunsuké's semi-sacrificial self-destruction, an act of questionable creativity that would be echoed in his maker Mishima's own dramatic demise twenty years later. Both Shunsuké's and Mishima's final acts were self-absorbed endeavours to unite art and life, to destroy any boundary between them. However free Yuichi believes himself to be when he imagines how many flowers he can buy for ten million yen, Shunsuké's suicide and bequest mean the puppet will always be bound to the puppeteer as his artistic progeny. Every bud, blossom, and bloom he buys will be proof of that unbreakable chain.

Mishima, in his 'artistic' suicide, both cemented his fame and risked, in that very act, making it the one of his artworks that people most talked about (the life taking on an autonomy from the art). But then, that is surely exactly what Mishima the self-aggrandizer wanted. His death might well be his most discussed artwork, often frustratingly so at the expense of his fiction, but it would also be one that would send people, again and again, to all the others. It was the ultimate publicity stunt, the definitive advertisement for art, and one which bound the work forever to the life.

In writing *Forbidden Colours*, Mishima was clear that he was not only exploring various forms of his literary inheritance but also scrutinizing numerous sides to his own personality, creating – as he put it – a debate among his many assorted selves. The book allowed him to go further in art than he often wished to in life: in cynicism, in discrimination, in lust, in anger. It also allowed him to time-travel. Shunsuké was a dreadful revelation of a potential future self, one that was treacherously close to hand. Yuichi was a prettier version of himself, an incarnation of an alternative Yukio, perhaps one who would have been happily exquisite in the Athens of centuries past, a simple model for an older sculptor who might immortalize him in stone.

For all its celebration of the plastic arts, however, and its protagonist's pessimism surrounding the novel as an art form, ultimately it is as a work of intense psychological literature that *Forbidden Colours* succeeds, as a work of profound insight into the destructive influence of not only sex, love, and hate but the written word too. For all his gleeful malevolence and nastiness, we should surely celebrate Shunsuké for his own magnificent ability – like Mishima's – to use words as powerful, poisonous tools.

In this chronicle of spiritual corruption of the young by the old, Mishima extended the definition of a work of art to include the artist's own life. Now an artist could be author of their own fate *and* a memorable, organic, and unified heroic character in the literature of life, one (following Nietzsche) without any superfluous or unnecessary features. The artist both writes and features in his own dramatic creation. It makes a mockery of Wilde's celebrated remark 'I have put all my genius into my life, I have put only my talent into my works'[45] – the boundaries between life and art have been exploded. For Mishima, there could be no distinction between the two.

It was a radical, even life-threatening, aestheticism that would have profound implications for the journey and destiny of Mishima's own existence.

---

45   Which Mishima has a successful businessman, hopelessly under the sexual spell of Yuichi, actually cite near the end of *Forbidden Colours*. According to Mishima's harsh analysis, Wilde wilfully, even masochistically, authored his own demise, but kept his life as a creation distinct from either his prose fiction or those works he wrote for the London stage. For Mishima this was both a critical and a vulgar error: commonplace, and lacking in aggression, sedition, or perversity.

Chapter Four

The Sound of Waves
GREEKS BEARING GIFTS

The twilight clouds glowing like a gilded helmet in the western sky, the departing sun a dazzling fire on the mountains, a plane crossed the Ionian Sea and Gulf of Corinth to bring Mishima to Athens. It was the penultimate leg of a five-month world tour between December 1951 and May 1952 that had taken in San Francisco, Los Angeles, New York, Miami, Rio de Janeiro, São Paulo, Paris, and London (Rome would be the last stop). Seeing the Hellenic landscape of his dreams unfolding beneath him, he cried out a single word: 'Greece',[46] breathing the magic of the name and all that it meant to him.

One aspect of the visit Mishima relished, along with the savage blue of the Greek sky, was the asymmetrical splendour of the ruins he explored. The writer was fascinated by the way time (and sometimes more deliberate destruction) had created

---

46　ギリシャ, 'Girisha'.

an irregular, uneven perfection – akin to many of the stone gardens in Kyoto, where rocks of unequal size are arranged within linear sweeps of smooth pebbles. The empty, lopsided shrines and limbless marble youths of Athens had been arrived at via the accidents of history, whereas Japanese designers had relied on intuition to find something unique, exceptional – an inimitable composition, not a universal model or copy. The aims had been different, but the results were the same: an incitement to meditation, reflection – and further artistic creation.

Pottering around the tumble-down temples, as he recorded in his journal,[47] Mishima pondered how just as Japanese art and poetry is highly suggestive, with buried and concealed meanings, so the Greek ruins invite, even demand, the observer rebuild the structure of the ancient edifices in their imagination, filling in the vanished architecture, the lost stones, the missing and misplaced ideals and traditions. Onlookers, like readers, have to become new architects, new masons, new visionaries, as they recreate and revisit the past via the Parthenon or Theatre of Dionysus, just as readers must dynamically reinterpret literature with each successive generation.

In Mishima's literary career – which sought to combine traditional and modern elements, while also affirming cross-cultural bridges between Asia and Europe – ancient Greek tragedy and poetry played a key role (he even undertook a course in the language and attained a working knowledge). Greek mythology, now supercharged by his presence in the cauldron of its creation, had long been one of Mishima's passions, and in seeing the ruins of Athens and Delphi he was intoxicated by happiness, enjoying the mixture of physical and intellectual

---

47   Which became his non-fiction travelogue, *The Cup of Apollo* (1952).

sunlight, his poetic imagination guiding those two solar horses like an antique charioteer.

He had already recently written a short story based on Euripides's *Medea*,[48] as well as a satirical play taken from Greek myth,[49] and on returning home from Europe he conceived of a new novel reworking Longus's second-century tale of Daphnis and Chloe into contemporary Japan: *The Sound of Waves* (潮騒, 'Shiosai', 1954).

༈

Back in Japan and undertaking research for *The Sound of Waves* in March 1953, Mishima visited Kamishima,[50] an isolated island at the mouth of Ise Bay, off the south-east coast of Honshu. The writer had wanted to see an old fishing village on a small island as the setting for the novel, one not influenced by big cities, with beautiful scenery but not economically stagnant or obsolete: relative prosperity would be a key element to his new text. Having been met by the head of the island's fishermen's association (Mishima had received an introduction via his father's contacts in Tokyo), he stayed with this local leader for nearly two weeks, generally observing life but noticing in particular the family's peculiar use of an oil drum as a bathtub – something soldiers had been known to do, during the al fresco campaigns of WWII.

He was also keen to see the island, and its surrounding seas, in rough weather, especially during a storm, for the climactic scene of the novel. He informed his hosts of this desire and

---

48 'Lion' (獅子, 'Shishi', 1948).

49 *Niobe* (ニオベ, 'Niobe', 1949).

50 神島, literally 'God Island' and referring to the Shinto shrine located there.

asked that they contact him in the summer when a typhoon was on the horizon. A few months later, in August, he received a telegram alerting him to a looming storm. He rushed down the coast but on reaching the ferry to take him from the mainland to Kamishima found most of the bad weather had passed. The seas remained high, however, during the crossing, and Mishima thrilled at the white-knuckle ride up the mountainous waves before the heart-stopping plunge to the bottom of their aquatic valleys. Once back on the island, which was as remote and free of urbanization as he had remembered from the spring, he set about his meticulous process of surveillance. A month later, in September, he began to write *The Sound of Waves*.

This coming-of-age tale, this Bildungsroman, is an alternate reality and sometimes seems to come close to gentle fantasy. In many respects – not least in the context of Mishima's wider work – it reads like a fairy tale: one with a (semi-) orphaned hero and an optimistic ending. Its positive, buoyant nature feels disconcerting coming from Mishima's pen, with its more conventional love story devoid of the lurid baroque agonies of *Forbidden Colours* (1953) or the tortured obsessions of *Thirst for Love* (1950). Yet it is this very simplicity and absence of histrionics which makes the text so intriguing, its more placid surface concealing a surprising tide of tensions, discussions, and stubborn negotiations.

Although *Waves* is technically set in Japan – its Utajima ('Song Island') is closely modelled on Kamishima[51] – it could be

---

51 Part of Mishima's reasoning for setting his novel on Kamishima/Utajima was the profound connection between Kamishima's shrine and the nearby Ise Shrine in Mie, dedicated to the solar goddess Amaterasu, Japan's most revered Shinto monument and a vital link with the nation's creation myths as well as the aura and charismatic inscrutability of the imperial line.

set on the moon, given its immense distance from the bourgeoning industrial post-war Japan, a nation rebuilding (with American dollars) and extending its ugly urban sprawl. And yet, of course, it is crucial that Utajima both is and is not in Japan: the island, like all islands, is a liminal, potentially idyllic, space. The novel opens with a wonderful prolonged description of the setting, emphasizing not only its predictable beauty but its spiritual and physical isolation from the rest of the country. Utajima is but a dot in the (literal) ocean, its inhabitants sincere participants at the island's shrine, a dutiful, pious attribute noticeably lacking, it is implied, from contemporary Japanese life, with its beer bars and pachinko parlours.[52]

Beyond the devout worship of the islanders, however, is the novel's stress, especially at its outset, on the physical environment itself, the immense beauty of the land-, sea- and skyscapes, along with the mutually beneficial connection between humanity and the natural world. The islanders exist mainly as fisherfolk, adjusted and accustomed to the rhythms of the seasons, the fluctuations in the weather, the homespun traditions that have long existed among their community, tying them to both each other and their location. They are all outsiders, almost a society of outcasts, with only glimpses, and usually negative ones, of the real world beyond their ostensibly serene shores.

---

52   A particular bête noire for Mishima: *pachinko* – a type of pinball gambling game imported from the USA in the 1920s – stood for everything that was vulgar, alien, and corrupt in contemporary Japan. The machines remain wildly popular to this day, filling the betting niche in Japan that fruit machines do elsewhere: low stakes, low skill, low strategy – and highly addictive. For Mishima, the pachinko machines' nickname, 'one-armed bandits', did not nearly come close enough.

The plot itself maintains this sense of isolation, of remoteness, taking up an ancient Greek myth and many of the familiar figures, images, and events of the fairy tale: the industrious young hero who must prove himself through a series of trials – both physical and emotional – in order to win his beautiful bride (and revive his community). The heroine, naturally, has a domineering father who is not only controlling of his daughter and her potential suitors but occupies a conspicuous, high-flying social and economic role in the community, bringing class and coin into the equation. Whether in antique Athens, medieval Europe, or twentieth-century Japan, the tropes and traits endure.

Our hero is Shinji, a poor handsome fisher boy whose father was killed as he fished, strafed by the US Navy's machine guns toward the end of the Second World War. The heroine is Hatsue, recently returned to the community after an enforced exile, and the daughter of the richest man on the island, significantly the owner of a boat. The two fall in love early on in the novel, and after various trials and tribulations – including traumatic meteorological events, heroic deeds, social prejudice, green-eyed rivals, erotic temptation, and sexual violence – the lovers become betrothed, and the story ends happily.

Written under the influence of Mishima's intoxication with Greece – his 'Greek fever', as he called it – *The Sound of Waves* was to be a classical utopia of love, transferring Daphnis and Chloe to a Japanese island. Mishima wanted to render not reality, not the messy mechanics of true adolescent sexuality, but something idealized, a beautiful picture of aesthetic perfection.

And virtue – for the novel constantly teases the reader's sense of erotic anticipation, expectation and realization. Descriptions of sexual encounters and the body tend to be highly artificial: characters are icons of beauty discussed not as complicated, three-dimensional individuals but as if they are Greek sculptures, paintings, or literary archetypes.

In the context of this prelapsarian island world, the pastoral form Mishima employs not only stresses innocence to an exaggerated degree (to such an extent that it is clearly intended as artifice) but makes more than implicit the distinction between its rustic purity and the fallen world of the mainland (which is almost to be viewed as one vast unending mono-metropolis – something that often feels the case, as anyone who has ever travelled on a train west out of Tokyo can attest to).

Famously, *Daphnis and Chloe*, like *Waves*, opens with a long and detailed rural description. In the Longus, we witness the nymphs' grove and its dedicatory picture representing the history of love in the Lesbos countryside, before an unforgettable portrayal of urban Mytilene and then a change back to the pastoral scene. Tensions between town and country were a common feature of ancient Greek novels (not to say most global literature), which tended to represent the countryside as a dangerous, destitute place from which a temporarily displaced hero and heroine would escape back to urban(e) civilization.

Daphnis was different, however, in presenting its protagonists as preferring their rustic environment, even when the rural foundlings are revealed as genuine elite citizens – though Longus is keen to destabilize any superficial or naive commemoration of the countryside. The Greek text intimates that the ideal is actually to be found in a mixture of straightforward rustic nature and artful city culture. Mishima felt a more clear-cut fondness for traditional rural life, which his novel makes unambiguous (even if he also knew the poverty and ignorance that country life could breed).

Throughout *Waves*, Mishima makes Utajima a symbolic substitute for Japan itself, the island nation off the coast of the rest of the world. Two locations in the novel, presented in its first paragraphs, offer the islanders extraordinary views: the shrine and the lighthouse. But while the former is a holy place, the latter is a dangerous site of urban encroachment, Mishima's parallel for the Mytilene of *Daphnis*. It seems to exist less to caution and advise sailors than vice versa, warning islanders of the treacherous world beyond their own hazardous yet protective coastline.

Crucially, the hero and heroine, unlike Daphnis and Chloe, are native to their island. Hatsue symbolically readopts her homeland at the outset, after a spell elsewhere, and partakes in the prototypically inward-looking yet bountiful activity of diving for shellfish, much to the astonishment and occasional vexation of her colleagues. Shinji himself never leaves the island – except in the test of his gallantry and resolve at the novel's climax, a single voyage (it's all that is needed).

Although it can, as with the kind of lazy patriotism Mishima was often prey to, especially in his later years, be insular, narrow-minded, and its own form of dangerous, in *The Sound of Waves* island life – rural life – is to be regarded as the best life, and islanders the best kind of people. The outside world of the mainland, with its glaring neon signs, intimidating tall buildings, filthy cars, and chaos, is a negative, detrimental space, an urban threat to order and harmony. Chiyoko, the restless, fretful, invidious daughter of the lighthouse keeper, has – with lovely Mishimian irony – been to Tokyo to receive an impractical and superficial higher education in literature, returning home unfulfilled, a purveyor of gossip and lies: her metropolitan learning has taught her nothing but envy for simplicity and a desire to exploit rural moral attitudes. Similarly, local boy Yasuo's frequent trips to the mainland – made possible by a comparatively wealthy family – have merely made him a sexual predator, a licentious bully and bore.

Whereas, notoriously, in *Daphnis and Chloe* the suggestion is that rural children, left to their own devices, will simply turn to sexual experimentation and debauchery, copying the rams, ewes, billy goats, and nanny goats, in *The Sound of Waves*, the scene where Shinji and Hatsue confront each other naked is an exploration of temptation tamed. They impulsively embrace, but Shinji's passion is checked by Hatsue's realization that they should wait for marriage (even if that union is, at this point, an unlikely one). Rural ignorance is not at work here, but rather a conscious, elegant desire to conform to the ethics of their community. We might scoff with suave superiority at the ardent young lovers denying themselves pleasure, but given the pastoral form of the novel, it is us who are the unsophisticated, leering hoi polloi if we do so.

Given the close ties between the island community and nature, for Shinji and Hatsue to withhold their sexual desires until uniting themselves with each other (and, by extension, that community) is ultimately an engagement with and to nature, not a denial of it. In *Daphnis*, Dorkon attacks Chloe disguised as a wolf, a creature classically representing rural violence, with his assault foiled because of his own dishonest imitation of nature: his wolf's apparel attracts the lovers' biting dogs. Mishima's equivalent scene, when Yasuo schemes to rape Hatsue at the well, is similarly thwarted by nature – in this case, swarming hornets – acting in its expected, biological manner, rather than by concealment or subterfuge. Moreover, the hornets' aggravated but ultimately salvific attack is prompted by an unnatural force equivalent to Dorkon's lupine garb: the phosphorescent glow-in-the-dark glare of Yasuo's city-bought watch, a material symbol of flaunted wealth and urban corruption.

The pastoral form allows Mishima's sparkling, hygienic narrative to proceed – even if its status as a morality tale rather than a realistic advert for island life has frequently been missed. Clearly internal dishonesty and local moral laxity exist, and it is both wrong and dangerously convenient to always blame ethical breaches on external influences. Yet the formulaic context is crucial to the wider celebration of, and respect for, nature (and condemnation of urbanization) *The Sound of the Waves* observes. The shape and forces of the natural world define life on the island, along with the plot of the novel, and through trying to embody nature's fusion of clarity, strength, flexibility, resilience, and beauty, humanity can exist in harmony with it, not antagonism.

Both Shinji's and Hatsue's professions – fisherman and diver – require a close engagement with and understanding of how nature works if they are to succeed in their work and avoid its inherent dangers. Hatsue's activity, plunging into the depths for treasures hidden in rough exteriors, might also suggest a metaphor for her would-be husband, though his roughness is a physical durability and working-class background rather than any moral or verbal coarseness. Inside we know he is a pearl.

Consequently, it is the ultimate exhibition of nature's wrath and power – a typhoon at sea – which is required to obtain the ultimate exhibition of human love and happiness: marriage. Shinji is invited to join the crew of the *Utajima-maru*, the merchant ship owned by Hatsue's father. During a storm,[53] a crucial cable snaps, and Shinji volunteers to swim into the raging seas to reattach it, something he completes with his years of maritime knowledge as a guide. He does not confront nature but engages with it in a positive, adaptable, and respectful manner which marks both his moral and physical strength, replicating the power of the natural world, and in so doing saving not only his own life but those of his shipmates.

The sea, that definitive and supreme romantic image, a realm of ambiguity, obscurity, and promise, was the ideal setting for the novel, as well as the scene of its climax. It is both a ghostly monarchy of mystery and a place of hard, dangerous work. Those who earn a living by or on the sea will come back to haunt Mishima's oeuvre with varying degrees of irony and sincerity: there is the eponymous mariner of *The Sailor Who Fell from Grace with the Sea* (1963) and the lighthouse keeper Tōru of *The Decay of the Angel* (1971), the final part of the *Sea of Fertility* tetralogy, who exchanges a fresh-faced, clean-living existence for one of social advancement and depravity.

Although it never approaches pantheism per se, *The Sound of the Waves* is distinctive in both its reverence and its respect for nature as well as its relative textual absence of gods. In *Daphnis in Chloe*, the gods appear in visions and dreams to influence events, with the persuasive holy trio of Eros, Pan, and the nymphs manoeuvring

---

53 This occurs, symbolically, off the coast of Okinawa, an island prefecture in the far south of Japan, which, at the time of the novel, remained under American administration. It was eventually returned to Japan in 1972, though thousands of US armed forces controversially linger to this day.

the story toward its contented conclusion – something dutifully acknowledged by the human participants. By contrast, although the protagonists of *Waves* sometimes pray at the island's shrine or leave offerings, the gods are not seen to reciprocate these human submissions, being less overtly obliging in assisting the young couple.

Instead, through venerating nature as a divine force in itself, Shinji and Hatsue are able to help themselves – and to congratulate themselves accordingly at the novel's close. Hatsue quietly insinuates that a picture of herself she gave Shinji helped protect her lover on the perilous voyage out to sea, but Shinji recognizes that it is his own strength, built through and maintained via a deferential engagement with nature, that won the day.

The Japanese word 'chikara' (力) – 'strength' – is a key one for Mishima and echoes the term Hatsue's father uses in the novel's penultimate chapter when commending Shinji's exploits at sea and approving of the young man's marriage to his daughter: 'The only thing that really counts in a man is his get-up-and-go.' Texan translator Meredith Weatherby's mid-1950s rendering of 'kiryoku' (気力) as 'get-up-and-go' is – perhaps with unintended irony – heavily Americanized, representing a kind of bootstrap philosophy. A more literal rendition would be 'mental/spiritual strength', whose second element, as we can see, contains the same Japanese character as that for 'strength' just alluded to.

A further translation of 'kiryoku' seems even more important and not only brings us back to Mishima's trip to Greece, as well as his dethronement of the role of the gods in humanity's activities, but demonstrates that *The Sound of Waves* is a more significant work in this writer's canon than many, Mishima included, have given it credit for: 'willpower'. In Greece, Mishima sought an escape from what he saw as his romantic affliction, his 'katagi' (気質) – 'temperament, disposition or nature' – as he called it in 1959, which was partly sexual, partly intellectual, partly spiritual. He desired the hot, absolving sun of Athens, the endless sky, somewhere uncomplicated and exuberant. As he gazed at the ruins and statues in the abundant, contagious sunlight, he exulted in the celebration of the physical the Greeks made manifest. It was a cathartic experience, a lesson that ethics and beauty were the same, and moreover that – for Mishima – personal and literary aesthetics were to be ethically indistinguishable.

Mishima claimed that the world tour, and especially its Greek element, had purged him of his self-hatred, his loneliness, awakening in him what he called a 'will to health' in the Nietzschean sense of a 'will toward power', which incorporates the death of God and the Übermensch. Mishima, as he embarked on writing *The Sound of Waves*, saw himself in a far more confident light than he had previously supposed, sure that self-hatred and loneliness could no longer hurt him. This was wishful thinking, perhaps; certainly it was naive. But it contained a truth and an optimism that he carried over into his new novel, a new belief in, and destructive obsession with, personal strength and determination – even if those twin deities would ultimately cause much of his own future collapse.

The Sound of Waves derived from Mishima's desire to transform himself both as a man and a writer, artificially and aesthetically, physically and psychically. The trip to Greece was a catalyst in this unobtainable, unrealistic, process – an idealism Mishima himself was only too aware of. On 14 January 1955, his thirtieth birthday, as potent an occasion as any on which to attain an epiphany, Mishima invited two literary friends to his house for drinks. He was now too old to die beautifully, via suicide, he claimed, before showing them a name card on which he had written what was pronounced as 'Yu-ki-o Mi-shi-ma' but written with different Japanese characters, characters which meant something akin to 'Mysterious-devil-tail devil-bewitched-by-death'. It was a disturbing joke, met with an awkward silence, and typical of Mishima's endless buffoonery, but proof that he was not over his death wish or obsession with the grave, which he had hoped *The Sound of Waves* (and Greece) would help banish. A rusty nail might as well convince itself that tomorrow it will become a rose.

In the book itself, we witness not only a desire to present a less anguished story than in his previous novels but a further exhibition of Mishima's desire to become a master of both style and styles, rejoicing in the variety of his output, revelling with a Joycean bravura in the wearing of many literary masks as well as his immense gifts as a writer of Japanese. He luxuriated in the richness and variety of the language, its elegance and allusive power.

Although Mishima would later claim *Waves* to be his own 'joke on the public', the novel itself wears that (potential) irony as a mask: any hint of sarcasm, satire, or insincerity is absent from the text, and we need to treat Mishima's pronouncement with caution. It is true that the whole work might exist as a tongue-in-cheek shrug by its author, a mockery of its celebration of youthful beauty and romantic optimism, but we – and he – can also appreciate it on its own, honest and unironic, terms as well. For Mishima, with his complexity and chameleon-like personality and literary style, it is easy to see how he might come to disown, or at least disparage, the novel, but we can also see where it fits in with many of his wider ideas of personal, social, and communal integrity, concepts that need no mockery or derision.

The intensity – natural, sexual, emotional – of *The Sound of Waves* is both distinctly Mishimian and an antidote to the miasma of listless misery which had inhabited so many of his recent protagonists (in many ways, symbols of the defeated Japan, bewildered and lost in its post-apocalyptic, post-atomic haze). This work is full of passion, light, and life – a world away from the desolate, scheming sexual manoeuvres of *Forbidden Colours*. Although Shinji and Hatsue supress their amatory impulses, this gives the novel an immense erotic insinuation, a highly charged sensual sovereignty – naive, profoundly virtuous, and anticipatory beings swirling with sexual potency. Read this way, there is nothing chaste about *The Sound of Waves*.

To accentuate and realize this emotional, physical force, Mishima necessarily created flatter characters than we might expect, along with stereotypically attractive figures, conventionally beautiful imagery and scenery, and a setting that is a powerful character in itself, as well as a structure and narrative arc that is entirely conventional – or, rather, traditional, since it was a celebration of and homage to Mishima's beloved Greek myths. The conservative, orthodox vessel was intentional, necessary, radically sublime, required in order for the radiance of the themes to shine. This was the point of the novel's construction and execution, something that Mishima himself later seemed to have missed. Or was his claim that *Waves* was a 'joke' on the public merely another gag, another mask, another layer in the irony with which he continually played?

If the novel's sometimes saccharine elements, and its basic categorization as a 'romance', led to its ostracism by those unable to peer beneath its surface charms and into its more complex depths, or those who believed that only dark and disturbing art was worthy of consideration, it also accounted for its instant and immense popularity.

Published in June 1954, *The Sound of Waves* went through seventy impressions in three months, selling in its hundreds of thousands; three major film studios optioned the book; the Ministry of Education adopted it as a set text for schoolchildren; it won the 1954 Shinchō Prize and two years later became the first of Mishima's works to be translated into English, for Knopf in New York.[54] The success of *Confessions of a Mask* (1949) had already made Mishima well-known and widely respected (in 1953, his principal publishers, Shinchōsha, had brought out a six-volume *Collected Works*, a rare honour for a writer still under thirty), but *Waves* turned him into a national celebrity.

But for those who feared that the consummate, challenging author of 'Death in Midsummer' (1952) and *Forbidden Colours* (1953) had turned into an insipid, antiseptic writer of sanitized popular romances, there was a clever but quietly understated network of symbolism at work in *The Sound of Waves*. The San Francisco Peace Treaty of 1951, effective the following year, had ended the American post-war occupation of Japan, marking a new beginning for the nation and giving fresh impetus to its economic miracle and global resurgence. As if to solemnize this rebirth, the protagonists of Mishima's *Waves* each bore a potent

---

54   Two months after it first came out, and with sales rocketing, the publishers released a limited edition of two hundred copies for 2,500 yen, a staggering sum for a book in 1950 (and equivalent to around $100 or £75 today).

element to their name: 'new' ('shin' in Shinji) and 'first/beginning' ('hatsu' in Hatsue), each standing, like the island setting of their novel, as a representation of a revitalized Japan, but one ironically rejuvenated through reconnecting with its traditional values.

Shinji, a flat and happy hero, in many respects anticipates the simpler, resolute protagonists (Ryuji in *The Sailor Who Fell from Grace with the Sea*; Isao in *Runaway Horses*) who inhabit much of Mishima's later fiction, with its precarious nationalism, in contrast to the more nuanced and realistic characters he created in works like *Thirst for Love* (1950). In *Waves*, the community and the setting are perhaps more important than the characters, as is nostalgia for a disregarded, non-existent, rural realm of the forgotten past, a hearty, healthy, pre-modern, pre-capitalist fabrication that Mishima on occasion – along with countless other writers, artists, and thinkers from around the world – yearned for.

All this, however, is not to suggest Mishima's novel is empty, ironic. Quite the reverse: it is an immensely potent symbolic vision. In many ways the brightest and most optimistic of all his major works, *The Sound of Waves* has a simplicity, even a naivety, that belies its hidden depths, strengths, and range of meanings: social, sexual, political. By adapting a tale from Greek myth into contemporary life, Mishima modified the literary past to represent the shifting realities and contradictions of post-war society. Using a classical association created a sense of distance, intensifying the sense of yearning for a lost world – a mythical, nostalgic, largely imaginary, pre-war past – while also amplifying the apparently intolerable breach between traditional and contemporary Japan.

Like James Joyce in *Ulysses* or T. S. Eliot in *The Waste Land* (both 1922), Mishima contrived an unremitting correspondence between antiquity and modernity: a degree of organization, stability, shape, and significance are granted to the futility and anarchy of present-day life by reworking and bringing together the past. There is a deep irony, perhaps even illogicality, in all this: while Joyce revised and modernized a foundational Greek myth (Odysseus) from within his own broad European culture, Mishima seized upon an alien culture to evoke and explore the vanishing image of a traditional Japan at a time when it was being pressurized by new, Western, paradigms.

Yet this paradox is only superficial, and *The Sound of Waves* instead reveals Mishima – like Joyce and Eliot – as a protean, versatile artist, adapting and reworking a range of motifs and models from several literary traditions in a manner which defies labels and static definitions, and using that variety and variability to investigate his own uncertain understanding of the dialogue between East and West, tradition and modernity.

Greece bore Mishima the gift of *The Sound of Waves*, even if it did not cure him entirely of self-loathing and isolation as he had hoped. And as ever, we, too, should beware Greeks bearing gifts, for there is a density and complexity to this apparently unassuming Japanese Trojan Horse that needs caution and close scrutiny.

Chapter Five

The Temple of the Golden Pavilion
BEAUTY & NOTHINGNESS

2 July 1950. 2:30 a.m. A twenty-two-year-old apprentice monk and university student, Yōken Hayashi, walks silently through the summer night, gliding through the dark paths and woods for several minutes before reaching his destination: a three-storey construction whose upper two floors are entirely covered by gold leaf, then crowned by a golden phoenix, who perches at once defiant and serene. The building stands upon a lake, in which is reflected an image of the structure itself, a flawless synchronization of art and nature. It is, of course, Kyoto's Kinkakuji – the Temple of the Golden Pavilion – a five-hundred-year-old Zen Buddhist temple, and a masterpiece of mixed architectural styles, fusing forms in a proud display of exquisite harmony and unimpeachable beauty.

A few minutes later, this gem of Japanese culture, which had survived centuries of typhoon, war, and earthquake, was ablaze, lit from within by a disturbed young man's kindling. Intending to burn himself along with the temple, at the last moment Hayashi lost his nerve and fled to the surrounding hills, where he watched the inferno for a time before swallowing sleeping medicine and stabbing himself.

By four o'clock the building was gone, reduced to a scorched skeleton.

Many motives were sought in order to comprehend this psycho-cultural tragedy which shocked Japan and the world, but they all remained unclear, incongruously insufficient. At his trial – he survived with only superficial wounds – Hayashi maintained he was disgusted by the commercialization of both the temple and Buddhism more widely, revolted by the tourists gaping and gawking at this sacred place. Other motives touched on both the monk's complex vocational relationship with the temple and his many-sided love/hatred for the beauty of the building. His mother claimed he had a short temper and terrible shyness; assorted medical opinions professed that a mixture of schizophrenia and latent dementia had led to the catastrophic events that July night (in which, at least, no one lost their life).[55]

Whatever the exact reasons for Hayashi's crime, and they are unlikely to ever be fully established, the event – and its instigator's curiously elusive personality – presented exactly the straightforward plot and strange hero Yukio Mishima needed for his next work: *The Temple of the Golden Pavilion*

---

55   Sentenced to seven years' imprisonment, Hayashi was released after five but died only months later from tuberculosis.

(金閣寺, 'Kinkakuji', 1956).[56] This was to be a peculiar but immensely compelling blend of various forms of the psychological, philosophical, and aesthetic novel – with a dash, but only a dash, of good old-fashioned thriller both igniting the mix and balancing the more reflective aspects of the text.

Although many emotional, physiological, and incidental correspondences exist between the inspiration, Hayashi, and Mishima's hero, Mizoguchi – such as his physical unattractiveness and debilitating stutter – *The Temple of the Golden Pavilion* develops its leading character far beyond anything which existed in reality. What is more, writing in a first-person confessional style, Mishima thrillingly merged his own dreams and experiences with those of his protagonist to create a novel of profound personal introspection with some alarming insights into Mishima's own psyche, his own deepest thoughts and feelings concerning love, desire, otherness, isolation, death, violence, and beauty.

Readers coming to this book expecting a true crime page-turner (or even a more sophisticated realistic approximation of a shocking occurrence – such as Truman Capote's 1966 masterpiece *In Cold Blood*) will be disappointed. The incineration of the temple itself only takes up the final few pages of this meditative medium-sized novel: most of the text deals with the protagonist's mixture of adolescent angst and philosophical musing. Yet, of course, it is precisely the employment of a real-life event that makes so much of the text thrilling: most readers are bound to know the ending long before they pick up the book. This makes

---

56 A recent rediscovery of Mishima letters, exhibited at Tokyo's Museum of Modern Japanese Literature, indicates he originally planned to call the book 'The Human Disease' (人間病) or even 'The Human Hospital' (人間病院), writing to an editor in June 1955 that his new novel was about 'the treatment of the disease called human existence.'

us hyper-alert to detecting (or thinking we detect) the tiniest clues of the terrible crime ahead, as it rushes with unstoppable momentum toward us. Every exquisite description, every eloquent metaphor of the building, in all its architectural and metaphysical splendour, becomes an ominous ironic anticipation of what is to come in its destruction.

By constructing his book in this way, with the one great main event looming at the novel's conclusion and dragging the narrative inexorably toward it like a supermassive black hole, Mishima also allows for far more philosophical density within the text than many of his other novels. This is evident not only in the Zen conundrums that pop up from time to time, but also in the extended musings on death and beauty which Mizoguchi imposes on us. Many readers, alas, perhaps skip over these wonderful passages, or let them slide largely unnoticed through their mind, but given the wider context of their appearances they are unmissable: crime scene evidence, witness statements, manifestos.

At the tortured heart of *The Temple of the Golden Pavilion*, and surely the initial great fascination for Mishima in writing it, is the exquisite irony that a monument of such boundless beauty and uniqueness could be obliterated by a particularly ugly and unremarkable figure. It was a marriage of great opposites which Mishima always relished. But he also saw the opportunity to arouse our compassion for this ostensibly unpleasant and outwardly inarticulate young man who, over the course of this novel, takes us deep into his mind, his soul, his essence. By the end, against our better judgement, we are urging him on to commit his crime, sharing his lack of concern for the personal or ethical consequences – just driving him on relentlessly to the scandalous act which must now be performed.

If Hayashi the monk was an unexceptional, unsympathetic figure, Mishima's Mizoguchi is absolutely unforgettable. He is the ultimate anti-hero: the weird romantic lead at the heart of a bizarre and captivating love story.

⛩

Visiting the rebuilt pavilion in 1955, in preparation for writing his novel, Mishima was struck by the very thing many had complained about. While they criticized the 'movie set' gaudiness of the shiny new building, the writer marvelled at its freshness, the glitziness of its gilt which surely recaptured, like a cleaned-up old master painting, the spellbinding vision of the original builder. Prior to its fiery demise in 1950, Mishima felt the temple had become tired-looking and decrepit (those fundamental Mishimian fears), its gold leaf peeling off, the whole appearance dull and uninspiring. While scarcely supporting the destruction of the previous building, Mishima the advocate of eternal youth and rebirth could see many advantages to this new state of affairs.

On site, despite – or perhaps because of – his fame, Mishima was not permitted to drop in on any private or sacrosanct areas of the temple for his research. Indeed, the resident monk was obstinate, deliberately uncooperative, granting neither an interview nor any special permissions: for him, it was deplorable that such a catastrophic event was to be turned into cheap entertainment. Here we encounter one of many ironies in the whole tale. Not only is Mishima's novel about as far from cheap entertainment as his work gets (and, as we have seen, he was certainly not above producing some fairly tawdry material), but it was to be a profound reflection on the place of the temple, Buddhism, and the spiritual in society, especially that of post-war Japan. What is more, it was, arguably, the temple administrators themselves who had demeaned and devalued the temple, opening it up to mass tourism and the leisure industry, an ornate, must-see cog in the vast recreational infrastructure – potentially encouraging precisely the act of pyromaniacal vandalism which intrigued the writer. But then, the Kinkakuji's resident monk was hardly the first hypocritical member of a religious institution.

Not to be thwarted, and in another smirking irony, Mishima had to explore the temple in exactly the manner the monks claimed to loathe: as a tourist, permitted no more access than the Japanese day trippers or global sightseers who to this day swamp the Golden Pavilion, ready to turn it into their latest selfie backdrop or social media post. Mishima made good use of his time, however, exploring every nook and cranny, inspecting every strange angle, and gathering any titbit of information that might prove useful, then retiring to a traditional local inn for the evening to sort and assess his burgeoning material.

He travelled to Hayashi's hometown and to an assortment of shrines that might prove beneficial for details and atmosphere. He also visited other places of worship near the Golden Pavilion, not only in order to capture their flavours but to help differentiate the particular aroma and piquancy of the Kinkakuji. One, the Myōshinji temple, agreed to let Mishima spend the night, so that he could observe, in situ, the activities of the young monks in training. It proved a fascinating experience – not least because he discovered that these holy sites were not only places of instruction and meditation but in use as handy retreats for middle-aged businessmen recovering from nervous breakdowns after their messy divorces.

Themes of withdrawal and escape are fundamental concerns of Mishima's fiction, and *The Temple of the Golden Pavilion* is no different. Within a contemporary context, that of Buddhist priests in post-war Kyoto, it explores the possibility of alternate, even substitute, worlds, mixing realism and romance in its metaphors, narrative, and characterization, showing its curious protagonist wrestling with the desolate, disappointing historical reality he faces. Lust and longing arm this private war, this personal chaos, with the object of Mizoguchi's desire being the centuries-old temple, the sentimental aesthetic exquisiteness of which represents his yearning to escape from crushing reality. This tension, this frustrating desire, is what drives both him and the novel until (unable to contain itself and with many obvious sexual-psychoanalytical subtexts) it explodes into an act of violence.

Mizoguchi is the quintessential romantic, adrift in post-war Japan, with its guilt and privations, defeat and defiance, its fractured masculinity and bottled-up ferocity. His tragedy is that he is burdened by his own reality, his own shortcomings – in courage, appearance, diction, and sexual know-how – so that he is maddeningly unable to reach for the other world he desires, except through a dangerous, malicious undertaking of pure empty action free of the self. The unappealing, stuttering boy craves – and loathes – that which he lacks: beauty, a frenemy both symbolized and embodied with unqualified perfection by the Golden Pavilion.

Compulsive, introverted, narcissistic, disaffected, and with several inferiority complexes, Mizoguchi possesses a ferocious and resourceful imagination that threatens to overcome him yet also plunges him forward, away from perpetual despair and ennui. As with Shunsuké's manipulation of Yuichi in *Forbidden Colours*,

Mizoguchi comes to see the temple, or rather his destruction of it, as a creative project, both active and intellectual. He seeks an artist's godlike power of life or death over the temple as if it were his own creation. This union of subject, object, form, and content makes *The Temple of the Golden Pavilion* perhaps Mishima's art in its purest distillation.

In psychological terms, Mizoguchi seems like a sociopath, fitting the classic prototype in terms of alienation and social unease. Yet, like many – but not all – sociopaths, he is also quietly reflective, methodical, scrupulous in his reasoning, and possessing a rare sensitivity toward aesthetic forms and ideals (whether architectural or narratorial). Whatever our need to suspend disbelief as to the exact circumstances of the creation of the book we are reading, he also has extraordinary powers of textual articulation (in contrast to his stuttering incoherence in spoken language) since he has consciously created the written work of literature we possess. At times, in his petitions and deviations, the words of Mizoguchi seem more those of the young Mishima – but we do not need to divorce them. Mishima, and Mizoguchi, convince us of the complete identification of the one with the other, efficaciously relocating the spiritual, psychological, and artistic responses of a writer of genius into a youth of less obvious gifts.

⁂

It is this dual ability to articulate in both the composition of his narrative and his quasi-artistic project of the temple's annihilation that reflects – though ultimately transcends – the sad irony of Mizoguchi's powerlessness to verbalize effectively in oral communication. The vocal ugliness of his speech impediment represents the otherness at the heart of his personality.

In part, it is this stammer which has caused him to flee to the temple, to a place where – initially, at least – he is not bullied or intimidated in the same way as in the real world. This is especially so early on in the novel, during the war, since tourists and priests are largely absent, allowing Mizoguchi to exist and expand almost on an atoll unto himself amid the idyllic impeccability of the Golden Temple. Later on, with the return to the environment of peacetime and then the start of his university studies, those threats begin to re-encroach with increasing vehemence and devastating repercussions for Mizoguchi's mental stability.

In literature, stereotypical disfluency has long been used not only as a symbol of language's persistent vulnerability to collapse, rather than cohere, communication but also as a metaphorical indication of a character's inherent weakness or flawed nature, especially their social alienation or repressed sexuality. Sexual inexperience/impotence and stuttered speech are commonly coupled as consistent, even causally linked, forms of obstruction, observable in the double meaning of the verb 'to ejaculate': both to emit seminal fluid at the moment of sexual climax and, in its rather more dated form, to say something quickly and suddenly.[57]

Notably, the eponymous sailor hero of Herman Melville's unfinished novella *Billy Budd* (1891) has a youthful attractiveness and physical prowess which make him an object of desire and envy amid the homoerotic tensions of a warship during the French

---

57 Notoriously, Arthur Conan Doyle's Sherlock Holmes stories include twenty-three instances of the word and its various cognates. In the canon, Dr Watson ejaculates twice as often as Holmes, while in 'The Man with the Twisted Lip' (1891), Mrs St Clair's husband does so from a second-floor window.

Revolutionary Wars. Yet his virginal innocence is also seen as an indication of his being a 'barbarian' (a word linked etymologically to his stutter). Through his good looks, naivety, and tendency to stammer when emotionally roused, the fatal 'flaw' that will directly proceed to his downfall, Billy is infantilized and feminized, and essentially emasculated, with brutal consequences. Sexual and verbal repression lead to a violent physical ejaculation that kills the evil Claggart, in a scene filled with erotic insinuations, the verbal and sexual connotations furiously interacting on the page.

Mishima knew the story and even saw a production of Benjamin Britten's opera based on it at Covent Garden in London not long before he embarked on his own work featuring a sexually inexperienced/impotent stammering hero who is compelled to express himself via a violent act. Where Melville's Billy is a feminized beauty, however, Mishima's Mizoguchi is unsightly, 'conventionally ugly', as well as physically frail – something he sees, initially at least, as part of the cause of his stammering, a perceived defect that creates an insurmountable chasm between him and the real world, while also anchoring him in it, desperate for escape.[58]

Although Mizoguchi sees his stammer as a function of his generalized infirmity, and unambiguously states early on in the novel that he has had the condition 'since birth', contributing factors may have exacerbated it. One is his increasing awareness of his own physical unattractiveness and the other is his mother's infidelity: she engaged in intercourse with one of her own relations while both her thirteen-year-old son and (dying) husband were

---

58   Mishima's character's name underlines the point: 'Mizoguchi' (溝口) in Japanese literally translates as 'estrangement mouth' or 'division mouth'.

ostensibly sleeping in the same room – a complex incestuous, Oedipal frisson bound to have certain sexual-textual ramifications.

Though it is clear from his own words that his disfluency existed in some form prior to his mother's betrayal, the trauma of this event, along with the domineering, even demeaning and derisive, attitude of his mother throughout his life, has aggravated and exaggerated Mizoguchi's stammer and has become pathologically linked to his feelings of sexual inadequacy and impotence when encountering women. He is unable to verbally express himself, and his congested, frustrated speech is continually associated with his prolonged status as a virgin, something naturally intensified as he begins his university career, stepping back into the harsh real world that time at the temple had to some extent alleviated.

Only by the end of the novel, and immediately prior to his act of arson, is Mizoguchi able to lose his unwanted standing, sleeping with a prostitute – which also (temporarily) releases him from his stutter, the clearing of the sexual organ clearly leading to the unclogging of his verbal one too.[59] For Mizoguchi, his disfluency and impotence are closely connected to his wider inability to act, an incapacity that can now be overcome in the grand and liberating discharge of burning the temple, freeing him to live (as the novel's closing line makes explicit).

Mizoguchi's relationship with, and impulse to destroy, beauty is thus fundamentally linked to the divisive nature of his stutter, since it detaches him from life and people, heightening his incapacity by leaving him unable to act. The extreme beauty of the temple (which is only the ultimate in a line of beautiful

---

59 Another literal meaning of 'Mizoguchi' in Japanese might be 'gutter entrance'.

objects he encounters, from a soldier's sword to numerous idolized and idealized women) is not only something of which he is incapable of attaining, but comes to represent a hostile and suppressive force operating against his ability to act / speak / have sex – in short, to live.

The protagonist's preoccupation with internalized, unspoken words has, as we have seen, worsened his inability to act – and as such it bears a strong connection to his creator's own enduring over-absorption with the conflicting disposition of words and action. This crucially distorts convenient distinctions between disfluent and normative speech, highlighting that all language is vulnerable to failure, equivocation, and limitation. For Mishima, words and actions had long existed as opposing forces, the former constraining the latter. This was a paradox he sought to evaporate in his proud mixture of literary and martial arts, combining the two opposites in a revivification of traditional Japanese ideals (expressed in both his 1968 autobiographical essay *Sun and Steel*, subtitled 'Art, Action and Ritual Death', and elaborate suicide two years later).

For Mizoguchi, the words/action dilemma becomes an unbearable internal struggle concerning the destruction of the holy building he reveres but also despises. But it is a predicament he eventually resolves into a (destructive) decisive action that will also release his flow of words and the (creative) literary enterprise of *The Temple of the Golden Pavilion*.

Combustive, sometimes creative, opposites occur again and again in *The Temple of the Golden Pavilion*, as they do across almost all

Mishima's writing: language and action, beauty and ugliness, life and death, harmony and violence, desire and repression. Yet, like *Hamlet*, with which it shares a preoccupation with words versus deeds, *The Temple of the Golden Pavilion* is a literary work propelled by doubles and duplicity.[60] Indeed, given its status as a semi-fictional novel directly inspired by real events, *The Temple of the Golden Pavilion* itself is a two-faced twin, existing both inside and outside reality. Operating as not just antinomies but disturbing parallels and collaborators, duos haunt and stalk Mishima's text in sinister pairs, elaborating its themes and helping weave its wider textures. We might now consider three particular doubles in characterization which exemplify this disturbing tendency: two fathers, two prostitutes, two friends.

Mizoguchi's biological father is an unimpressive country priest, a cuckold with a weak constitution, a feeble figure who nonetheless represents knowledge, mysticism, and the sacred (just as Mizoguchi's domineering adulteress mother stands for ignorance, materiality, and the profane, especially in sexual

---

60   In Shakespeare's tragedy, to name only a few instances of character doubles, there are two Hamlets (father and son), two ambassadors (Voltemand and Cornelius), two comically indistinguishable friends (Rosencrantz and Guildenstern), two wronged women (Gertrude and Ophelia), two kings (with the parts of Claudius and the Ghost often played by the same actor, creating a further performative doubling), plus a pair of avenging sons – Fortinbras and Laertes – alongside Hamlet himself. In addition there are various doppelgangers encoded within the text, creating multiple linguistic, thematic, and narrative doubles: puns, hendiadyses, euphemisms, anaphora, alliteration, binary consciousnesses, dilemmas, duels, the play-within-a-play (which has its own dumbshow duplicate, creating a Russian doll in drama), plus the most famous verbal repetition of them all: 'To be or not to be'. (Kenneth Branagh's 1996 film, in which he also stars as the Danish prince, takes the theme of doubling so seriously that the entire set of Elsinore is covered in mirrors, generating an abundance of optical twins. I am indebted to Steven Lally for this insight.)

terms). Yet Mizoguchi also has a second father, the Golden Temple's superior – and he is more than simply a symbolic or figurative paternal force, since the relationship between a priest and his acolytes is a powerful and often highly ritualized one. These two fathers are further closely linked not only because they were student clerics together, undertaking acts of a most unpriestly nature, but since it is Mizoguchi's biological father who introduces his son to his surrogate at the temple, leaving his future in the care of his old friend.

(In a curious sense, the Superior is also a second mother to Mizoguchi as well as a second father, less in an interpersonal manner than a behavioural one, since his conduct frequently mimics or echoes Mizoguchi's mother's actions: occasionally overbearing and sexually uninhibited, he also quietly scorns his stuttering, insubordinate temple charge. Mizoguchi's mother is also the one who plants the idea in her child of becoming the next superior himself, thereby truly possessing the Golden Temple, a destiny thwarted by the present occupant of this position in a disturbing pseudo-maternal frustration of her son's desires.)

The Superior is one of the great enigmas of the novel, as well as a source of intermittent comedy in what is, for the most part, a relentlessly intense text. For one thing, his sheer physical size Mizoguchi finds strange: he initially thinks it odd that a Zen priest could have a body at all. Plump, pompous, promiscuous, elusive, and a slight eccentric (though lacking a magnanimous sense of humour that might humanize him more), the Superior is an erudite but unethical figure, abusing his position as leader of a rich and famous institution for his own fleshly profit. Yet for all his flaws, the Superior is shown to be a good man: he displays a great deal of patience, nobility, and compassion toward his acolyte but ultimately cannot cope with Mizoguchi's apathetic attitude toward his academic work and the petty campaign of vengeance the boy pursues. Accordingly, he treats him much as the boy's mother has, as an outcast. The caring and romanticized paternal figure is thus warped into the treacherous reality of the maternal one.

For this reason, the Superior is contrasted near the end of the novel with a visiting colleague, Father Zenkai, a ghostly rebirth of Mizoguchi's deceased father, who so nearly brings the wayward son back to his priestly vocation but, even more significantly, also inadvertently lets Mizoguchi fulfil his true destiny. This fate – the burning of the temple – will not only allow the acolyte to live but will serve the twin role of both avenging his mother's infidelity and setting right the Superior's snub. But, much more than this, by trying to make himself understood by someone else, Mizoguchi begins to feel free of his self and to experience personal emptiness – blank and happier than he had ever felt. This encounter with nothingness prepares him to experience it fully in his act of arson.

The complex sexual politics swarming around his parents and the Superior – a menacing *double double* – are explored in less intense, but no less significant, fashion by another sinister pairing, the two sex workers that come into Mizoguchi's life: first, a GI's pregnant prostitute lover; then Mariko, the brothel inmate to whom Mizoguchi finally loses his virginity. The American soldier pressures and then manhandles Mizoguchi into vehemently stepping on the GI's lover's stomach in order to cause a miscarriage, something which, although it has consequences in undermining Mizoguchi's reputation in the eyes of the Superior, also represents a significant *action* on the boy's part amid a life of stasis and indecision.

A repulsive undertaking, it is a merciless – if coerced – unconscious enactment of Mizoguchi's desire to damage or destroy beauty existing in the female form (of which, with its graceful lines, the Golden Temple evidently partakes too). Not only does the GI's lover seem to be a reactive reincarnation of Mizoguchi's lost adolescent fantasy, Uiko – his first experience of beauty, who mocked his attempts to love her – but this incident exists in the same chapter as both his mother's visit to the temple and the recollection concerning her infidelity. The American GI is representative of hostile forces that must be destroyed, and the vile deed Mizoguchi performs on his accomplice/lover subtly begins to free Mizoguchi from his inertia, and ethics, which will then be repeated in his finally losing his virginity with Mariko toward the end of the novel – which, as we discussed above, liberates him into another act of violence against beauty, the ultimate one of his attack on the temple.[61]

Although many of Mishima's heroes' friendships have a homoerotic edge, none seems to exist with either of Mizoguchi's two friends – Tsurukawa and Kashiwagi – who form an ominous third double act in *The Temple of the Golden Pavilion*. In straightforward terms, they might seem to be embodiments of Good and Evil: the luminous and positive Tsurukawa 'an alchemist who could transform tin into gold'; Kashiwagi the deformed cynic and dangerous manipulator, perilously convinced of his own importance. Yet Mishima is careful to make things much more complicated than this, showing each of the friends

---

61 Intriguingly, and in obvious ironic anticipation of the conflagration to come, the strange and intimate scene with Mariko overflows with water imagery: not only is it the rainy season, and the low-hanging air 'moist', but the brothel is called Otaki ('Great Waterfalls'), and Mariko mockingly refers to Mizoguchi as a 'water drinker'. Moreover, during the actual sex, an aquatic language is frequently employed ('immersed', 'melt away').

to be complex and enigmatic creations, as elusive, ambiguous, and paradoxical as the Golden Temple itself.

During the last year of the war, Mizoguchi is at his happiest, enjoying his most intimate relationship with the temple. He hopes and fears it (and he) will together be destroyed in an apocalyptic bombing raid: it takes on the same air of vulnerability and finitude as anything else, and the apprentice's inferiority subsides. It is at this time that fellow acolyte Tsurukawa comes into Mizoguchi's life. One of the most genuinely congenial of all Mishima's characters, he is easy-going and relaxed – 'fitting perfectly into the pattern of his life, like a chopstick in its box' – a positive figure to Mizoguchi's negative inverse. His friendship and kindness exist as an avenue to a new world of light and life, a conduit to the outside away from Mizoguchi's internal demons.

The hope that the temple will be obliterated by an external force ends with the war, as does the relationship with Tsurukawa. Mizoguchi rejects his friend's influence in favour of renewed alienation: he must discard the beauty suggested by Tsurukawa's assertion of light and life so that he may seek to possess and destroy the more threatening form of beauty embodied in the temple. It is a pattern many Mishimian heroes enact, rejecting a deficient world of friendship, attachment, and society, instead pursuing a world of isolation that alone is sufficiently intense to meet their desires.

Unable to greet the alternative reality that Tsurukawa offers, Mizoguchi inevitably seeks out its opposite in the shadowy Mephistophelian spirit Kashiwagi, a perverted relationship that propels him to his final devastating deed. A fellow university student, Kashiwagi has clubbed feet that he exploits to manipulate others, especially women into sexual sympathy; he also plays the flute with an exquisitely demonic refinement and precarious moonlit magnetism. Kashiwagi is full of didactic sophistry and youthful arrogance, and his vision of the world is as dark and ugly as Tsurukawa's was bright and beautiful, turning everything sour and misshapen, just as Tsurukawa turned 'tin into gold'. Yet it is a world equally unobtainable for Mizoguchi, and one which he must surpass and rise beyond. (Appropriately, it is after a disastrous early excursion with Kashiwagi that Mizoguchi learns of Tsurukawa's death in an apparent road accident.)

We are offered a sly hint as to the inadequacy and problematic nature of Kashiwagi's cosmos, as well as his own flawed and hypocritical nature, when he chastises Mizoguchi for asking for a loan (a disingenuous transaction that will ultimately lead to the novel's climactic events). Kashiwagi haughtily cites Shakespeare – and gets it wrong. Recalling the pompous Polonius's platitude in *Hamlet* 'neither a borrower nor a lender be',[62] Kashiwagi erroneously claims that Polonius's son, Laertes, gave this advice to his own son, a blunder revealing that the student's proud reliance on knowledge is not all it's cracked up to be (thus also endorsing the romantic Mizoguchi's/Mishima's assertion that it is not knowledge which transforms the world but action).[63]

A brutal, destructive force – especially when it comes to beauty and traditional Japanese culture – Kashiwagi also destroys Tsurukawa's memory when he divulges to Mizoguchi that not only did he know Tsurukawa but that his seemingly inadvertent death under the wheels of a truck was, in grim reality, a suicide – a

---

62 In the First Folio version of the play, they occur at I.iii.75. Like *The Temple of the Golden Pavilion*, *Hamlet* is of course a work preoccupied by hesitant sons; absent, cuckolded fathers; and potentially promiscuous mothers.

63 Mishima's text, in Ivan Morris's translation, reads "'Do you remember the advice that Laertes gives his son in *Hamlet*? 'Neither a borrower nor a lender be.'"

negation of all that the sunny boy stood for. The sinister double of these two, grotesquely interlinked, friends now also seems to operate, along with the protagonist himself, as a perverse trinity, an unholy alliance of forces which precipitates the action toward the inevitable inferno that will transcend reality and liberate Mizoguchi.

Our hero might have chosen Kashiwagi's charismatic but essentially empty path of passive surveillance, cynical exploitation, and static wisdom. Instead, he enters into romantic action, overcoming a final vacillation at the last moment and setting fire to the temple.

Kyoto's Temple of the Golden Pavilion is a Zen Buddhist temple, and the faith of which it is both a symbol and a participant is a continual presence in Mishima's novel, from its famous opening line regarding the Kinkakuji's beauty to its close and the hero's desire to go on living. Just as Mizoguchi – and Mishima – struggle with reconciling word and action, so the hero's stutter is also a reflection of Buddhism's awareness that reason (i.e., language) is both a trusted and a slippery friend, constantly deceiving us and maintaining our perpetual state of suffering and unhappiness.[64]

Accordingly, the novel charts Mizoguchi's journey along an emblematic process of (Rinzai) Zen illumination involving refutation and failure in order to build up doubt which leads to despair and the eventual death of the self. If Mizoguchi does not perhaps achieve a full liberating enlightenment, or satori

---

64   A concept known in Buddhism, Jainism, and Hinduism as dukkha.

(the Japanese Buddhist term for deep comprehension and understanding, where one sees into one's true nature), he does at least go through a comparable development.

Across the novel a notorious Zen kōan, or riddle, known as 'Nansen Kills a Cat', appears three times, yet with each successive reappearance and attempted explanation, it eludes elucidation. Many readers of *The Temple of the Golden Pavilion* perhaps mistakenly believe they need to 'solve' the problem of the cat kōan in order to proceed with or comprehend the novel, but kōan are meditative exercises intentionally designed to lie beyond rationalization. Mishima ran the risk of tripping and confusing some of his audience here, but he knew this danger was an intrinsic aspect of writing a philosophical novel, not least one set in the world of Zen Buddhism.

Yet the very insolubility of the cat kōan points to the wider mystery and impenetrability of the temple, as well as its namesake novel. Just as a kōan eludes explanation, the temple's beauty escapes and bewilders Mizoguchi. When he first sees the temple, the sight of it cannot match the image of beauty he has held in his mind for so long – the building's 'true beauty' must be concealed, so he sets about trying to uncover it. The more he tries to locate this mysterious magnificence, the more it evades him, just as the meaning of a kōan slips further away the harder one attempts to decipher it.

Images of the temple, and Mizoguchi's attempts to locate its true beauty, intensify his failed attempts to find an equilibrium between his inner and outer worlds, making him at once disenchanted by the building and possessed by it. The unequalled beauty of the temple hints at eternity – which merely serves to emphasize to Mizoguchi not only his ugliness but his boundedness and irrelevance. Such tensions and revelations leave him only one choice: to destroy the temple, freeing himself from its curse. But before he does so comes a final disclosure which allows him to overcome a last-minute hesitancy and commit himself to action.

The hostile, serene, marvellously *indifferent* refusal of the temple to relinquish its sublime beauty to Mizoguchi is, as we saw earlier, connected with both his stammer and his sexual inexperience/impotence, all of which are to be ostensibly resolved in a final series of decisive, but destructive, acts. It is then, at the moment of the temple's annihilation, that Mizoguchi realizes that the true beauty of the building lies not in any particular part (a pillar, the roof, the phoenix) but in the often contradictory and sometimes disharmonious relationship between the individual parts and those parts' relationship to their overall setting.

Thus beauty resides only in the complete and incorporated whole, whose fundamental nature is not its constituent elements but an emptiness. Greater than the sum of its parts, the whole is unknowable, indefinable, a void, an empty embodiment. The Temple of the Golden Pavilion's beauty is essentially a nothingness, rather than a substantial entity, but it is a nothingness in which Mizoguchi can participate by destroying it, freeing himself from the temple's cursed spell over him.

After he starts the fire, Mizoguchi tries to die in the upper floor, the tiny Kukyōchō, but its door is firmly locked. His desperation to enter this radiant little room, to experience its golden beauty at the moment of his death, reaches a climax of desire and frustration, but there is no escape from life, even in death. Compelled to leave the burning building, he emerges to a new existence – scratched and scorched but no longer willing to die, desiring only life.

As with Etsuko's deliverance in *Thirst for Love* and Yuichi's in *Forbidden Colours*, the extent of Mizoguchi's freedom is one which *The Temple of the Golden Pavilion* leaves open at its close – though the very existence of the book we have been reading suggests that Mizoguchi has achieved a great degree of liberation and the momentous union of words and action in a new animation.

༈

Midway through the first chapter of *The Temple of the Golden Pavilion*, Mizoguchi describes, in some of the novel's most exquisite prose, the magnificent phoenix which crowns the building. It is a paragraph of lyrical magic, the text on fire, as Mizoguchi wonders about this mysterious but beautiful bird that never crows at dawn nor flaps its wings. Like the temple itself, its beauty lies in its nothingness and its ability to fly not through the air but through both the mind and eternity. Beyond, or indeed because of, the sheer beauty of the writing, it is an important early clue as to what will need to be achieved many pages and years later at this same place. The phoenix, too, is itself an important symbol: an emblem of obliteration, of rebirth and eternity, a bird which nests just before it dies (just as Mizoguchi will prepare a strange nest of all his belongings in the temple prior to torching it and obtaining his own epiphany concerning beauty and nothingness).

The building upon which the phoenix stands aloft, with its serene defiance, its motionless anger, is a ship on the sea of time. By day, it is anchored, innocuous, acquiescing itself to tourists and crowds. By night, it can travel into infinity, through the immense darkness of space toward an end one cannot predict, floating away, 'its roof billowing like a great sail.'

Yet the Temple of the Golden Pavilion is more than just a time machine. It is also a mirror, inviting us to examine ourselves but not caring if we do not like what we see. It is a black hole, a creative and destructive force of immense gravity and power. It is Pandora's box, bringing both great trouble and great hope. It is a prison and a paradise, a weapon and a tool. It is useless and yet no limit can be set upon its uses.

Mishima's great novel explores all these aspects and countless more. For many, this writer included, it is his masterpiece, the balance and articulation of his themes matched only by his much larger and more complex four-novel cycle *The Sea of Fertility*. Its mastery of language is astonishing (all being well, much of which is conveyed across the fertile obstacle of translation). Its words seem to inhabit a variety of forms, at once stable and fixed, then volatile and unpredictable, elegant and effortless, almost operating as classical elements – earth, water, air, fire – urgently trying to explain the nature and complexity of existence.

Its moods shift with alarming ease and dazzling dexterity, from the melancholic and choleric to the ecstatic and optimistic. Its grasp of experience and the workings of fiction operates in defiance of customary expectations concerning plot and character, confusing many with its refusal to submit to routine requirements in motivation, point of view, or perspective. Yet the integrity of its intellectual framework is extraordinary, a liquid and organic structure that can shift and evolve across the decades and around the globe to reach innumerable people of all times and places, outlooks, and creeds.

The Temple of the Golden Pavilion makes you hunger to set eyes upon the graceful construction of the Kinkakuji while simultaneously never wanting to disturb the majesty of the form which exists in your mind. Transcendent and outrageous, human and divine, this is a novel in which everything and nothing happens, a work that plays with several forms of reality and explores never-ending layers of meaning. It is literature at its most exquisite and commanding, taking on the properties of other art forms – the ambition of architecture, the intimacy of theatre, the exhilaration of cinema, the abstraction of music – to celebrate and confirm the extraordinary power of the written word.

PART TWO

THE MIDDLE WORKS

Chapter Six

After the Banquet
DOMESTIC DIPLOMACY

After the gruelling candour of his early works, and before the sweeping zeal of *The Sea of Fertility*, during his diverse middle period Mishima wrote something rather unusual for him: a political satire, the often overlooked gem *After the Banquet* (宴のあと, 'Utage no Ato', 1960). Although on the surface an alien work in the Mishimian terrain, its scathing assessment of politicians, their associates, and political life in general not only is part of the fabric of his deeper textures and future discourses but maintains and extends many of his most persistent themes – around time, love, freedom, mortality, and solitude – necessitating its place within the canon.

The 'political novel' itself is a curious, indefinite, and widespread phenomenon with a long history in many societies. Given the unavoidably broad nature of politics, most if not all novels might, in some way, be considered political. However, some thanks to their themes or scenarios require a more specific genre label; they seek to address political systems, theories, or events. In Britain, George Eliot's *Middlemarch* (1871) inspected in exquisite detail every shade and gradation of Victorian advancement, in both economic and ethical terms, while Anthony Trollope's *The Way We Live Now* (1875) angrily denounced the corruption of contemporary London society. Robert Tressell's *Ragged-Trousered Philanthropists* (1914) explored the early days of the labour movement; Thatcherism's excesses and dissipations were brilliantly dissected in novels as diverse in time and style as Martin Amis's *Money* (1984), Jonathan Coe's *What a Carve Up!* (1994), and Alan Hollinghurst's *Line of Beauty* (2004), while the origins and foibles of Brexit are just beginning to find their way into fiction.

In Japan, the political novel has existed arguably since at least Shōnagon's *Pillow Book* and Murasaki's *Tale of Genji* in the eleventh century, with their superb considerations of Heian courtly life. More recently, in the proletarian literary movement of the 1920s and '30s, novelists like Takiji Kobayashi and Ineko Sata sought to promote the rights of workers and women, while after the war anti-nuclear political themes interested, among others, Mitsuharu Inoue and Kenzaburō Ōe (the latter eventually winning the Nobel Prize, in part for his pacifism).[65] Mishima himself is famed for the ideological nature of his later writing, in particular the monumental tetralogy *The Sea of Fertility*, with its often alarming discussions of spiritual renewal, militarism, and imperialism. But before that, political concerns certainly enter into his work – and on occasion he could be a sly cynic and pleasing satirist of contemporary governance, policy, and power.

65　To which can be added, as we will see in chapter eight, Mishima's own anti-nuclear novel, *Beautiful Star* (1962).

Chief among these earlier political texts is *After the Banquet*, an apparently innocuous little novel that contains savage send-ups of post-war political life and electioneering, the Machiavellian manoeuvring and ineptitude we all know only too well. Indeed, at times it is wretchedly familiar, skewering empty political rhetoric that would not feel out of place on the campaign trails today – from Tokyo to Tangier, Birmingham to Buenos Aires. Yet Mishima is not content to merely ridicule state administrators or lampoon the political absurdities of modern democracy. If *After the Banquet* lacks the radical idealism of his later works or the demanding realism of his earlier ones (a twin absence which might well appeal to many readers), it nonetheless touches on many familiar Mishimian subjects – something it shares with *Kyoko's House* (鏡子の家, 'Kyoko no ie', 1959), which he wrote just prior to *After the Banquet*, and which, as we will see, offers illuminating parallels to the later book.

Beyond its caustic swipe, *After the Banquet* is a delicate tale of love and loss, of identity and personal discovery – a story about feminine folly and resource, with a central character of audacity, strength, and credibility. Although the texture of *After the Banquet* can be frosty, this only serves to intensify the warmth and empathy of the much more sincere human story (replete with impeccably observed details of clothes and cuisine, nature and people) which encloses the hard, world-weary political centre of the novel.

Mishima was an enormously wide-ranging writer, not least in his middle period during the early 1960s, when he embraced a far greater assortment of genres as well as innovative structural experiments – as he declared, he never wished to write the same book twice – as he journeyed toward the grand summation of his literary life: *The Sea of Fertility*. And yet, for all the variety, he always maintained a sense of his own identity, his own leitmotifs, his own essential personality and style. For, reading *After the Banquet*, no one can be in any doubt that they are perusing a novel by Yukio Mishima.

The period between *The Temple of the Golden Pavilion* (1956) and *After the Banquet* (1960) was one of the most significant in Mishima's life, and requires a little unpacking, as both his life and art began to travel in important new directions.

One of the defining works of post-war Japanese literature, *The Temple of the Golden Pavilion* secured Mishima's place in the literary elite not only of his own age but arguably of all time. It is, in many respects, the apex of his art, representative of his unflinching vision of the world, as well as a decisive reflection of the guilt and self-reproach that lingered on in Japanese society after the war. Yet it was also a novel about art, about language, about Mishima's own bourgeoning belief that words were insufficient – worse, they were dangerously disengaging him from life, an addiction severing his attachment to reality.

To some extent this was true: at the time, Mishima's literary outpourings, in both quality and quantity, continued at an astonishing rate. Plays, novels, stories surged out of him, some deadly serious, some more light-hearted and even a little frivolous. Yet he was never entirely trapped in a compulsive cycle of writing: relationships and travel continued, though he would now begin to take a more fervent interest in specifically non-literary pursuits, especially martial arts and other physical activities (the eventual implications of which the world now knows).

Impotence, both literal and figurative, lay at the heart of *The Temple of the Golden Pavilion*, and it was a fear rarely far from Mishima's mind and his own notion of masculinity. In a bizarre incident during the writing of the novel, Mishima telephoned a literary critic at two o'clock in the morning to excitedly, drunkenly, tell him how he had just been able to sexually satisfy a woman (his then-girlfriend Sadako). But with this success came a problem: If he lost his impotence (or rather, his fear of impotence), would he also lose its ostensible substitute, his imaginative powers? Would a 'normal' life of marriage and children mean he could no longer be a radical creative artist? He was in a familiar, Flaubertian, bind: on the one hand anxious his art was cutting him off from life; on the other afraid that committing himself to life would diminish his abilities as an artist.

For the time being, art won. He broke off relations with Sadako and committed himself further to writing. A rather bitter short story, 'The Memory Boat' (1956), from this time seems to outline his fears: a father recalls to his son how he became 'infected' by the world's conventions and was pleased when his wife died. Some of this was connected to Mishima's complex sexuality, but he was hardly tortured by his attraction to men; it was more about his fear of what being married to a woman might entail.

So, rather than a betrothal to Sadako, he became engaged in muscular activities. First there were traditional Japanese festival sports and games, and then the ultimate test of bodily skill and power: boxing. Like Nabokov, Mishima loved the sport, but, despite a significant recent bulking up, he was not strong enough to compete and took many whacks and wallops before 'retiring' a year later (though he never lost his fascination with boxing, appreciating both its beauty and simplicity, its unswerving commitment to proving that one is, for now, alive).[66]

The Temple of the Golden Pavilion was a huge success, critically and commercially, as were the lighter novels of this period. Combined sales ran into the several hundred thousand, an achievement supplemented by numerous successful runs of his plays; English translations of his works were also beginning to appear. Looking for a change of scene after breaking up with Sadako, between July 1957 and January 1958 Mishima went on a six-month tour of North and Central America, including a few weeks in Mexico and the Caribbean. In Uxmal he surveyed ancient Mayan ruins, and contracted a fever; in Port-au-Prince he sought out 'real' voodoo but had to be satisfied with the slightly sanitized tourist version; in hedonistic Havana, with its blue skies and dark eyes, he thrilled to the atmosphere of grenades and nascent insurrection just over a year before Castro's takeover.

Back in the States, he enjoyed plenty of stage entertainment in Manhattan, especially Broadway shows like *My Fair Lady* and *South Pacific*. He was impressed by the music and fight scenes of Bernstein's *West Side Story* but found the love story itself mawkish and unadventurous; Kurt Weill's *Threepenny Opera* he thought a brilliant piece, not least because of the masterclass in sung acting he witnessed. The New York City Ballet was on the menu, too, Mishima savouring above all Debussy's *Prélude à l'après-midi d'un faune* and Stravinsky's *Apollo*; the synthesis of art and athleticism at such a high standard delighted him.

---

66   In the autumn of 1958, Mishima would take up the sport that perhaps meant most to him, containing as it did the perfect harmony of body and spirit: the great martial art of kendo. As a child, he had hated it; as an adult, it helped forge the identity of his later years.

There was also work: in particular, attempts to stage his freshly translated *Five Modern Noh Plays* (近代能楽集, 'Kindai nōgakushū', 1956) in a small off-Broadway playhouse. Despite Mishima's fame and significant interest from locals,[67] the project failed to receive enough backing; on top of this, the actors were unwilling to embrace the unexpected demands of Mishima's theatre. Despite this frustration, America had galvanized his state of mind. At a gay bar in Greenwich Village during Christmas 1957, Mishima met up with an old friend: the writer Mitsuru Yoshida, officer and survivor of the catastrophic sinking of the Japanese battleship *Yamato* at the end of World War II.[68] He told Yoshida that in the coming year he would write a huge and important new novel, build a house, and marry. After returning to Japan in January 1958, following brief visits to Madrid and Rome, he set about realizing all three goals.

To please his parents, Mishima decided a traditional arranged marriage would be the most efficient way of wedding an appropriate girl. Applications were sought and flooded in, but most were rejected. (Many rebuffed him, too: muscled like an irascible bulldog and with a shaven head, his appearance was not to everyone's taste.) There was talk of marriage to Michiko

---

67 Not least from a wealthy entrepreneurial friend of Saul Bellow, already the author of one of the great American novels, *The Adventures of Augie March* (1953), and destined for the 1976 Nobel Prize.

68 Mishima had, in fact, been the first person to read the manuscript for his friend Yoshida's epic *Requiem for Battleship Yamato* and wrote a touching tribute upon its publication in 1952. The *Yamato* itself was the most formidable warship of World War II and came to symbolize both the power and might, as well as the tragedy and futility, of the imperial forces. It eventually succumbed during a suicidal mission to defend Okinawa in April 1945. Jan Morris has written an exquisite short book on the subject: *Battleship Yamato: Of War, Beauty and Irony* (2017).

Shōda (who ended up marrying Crown Prince Akihito, eventually becoming his empress), but on 1 June 1958 Mishima married Yōko Sugiyama, the daughter of a prominent painter (meaning she would be under no illusions about what marriage to an artist entailed). They would have two children together. Smart, pretty, but fulfilling Mishima's requirement that his spouse have zero interest in literature, she was the companion he wanted and probably needed: a faithful friend, supporting him and his work. It was never going to be the romance of the century, and an 'arranged marriage by choice' seemed to satisfy everyone.

Wedding and honeymoon ticked off, next came the house.[69] Mishima treasured traditional designs but knew he would be more comfortable in something modern, where he could sit in his stylishly washed-out jeans and aloha shirt on his precious antique furniture. Constructed in consultation with the hot-tempered young architect and artist Yasuo Hokonohara, it would be a huge Western-style house, eventually three storeys high and featuring a piano, an ivory staircase, Louis XIV dining chairs, and a rooftop terrace overlooking Tokyo Bay, along with his vast library of books, papers, and pamphlets. (A modest Japanese-style granny annex, complete with a charming little garden and private entrance, was built for Mishima's parents next door. He would visit them most evenings when he could.)

---

69   During their honeymoon, the newlyweds saw the film version of *The Temple of the Golden Pavilion*. Directed by Kon Ichikawa, it was retitled *Conflagration* to appease the priests in Kyoto and won a minor prize at the Venice Film Festival in 1959. It remains probably the most cinematically successful and aesthetically pleasing of all adaptations of Mishima's works and is well worth tracking down to experience how even such an astonishingly literary novel as *The Temple of the Golden Pavilion* can nonetheless be fruitfully transferred to another medium.

The house would take a year to construct, however, and in the meantime he still had to fulfil the third of his three pledges to that friend in Manhattan. After busy days of martial arts, sunbathing, social engagements, and publishing commitments, at night he would retreat to his spartan writer's studio, relishing the isolation and austerity in which to write his ambitious new novel, a work he hoped would both meticulously reflect his own era and majestically transcend it.[70]

Kyoko's House (鏡子の家, 'Kyoko no ie', 1959) is a vast, gloomy, elaborate, and important work, exquisitely assembled and portraying a society-wide existential emergency, though not yet translated into English – hence the lack of a separate chapter devoted to it in this book. Nonetheless, it warrants a little space of its own and, far from parasitizing this chapter on *After the Banquet* (1960), can help illuminate some of the darker themes of Mishima's political novel.

Set between April 1954 and April 1956, with both the Korean War (1950–53) and Japan's official 'post-war period' at an end, the eponymous heroine of *Kyoko's House* yearns for the time of her country's immediate defeat, for the strangeness, freedom, and opportunity it seemed to offer. She kicks her husband out of the family home and opens it up as a fashionable salon to which are drawn four men whose interconnected stories form

---

70 The Mishimas eventually moved into their grand new house on 9 May 1959. Yōko gave birth to their first child, Noriko, on 2 June, and the novel was completed seven weeks later, on 29 June.

the principal basis of the narrative: a businessman, an actor, a painter, and a boxer.

Each incontestably signifies a competing side to Mishima's personality, and each is successful in his field, but all four of the *Kyoko* quartet are unsatisfied, discontented, facing a profound existential crisis. This novel was a nihilistic nightmare that came straight from its author's pessimistic heart. There is the narcissistic bodybuilding actor and the athletic purity-minded boxer. There is the sensitive painter of traditional Japanese styles, who finds the real world disintegrating each time he creates a work of art, the infinity of the one and the boundedness of the other in tense competition. And then there is the enigmatic, negativistic salaryman, going through the daily motions of life yet all the while disdaining the bourgeois hypocrisies of reality.

The hard honesty of *Kyoko's House* reveals at least as much of Mishima as any of his demanding, candid works from the earlier 1950s. In taking these four explicit aspects of his character, each of which was endowed with a multifaceted, complex personality – none is mere stereotype – their author was able to powerfully express his own intricate, composite range of selves more directly than his fiction had hitherto allowed. (By the end of the 1960s, and *The Sea of Fertility*, he would increasingly allow this to come to the fore.) Although he could certainly identify with Etsuko in *Thirst for Love* (1950), Shunsuké and Yuichi in *Forbidden Colours* (1953), Shinji in *Sound of Waves* (1954), and, of course, Mizoguchi in *Temple of the Golden Pavilion* (1956), the male figures in *Kyoko's House* (1959), which closed the decade, came direct from Mishima's soul, barely veiled by fiction. When they spoke, they spoke for their creator.

Eerie, disconcerting, occasionally disjointed, *Kyoko's House* is, in hindsight, an uncanny prophecy of the troubling times that lay ahead for Mishima. Confusions between truth and illusion, blurred in the book, were blurring outside it too. Narcissism, masochism, aggression, and masculinity clashed with one another in their pursuit of purity and pain; their quest for beauty and reality is made manifest only in the moment of their own destruction (a theme familiar from *The Temple of the Golden Pavilion*). Although the artist in *Kyoko's House* recuperates and avoids embracing the dark right-wing ideologies the boxer does, the performative suicide of the actor might seem an obvious premonition of what was to come for their author. Even so, unnervingly mirroring the fact that his own ostentatious death had not yet occurred, Mishima is careful not to show us this scene directly, instead allowing us to hear about it second-hand, forcing us to create it in our own minds.

Kyoko's House was a book on which Mishima worked tenaciously, mercilessly, for over a year of night-time scribbling, going to bed only after breakfast.[71] But his reach had probably

---

71 During the writing of this very personal, and enormous, book (which was to appear in one go, un-serialized), Mishima kept a diary charting the astonishing willpower it took him to complete it. And this was no secretive journal: a self-aggrandizer's chronicle, bits of it were published long before *Kyoko's House* came out. On 10 March 1958 we witness the honey warmth of the afternoon as work gets underway; a couple of weeks later, a 'heavy, unpleasant' feeling surfaces, a common sensation for Mishima when starting a novel, though by the next day the book is in splendid motion. Later on we see fever and light-headedness assisting the composition of boxing scenes; a typhoon and power cut help add atmosphere to some oppressive central pages; a hangover and malingering party guests on New Year's Day threaten headway. The diary, at times painfully honest but full of wry humour and snarky self-doubt, is a magnificent portrait of the artist at work: the great joys of literary creation along with the considerable lows generated by slow progress or inertia. *Kyoko's House* was finally complete at 3:30 a.m. on Monday 29 June 1959 – when we are treated to a vast and detailed entry, including Mishima's account of the lovely bath he had when he had finished writing.

exceeded his grasp. It contains four of his most interesting characters – together a fascinating composite hero – along with some of his bleakest and most compelling prose, and the novel is a superb poly-sided portrait of mid-century torment and despair. And yet, for all its potential and brilliance, it could not quite succeed. The book sold in excellent numbers; of course it did: everything Mishima wrote did. But it was his first real failure, its tone out of step with the times he had been hoping to capture. He wanted to maintain the post-war gloom with a devastating social panorama; everyone else wanted to move on – by 1959 the economic boom years had arrived for Japan.[72]

For all the male angst and alienation, however, all the various roads that lead to nihilism, *Kyoko's House* is bound together by Kyoko herself, an absorbing if functional heroine who not only sets the plot in motion but creates the circumstances for the four principals to exist. If the men are a quartet of 'I's', the protagonist Kyoko is an era – as the logogrammatic kanji characters of her name suggest: the name Kyoko (鏡子) can be literally translated as 'mirror child', i.e., the reflection of the age. Yet Kyoko is also a self-willed and independent-minded woman, crafting, in the salon-like open house of the title, a particular and peculiar social world for pleasure, discussion, and connectivity.

It is this which links Kyoko to the great heroine of *After the Banquet*. But in this later novel Mishima does not simply create a flattish metaphorical figure. Instead he crafts one of his finest leading roles, one inhabiting a flourishing contemporary Japan, replete with scepticism and distrust of the ruling classes. Written

---

72 The reproach was by no means unanimous: one leading literary critic, Takeo Okuno (1926–1997), admittedly also a friend of the author, hailed *Kyoko's House* as a 'model of classical psychological fiction' and thought it Mishima's finest work since *Confessions* a decade before.

with exceptional intimacy and credibility, Mishima's new heroine would not be out of place amid the vibrancy and immediacy of *Madame Bovary* (1857), or within the sumptuous historical activity of *Sentimental Education* (1869). (Indeed, such is the veracity of both the character and her story in *After the Banquet*, it should not be surprising that both had a factual origin.)

This heroine is Kazu Fukuzawa, a convincing, three-dimensional individual who runs a fashionable Tokyo restaurant catering not, like Kyoko, for miscellaneous malcontents, but for high-ranking diplomats, legislators, and other influential policymakers. Harmless and inoffensive though it might seem, the novel would be Mishima's first major flirtation with politics – and would have significant consequences for his life, work, and literary legacy.

After the Banquet was serialized in *Chūō Kōron* – a major literary magazine established in 1887 and still going today – between January and October 1960, allowing Mishima to check the progress and reception of the novel as it appeared.

The failure of *Kyoko's House* meant the stakes for *Banquet* were higher, with Mishima keen to reconfirm himself as the preeminent writer of his generation. To an extent, he did, and the public warmed to this new tale, which avoided the overt pessimism of *Kyoko's House* and returned to some of the more effective and familiar elements of his first period. Utilizing recent real-life events, as he had with *The Temple of the Golden Pavilion*, he also included political melodrama, which his play *The Hall of the Crying Deer* (1956) had explored to widespread critical and commercial acclaim.[73] There was darkness in *Banquet* – to an extent, his nihilistic epic *Kyoko's House* cast a shadow over all his subsequent fiction – but it was not all-embracing, destructive, resorting to death and despair. Quite the reverse: not only was the gloom deployed solely when the narrative required it – when Kazu is forced to close her beloved restaurant – but it was used as a structural means for the heroine to then positively reassert and rediscover herself by the novel's happy close. (There is an exquisite symmetry to the ending of the book, in formal, moral, and personal terms, as we will see.)

So what, therefore, went wrong? Why did such an affectionately received, enchanting, and even uplifting novel turn out to be such a disaster for Mishima? This time, literary calamity was looming not in the form of churlish critics or an apathetic, distracted readership but in the seeds of the subject matter the author had chosen for his new book. The authenticity which made it work turned out to be its real-world undoing. Whereas the real-life person who had set fire to Kyoto's Kinkakuji and inspired Mishima's novel of the same name had died in March 1956, prior to that book's release, a character at the heart of *After the Banquet* was very much still alive – and didn't like what they read. Moreover, unlike the protagonist of *The Temple of the Golden Pavilion*, they were no mere ascetic acolyte but a powerful political force.

After the Banquet tells the story of how Kazu Fukuzawa – the middle-aged, self-made proprietor of her own trendy high-class Tokyo restaurant – falls in love with one of her guests: an elderly

---

73 Opening in November 1956, the play was enormously successful, running on tour around Japan for years before being turned into a feature film, several television movies, and even an opera by Shin'ichirō Ikebe (2010).

retired stateman and ex-cabinet minister, Noguchi. They marry, and he decides, with her help, to run to be governor of Tokyo. The campaign is a disaster, not least because of Kazu's well-intended, if overly ambitious and slightly naive, interference, and the election is lost. The restaurant has to be sold to pay for the debts, and Kazu betrays her husband by attempting to recoup the money via her husband's political rivals. They divorce, but Kazu is able to reopen her establishment, and the novel finishes much as it began, in an appealing, upbeat mood. (The final chapter is especially dazzling: mirroring the opening one, it ends delightfully with Kazu reading a letter in her charming garden – and with a wonderfully optimistic, compassionate closing line.)

The inspiration for Noguchi, Hachirō Arita (1884–1965), was a career diplomat in Europe before serving as Minister for Foreign Affairs three times before and during the war. He was the originator of the infamous phrase 'Greater East Asia Co-Prosperity Sphere', which presented an official language and agenda for Japan's expansive imperial desires of the 1930s. After the war, however, he had – like so many – refashioned himself as a left-leaning politician and, as a widower, had married for the third time: to Terui Azegami (1906–1989), owner of a pair of exclusive Tokyo eateries. The Japan Socialist Party put Arita forward as their candidate for the Tokyo governorship in both 1955 and 1959, in the latter campaign – as in Mishima's version – supported by election resources from his wife's restaurants: one was sold; the other, the Hannyaen, heavily mortgaged. When Azegami tried to sell the Hannyaen to raise more capital, the right-wing Liberal Democratic Party (LDP) government disrupted the negotiations, before the conservative establishment released a smear campaign, hinting at Azegami's colourful past while also suggesting her husband was critically ill. Losing the election by a whisker, the couple were lumbered with financial obligations. They quarrelled and eventually divorced – though with backing from, of all people, the conservatives, Azegami was able to reopen the Hannyaen.

Mishima, as can be seen, largely stuck to this chain of events in *After the Banquet* – and everyone could tell (most of the plot was public knowledge). But he was not producing salacious, malicious trash: this was a serious and meticulously researched novel from the country's leading young writer. With his editors Mishima had visited Azegami at her restaurant, spoke to her about the circumstances of the election, read her accounts of it. Arita's version of events, it is true, had not been directly sought, but he had, after all, recently published a book on the matter – and had sent it, autographed, to Mishima himself.

As serialization continued throughout 1960, Arita grew more and more twitchy, eventually demanding *Chūō Kōron* suspend publication. When Shinchōsha published it as a book in November, he snapped and sued Mishima for invasion of privacy. The long trial (April 1961 to September 1964) was, naturally, a huge event, bringing together as it did a major star of the contemporary literary scene and one of the towering figures of recent Japanese politics – like Margaret Thatcher suing Martin Amis, or Ronald Reagan, Don DeLillo. Arita was outwardly, and reasonably, distressed by the novel's voyeuristic bedroom scenes (though they are infrequent, hardly explicit, and crucial to the developing plot). Was Arita more concerned with Mishima's satirical portrait of an outwardly cultured political grandee who is actually embroiled in local, rough-edged antics, acting on occasion like a petulant child?

Either way – and despite Mishima's legal team producing the autographed book, in a dramatic moment surely engineered by their theatrical client, as proof Arita had not condemned him – Arita won. Substantial, if hardly ruinous, damages were awarded, though Mishima was not compelled to issue a public apology as Arita had demanded. Mishima and his publisher appealed, but Arita died during the process, and eventually a compromise was reached in which, crucially for us, not a word of *After the Banquet* was changed. The case, however, was a landmark in Japan, since it unquestionably made privacy laws more strict and circumscribed a great many artistic media, from novels and plays to comedy, films, and TV, making Japan's output to this day arguably more cautious and conservative than many comparable countries.[74]

For Mishima, the case soured his belief in many Japanese institutions: politicians, the courts, the press. Arita's lies during the trial – he had denied sending the autographed book, for example – infuriated Mishima, as did the ageing politician's childish comment that the defendant was no writer of the calibre of a Sōseki or Ōgai. The case had dragged on, causing immense psychological pressure, distracting Mishima from his work, and turning his fine novel into a circus. It also alienated much of the literary establishment from a writer many already enviously considered too wildly successful. (Even his great colleague Yasunari Kawabata was somewhat evasive in supporting his friend in his hour of need.)

The *Banquet* fiasco was doubtless part of the reason Mishima would fail to win the Nobel, despite his reputation (and several nominations). It was all injurious attention – there *is* such a thing as bad publicity. More than this, the affair tainted many

---

74 The phrase 'invasion of privacy' even entered the language, with the English word 'privacy' retained – プライバシー ('puraibashī') – since no precise equivalent was considered to exist in Japanese.

of Mishima's beliefs in his own country, helping accelerate his crossing toward a more alarming kind of politics that looked backward rather than to the future.

⁂

After the Banquet, for all its sporadic cynicism and the nihilism hangover from *Kyoko's House*, is a fine example of Mishima's ability to write glowing, affirmative fiction. And it is the memorable central figure of Kazu that lies at the heart of this rosiness, this luminosity, for she is one of the most admirable, engaging, and fully drawn of all Mishima's women – caught in the conflict between politics and love but shining through, a positive human being.

To some extent, fashionable restaurateur Kazu occupies an updated version of the realm of the 'books of the floating world' (浮世草子, 'ukiyo-zōshi')[75] explored in eighteenth-century Japanese literature, especially in Osaka, Kyoto, and Edo (Tokyo), by writers such as Shogetsudo Fukaku, Tomonobu (Ishikawa Ryūsen), and, above all, Ihara Saikaku.[76] Using sophisticated literary techniques, though a good deal of unfortunate misogyny, too, the gaudy, bawdy, snickering prose of the floating world peered into amorous, even erotic, subjects and settings usually

---

75   The 'floating world' (浮世, 'ukiyo') was originally a Buddhist concept, one of impermanence and transience – the fleeting life to be left behind. This then developed into a 'seize the day' or 'live for the moment' philosophy which ultimately became that of the more familiar floating world which involves urban lifestyles and culture, especially their pleasure-seeking aspects.

76   See especially Saikaku's *Five Women Who Loved Love* and *Comrade Loves of the Samurai*.

considered vulgar. The usual aristocratic victuals of courtship and nature were usurped by stories involving brothels, samurai, tradespeople, curious characters, and intriguing episodes that nonetheless maintained one of the key characteristics of the floating world: its realism, which, together with their detached, ironic tone, anticipated Flaubert by a century – and *After the Banquet* by two.

We all need to eat, so restaurants naturally also featured heavily in the ukiyo-zōshi, and Kazu's modish bistro, the Setsugoan, is their modern incarnation, albeit as an upscale embodiment. It is a ryōtei, a traditional Japanese establishment, one which often accepted new clients by invitation only and offered an inconspicuous location for high-level meetings or discreet get-togethers. In *After the Banquet*, Kazu's Setsugoan is less unobtrusive: indeed, it is the chic and stylish venue where the moneyed and elite go to wine and dine, where affluent and powerful Tokyoites go to see and be seen. It is the only place in town to impress colleagues, to commemorate the past, or to look forward to the future. With Kazu and Noguchi, it is the third main character of the novel, and Mishima presents a rich and sumptuous portrait of a rich and sumptuous setting, with its magnificent garden a particular highlight – both as a dazzling al fresco space for Kazu's clientele and as a haven into which she can escape for peace and reflection.

Kazu is the audacious, self-reliant queen of the restaurant, monarch of all she surveys and, like many of Saikaku's heroines, is ardent, enthusiastic, effortlessly tearful, combining what Mishima sees as a masculine determination with a feminine zeal. Moreover, and in the vein of many of the female protagonists in the floating world, her love leads many a man toward his own destruction, never exalting him or generating success, but leading only to an inevitable decline. Kazu is not malicious, still less evil, but her spontaneity and occasional hot-headedness go with her careless amorous nature – she prefers to love rather than be loved.

We see all these qualities in both the whirlwind romance between passionate, sensitive Kazu and poker-faced, supercilious Noguchi as well as later in her husband's gubernatorial campaign, into which she is irresistibly drawn. Frustrated by her potential lover's aloofness, despite their clear friendship and indications that it means something more to them both, she hastily writes a letter chiding him for his coldness – a detachment which has in fact only served to romanticize him in her eyes; she misconstrues his impassivity for a mysterious aura. Thus, when she has captured her prey, their marriage is something of a disappointment, flat and unexciting: it is the chase which gratifies Kazu, not the fulfilment. Similarly, just as the unpredictable excitement of the pursuit led to an anticlimactic union, the impulsive, volatile exhilaration of the governorship campaign leads to the disappointment of their election defeat – though with a pleasing irony it is also the event which allows Kazu to depart the marriage and return to running her beloved Setsugoan.

A peculiar political satire lies at the literal, if not figurative, centre of *After the Banquet*. An exquisitely constructed novel, it situates the problems of mind and body, affection and animosity, freedom and constraint, within the apparently unusual (at least for Mishima) context of a contemporary political campaign. It is replete with scathing details concerning the hubris and ambition of all involved. Such is the animation and authenticity of Mishima's telling, it will feel recognizable to anyone that has recently sat through an election season, with its sound bites and backbites, vulgarity and skulduggery.

For all the wry observations about the nature of political campaigning and the folks who yearn for and then become involved in it, in truth these aspects of *After the Banquet* are there only to serve as the means for Kazu's quest, a typically Mishimian mission of self-discovery and self-fulfilment. Neither are to be found in her husband or the political sphere. The politically charged environment encircling the two central characters is an element which deflects the conflict between Noguchi and Kazu (and between mind and body, love and animosity, freedom and constraint), bending its harsh light into the harmonious resolution of divorce – whereas a normal domestic life might have led to years of umbrage and resentment. The intensity of the gubernatorial campaign exposes, as Kazu rightly testifies, the polarities of both political life and her marriage:

> Policy and such are secondary. All you need for an election is money and feeling. I am an uneducated woman. I mean to slug it out with only those two things on my side.

Kazu is an intuitive, demonstrative, spontaneous – sometimes even irresponsible – heroine, an embodiment of a certain kind of instinctive intelligence and aptitude. Her husband, Noguchi, is cerebral, senescent, fond of books and posturing, pedantically. He's dull, an intellectual poseur, and always afraid of being exposed as such. He's also vicious, striking his wife when he feels his honour is betrayed by her generous, unconstrained actions to help his election prospects (mortgaging her beloved restaurant, distributing posters, giving speeches, and so on). The carefully constructed scene where Noguchi commits an act of domestic violence, not least because of the satirical atmosphere of much of the novel, is shocking, appalling, *nasty*.[77]

Their differences had led to their initial mutual attraction, but the damage they cause soon inevitably turns Kazu and Noguchi against one another, with bickering leading to more detrimental hostilities. Yet because of their entirely dissimilar characters, and the fact that each is firmly affixed to their particular social sphere, Kazu and Noguchi do not extinguish each other in acts of total ferocity, even if they are eclipsed in one another's hearts. Blood is not shed, even if tears are. It is this relatively tame resolution to *After the Banquet* that has caused many seasoned Mishima fans to ignore or dismiss the novel, their bloodlust seemingly not sated.

The ending to this story, however, is one of the most plausible, and even representative, despite the lack of murder and mayhem, in all Mishima's work. Kazu's realism and complexity demand an authentic conclusion to her tale – which she receives, with her restaurant and the life that went with it back under her control. But it would be misleading to say she is simply back where she started. She has undertaken a personal journey across the stormy seas of love and politics and come through with grace and style. Some of the Weltschmerz of *Kyoko's House* is certainly apparent in *After the Banquet*, colouring (though not tainting or contaminating) the story. Politics will do that to you. But the strength and resolve of Kazu's character overcome any

---

77   It is perhaps these two aspects, the affectation and the aggression, that the real-life Arita, not unreasonably, took exception to when he read Mishima's work.

attempt to undermine it, allowing her and her novel to radiate their special light.

ॐ

Just as there were generational tensions between Mishima and Arita in their court case, there are naturally some between the older Noguchi and his younger wife. More significant, however, is class difference. Like Arita, Noguchi is well-educated and has had a distinguished diplomatic career; he, perhaps a little pompously and elusively, enjoys European literature and culture. Like her originator, Terui Azegami, Kazu has found success the hard way, her air of rustic simplicity and fleshy fondness concealing her pitiless determination.

Kazu's modest birth further confirms her status as a member of the neo–floating world and of a twentieth-century demi-monde, whose protagonists are apt to be low-ranked, scorning the pomp and pomposity of the upper orders. Mishima himself found the roughness of the working classes alien to him, tending to admire the generally courteous grace of the nobility, but he had a certain romanticizing envy for the bucolic energy of those who existed in society's underbelly. Moreover, the upper crust tended to have something concealed beneath their elegance and refinement, and if it wasn't unequivocally venal behaviour, it was, for Mishima, arguably worse: sterility and banality.

Mishima's ambivalence toward the working class and the aristocracy, simultaneously offended and welcoming to both, seems to some extent projected in Kazu's personality herself. Kazu is plump, exuberant, her expansive body a reflection of her capacious nature; Noguchi is intellectual, cultured, frigid, wont to spend the evening with a good thick German novel his wife can't begin to understand. Yet her husband's cold cerebral disposition hypnotizes Kazu, especially early in their courtship. She idealizes his patrician etiquette, his knowledge of and love for foreign literature, even his occasional wrath and rudeness: his acerbic reprimands become regal expressions of his noble nature.

Kazu is hardly the first pedestrian to be taken in by the magnetic icy charms of the aristocracy, and soon she begins to tire of Noguchi's tedious temperament, seeing that his solemnity and hauteur are not an innate aspect of his personality, before the election campaign allows him to shine a little in her heart again. (As does the delectable prospect of being the governor's wife – a station which excites both Kazu's insecurity and her upwardly mobile pretensions but which we know would betray her truer, freer self.)

Here we witness some of the wonderful authenticity and complexity about Kazu, her truth as a character and a human being. Although she wishes to be the one to love, rather than be loved, to be active, not passive, she takes a quiet pleasure in being patronized (and worse) by her husband, enjoying his stubborn deportment. Noguchi refuses to be controlled by a woman, yet in her way, by declining to allow his obstinate conduct to disturb her, she is maintaining her own dynamic position – and continues to be the one to love, by undertaking her own private initiatives for his election campaign.

If, for some readers, her sudden changes from belligerent political crusader and outgoing restaurateur to meek and deferential housewife are a contradiction or even a betrayal, we should remember that all these sides to Kazu's personality are autonomous to her own personality – not her husband's coercion. Mishima magnificently realizes the fluidity and swiftness of these shifts, confirming the instinctive reality of his creation as well as the veracity of her superficially inconsistent mindset.

Moreover, when Kazu, as he sees it, deceives Noguchi, by seeking money from his political rivals to reacquire the Setsugoan, she continues to act as the one to love, in wider best interests. She uses her aquatic arsenal, tears,[78] to confront her husband's political enemies and eventually to extract money from him in order to reopen the restaurant. In some ways it is an emblematic transformation, from a virtuous geisha-wife to an unscrupulous adulteress, though the dichotomy is never apparent in Kazu's self-conscious behaviour. Her 'betrayal', such as it is, is selfish and self-interested but sovereign and self-sufficient, too, authentically so. In fact, of course, her actions seem, consciously or not, to be in everyone's interests: not only because the marriage is a bad match for both parties but also because Tokyo has yearned for Kazu and the Setsugoan to return to the contemporary socio-gastronomic scene.

Kazu's ruthlessness, using whatever weapons are to hand, be they weeping or instinctive determination, is obviously linked to her humble origins and her need to survive, as well as her need to confirm a place for her existence after death. Throughout the novel we are told of her conflict between being interred in the grand, oft-visited Noguchi tomb, with its insincere confirmation of status and surrender, and a remote, forsaken burial place, unloved but honest. The former offers security which is only imprisonment, both in marriage and eternity. An unmarked grave in some desolate cemetery, however frightening, is also freedom – the freedom she held by running the Setsugoan.

Choosing the secluded grave and retrieving the restaurant are courageous acts, proof of Kazu's immense inner strength

---

78   Cf. 'Women's weapons, water-drops' – *King Lear*, II.ii.466.

and quiet conviction, which persist despite her own fears of a lonely life and lonely death. Her action carries the vigorous pre-eminence of Mishima's favourite heroes, which still lay a few years in the future. Already, in *After the Banquet*, and in the unlikely character of an upmarket restaurateur – chubby, cheerful, middle-aged – Mishima was anticipating those active, moody young protagonists – Kiyoaki in *Spring Snow*; Isao in *Runaway Horses* – that his later fiction would elevate into his highest pantheon.

The cosmic black hole of *The Sea of Fertility* was beginning to exert its disturbing gravitational influence.

Chapter Seven

The Frolic of the Beasts
NOH EXIT

Beethoven's only opera, *Fidelio* (1805; rev. 1814), depicts the rescue of a political prisoner by his wife in eighteenth-century Spain. Various intrigues and complications – romantic, ethical, and otherwise – take place as she tries to secure his release. Filled with some of the great German's most noble, touching, and heroic music, this complex generic hybrid (taking in opera, oratorio, Singspiel, and melodrama) was one of Mishima's favourite stage works, one that appealed to many of his deepest sensibilities surrounding love, violence, freedom, sacrifice, political machination, and dramatic form. He later claimed that it was actually during a performance of *Fidelio* that he was finally able to resolve some tricky structural and thematic issues for his next novel.[79] This was *The Frolic of the Beasts* (獣の戯れ, 'Kemono

---

79 During his third world tour, in January 1961 Mishima saw a production of *Fidelio* at La Scala, Milan, conducted by Herbert von Karajan – and

no tawamure', 1961), an intense psychosexual drama revolving around a tragic love triangle, which, like *Fidelio*, involves prisons as sites of physical captivity in addition to emblems of moral and spiritual confinement.

In terms of design, *Frolic* is one of Mishima's most stimulating works. Taking advantage of a slightly shorter form (it's around 160 pages), he constructed a complex non-linear narrative that flashes backward and forward after an extensive, purposely elusive prologue, whose shadowy secret is only gradually revealed to us, piece by bleeding piece. The prose employed within this unusual architecture is languid, luminous, often exquisite, sometimes disconcertingly ironic. The elegance of this language operates as a mask to conceal tensions, while also helping create three sharply defined central figures: a husband, his wife, and her lover. Each intrigues but ultimately eludes the reader. And, as we will see, part of the subtlety and mystery of this trio derives from their origins in traditional Noh theatre – and the book as a whole is a teasing, complex negotiation with its own aesthetic heritage.

Although something of an outlier among Mishima's novels, *The Frolic of the Beasts* is gradually becoming better known, not least as readers discover how its dark themes echo or anticipate many of those found in more familiar works such as *The Temple of the Golden Pavilion* (1956), *The Sailor Who Fell from Grace with the Sea* (1963), and *The Decay of the Angel* (1971). As with these books, *Frolic* is a nihilistic tragedy, a gloomy catastrophe, but one shot through with the most radiant light, particularly the dazzling sun of the Japanese coast. Indeed, as in *Sailor*, *Frolic* makes extensive use of the sea – that pervasive presence surrounding the island

---

with a legendary cast, including Birgit Nilsson as Leonore, Jon Vickers as Florestan, Franz Crass as Don Fernando, and Hans Hotter as Don Pizarro.

nation of Japan – as both a setting and symbol. An insignia of both simple and complex being, the sea is an immense, formless reality, often dark and unfriendly, a threatening force as well as a welcoming one. It forms a counterpart to the monotonous, closed-off world of the prison, offering freedom and variety, fantasy and reality. Lives gush and erupt like ocean waves before sinking back, inevitably subjugated and overwhelmed, to be reabsorbed in the waters of time.

Aggression and incarceration structure and colour the narrative of *Frolic*: a vicious act imprisons one character in jail and another in his own body, before a further monstrosity leads to the deaths of two characters and detention of a third. Violence abounds, lurid and inexorable as the novel's troubled characters try to impose their needs and ideals onto an empty and impervious, even paradoxically resilient, world. They struggle, they suffer, they confront and contest. They are compelled to commit crimes against the conventional morality which resists their strangeness.

Yet these figures are not mere delinquents, or self-indulgent firebrands against a humdrum status quo. They offer something more positive: an assertion of defiance and change, something to transcend what Mishima saw as the barrenness and commercialism of post-war Japan (an antagonism which would grow during the 1960s into outright political radicalism). In his art, as in his life, Mishima presented perversions, even criminal actions, as statements of insubordination and anticipation in the face of an indifferent cosmos and ephemeral human existence. The 'beasts' of this teasing, intangible novel behave with brutish malevolence – but their 'frolic' offers strange avenues of hope, peculiar routes to certain kinds of liberation.

Ippei, an urbane Tokyo porcelain dealer fond of luxurious Italian suits and upmarket hair salons, also moonlights translating and reviewing German literature (his former profession was as a university lecturer, before he inherited his parents' ceramics shop). A dandy and a philanderer, he has numerous affairs, to which his wife, Yūko, turns a repressed blind eye. One of his shop's new employees, Kōji (who is also one of his former deutsche lit students), is a typically handsome and antagonistic Mishimian hero, who then embarks on an affair with Yūko, falling in love with her in the process. A few months later, the lovers discover Ippei with another mistress. A quarrel ensues, and Kōji strikes the husband over the head. Ippei is severely incapacitated, developing speech and motor problems, but survives.

Kōji is imprisoned for two years. Upon his release, at which point the novel's first chapter opens, he joins up with his lover and her husband again, and the three live out a strange existence, with Kōji working in the greenhouse that Ippei has opened on the Izu Peninsula (having been forced to close the Ginza ceramics store). Various erotic and emotional entanglements[80] ensue before, eventually, Yūko and Kōji strangle Ippei. He is sentenced to death; she is given a life term. Kōji and Ippei are buried next to one another, with a plot between them reserved for Yūko when her time comes, a macabre but oddly satisfying final state of affairs.

This is a deliciously titillating work of sex, slaughter, and subjugation – it brings to mind many a cheap thriller as well as more sophisticated works like Zola's *Thérèse Raquin* (1868),

---

80 'Beastly Entanglements' is a further possible translation of the Japanese title, 獣の戯れ, 'Kemono no tawamure'.

Nabokov's *King, Queen, Knave* (1928), and Mishima's own *Thirst for Love* (1950) – and here the novel's plot has been retold in relatively straightforward linear form. But in Mishima's book, the narrative undergoes a series of shifts in time, leaping ahead before retracing its steps (something its subplot, involving Ippei's employee Teijiro and his daughter, also undergoes, before itself being gradually incorporated within the main narrative). An unusual prologue and epilogue add to the uncertainty, depth, and scheming – of both Mishima the novelist and his protagonists.

It is an inspired technique, refined and experimental. But *Frolic* never flaunts its unusual methodology merely for its own sake; rather it seeks to disorientate our sense of action and motivation, chronology and morality. By having to piece together the outline of the work, we must continually reassess our attitudes toward this beguiling set of characters – personalities, like toddlers near traffic, we shouldn't let wander off for a moment.

Creating this short but intricate work of art took Mishima a little time to get just right. As we saw above, solutions to its overall structure only came during the curious but perfectly reasonable circumstances of a performance of *Fidelio* in Italy in January 1961. Several months before, in August 1960, Mishima had travelled south and west of Tokyo on a research trip to gather details and background information for the novel. He visited Hamamatsu, to see the airbase and drop in on a musical instrument manufacturer,[81] along with the fishing port of Arari, in order to observe a seaside plant nursery – all of which was required to depict particular settings and events of the novel.

Indeed, even in this comparatively short novel, the wealth of details Mishima provides is astonishing, convincing us with charming, though occasionally sinister, minutiae (not least regarding the plants in Ippei's new business). Mishima knew the power of his prose as well as of his imagination, but he was never so arrogant to believe that he could invent details out of thin air or without sufficient research. And it is these details which provide his narratives, especially *Frolic*, with their troubling authenticity within which so much of his distinctively disconcerting material is situated.

With these details secured and ready to be incorporated into his evolving new novel, Mishima could return home. He finished *After the Banquet* by the end of August, before embarking on one of his most (in)famous short stories: 'Patriotism', which he completed in mid-October. On 1 November 1960 Mishima and his wife, Yōko, set off on a round-the-world tour (the writer's third). They would be away three months and visit Hawaii,[82] Los Angeles,[83] New York, Lisbon,[84] Madrid, Paris,[85]

---

81   The significance of which this writer will leave the first-time reader to discover for themselves in Mishima's text.

82   In Hawaii, voting in its first presidential election since joining the union a year before, they saw, on a hotel TV, Kennedy defeat Nixon 303–219 in the Electoral College vote.

83   After visiting Disneyland, California, Mishima wrote breathlessly to Yasunari Kawabata back home that he never believed such an exciting place could exist.

84   Which Mishima, with some reason, thought one of the most beautiful cities on earth.

85   Where he had dinner with poet, playwright, novelist, designer, film director, visual artist, critic, and all-round contemporary Renaissance man Jean Cocteau.

London,[86] Rome,[87] Milan, Athens, Cairo,[88] Karachi, Kolkata, Bangkok, and Hong Kong,[89] before arriving home in Tokyo on 20 January 1961 (just as JFK was being sworn in as the thirty-fifth American president in Washington, DC).

In New York, Mishima's own celebrity status sanctioned get-togethers with stars such as Greta Garbo, but the main excitement of his time in Manhattan was the staging of two of his *Five Modern Noh Plays* (1956), which had been ignominiously abandoned during a previous trip to the States.[90] Presented as part of the American National Theater and Academy (ANTA) at the Theatre de Lys – Samuel Beckett and Eugène Ionesco were also on the bill – the 'versatile, subtle and effective' Noh plays impressed *New York Times* drama critic Louis Calta, confirming for him why Mishima was considered by many to be Japan's leading contemporary writer.

---

86   In London he met the poet and essayist Stephen Spender, a Japanophile who had visited the country twice, in 1957 and 1958, travelling all over the islands and paying his way by giving lectures. Mishima also met Arthur Waley, at that time the only translator into English of *The Tale of Genji* (and who, perhaps not entirely unreasonably, refused to visit Japan lest it spoil the 'ancient, uncorrupted' picture of the country he held in his imagination).

87   On New Year's Day in Rome, Mishima visited the sculptor Giovanni Aldini, who made for the writer a replica of a statue of Apollo owned by the city. Weighing over half a ton, it arrived in Tokyo six months later; Mishima eventually installed it in the middle of his garden.

88   The Great Pyramid of Giza, one of the Seven Wonders of the World, Mishima thought 'an indecent monument'.

89   Where Mishima visited all sorts of iniquitous places, from opium dens to brothels and bars.

90   The plays were *Hanjo* and *The Lady Aoi* (though the latter was presented as *The Lady Akane*, since 'Aoi' was regarded as unpronounceable for delicate American tongues).

The Noh play was an important literary form for Mishima: not only did he write eleven of them himself, but their style and structure influenced a good deal of his prose fiction, too, not least *The Frolic of the Beasts*, which is, in part, a parody of an early Noh play. The oldest theatre art form still regularly performed today, the highly specialized dance dramas of Noh[91] originated in the fourteenth century and were based on tales from traditional literature, usually with a supernatural being narrating the story after being turned to human form. Staunchly codified, performances are characterized by their integration of costumes, props, and gestures with their most defining and iconic feature: masks. Made from Japanese cypress wood and highly stylized, they signify the age, gender, and social rank of characters, turning them into quasi-archetypes and playing with our sense of both prejudice and expectation. The masks' very specificity paradoxically generates a wealth of ambiguity surrounding their true nature and role within a given play, stimulating the audience to imagine for themselves the range of expressions and emotions occurring beneath them.

In *Frolic*, these masks are frequently referenced, and each of the three main characters is presented in ways that recall them. When we first encounter Kōji after the prologue, his face is described as being 'like a well-crafted, carved wooden mask'; Yūko habitually wears thick dark lipstick giving the impression of the classic 'young woman' Noh mask; Ippei, after Kōji's attack, wears an 'interminable smile', evoking the immobile beaming countenance of many of the more sinister grinning masks.

91　The kanji for Noh (能) means variously 'skill', 'craft', or 'talent'.

The plot and design of *Frolic*, too, are related to Noh, since the book is a partial parody of the fourteenth-century Noh play *Motomezuka* (求塚), which also utilizes a framing device surrounding a love triangle story. Written by the father of modern Noh drama, Kan'ami (1333–1384), *Motomezuka* tells of how a priest and his companions, travelling from the western provinces to Kyoto, are told the tale of a woman named Unai. In the story, two men declare their love for Unai, but, unwilling to incur either's wrath or jealousy, she turns them both down. The suitors compete for her hand, but each contest ends in a draw. Tormented, Unai drowns herself; her wooers commit suicide at her funeral, and her soul endures in eternal agony (which Mishima sharply alludes to with Yūko's life imprisonment at the end of *Frolic*, though the novel offers a more promising vision of the afterlife). Clearly, too, the Unai love triangle references those at work in Mishima's text (Yūko/Kōji/Ippei, as well as the subplot trio Kimi/Kiyoshi/Matsukichi), though each triangle exists in its own particular way, inviting multifaceted comparisons. Moreover, the refreshingly topsy-turvy nature of Mishima's non-linear narrative connects his work to the hallucinatory otherworldliness (in both time and space) of Noh.

By offering these links to an ancient, though enduring, dramatic form, Mishima alters our relationship with his writing, coercing us to re-examine the motives and morality of his characters. He compels us to see them less as personalities in a series of modern situations than as wider, representative figures. Given their frisson of Noh, Mishima's characters are less guilty of lust and wrath, less responsible for their swathe of crimes. Instead, they resemble more edifying, cautionary, forms from time immemorial. In a contemporary setting, we are far more likely to judge and denounce; in an ancient tale, our empathy and receptivity to enlightenment are heightened.

The prologue and epilogue, while also associating the novel with Noh structures, further this sense of artificiality and instruction, and the prologue is an especially ingenious construction. It teases our expectations, preloading the novel, first offering a comprehensive description of a static, isolated, mask-like moment in time (a photograph of the three principal characters in the sun by the sea) before ending by describing the graves of the three protagonists (only two of which are occupied, an agonizingly thrilling detail). In between we are told a few details about the lives of the threesome in the picture, as well as of a 'wretched incident' that will take place only a few days after the snapshot was taken and which will lead inexorably to the three graves, which are themselves unwelcome recent editions to the local neighbourhood. All is linked, but all is elusive too. Something is odd, amiss; everything is too intimate, too knowing.

After five chapters, a curious first-person epilogue closes the novel, in which a folklore researcher on vacation recounts his visit to the region and his meeting with a priest who told him the tale of Ippei, Yūko, and Kōji: how the latter two had confessed to murdering the former, who himself yearned for death to release him from his harrowing, debilitated existence.[92] The scholar takes a photograph of the graves to Yūko in prison, where she is satisfied that she can serve her sentence in peace before a joyful reunion in eternity with Ippei and Kōji.

In strong contrast to the mysterious prologue, everything in the epilogue feels obvious, even superfluous, matter of fact (even though of course it crucially reveals the ending to the story

---

92   'Death. I want to die.'

for us). Along with the eminence of Mishima's prose and the elegance of his complex construction, such teasing, mischievous frankness induces us to read more into what is being said, to make connections to the Noh heritage and its implications, to recognize this as far more than awkward erotica or shoddy whodunnit, but as something more profound – a modern myth, a contemporary folk tale.

Connected to this is the passion tangle at the centre of the plot. Love triangles are one of the great mainstays, even clichés, of all kinds of literature: from ancient legend and fable to the hammiest present-day potboiler. As a narrative device they are inherently intriguing, fundamentally dynamic, their three sides working to create endless conspiracy, drama, and pain. Moreover, unwittingly or not, most of us have probably been involved in one, one way or another: they are personal, ordinary, even commonplace. And yet there remains something inherently curious, even exotic and elusive, about them. So, too, in Mishima's novel, where the figures of Ippei, Yūko, and Kōji, as well as the much more minor ones of Kimi, Kiyoshi, and Matsukichi, linger in our imagination long after we have closed the pages of this short novel.

It is a haunting work, cryptic and enigmatic, an unsettling jewel.

⁂

At the centre of *The Frolic of the Beasts* resides an object not only upon which the plot hinges, but that stands as a fundamental symbol for many of the novel's profounder connotations, bringing further metaphysics and philosophical depth to this magnificently sordid story. One day, early on in his affair with Yūko, Kōji is out walking with her and discovers, lying on the ground, a heavy black wrench. Not really knowing why, and in a fashion akin to a Sartrean or Camusian protagonist – the Roquentin of *La Nausée* (1938) or the Meursault of *L'Étranger* (1942) – he picks up the mysterious dark tool and puts it in his pocket. Later, this will be the implement with which he strikes Ippei, causing his boss and love rival devastating permanent brain damage that turns him into a grinning ghoul who requires long-term care from his wife.[93]

In prison, with time on his hands as well as blood, Kōji reflects on the incident, suffusing it with metaphysical significance and concluding that the wrench was a manifestation of some primal 'will' turned tangible which then strove to propel reality's order into anarchy and disarray. It was not actually him, Kōji, who chose to grasp both the tool and his destiny; this act was determined by an auspicious chaotic force. It's a classic adolescent excuse, of course, unusable as a legal defence, but reassuring to the disgruntled romantic jailbird – though it also has more profound implications for interpreting Mishima's text.

Kōji, like many a disaffected youth, for all his bouts of languor and aggression, still remembers patches and flashes of his learning – in his case, German philosophy and literature. Certain Schopenhauerian ideas of the will spring to mind (even if they are not explicitly mentioned), especially the German philosopher's declaration that everything is a manifestation of a fundamental, inherent, and singular will – a cosmic will, one without goodness or morals, a dynamic, furious, and pitiless

---

93   Just as *Frolic*'s tale of aberrant love and moral transgression connects it with the plot of *Thirst for Love* (1950), so the wrench links it with the earlier novel's own murderous tool, the garden mattock.

force. As he ruminates in his cell, it is natural that Kōji might call to mind some of these ideas and implant them within the mysterious (in reality, mundane and mendacious) black object which caused him and others so much pain.

Kōji had hoped the skirmish involving Ippei, his mistress, and his wife would lift the veil on existence, leading to an exposure of the perversity at the centre of humanity. Instead, it merely exposes the pathetic, conformist nature, and the inclement intransigence, of our predictable species. We are shameful but ashamed, keen only to maintain appearances and face: Yūko reacts to her husband's infidelity not in grand romantic terms but in the hackneyed fashion of the slighted wife. For Kōji, this creates a dangerous internal imbalance, causing him not only to recoil, then strike out with the wrench, but to later envisage that object as the majestic embodiment of cosmic resolve.

Kōji repents enough of his misconduct to be released from prison after two years, and to resume his peculiar existence with Ippei and Yūko, but the incident seems to confer upon their unusual lifestyle a status of something more than the perfectly ordinary, slightly sleazy ménage à trois it is. The violent deed has operated as an essential, and rational, corrective to the terror of obnoxious banality, the 'cold, hard, black logic of iron' overcoming the rotten world and confronting the futile, empty nature of reality. The action alters the course of time, space, and destiny to overcome mediocrity, to transcend convention and immortalize the three protagonists. Though they are reviled by the locals, their strange and vexing story – like that of Unai and her suitors in the Noh source of the novel – will endure.

It is right and proper that the trio lie shoulder to shoulder in their three graves, perhaps now no longer wearing their three masks.

Chapter Eight

Beautiful Star

A SPACE ODDITY

1962 was a good year for literature – even a miraculous one. As a distraction from the atomic nightmare of the Cuban Missile Crisis and the death of Marilyn Monroe, bookworms and bibliophiles could plunge into Vladimir Nabokov's radical reinvention of the novel, *Pale Fire*, or disappear into *Labyrinths*, Jorge Luis Borges's maze of mayhem and metaphysics. Aleksandr Solzhenitsyn's *One Day in the Life of Ivan Denisovich* and Zofia Posmysz's *Passenger* offered glimpses of recent history, while Philip K. Dick's *The Man in the High Castle* and Anthony Burgess's *A Clockwork Orange* peeped at contemporary alternatives. If the world seemed insane, novelists were on hand to concur, with Doris Lessing's *The Golden Notebook*, Len Deighton's *The IPCRESS File*, James Baldwin's *Another Country*, and Ken Kesey's *One Flew Over the Cuckoo's Nest* presenting four very different chronicles of mental instability.

In Japan, a book came out that was not only extraordinary but almost inexplicable, for Yukio Mishima wrote something which sticks out, even now, like a sore thumb: a work of science fiction. For some, it's like discovering Wagner wrote nursery rhymes or Walt Disney repainted the Sistine Chapel. In fact, Mishima was an inveterate afficionado of SF, just as he was an ardent admirer of graphic novels and other literary genres habitually dismissed with a sniff.

Mishima's new book, *Beautiful Star* (美しい星, 'Utsukushī hoshi', 1962),[94] had flying saucers, a middle-aged man from Mars, and a young woman from Venus. It was provocative, sardonic, avant-garde. Yet it also carried the conviction of reality, presenting plausible human beings both in every detail and in unremarkable situations, and taking as its subject matter contemporary anxiety over imminent nuclear annihilation. As such, it blended the real and the anti-real in a distinctive fashion to create something disturbing, disconcerting, clearly ironic and humorous but with a hard edge that was as troubling as anything Mishima had yet written.

In many ways, the approach – satirical, surreal – was ideal for tackling the very real but equally otherworldly and inconceivable prospect of atomic Armageddon, which both intruded on everyday life and yet was so vast, mind-boggling, and incomprehensible that it seemed to exist only in fantasy or dream. (Given the book's generally bleak assessment of pending obliteration, it was fortuitous that *Beautiful Star* in its book form was first published on 20 October 1962, day five of the aforementioned confrontation in the Caribbean.)

---

94   In the novel, the title refers to Earth, though it might also be a sardonic reference to a nuclear blast.

The novel is far from flawless, not least in its fifty-page 'cosmic dialogue', which approaches the great philosophical debates of Dostoyevsky, especially the 'Grand Inquisitor' section in *The Brothers Karamazov* (1880), yet feels rather cumbersome in Mishima's text. For all that, this novel makes an interesting diversion from this author's more familiar material, while at the same time reconfirming and broadening many of his most enduring themes. It's a funny book, a strange book, an angry book, at times a little awkward, a little stubborn, but full of passages of consummate lyrical splendour – especially when pondering the heavens – and these more than justify our time spent with it.

Beautiful Star was a risky project for Mishima to undertake – and given the vindictiveness directed against them within its pages, the public understandably weren't much interested in it (though such leading writers as Jun'ichirō Tanizaki, Kōbō Abe, and Shōhei Ōoka praised it). Nevertheless it is a novel which repays repeated visits: for its dark moral and metaphysical acumen, for its witty insights, for its endearing frustrations, and for the ferocious scorn it levels at modern society and the recklessness of the human race. Under the cloak of science fiction, Mishima wrote one of his most realistic works of all.

On 30 October 1961, the Soviet Union exploded a new kind of thermonuclear device over the remote archipelago of Novaya Zemlya.[95] By far the most powerful weapon ever made, the

---

95 A name and place which Nabokov ironically references throughout *Pale Fire* with his fictious 'distant northern land' of 'Zembla'.

so-called Tsar Bomba weighed nearly thirty tons and was so large that the aircraft which released it had to have parts of the fuselage removed to accommodate it. The test itself yielded the equivalent of over fifty megatons of TNT, nearly four thousand times the strength of the bomb which devastated Hiroshima, and its seismic wave circled the globe three times. Its orange fireball was eight kilometres wide and the accompanying mushroom cloud seventy kilometres high (seven times the height of Everest and well outside the earth's stratosphere). Had the bomb detonated over a municipality the size of Paris, it would have destroyed the city to a radius of thirty-five kilometres. It was an awesome display of humanity's ingenuity, might, and folly.[96]

The test heightened the already tense nuclear confrontation – and contest – between the United States and the Soviet Union. Political posturing and military goading attained startling levels, and global unease over the possibility of an all-out war, with no winners and no survivors, reached an intense state of agitation. It was something reflected in the culture of the time – including by filmmakers as diverse as Ingmar Bergman (*Winter Light*, 1963) and Stanley Kubrick (*Dr. Strangelove or: How I learned to Stop Worrying and Love the Bomb*, 1964), the latter a movie which took black comedy to new pitches of obsidian humour to match the extremity of its subject matter. As a citizen of the only nation to have nuclear weapons used in anger against it, Mishima was well-placed to offer his own perspectives, fictional and otherwise, on atomic warfare.

---

96 The USA's Castle Bravo (1954) yielded the equivalent of just fifteen megatons of TNT; no device has even been devised to exceed the Tsar Bomba, and current treaties mean it is unlikely to be surpassed.

In January 1962, several stories by Mishima appeared in
the monthly magazines (as did the first instalments of *Beautiful
Star*'s serialization). One of them, 'Flowers on a Hat' (帽子の
花, 'Bōshi no hana'), was obviously inspired by the author's trip
to California the previous September – indeed, it often feels
less like fiction than a ferociously exquisite diary entry, offering
Mishima's reflections on living under the constant threat of
collective eradication. In the tale, the first-person narrator sits in
Union Square, San Francisco, overhears news of UN Secretary-
General Dag Hammarskjöld's death,[97] and has a hallucinatory
vision of nuclear catastrophe. All the details of the scene – the
crystal-clear late-summer sunlight, a mother knitting, a man
with a cane – are exquisitely captured in prose so that they can
be frozen in time by the cataclysm.

Another significant piece from this time took the form of
an essay Mishima wrote for the *Mainichi Shimbun*, 'Eschatology
and Literature',[98] in which he discusses how, in the past, religious
and philosophical thought on the end of the world had a deep
connection with classical literary forms. This is contrasted with
the uniqueness of modernity, where global annihilation, in the
form of nuclear weapons, is no ally of literature, indeed is its
mortal enemy representing something entirely mutually exclusive:
the hydrogen bomb presupposes a mechanical view of the world
that true literature cannot abide. But, Mishima concludes, serious
literature cannot ignore present-day realities, escaping *only*
into fantasy or absurdity; authors must assert and maintain the

---

97   Hammarskjöld died in a plane crash on 18 September 1961. Three official
     inquiries failed to conclusively determine its cause, including foul play or
     an assassination attempt, though at the time of the incident speculation
     was understandably rife.
98   Published in the evening edition on 4 January 1962.

reason for their existence, by attempting to confront the horrors. Accordingly, in *Beautiful Star*, Mishima located a means through which to tackle the nuclear predicament by navigating neatly between reality and make-believe, fact and science fiction, toying with the tension between them.

Mishima had long been interested in both speculative literature and paranormal phenomena. He attended seances and kokkuri (a form of divination meeting not unlike those using a Ouija board) and, in 1956, joined the Flying Saucer Research Association of Japan. He became passionate about the detection and observation of unidentified flying objects, which, in the new era of satellites and jet aircraft, were naturally becoming more and more common. During meetings of the society he claimed to witness several anomalous occurrences, including a cigar-shaped object he saw while on a rooftop with his wife (though he stopped short of declaring them to be alien spaceships). He consumed a vast quantity of both popular and more technical literature on the subject, travelling the country in search of sightings or to discuss matters with fellow enthusiasts.

In many ways, of course, such speculation was an instinctive reaction to the turmoil of the nuclear threat, as well as a natural extension of other scientific advances of the age: After all, if humanity could put objects in space, could not other civilizations? For Mishima, it was also a furtherance, even a putting into practice, of his long-cherished love of science fiction stories; he recognized that UFOs were largely an artistic conception rather than an authentic phenomenon (however much their existence could not be ruled out). Since childhood he had enjoyed the style, inventiveness, and excitement of SF, appreciating its ability to not only maintain but advance our innate curiosity and wonder, so often mislaid in our maturity, while relishing, too, its ability to overcome many of the problems of modern humanism/ atheism and the godless cosmos. Arthur C. Clarke was a great contemporary favourite, especially his novel *Childhood's End* (1953), which Mishima considered 'the greatest masterpiece' and a wonderful example of the compassion and humanity at the heart of the best science fiction.

It was this potent mixture of the current political climate and his interest in an often denigrated literary genre which fuelled Mishima's aim to combine them in a new novel. This book would be a semi–science fiction as well as an innovative kind of political novel, exposing the follies and foibles of governments around the world as they tried to exploit or contain the nuclear threat they themselves had created.

On its release, the novel was a little forgotten in the book charts as changing literary tastes in Japan pursued Mishima's great contemporaries Kenzaburō Ōe and Kōbō Abe, and it was not published in English until 2022. But Mishima had great fun writing *Beautiful Star*, taking pleasure in the oddity and conceit, and believed it to be one of his best works. He knew it to be a strange book, somewhat different to everything he had written before, taking him and his readers to some peculiar places. For all that, it still touched on and deepened many of the themes of his earlier work, while also anticipating both the shadows and principles of his later novels, especially those in *The Sea of Fertility*.

A family of four – mum, dad, son, daughter – live comfortably with inherited wealth in a small provincial Japanese city, Hannō, some fifty kilometres northwest of Tokyo. The kids are university students living at home, while the mother cooks and generally looks after the household. Father is a casual intellectual, unemployed and with too much time on his hands, spending his days in idle dreaming. They go on family walks, eat meals together, shop, quarrel, sleep. So far, so normal. Except that each of them thinks they're from a different planet: Mercury (son), Venus (daughter), Mars (dad), and Jupiter (mum).[99] They are all extraterrestrials (or, more precisely, humans whose minds and bodies are controlled by extraterrestrials).

They have, variously, seen unidentified flying objects from space, interplanetary vehicles from their home worlds. The father (a slightly odd, subdued version of one of Mishima's active heroes) becomes convinced that it is his mission to save humanity from the impending threat caused by nuclear weapons, so he establishes a society lecturing on UFOs and atomic annihilation, becoming something of a conspicuous celebrity in the process. This draws the attention of a curious troika of malevolent misanthropes – an assistant legal professor, a barber, and a bank clerk – who believe themselves to be from a planet orbiting the binary star system 61 Cygni and destined to save humanity by doing the only decent thing: euthanizing it via nuclear destruction.[100]

Such is the essential plot of *Beautiful Star*, for little actually takes place in this moody, meditative, static novel, save some intriguing trips by various family members to explore their origins,

---

99   In Japanese, the classical planets are associated with the five elements: Mercury, 'Suisei' (水星), literally 'water star'; Venus, 'Kinsei' (金星), literally 'metal star'; Mars, 'Kasei' (火星), literally 'fire star'; Jupiter, 'Mokusei' (木星), literally 'wood star'; Saturn, 'Dosei' (土星), literally 'earth star'.

100   Observations in the 1950s caused speculation that the 61 Cygni star system had unseen low-mass companions – planets or a brown dwarf – which gave rise to several works of science fiction, including Hal Clement's *Mission of Gravity* (1953).

identities, and destinies. Nevertheless, some of the internal set pieces are enthralling to follow – not least the novel's wonderful opening chapter in which the family climb a local mountain at four o'clock in the morning to try to make contact with a flying saucer that is due to make an appearance. Mishima elegantly and unobtrusively introduces this strange tale to us with some exquisite writing describing their nocturnal perambulation under the stars, gradually revealing the peculiarity of his plot. By the end of the book, no lavish laser-and-explosions finale has occurred between Papa Mars and the 61 Cygni trio: instead, a grand (and grandiose) 'discussion' takes place – a vast fifty-page cynical scream of pessimistic despair – before a muted, very human, conclusion that raises many more questions than it answers.

Mishima seemed clear that the father – and by extension everyone else in his family – was suffering from a delusion. He was someone given to much work-shy time, making him suited to fantasizing, hallucinating, fabricating. But he contaminates and consumes his family with this belief too. And evidently he is not an isolated case, since the three evil men in their own personal misery and loneliness (which are carefully delineated for us) have concocted their own cosmic backstory in order to give some meaning, and perhaps a little hope, to their particular brand of anguish. After all, one way to relieve yourself of the itch of being, the ache of existence – or the dread of not fitting in – is to convince yourself you're not a human being at all.

For Mishima, *Beautiful Star* was not strictly science fiction, since part of the appeal of the novel lies in the subtle tension the reader feels between believing, for the sake of the story, that the protagonists (and their antagonists) *are* humans governed by alien souls and knowing their belief to be an aberration. And, more than this, an aberration derived from the plausible, highly intelligible fear of nuclear apocalypse: how comforting it would be to have a spaceship to whisk one to the stars, away from the hubris and madness of mankind! In this sense, *Beautiful Star* is not merely a fable, a warning about the danger of unchecked destructive devices. It is a psychological novel about the devastating mental and emotional impact of disastrous political decision-making – not least as felt in Japan, the only country to suffer the consequences of an atomic attack.

Seeking to protect his family from thermonuclear catastrophe, the father appears to have devised an elaborate myth of his family's origins, lending little details (like their each coming from separate planets) to give credence to his story and to perhaps explain their usual human differences. Although clearly well-intended, it has had the effect of forcing his family to encounter their own individual isolation, to discover the overwhelming desolation and blankness within, where only deceits and illusions live: their hitherto happy-go-lucky, privileged lives have not taught them introspection like this. The Venusian daughter, haughty and gorgeous, seeks comfort in a lover claiming to be from her home planet, only to discover he has exploited her own delusions.

The father's affliction in the final chapter – he receives a stomach cancer diagnosis – deepens the pathos of the situation, as does the family's absconding from the hospital, where the species-wide fear of universal annihilation is attached to their own personal sense of suffering and loss. They take him from his sickbed to a nearby hill where, as the novel ends, a 'silver-grey flying saucer' appears to arrive. It is a terribly sad image of false hope – but one tinged by genuine optimism because of the intricate tensions between reality and unreality, truth and fiction, that Mishima has given his story. Unable to save humanity, are the family escaping our globe to return home, or are these cognitive illusions, imprisoning them in their hoodwinked minds as well as on Earth?

Mishima develops the psychological aspects of *Beautiful Star* alongside the political by ingeniously including a perversely equal and opposite 'family' in the three evil men bent on global destruction. Again we experience a delicate discord between the fictive reality of their stellar origins and their delusional states, the multifaceted schizophrenic disorders resulting from their miserable and disillusioned lives that have led them to create complex intellectual constructions (and to try to convince similarly afflicted people). None of the three evil men nor the family is blatantly insane, disenfranchised, stricken by substance abuse or destitution. They have money, jobs, needs, desires – and no supernatural powers. They are disconcertingly *normal*, an ordinariness which gives the novel so much of its anger and sadness as well as its transcendent beauty.

The climax of *Beautiful Star* (the long debate about saving or annihilating humanity, which occurs between the father and the principal member of the wicked trio) has often been criticized – not least by Mishima himself. It takes up a fifth of the book, and its author appreciated it was awkward, overlong, unmanageable, knew it would leave quite a few readers speechless. This is unsurprising given the pages' gigantic ejaculation of egotism, despondency, and pessimistic disgust, which seem to come straight from the author's own cynical soul. But Mishima also wanted the section to carry a teasing tragic-comic flavour – something hinted at when a playwright named 'Yukio Mishima' turned up a little earlier in the text – with a sense of the tensions between fiction, falsehood, and reality. What is more, the sheer anger of the prose forces the reader into confronting some uncomfortable home truths while at the same time it urges them to defend humanity against the volley of assaults ranged against it.

From God to love, shopping to sex, everything and anything comes under sustained verbal attack, as the foolishness and hypocrisies of the species are exposed. Although the arguments are not entirely extraneous to the mouths of the speakers in context, it is clear that they are actually laying forth much of Mishima's own condemnation of modern people and modern life, as well as the idiocies of the human race throughout its glorious problematic history, and along with the writer's own private inner war between Eros and Thanatos.[101] For all the debate's unwieldiness – and in truth it is probably too long, undermining its own power and purpose in the novel, though many of us wouldn't be without a line of it, such is its delectable virulence – there is a sense of Mishima broadening the horizons of his fiction here, while also preparing for the troubled texts of his later years. And the fundamental question of the debate – Is humanity worthy of redemption? – is surely worth asking, and repeatedly.

The piercing prose and eye-catching individual arguments of the discussion are fertile, pertinent, and prescient, firing from the page like dynamite, their invectives striking blow after blow as the diatribe hits home. At times it carries all the conviction and substance of Dostoyevsky, Nietzsche, Sartre, or Thomas Mann, taking in many of their explorations of the troubled human

---

101 That is, the life drive and the death drive, which, according to Freudian theory, guide and direct human behaviour.

condition as well as their disquieting challenges to long-held social, cultural, and political assumptions. It is astonishing to read, and given the reflection of anxiety over the extinction of humanity which it was designed to reproduce, on this level it does work. No frivolous entertainment or 'mere' science fiction (though Mishima would be the first to point out the gravity of much of the genre), *Beautiful Star* was a serious philosophical novel, and this justified the protracted interstellar argument at its culmination.

For its author, *Beautiful Star*'s humour, jokes, and sometimes otherworldly qualities were designed to work in tandem with its deeper, more plainly serious and nihilistic passages, the combination alerting the reader to the importance of the questions riding on it. Much of the reading was painful – agonizingly honest – which is perhaps why so many readers have instinctively reacted against it. But it was necessary. As the father puts it in another context early on in the book: 'Someone must suffer. Someone must walk barefoot, bleeding on the shards of glass of this broken world.'

Beautiful Star broke many of the rules of Japanese fiction, juxtaposing elements of depth, irony, and play in ways which confused a number of readers and critics alike. If it wasn't perfect, the novel intriguingly suggested Mishima might develop his literary skills either as a comic writer or one dedicated to science fiction (though, of course, neither route ultimately appealed to him). The inclusion, or semi-inclusion, of planets and worlds beyond Earth seemed to reflect Mishima's wish to emblematically incorporate in the heavens those fundamental elements of humanity – (Venusian) love; (Martian) ire – which all his fiction tended to explore. If there was an ironical element to these otherworldly presences, a wry shrug at astrological gullibility or the limitations of pseudoscience, as well as an acknowledgement of the falsity of this symbolism, this was only part of the complex texture of his novel, which played several games with genre, form, tone, and expectation.

At its core, *Beautiful Star* rehabilitated or reinvented myths which humanity seemed to sorely need, which they had ignored in their pursuit of power, dominance – or a new electric kettle. These were huge, elemental questions of species survival, destruction, and destiny, and people needed lore and legend to comprehend the magnitude of what was occurring. This was a new kind of political novel for a new kind of political age. It fugally depicted the intricate psychological, constitutional, diplomatic, and administrative realities of new ideologies and tersely disparaged the blind spots too many post-war novelists and politicians had succumbed to, attitudes which had ignored the murky and decisive issues at stake.

The shimmering hope on the final page of *Beautiful Star* is, at best, ambiguous, the provocations of this blend of social satire and science fiction enduring to the end. Intermingling gloomy nihilism with a childlike optimism was a masterstroke of deception and persuasion: deflecting attention while tightening the noose. Through an unlikely instrument, further groundwork for Mishima's ultimate amalgamation of darkness and idealism, *The Sea of Fertility*, was being carefully laid down.

Chapter Nine

The Sailor Who Fell
from Grace with the Sea
BLOOD, WATER, GLORY

In the 1950s, Mishima's books sold in the hundreds of thousands; by the end of the decade and the early 1960s, novels like *Kyoko's House* (1959) and *Beautiful Star* (1962) were managing barely 10 percent of those figures. Younger readers, in particular university students and recent graduates, were hunting for something new – which they found in the brilliantly distorted caprice of Kenzaburō Ōe's *Nip the Buds, Shoot the Kids* (1958) and Kōbō Abe's weird hypnotic masterpiece *The Woman in the Dunes* (1962). Perhaps with a view to reversing this trend, for his next book Mishima turned to something thoroughly familiar yet universally strange: that archetypal romantic icon, the sea.

As a setting and a symbol, the sea is both a dream and a nightmare, a fantasy and a reality, a beginning and an ending. It has inspired countless composers, artists, and writers down the centuries, stimulated and seduced by its beauty and immensity: Britten's *Billy Budd* and *Peter Grimes*, Sibelius's *Oceanides* and Debussy's *La Mer*; Turner's *Temeraire*, Hokusai's *Great Wave*, and Aivazovsky's *Ninth Wave*; Homer's *Odyssey* and Shakespeare's *Tempest*. Then the great novels by Melville, Murdoch, Stevenson, Defoe, Conrad, Verne, Hemingway. A liminal but limitless realm, the sea encompasses all, signifying fluidity, variation, and the unfathomable as well as stability and eternity, its essentially unchanging nature a constant presence (not least for an island nation like Japan).

The original Japanese title of Mishima's own key contribution to this body of aquatic art, 'Gogo no eikō' (午後の曳航, 1963), hinges on an untranslatable homonym, eikō, the word for both 'glory' and 'tow/drag', so that it could mean either *Afternoon Drag* or *Glory in the Afternoon* (a typically Mishimian irony, given the book's exploration of pubescent ennui, and its gory climax). When discussing possible English titles with his translator, John Nathan, Mishima commented that it would be interesting to have a long title akin to that of Proust's magnum opus, *À la recherche du temps perdu*. The author suggested a dozen or so and, hearing them read back to him, chose *The Sailor Who Fell from Grace with the Sea*.

It was a slightly awkward but intriguing and achingly romantic title: appropriate given that, in many ways, *Sailor* is the quintessential Mishima novel, a tense, intense, and timeless tour de force. It stands at the near-literal and certainly symbolic centre of his work, looking both forward and back, radiating its romance in all directions. The book both returned to some of the themes of his earlier writing – dreams of glory, adolescent tribulation, idealized beauty – and prepared further ground for the metaphysics and aesthetics of his final work, *The Sea of*

Fertility: the obsession with opposites, borders, transitions, and repetitions; the complex, shifting positions of heroes.

In *Sailor*, as in *The Temple of the Golden Pavilion*, *After the Banquet*, *The Frolic of the Beasts*, and *Beautiful Star*, Mishima focused on an identifiable historical reality through a more romantic lens, exploring through extraordinary narrative configurations and poetic imagery the empty, narcissistic materialism which he felt was controlling the new Japan. And in *Sailor*'s pair of protagonists, the eponymous mariner and his teenage stepson, Mishima found two of his most representative masculine heroes. In the novel, they would switch roles, one voyaging from active hero to passive coward, the other from docile voyeur to dynamic villain – something underpinning both the design and motifs of the book, a text dominated by both doubles and curiously asymmetrical triangles.

The two egotistical heroes of *The Sailor Who Fell from Grace with the Sea* share interwoven frustrations and desires, antagonisms and ideologies, travelling in different directions but carrying disconcertingly similar goals. They seek to reorganize the unsatisfactory and unfair world which surrounds them. They are quasi-artists obsessed with creating their own violent visions of a replacement reality. They are damaged, dangerous – and irresistible.

The Sailor Who Fell from Grace with the Sea is a relatively short novel, and most of its story is easy to relate. A sailor is admired by a teenage boy as a nautical hero, a great figure of the sea, a true man of adventure, romantic exploits, and escapades, a mariner motivated by his own elusive desire for glory and fixation on ideal beauty. Later, that hero marries the boy's widowed mother and tries to make a new life for himself on land, dressing himself in foreign clothes and learning English conversation skills. Disappointed, disgusted, and dismayed by this betrayal, the boy and his gang of precocious friends plan to horrifically murder the sailor as punishment.

Beyond this essential plot, Mishima's book has a basic division into two halves, marked 'Summer' and 'Winter', the first and most obvious of its complex engagement with mirrors and opposites, binary pairs from both within and without the text. At a glance, they might seem obvious, innocuous, banal – but many of these couples attach, disconnect, or recombine in surprising and often uncomfortable ways. They include, but are certainly not limited to:

male/female
mother/father
light/dark
day/night
land/sea
life/death
inside/outside
emotion/intellect
fertility/sterility
Apollo/Dionysus
civilization/nature
modernity/tradition
East/West

Amid these sets, *Sailor* also offered a contemporary update to one of Mishima's long-held preoccupations: the sadomasochistic martyrdom of Saint Sebastian. We revisit the enigmatic hero's ritual sacrifice in a shower of arrows, but his tale is now given a sombre Oedipal perspective, as both the author and his characters confront the shifting realities of fatherhood (not unrelatedly, Mishima's only son was born in 1962).

The self-generating, self-referential texts Mishima pens are complex systems. They were stimulated by and, in turn, stimulated his own biography, insinuating back on themselves, removing convenient borders between life and art like a Möbius strip – entrance and exit, beginning and ending, intimately, infinitely, allied. It is an incestuous web, an intertextual dialogue not only among individual works but between creator and creation. Accordingly, a consideration of *Sailor*, with its meticulous examinations of childhood, parenthood, and nascent maturity, necessitates a brief revisit to some areas of Mishima's upbringing and family history to enrich our understanding of his novel.

Mishima came from a long line of relatively distinguished and imposing male ancestors. Many of them had been samurai, governors, administrators, lawyers, and legal representatives. From his mother and grandmother, Mishima was exposed to the art and literature of both his native Japan and Western traditions. Thus a clear, if crude, male/female division was made in Mishima's life which strongly linked the rational or Apollonian with the masculine, and the emotional or Dionysian with the feminine. Mishima's work would not cling to these partitions, and indeed would often thwart, confuse, or conflate them, but these early attachments nonetheless inform many of his most recognizable literary networks.

Dominating this feminine side was Mishima's grandmother, Natsuko, who took her grandson to his first kabuki play while also effectively confining him to her domestic sanatorium for most of his childhood, sanctioning only girls as playmates and sometimes even dressing him in clothes more usually worn by young women. Rather than experiencing the rough and tumble of outdoor reality, Mishima catered to his grandmother's whims, while also exploring the inner world of literary fairy tales and discovering the dark imagination he himself possessed.

Whatever the obvious rightness and wrongness of this cosseted, restricted, and often spiteful 'nurturing', it birthed a number of fixations and contradictions within Mishima's life and art. Perhaps chief among them was the difficult relationship between inside and outside – be it rooms, buildings, or bodies – so that the interior represents both safety and threat, the exterior both danger and illicit excitement, peril and temptation. By extension this compulsive uncertainty broadens to borders and transitions more generally, to the vast number of mirrors/opposites/dualities recorded above and to which *Sailor*, and Mishima's other work, so obsessively returns. Thus the boundaries between, say, male and female, homo- and heterosexual, day and night, civilization and nature, become increasingly eroded, their transitions gradually windswept and worn to create not only alarming ambiguity but a troubling complexity, some of which could be manifest as misogyny or idolization, homophobia or homoeroticism.

Such an unusual childhood – even by the standards of the day – was bound to engender some of the more worrisome but enduring aspects of Mishima's personality that were also manifest in his work: the heightened self-consciousness and its related self-absorption and egotism; the piercing sense of estrangement and disaffection; his fascination with sexuality and violence, especially of a sadomasochistic kind; the intense gulf, even contradiction, he felt between mind and body (all of which, of course, would conclude with his suicide).

This inside/outside ambivalence has a special relevance for *The Sailor Who Fell from Grace with the Sea* since so much of the novel takes place not only indoors but in bedrooms and, even more tightly, within a drawer (the inside of an inside of an inside) and yet with the constantly looming, infinite presence of the ultimate outdoor space: the sea. Images of, and settings in, nature recur throughout Mishima's work, but *Sailor* turns the marine environment into a vast and seductive force linking the outside world with illusion and emotion in often destructive ways, culminating in a gruesome homicide by children.

Noboru, the thirteen-year-old protagonist, is locked in his bedroom each night by his thirty-three-year-old mother, Fusako, ostensibly as a reprimand for his once sneaking out with his mates. Exploring both his criminal tendencies and his bourgeoning sexuality, Noboru has discovered a peephole in a chest drawer in his bedroom, through which he can spy on his mother undressing or making love to her handsome sailor during the warm summer night. Later, in winter, after the sailor has returned from another long sea voyage, he marries Fusako, giving Noboru more opportunities for voyeurism.

One night, inevitably, he is caught in the act. His mother drags the now sleeping child out of his hiding place and expects his new father to punish him, to perform the masculine, patriarchal role of disciplining wayward behaviour. But the sailor is embarrassed and unable to, offering only banal clichés – which has the effect of furthering Noboru's disrespect for him. Noboru's opinion is already low after what he sees as the man's craven renunciation of the outside world, of the majestic ocean and the (as the child imagines it) exhilarating life of a mariner. Noboru's habit of voyeurism stems from both desire and fear, a yearning for the freedom and thrill of sexuality (and by association the outside world), yet a fear of its power (not least within the semi-incestuous context of spying on his own mother in her bedroom).

Through his peephole, Noboru looks both forward and backward in time, as well as inward and outward in space. Gazing upon his mother's nakedness and erotic activities is an anticipation of Noboru's own sexual life and a glance back to his conception and birth, as well as a journey to the terrifying unguarded outside world and a glimpse into his own corrupt soul. Everything – emotion, sexuality, location, relationship – is dangerously heightened and inverted, twisted into a ghoulish series of alarming distortions. Yet these deformations and disfigurements are not limited to Noboru himself. They seem to infect the sailor, Ryuji, as well, confusing his sense of his own being, his purpose in life, his somewhat ambiguous and naive pursuit of 'glory'. Each becomes confused by Ryuji's complex interrelationship with Noboru, the boy's mother, and his, as it turns out, fatal decision to leave the sea behind for the land (the latter a static realm which, we know early on in the novel, he despises for its immobility, 'the eternally unchanging surfaces').

So, too, become contaminated the novel's wider arrangements of time and space, darkness and light, summer and winter, inside and outside. At the end of the first chapter, with his first nocturnal tryst with Fusako, Ryuji's glittering body matches the shimmering midnight moonlight. Yet each is altered by small but suggestive elements of darkness – just as at the opening of the book, Noboru's drawer is a semiprivate abode of illumination and shadow. Indeed, the whole of part one is a journey of light's transition, from the abundance of brightness in early summer to the increasing darkness of the season's end, which also closes at sunset with Ryuji's departure for his final sea voyage.[102]

If, in the summer section of the novel, light is dominant over darkness, darkness is still granted a powerful role, not least in bestowing Fusako and Ryuji the night-time with which to make love. The opposite is also true in part two: winter, the season of darkness, nonetheless confers light a formidable function – seen first when, two days after his arrival back in a typically damp and drizzly Yokohama, Ryuji celebrates the first sunrise of the New Year with Fusako. The intimacy, and tragedy, of their love is watched over not just by an adolescent peeping Tom but by the universal cycles of the heavenly bodies, as days and years begin and end.

The ambivalent role of space is also a crucial structuring and thematic principle of the novel. Part one begins within the claustrophobic, and alluring, closed spaces of Fusako's house, its bedrooms, and Noboru's drawer, each providing an intricate combination of safety, danger, and excitement. By the end of part one and the farewell to Ryuji, Yokohama harbour offers a further, larger, temporary haven before the sailor is cast, one final time, into the complex sanctuary of the sea, a realm with its own mixture of security and suffocation. Sailing is a steady and reliable life, though one that is also, on ship, an asphyxiating prison. By

---

102 The name of Ryuji's boat, the *Rakuyo*, is a homophone in Japanese for 'setting sun'.

the end of part two, and Ryuji's murder, the location is shifted far from Yokohama, to a distant cave, a space of elemental protection and terror, one which liberates the scene, and the novel, onto a cosmic scale, travelling beyond our restricted spatio-temporal sphere and into something more infinite.

Whatever pleasing patterns and attractive echoes Mishima offers throughout *The Sailor Who Fell from Grace with the Sea*, it should be clear that they are not fundamentally congruous or even constant. Rather, they are intentionally spoiled or unsettled, as a series of poignant and peculiar kinks are advanced into the design of the narrative: Dionysus re-exerting his influence over Apollo. For Nietzsche, a writer Mishima consumed in enormous quantities when he was young, the conflict between the Apollonian and the Dionysian, between order/rationality/discipline/spirit and chaos/emotion/spontaneity/flesh, was the mainspring and animator of Greek tragedy. For Mishima, such an engagement also extended to the encounters between masculine and feminine, as well as to broader geo-cultural divisions.

In this world view, the West stood for a patriarchal, controlling order, one attempting to dominate and subjugate the – as Mishima saw it – passive, effeminate, and all too often weak contemporary Japan. It is clear that the psychosexual conflicts within the author that drove his own texts were also driven by his complex engagement with the non-Japanese world, something discernible in the way his narratives embrace Western literary styles and techniques, and for his treacherous, often highly romanticized vision of a traditional Japan. The result is a complex series of ironical, equivocal, and often paradoxical relationships between different sensibilities and principles – be they Apollo/Dionysus, East/West, masculine/feminine. Yet it is these kinks, these ironic twists, which drive the narratives, not least *Sailor*'s, where, as we have said, order is continually disturbed by chaos.

Parts one and two of *Sailor* each occupy roughly half the novel but have eight and seven chapters respectively, a minor disparity which slightly disturbs the balance of halves and thus hints at the book's tragic climax, in which stability is upset by disorder. Further examples of this destabilization abound: When, in part one, Noboru and his gang infamously kill and dissect a kitten, something which horrifically anticipates Ryuji's murder, it occurs on a warm August day but inside a murky shed operating as a torture chamber. Ryuji's departure on his final sea voyage is, as we have said, not only at sunset but at the end of summer – and, prior to disembarkation, his ship discharges ominous black smoke. The light and life of the summer section of the novel are disrupted and disturbed by the invasion of death and darkness. So, too, the whole narrative, and Ryuji's pursuit of glory, are disrupted by the ultimate ironic twist as that exaltation is achieved only in violent death.

Sailor also features a troubling thematic relationship with the (odd) number three, which lends curious twists and ironic crinkles to various aspects of the text. The novel is a semi-incestuous love story, among not two people but three – an Oedipal triangle between the mother, her son, and the sailor. Noboru's age is unlucky thirteen, Fusako's thirty-three. The mother's bedroom mirror has three sides; the horn on Ryuji's departing ship blasts three times. Although these are often coincidence, or mischievous Mishimian play, they also lend a sinister edge to the story, an asymmetry and misalignment which constantly fights against its neat configurations of doubles and opposites.

Both Ryuji and Noboru dream of, and indeed are obsessed by, an unattainable, indefinable 'glory' – something beyond the mundane world, something composed of sun, sea, sex, and violence. Ryuji is a prototypical young romantic who fantasizes of obtaining glory on the sea. Unlike his (step-)son and twin, the precocious Noboru, Ryuji is entirely unintellectual, his attractive looks and exciting life initially sufficient for happiness. These encourage him in sentimental romanticization, his only real form of mental articulation. But, over time, the sailor begins to resent the confinement of the ship, yearning for an unattainable, and ill-defined, romantic dream of glory, one closely connected with apocalyptic notions of destiny combining the sea, sex, and death.

When he submits himself to the land, and to love, his chance for glory is thwarted – or, rather, postponed. And when he achieves it, it is hardly the glory he had been searching for, but that in itself was a nebulous, even naive ambition, vague and immature. Whether his death can be a satisfactory glory is a question the novel, and Mishima in general, poses (as is the related interrogation into the disposition of romanticism itself). Nevertheless, before the hero can be martyred, not only must he and his dreams be pacified, but his twin, the novel's other romantic protagonist, must undergo his own transformation. Their destinies are linked.

In the process, Ryuji becomes not only land-based, terraformed, but domesticated, almost turned into his wife's pet, compelled to dress differently, act and speak in a new way, repressing his cruder, more romantic self – which, ironically, was what initially attracted Fusako in the first place.[103] To begin with,

---

103 He also becomes involved in his wife's business, a high-end foreign clothes store – the epitome of banal materialism and the opposite of rugged romanticism.

Ryuji is described to us in terms of religious architecture, with obvious links to the not dissimilar narrative of *The Temple of the Golden Pavilion*, where Mizoguchi dreams of an apocalyptic glory. Before the sailor is flattened through the comforts and conventions of married life, the peeping Noboru observes that Ryuji, about to make love to his mother, has shoulders as 'square as the beams in a temple roof', 'a thick mat of hair', flesh that is not only 'golden' but 'like a suit of armour', and – of course – a membrum virile which soars 'triumphantly erect' like a 'lustrous temple tower'.

That Noboru witnesses this scene is crucial, for we observe Ryuji through the boy's romantic eyes, linking forever the two heroes in their respective journeys and destinies. Like Ryuji, Noboru dreams of something 'terrific' – which he finds when he spies on his mother and her lover. For the boy it is like being part of a miracle, an ecstatic and extraordinary experience of sprouting juvenile sexuality. It is a dangerous, magical world lying, literally and metaphorically, just beyond his reach. Denied access (through both his age and intellect), as an alternative Noboru attempts to manipulate and command the enchantment, becoming a precarious adolescent sorcerer.

Noboru, the passive spectator, in due course proceeds to creative decision and action, perversely assisting the sailor in his attainment of glory. It is a resplendently Mishimian paradox, the passivity and voyeuristic nature of Noboru's engagement with Ryuji compelling the adolescent observer into an active role against the man genuinely built for the ultimate action, procreation. In this sense, both protagonists are quasi-artists: one a stage actor, performing the act of love, before performing his role as dutiful husband and stepfather; Noboru, a pubescent Prospero as he perceives himself, the talismanic author of events, creating and controlling the magic around him, though with catastrophic consequences.

Like most artists, Noboru is a magnificent egomaniac, his self-aggrandizement a decisive aspect of his creativity. But although the ur-encounter in the drawer, witnessing the sailor and his mother make love, transpires in the novel's first chapter, action, control, and manipulation do not come naturally to him. Instead they must be occasioned, then hastened by an elaborate sequence of occurrences – the tense narrative of the novel – along with the peer pressure of his equally precocious and disillusioned friends.

Noboru and his gang, led by the arrogant boy they call 'Chief', are – even by Mishimian standards – tremendously aware of the boundaries of the world around them, cynically dismissing what it and its inhabitants have to offer. They expand grandiloquently, and occasionally eloquently, on the mass failings of society, the shortcomings of fathers in particular – a critique that will have consequences for the novel's false father, the sailor. In this bleak view, fathers are failures with inferiority complexes, consumed by their unrealized aspirations, resentments, ideals, and weaknesses. When they're not absent, as Noboru's is through death,[104] fathers are inadequate – as Ryuji will prove to be, when he is tasked with penalizing his stepson's transgressions.

Wardens of the wilderness that was, for the author, contemporary Japan, fathers stand in Mishima's fiction for much

---

104 Though he lives on through the ghoulish, ironic name of his luxury clothing business, which his widow now manages: Rex – the Latin for king.

of what he despised. They are not evil as such; they are passive, insufficient, smothering dreams through their own incompetence and hopelessness. Their wickedness takes the inert form of their sterility, their compliance and conventionality, their lack of passion and action. They create and maintain a dull, monotonous bourgeois existence. This (perhaps rather unfair) figure of the drab, colourless father, doubtless trapped in a dreary company department, stands in opposition to Ryuji as we first find him – the man of an unhindered, apparently unimpeded existence, full of vibrant exotic ports and even more vibrant women (much of which, of course, is a false romanticizing, not least because the ship, as Ryuji knows, is as much a prison as an office is). In part, the sailor's tragedy is that he becomes a father, literally so as a stepfather to Noboru, but also in the poleaxing of his dreams, and in the conformist, henpecked nature of his marriage.

Ironically, the catalyst for his reclaimed glory is the moment of his submissive nadir: when he cannot punish Noboru for his voyeurism but only offer weak, cosy platitudes, making his stepson revile him further. It is this feebleness, this deterioration from his status as a great romantic hero in Noboru's eyes, that, in a delicious twist, leads to his tragic, violent death but also the attainment of his long-desired glory. Noboru and his friends pity the sailor for having become the very incarnation of the humdrum, tedious world, for having turned his back on the romantic realm; it is from this destiny that they must save him, sacrificing him on the altar of their own disillusionment.

Noboru's mother, like many mothers in Mishima and elsewhere, stands in opposition to this romantic destiny, a maternal, spousal shackle on the dreams of both her son and her new husband. Ironically, given her twin role in the novel as both life-giver and erotic emblem, she represents a controlling lifeless reality, far removed from the imagination and the fantastical worlds the mind can conjure. Fusako is the crucial second side of the glorified triangle – sea, sex, death – that the sailor yearns for, and she is presented to us as a formidably desirable woman. But she is also the proprietor of an upmarket clothes shop, its luxury and extravagance the ultimate representation of hollow materialism.

Moreover, it is due to her restrictive role – understandably concerned about family well-being and a happy domestic life – that she will unwittingly compel her son to enact his murderous plot against the sailor. Once an icon for Noboru, Ryuji is now merely a fraud, an obsequious land crab oscillating between specious sycophancy and vociferous oppression. The sailor is revealed to be a human being, not a nautical deity.

※

A devastating revelation requires a devastating resolution, a chance for the hero to be reborn in the image which Noboru, and perhaps the sailor himself, projected. Yet the manner of this rebirth – a violent death – is more than simply ironic: it is deceptive, even maliciously misleading. For although the complicities of the plot mean that, in some way, Ryuji does meet his end amid a mixture of sex and the sea, in truth his 'liberation' is a rather muted and tawdry affair, the antithesis of romance and the epitome of drabness.

There is no magnificent summer's morning, Apollo's sun shining in glory (Ryuji, with his golden tanned skin is an inveterate sun worshipper). Instead, the end comes amid a gloomy winter's afternoon. Neither is the climax at sea, in the realm of romance and exhilaration. It occurs just beyond an industrial landscape of bulldozers and dump trucks, in a cave in the hills, what the boys call their 'dry dock'; the sea is only a dull and distant sparkle on the horizon. The manner of his murder, too, is morbidly plain: a poisoned teacup, prior to his horrific dissection (which may or may not take place, outside the confines of the text).

For all this, Ryuji's death comes to pass because of both his love of the sea and a beautiful woman, since it is his relinquishing one for the other that directly leads to his demise. The glory he had sought has been found, though not in quite the way he, or we, might have expected. This is the delicious marriage of anticlimax and fulfilment, of anticipation and disappointment, that lends the ending of *Sailor* much of its disturbing, malevolent power. He is dragged, or towed, one afternoon to his death, which is also his glory, and the play on words that the Japanese title conveys is revealed to be the bottled essence of the novel.

Like so much of Mishima's work, both fiction and non-fiction, in *The Sailor Who Fell from Grace with the Sea* romance and realism are woven together into a cunning, subtle tapestry. From many standpoints, the sailor's dreams of glory are hopelessly unrealistic. They are a folly which, perhaps appropriately, ends in his semi-farcical demise, his delusions warped into horror by hard-hearted, over-intellectual juvenile agencies, fateful furies of vengeance.

Yet the romantic perspective of *Sailor* is never entirely degraded or destroyed. The romantic iconography and paraphernalia which surround Ryuji – his handsome looks and awesome body; his sentimentalizing of the sea; the glamorous harbours and adventures; his murder; even the structure of the novel into 'Summer' and 'Winter' – are continually subjected to the harsh, unforgiving glare of modernity. And yet they endure. The boys and the sailor, between them, have diminished the romance of the seafaring life to an unstable assortment of clichés, but these never quite lose their magic: for Noboru, for Ryuji, for us. They are stereotypes, romanticized formulas lifted from any infantile adventure story, and we know them to be untrue. Yet we cling to them, these dreamy and tender ideals, allowing them to assume a magnificent sway over us. Because it is not the clichés that we yearn for but our own state of fascination, our insistent attraction to the notion of glory and the romantic quest.

Desire is all. It is a concentrated and forceful longing which fuels Ryuji, just as it stimulates Noboru and his revolting band of brothers. As such, *Sailor* is no mere pessimistic exposition of the dangers of romanticism. It is an exploration of intense desire. The obscure, sentimental objects of yearning, the romantic accoutrements of the quest – glory, heroism, sex, death – are incidental, even disingenuous. It is the longing for them which persists in our memory.

Accordingly, the complex elicitation of a yearning restored in the book's final scene carries an immense pathos and poignancy. As the last chapter gets under way, we are assaulted with downbeat, pessimistic imagery – the dying, extinct, inconsiderate cosmos falling to earth. There is the dreary winter afternoon (the sun setting; the day ending); wood is rotting everywhere; uncultivated fields and mechanical excavators attack the soft tissue of the land; a rusty water tank is barren and dry; the English sign warning trespassers to keep out is lopsided and half submerged in the soil. The whole vista is one of death and decay, drabness and sadness, fertility turned to futility (a constant of Mishima's art).

The sailor, shorn of his flashy foreign attire and back in his grimy old clothes, is lured by the boys to their grisly hideaway, this site of melancholy sterility and degeneration. Oblivious to his impending death, he opens his heart and mouth with stories of his adventures, his desire reprised one final time. The tales captivate the boys, who are delighted to see their romantic hero reborn. He seduces them, but he seduces us, too, the romance doubly magnified through the twin lens of the sailor's and the boys' excitement. Suddenly we feel the prickle of desire and longing again, despite (and because of) the lacklustre landscape in which the stories are relayed.

As the 'Chief' hands Ryuji the tainted tea, do we not feel glad that the sailor has become, through the art of narrating stories, an adventurer again, saved from the doom of monotony and normality and granted glory at the moment of his death? But, as the novel's final lines attest, glory in the real world is bitter stuff, unsentimental, brutal, and attainable only through the allure of the imagination, through the romance of language, literature, and storytelling – through the book we hold in our hands.

Chapter Ten

Life for Sale
PULP FRICTION

During the autumn of 1964, Mishima worked as a special correspondent for Japan's three main daily newspapers – the *Mainichi*, *Asahi*, and *Hōchi* – covering the Tokyo Olympics. He brought his usual brand of lyrical prose to boxing, weightlifting, swimming, gymnastics, athletics, and volleyball, as well as to pieces for the opening and closing ceremonies. An article on the American sprinter Bob Hayes's victory in the 100 metres captures Mishima's hypnotic, almost philosophical fascination with the events, his words wondering at the skill and technique on display, at the mesmerizing way in which complicated human forms could travel through space with such divine speed.[105]

---

105 Officially the Games of the XVIII Olympiad (第18回オリンピック競技大会, 'Dai Jūhachi-kai Orinpikku Kyōgi Taikai'), the Tokyo Olympics ran from 10 to 24 October 1964 (to avoid both the city's oppressive summer humidity and the September typhoon season). Most of the events were held in Tokyo proper, with some stylish purpose-built venues showcasing

The 1964 Olympics were a final part of Japan's rehabilitation, the country at last joining the ranks of advanced nations who could afford – morally and economically – to put on this festive display of indulgence, diversion, and dexterity. They were a further sign of Japan's cultural recovery and growing technological prowess: the Shinkansen – or bullet train – had opened ten days before the Games as a practical means of transportation for the visiting droves but also as a symbolic gesture of national rebirth.

When the sporting circus and its hordes had departed, however, Mishima was left feeling wistful, hollow, writing a piece called 'All the Pleasures Are Now Over' about the depressed post-Olympic mood which seemed to have descended on him and the country. All was disheartened, unhappy, and blue, the exiting euphoria leaving only an abyss of money and adverts. Much as he had enjoyed the Games (and they inspired him to pursue with even greater fervour his bodybuilding craze), for Mishima they were indicative of Japan's contemporary malaise, the vacuum which he saw at the heart of his country, a nation increasingly devoid of its traditions, its emperor, its past. The 'lantern marches' to celebrate military victories had been replaced by a 'safe war', clean and sterile. Luxury was now a friend, citizens learning the false pleasures of peace: consuming, guzzling, indulging themselves in the role of host.

All the time more disgusted by his own comfortable, material lifestyle – the gated home, the antique furniture, the statues

---

contemporary Japanese architecture and design, including Kenzō Tange's über-cool Yoyogi Gymnasium, with its synthesis of sinuous lines and total absence of ninety-degree angles. The equestrian events took place in the forest resort town of Karuizawa and the sailing in Sagami Bay, with Mount Fuji the impressive backdrop. Tokyo had originally been awarded the 1940 Games, but Japan's invasion of China in 1937 meant they were passed to Helsinki, then cancelled anyway due to the outbreak of World War II.

in the garden – now more than ever, Mishima sought in his life and art to ask, if not answer, the question of how one can live – and die – well in a world so bereft of true meaning and value. Accordingly, a sense of meaninglessness is the central theme of *Life for Sale* (**命売ります**, 'Inochi Urimasu', 1968), a mischievous, self-aware, and surreal mongrel of a novel which exhibited Mishima's fascination with less sophisticated forms of literature as well as his gloomy sense of humour. *Life for Sale* is indeed ominously humorous, a shadowy, surprising, tongue-in-cheek work which also reflects its author's anxious vision of an absurd society in overwhelming – but possibly not yet unstoppable – moral, cultural, and political deterioration.

Given that its satirical target was cultural decline, the novel's origins carry a perhaps deliberate ironic burden. Initially published in twenty-one instalments by *Weekly Playboy* magazine between 21 May and 8 October 1968 (that year of tumultuous social conflict involving left-wing student protests and other uprisings which had begun in America and Europe but had spread across to Japan and had alarmed Mishima especially), it came out complete in book form from Shūeisha on 25 December. The somewhat salacious reputation of *Weekly Playboy* – with its celebrity interviews, scantily clad models, and manga cartoons – taunted readers a little, teasing their expectations (though *Playboy* itself has a rich literary heritage, publishing pieces by Arthur C. Clarke, Jack Kerouac, Ian Fleming, Alice Denham, Gabriel García Márquez, Vladimir Nabokov, Saul Bellow, Ursula K. Le Guin, and Margaret Atwood).[106]

---

106 週刊プレイボーイ ('Shūkan Pureibōi'). Japan's *Weekly Playboy* (1966–) was inspired by, though not affiliated with, Hugh Hefner's American men's lifestyle magazine, *Playboy*. (A Japanese regional variation of the latter – *Monthly Playboy* – arrived in 1975 after protracted legal disputes and ran until 2009.)

To an extent, Mishima's audience were led to assume, and invited to concur, that this was a more pulpy, flippant, or run-of-the-mill work. And it was: up to a point. But if *Life for Sale* does contain the accoutrements of less serious forms of fiction – hard-boiled dialogue; a bizarre cast of both stock and more memorable characters; an elaborate, cunning action plot that any thriller writer would be proud of – Mishima's novel employs that paraphernalia in the service of its own deeper complexities and complicities, in particular impeaching contemporary consumerist Japan, as well as to reinforce its connections to a range of authors and literary traditions. There are significant allusions to G. K. Chesterton,[107] Edgar Allan Poe, Bram Stoker, Arthur Conan Doyle,[108] and Raymond Chandler, along with echoes of the surreal experiments of Kōbō Abe, Franz Kafka, Clarice Lispector, Jorge Luis Borges, and José Saramago, as well as nods to Mishima's beloved manga and graphic novels (even sly anticipations of Quentin Tarantino's playful, stylized violence and audacious forms of cinematic storytelling).

Yet all this referential sport was to heighten the more insightful refrains at work, namely the motif of the meaninglessness of modern life and how it might be surmounted. *Life for Sale* toys with the tropes of pulp fiction – creating delicious textual tension and stylistic antagonism – but it would be a mistake to think that this is a forgettable anomaly, a facetious backstreet off the grand avenue of Mishima's other writing. It is precisely the way in which this novel engages with those genres that elevates it

---

107 Not least Chesterton's metaphysical thriller *The Man Who Was Thursday* (1908), with its bungling, blundering crime syndicate.

108 Especially the Sherlock Holmes stories 'The Adventure of the Naval Treaty' (1893) and 'The Adventure of the Bruce-Partington Plans' (1908).

to something more interesting, more significant, developing its themes along with its links to the rest of Mishima's oeuvre.

❧

Before completing the cycle of four novels that was to become his magnum opus – *The Sea of Fertility* – Mishima would pen several other works exploring the emptiness, the meaninglessness he felt beating in the heart of fatherless modern Japan. Chief among them were *Life for Sale* (1968) itself, the novel *Music* (音楽, 'Ongaku', 1964), the short story collection *Acts of Worship* (1965), and a curious but engaging social novel, *Silk and Insight* (絹と明察, 'Kinu to Meisatsu', 1964), originally called *The Father of Japan*, and based on a real-life labour dispute in 1954 at Ōmi Kenshi, a garment manufacturer.[109] It scrutinizes the role of a vigilant, protective, if rather possessive and controlling, patriarch, and supposed Japanese traditions of collective harmony and paternal guidance are symbolically stationed against the iniquities of 'Western' individualism and the dangers of unchecked workers' rights.

The novel's protagonist, the idealistic but domineering factory owner Komazawa, is placed in opposition to a Heidegger-and-Hölderlin-reading intellectual Okano, who is planted among the workforce by Komazawa's business rivals in order to incite a strike. Although Mishima is careful not to show Komazawa as a saint (indeed, as a direct result of his restrictions on his employees' activities, many of them die in a dormitory fire), clearly

---

109 The novel has been translated into English, by Hiroaki Sato, though it is sadly out of print and is not easy to find.

he is a trade and industry emblem for the emperor himself: an absolutist monarch who stands for traditional values against a Western-besotted Japan, one polluted by foreign ideas. Given the way in which Mishima's own work was deeply, profoundly, influenced by the European writers he loved and admired – Wilde, Nietzsche, Mann – there is a certain Mishimian irony (read: hypocrisy) at work here, but the way he concludes the novel offers a compelling insight into the developing direction his art was travelling.

Komazawa, the mysterious and semi-divine figure lying at the heart of the novel's drama, is defeated, and the smart young leader of the strike, Ōtsuki, is victorious: a triumph for youth and progress.[110] But against expectation, Okano, the imported intellectual, succeeds Komazawa as head of the company. As he lies dying after a stroke, Komazawa muses on the 'counterfeit jewel' of happiness that the workers have won, one which will, he contends, eventually leave them feeling empty, alone, and distrustful, without meaning in their lives. It is an ominous and disconcerting insight, that of the novel's title, and one with ramifications for both *Life for Sale* and *The Sea of Fertility*.

Although many of us might instinctively take the side of the workers, reasonably arguing for the importance of their rights, pay, and conditions, Mishima is shrewd in quietly showing the reader – that is, Japan, and the world at large – to be careful what they wish for. Undermining traditions and systems, hierarchies and pyramids, is not to be done lightly and potentially threatens the fabric of society. But beyond these complex sociopolitical

---

110 There are fascinating and potentially instructive parallels between Mishima's novel and Émile Zola's great study of a coal miners' strike, *Germinal* (1885), in which the workers are unsuccessful in their action.

discussions lie even deeper personal and philosophical ones (though, such is Mishima's point, they can barely be distinguished).

For Mishima, emptiness is a mental and emotional state in which meaning, especially that derived from a country's traditions and culture, has been misplaced, even evaded or squandered – again ironically, perhaps incongruously, a notion he wrought from Western, neo-Nietzschean, rather than Japanese ideas. Nonetheless, whatever the hodgepodge and all too often rose-tinted perspectives Mishima carried, did he not also have a point? Was modern society not too commercialized, too grasping and materialistic – too soulless? He conceded his own life had far more empty extravagance and acquisitive desolation than was good for it. And did the average life of the average salaryman, with his bland office and cramped apartment, need to be quite so drab, so grey, so utilitarian, so defined by transient, futile concerns?

Accordingly, and for his last novel (excluding the *Sea of Fertility* quartet), Mishima wrote a dark and trenchant satire, turning to a cross-breed and acerbic parody that condemned contemporary society through a series of spoofs and sardonic sport, the exasperated author still up for a fight as he indicted the modern world.

Hanio Yamada, a young, good-looking copywriter employed in swinging mid-sixties Tokyo, is besieged by the meaninglessness of his life and the world around him. His cushy, undemanding job needs little sweat or striving, and he is pained by the emptiness of not just his but all existence, with its bosses and wage slips, dull drudgery and routine. Thwarted by a botched suicide attempt after a series of disturbing (Kafkaesque or Lispectorian) visions, in despair – but also in a realization of his new-found freedom – he puts his life 'up for sale' via a local newspaper ad: 'Use me as you wish. Discretion guaranteed. Will cause no bother at all.'

This last clause proves to be less than strictly accurate, for several knocks come at Hanio's door and there ensues a comedy of the blackest hue – involving dodgy gangsters, contract killers, exotic foreigners, a toy mouse, an amorous vampire, an unhinged hippy, powdered scarab beetles, a semi-mythical secret society, a diplomatic mystery, and possibly poisoned carrots (as well as oceans of booze and mountains of hush money). Women leap into our hero's arms while men point their guns at him: it is all delectably melodramatic, absurdly fanciful, and eyebrow-raisingly *weird*.

Hanio's alarming initial ennui (which leads to this succession of eccentrics and escapades) takes us into the realm, not for the first time in Mishima, of Sartre's *La Nausée* (1938), into brute reality, contingency, an existential dread of meaninglessness. Like Roquentin on his bench under the chestnut tree, Hanio experiences a fit of world-weariness, a spasm of lassitude and disquiet. Hallucinating, he undergoes an epiphany when the letters of the newspaper he is reading turn into cockroaches: with troubling lucidity he realizes that the procedures and habits of his life are devoid of purpose, that existence is little more than a trivial collection of routines.

The disillusioned Hanio initially struggles with his unease, as well he might, realizing that if life is pointless, what is the point in continuing with it? Yet when his bid for oblivion fails, like Sartre's hero, Hanio realizes with a thrill that he is a free agent in a world empty of meaning. By rejecting modernity, he can exist in liberated rebellion against the conformist society which surrounds him, welcoming the world's emptiness, contracting out the need (or desire) to determine the path of his life and the conditions of his death. It is this which sanctions the sale of his life to anyone who wants it – and the bizarre sequence of events which constitute the bulk of the novel.

For all its craziness, however, the story is never entirely surreal or peculiar, but always just the right – albeit disconcerting – side of sanity. Were it even more peculiar, akin to fantasy or the realm of nightmare, we would expect the plot to develop in an irrational, erratic fashion, or to merely stagnate and deteriorate. But the reader of *Life for Sale* feels they are being drawn upon an inescapable narrative track, one building a sinister strength. Although the story is necessarily fragmented (partly due to its trance-like, madcap nature; partly because of its initial textual serialization) it is never merely a succession of independent, unpredictable sketches: together, each incident develops with delicious tension and equivocation into an intelligible climax exhibiting Mishima's great theme.

And that theme is decline. For all its material, economic, and technological success, Japan is perceived to be in terminal degeneration, regressing from its (idealized, sentimentalized) noble past into a world of new money, new crime, new manners (all bad), and filthy domestic routine, people living like cockroaches. Hence Hanio's retailing (and re*telling*) of his own existence is the decisive destiny of one locked into contemporary consumerism. Inner significance and meaning are absent, so even life might as well be put up for sale. Although Hanio never explicitly states so, and crucially he is no substitute for his author, amid the satire of *Life for Sale* is always the subtextual suggestion that Mishima himself is romantically yearning for the past. Vanished are the admirable warriors, the immaculate demeanour, the unimpeachable conduct and values which characterized so much of Mishima's personal historical Japan (which is obviously a fabled, even fairy-tale, conviction).

❧

The split between Hanio as character and Mishima as author is significant, for it allows the deeper meaning of the novel to emerge. Toward the end of the book, the murky organization which has loomed behind the text – the ACS, or 'Asia Confidential Service' – which might be a ruse or might be the criminal alliance pulling all the strings behind contemporary Japan, comes out of the shadows and into the foreground. The group appear to close in on Hanio – making his violent death, which he has spent the novel longing for, seem certain. Yet he rejects his doctrine of accepting or even embracing death, and tricks the gang into leaving him alone. He discards his principles, and his denunciation of the world is revealed to be – at best – a farce; at worst, a malignant hypocrisy.

Throughout at least the second half of the novel, after Hanio meets and embarks on a relationship with the affluent but unhinged hippy Reiko, Mishima has planted within the text the increasing suggestion that Hanio's mental state is deteriorating – that he is, in fact, a narrator not to be relied upon. Either Reiko's own idiosyncratic brand of delusions and insanity have infected Hanio or she herself is merely a manifestation of his own madness. Fearing himself pursued by the mysterious (and now likely illusory) ACS, who he has encountered or heard mentioned at several points, Hanio's grasp on reality becomes less and less secure.

The text of *Life for Sale* is keen to emphasize this to the point of self-mockery. When, near the end, Hanio tries to explain to a policeman that he has been abducted by a secret society, the officer politely rebuffs him, noting that it is 'not unusual for lonely men to suffer from delusions.' At the conclusion of the book, Hanio is alone and 'on the verge of tears', staring up at the stars, which blur into 'a myriad of lights blended into one.' Hanio the nihilistic lover boy and ladykiller has had his veneer, of accepting and applauding meaninglessness like a Camusian hero, torn away.

Mishima's twist – that old trick of everything being a nightmare or delusion – might seem a little hackneyed by now. But that is exactly the point, in a novel deliberately toying with tropes and expectations (in one early instance, a curious character tells Hanio, with a sly wink to the reader, that the ACS only exists in 'thriller mangas'). Significantly, of course, those tricks and tropes are exploited to serve the novel's broader thematic concerns. Mishima never believed in absurdist meaninglessness, and Hanio's apparent plummet into fantasy and then psychosis suggests what Mishima saw as the failure of embracing – whether consciously or not – meaninglessness, of living for nothing of value, the attitude which the author believed lay at the empty heart of modern Japan. Hanio's delusion is no different from the wider delusions of an entire society.

Life for Sale lulls the reader into a false sense of security, duping us via Hanio's adolescent fantasies into admiring, and perhaps envying, him – though the proliferation of gun-toting gangsters and sybaritic women keen to jump into bed should alert most of the audience to the textual games going on. We are tricked to concur with Hanio's initial bleak assessment of the world, and then to approve, even celebrate, his decision to undertake a life of absolute freedom unconstrained by orthodox ethics or normal expectations. (Mishima's joke being, of course, that his life is actually dictated by those he has sold it to, just as we ourselves every day sell our soul to this corporation or that conglomerate by buying their product or absent-mindedly clicking 'I agree' to their voluminous terms and conditions.)

For Mishima, to live a decent, virtuous, and respectable life is not to embrace emptiness, to mutiny against a meaningless world by adopting Hanio's sex-and-death quest, his über-nihilistic credo, but to submit oneself to a cause, through and toward which one may strive to achieve. Hanio seems to reach some insight with his realization of the desolation of modern life, but he fails to solve this problem appropriately. He accentuates that emptiness rather than fills it with value or meaning. He recognizes the need to renovate, to re-enact, himself, but he does so only within a context of accepting meaninglessness, rather than embracing the deeper values available to any of us should we wish to welcome them.

For Mishima, of course, those 'deeper values' lay in his interpretation of a mythical bygone Japan, of a ritualized life steeped in and dedicated to its customs and traditions. This was the paradigm that he adopted in his later years, a tragic template which in due course led inexorably to his own death in November 1970 – a death that contained its own dark mixture of emptiness and nihilism, and which drew the author back into the orbit of his hero Hanio. In this sense, Mishima himself ran counter to the profounder significance of *Life for Sale*, destroying his own life in contradiction of the values he wished to uphold (though, of course, this is not quite how Mishima would have interpreted his death, which he himself saw as maintaining those standards and ethics).

Surely even Mishima could not maintain the illusion that, however sincere or heartfelt, his military coup had any chance of succeeding; it was really a suicide mission, a pretence of the principled death for which he had hungered. And, for all the planning and ostensible solemnity of his demise, Mishima's death was a transgression of the traditional samurai values of honour and dignity, and more akin to a delusional publicity stunt. It was not a courageous sacrifice for the benefit of national redemption but a faintly comic aberration, one which tarnished much of his legacy, the extremity of his politics exposing his work to enduring suspicion and mistrust.

Nonetheless, a truth lingers at the close of *Life for Sale*, one which Mishima would explore on a much more far-reaching and impressive scale in *The Sea of Fertility*, his greatest, grandest, and final work (making this slim novel a kind of comic prelude). For although the complexities of his own life and death obscure the degree to which Mishima was able to endorse his rejection of emptiness and maintain his grip on meaningful ideals, there can be no doubt that in his art, and especially in its final phase, he did offer an eloquent, consequential, and profound revelation of the cosmos which not only embraced but embodied those precious values, exploring their nobility and fragility.

It is to that epic, ambitious, and world-enlightening vision, *The Sea of Fertility* – the work which Mishima had dreamed about writing since he was a boy – that the final part of this book will now turn.

PART THREE

THE FINAL TETRALOGY

Chapter Eleven

The Mechanics of Rebirth

INTRODUCING *THE SEA OF FERTILITY*

The Sea of Fertility (豊饒の海, 'Hōjō no Umi', 1969–71) stands as Mishima's crowning achievement and as the most majestic exertion of his creative imagination.[111] A commanding, challenging work of art, it is a literary venture with few contemporary contenders to match the scope and complexity of its ideas, the depth and range of its meanings, the sheer beauty

---

111 The first volume, *Spring Snow* (春の雪, 'Haru no yuki'), was initially published serially in the magazine *Shinchō* from September 1965 to January 1967, then in book form by *Shinchōsha* on 5 January 1969. The second instalment, *Runaway Horses* (奔馬, 'Honba'), appeared in serial form from February 1967 to August 1968, before complete publication on 25 February 1969. Part three, *The Temple of Dawn* (暁の寺, 'Akatsuki no tera'), was published serially from September 1968 to April 1970, and then complete on 10 July 1970. The final volume, *The Decay of the Angel* (天人五衰, 'Tennin Gosui'), was serialized from July 1970 to January 1971, before complete publication on 25 February 1971, exactly three months after its author's death.

of its language. A final masterpiece from Mishima's intrepid pen, it is a network of four novels which cover a vast stretch of culture, history, and experience – beginning in the early years of the twentieth century and ending in the mid-1970s, beyond even their own author's death.

A golden spider's web of symbols, stories, allusions, memories, metaphors, and mythologies, Mishima's tetralogy is open to a wide range of interpretation and reinterpretation. This includes, but is not limited to, as an interrogation of Shinto and Buddhist world views; as a cross-examination of Japan's emergence into modernity; as an indictment of the human condition, wherever one finds it, revealing our proclivities and blind spots; as a figurative commemoration of the function of art in life; and as a narrative of the various intellectual and emotional energies at work in its creator's own complex character.

Accordingly, the cycle encapsulates most of Mishima's principal obsessions and concerns, exploring his intricate, often zigzagging, philosophical outlook, his observations on society and history, his attitude toward impulsive and more rational heroes, taking them all to an exceptional level of literary refinement. But it is through the sophisticated intercourse of fictional genres, by coercing bleak realism to interrogate romance, fantasy, and myth, that Mishima is able to expand historical time into new dimensions, allowing for disquieting perspectives on the modern world.

Across the four books of *The Sea of Fertility* we witness how the transient beauty of existence is always under threat, how it is circumscribed by death and decay, time and reality, how idealistic visions deteriorate into humdrum experience and parodies of authenticity. As such, the cycle necessarily ends with a universal truth of entropic emptiness, expectation dwindling into disorder, chance, and uncertainty. It reads us before we read it, and we are shown the full extent of humanity's weakness and confusion, its limitless capacity for cruelty, delusion, and isolation. But the journey itself offers a less desolate and more optimistic aspiration, too, tendering tentative hope for transformation and renewal.

Mishima's great skill in *The Sea of Fertility* lies in contrasting the spectacle of the developing century with the intimacy of lives and minds. He shows us both the changing destiny of a nation and the individuals who inhabit it, exalting in the violence and mystery of the juxtaposition, while also searching for its panoptic implications. Accordingly, this work presents Mishima's complete cosmic and mythical vision, his final rendition of a dark, sterile universe which nonetheless contains the opportunity for the emergence and gradual ascendancy of our metaphorical, if not literal, souls.

Just as the Second World War had motivated Mishima's early writing – the knowledge of his, as he initially saw it, certain death in combat providing an urgent impetus to creativity – so he needed a provocation for the culmination and conclusion of his life's literary work. Being frigid, the Cold War, for all its dread and unease, was not the gallant crisis he required. So an emergency would have to be self-engineered, one which was guaranteed not only to terminate his life in blood, guts, and obstinate glory (since the military coup he would concoct was almost certain to end in failure), but which also offered the ultimate deadline for his final literary work.

In the 1960s, Mishima was undergoing an existential crisis, an alienation from the reality of the new world around him. He saw modern life as damaged, dangerous, but even more crucially empty, devoid of genuine significance and consequence (which could perhaps truly be located only in the imagination, as well as in an imagined past). As a result, he promoted a sense of meaning in his existence by performing roles in which he yielded to his sadomasochistic, militarist, and nationalist cravings. He found confidence and distraction in these, but they also provided energy for his literary undertakings.

He renewed his commitment to bushidō, the code of the samurai, as well as bodybuilding ventures, film projects,[112] theatre projects,[113] basic training with the Ground Self-Defense Force (Mishima feared the military threat from Communist China, especially after the Cultural Revolution in 1966), along with travel to America, England, France, Sweden, India, Thailand, Laos, and Cambodia.[114] There was a Beatles concert in Tokyo[115] – and the minor matter of the formation of his own private militia, the

---

112 Including writing and directing an adaptation of his short story 'Patriotism' in 1966.

113 Including the plays *Madame de Sade* (1965) and *My Friend Hitler* (1968).

114 In London in March 1965, he had lunch at the home of Margot Fonteyn (1919–1991), the great English ballerina – purveyor of an art form Mishima revered, with its mix of physical prowess and aesthetic grace – as well as dinner with the celebrated Irish author of *The Country Girls* (1960), Edna O'Brien (1930–2024). Mishima found Fonteyn to be a vivacious delight, endlessly entertaining and enjoyable, comparing her to Beethoven's Fidelio/Leonore, while O'Brien was 'typically Irish, full of gentle sensitivity and with a homey feel.'

115 Mishima was none too impressed with the music but was fascinated by the hysterical reaction of the adoring fans, the girls screaming themselves into a frenzy. 'Illusion is a frightening thing,' he concluded.

Tatenokai.[116] The last's odd collection of mercenaries and misfits was mainly composed of right-wing university students along with other disillusioned oddballs from mainstream society, who swore to protect the emperor with their life (and with whom Mishima would stage the coup d'état at the headquarters of the Self-Defense Force on the last day of his life).

But there was also, of course, his writing. At this time came many political, critical, and autobiographical books and essays, including *Aesthetics of Ending* (1966), *The Way of the Samurai* (1967), and *Sun and Steel: Art, Action and Ritual Death* (1968). *The Way of the Samurai* presented Mishima's interpretation of an early eighteenth-century manual on samurai spirituality, ethics, and behaviour, Tsunetomo Yamamoto's *Hagakure*,[117] and as such is an excellent companion piece to *Runaway Horses*, the second novel of *The Sea of Fertility*. *Sun and Steel* was a memoir of Mishima's relationship with his body, exploring the intense philosophical negotiations between his physical, emotional, and intellectual beings. A profound, often disturbing, portrait of a writer's troubled soul, it offers a deep insight into Mishima's state of mind, as well as a dark portent of his body's traumatic self-authored demise. Alongside these pieces of criticism and non-fiction, Mishima was also developing his final literary narrative work, which, like *The Way of the Samurai* and *Sun and Steel*, would

---

116 'Shield Society', so named as it intended to 'shield' the emperor from apparent left-wing activities.

117 Yamamoto narrated many of his thoughts to the samurai Tashiro, and these commentaries were compiled and published in 1716 as *Hagakure* (葉隠), which can be translated as *In the Shadow of Leaves* or *Hidden Leaves*. The book largely disappeared for two centuries before the growing nationalism of twentieth-century Japan rediscovered its appeal, and by the 1930s it was probably the best-known exponent of bushidō.

present his closing statement on the world, a departing vision of emptiness and fulfilment.

The death of the father we witnessed in *The Sailor Who Fell from Grace with the Sea* (1963) was connected closely with Mishima's pessimistic, romantic belief that the de facto death of the emperor – his de-deification after the war – had created the materialistic, nihilistic vacuum in contemporary Japanese society. For Mishima, the emperor was an authentic and definitive father figure, and his future divine restoration would renew a benevolent existence, not only purging Mishima the son and grandson of his own distant and disenchanting father and grandfather, but revitalizing the past for an entire nation.

Much of this glory might be achieved through direct military or political action, but it could also be attained through art – Apollo and Dionysus in creative collaboration (as we saw in *Sailor*). It was now that Mishima began to create one immense work: a 'long, long, long novel' that would not blindly pursue time but would transcend it, with multiple separate narratives all linking up to construct a vast circle. Just as an idealized emperor worship could provide the crucial, even strategic, key to the end of Mishima's earthly life, so reincarnation could be the motif central to the end of his creative life, the two quietly interlinked.

During the second half of the 1960s, this work would become, of course, *The Sea of Fertility*. It was serialized on a monthly basis from September 1965 on but could only be completed at the very end of its maker's life (in part because of the critical creative impetus his death would afford; in part because he wanted to incorporate all the 'contemporary vogues at the time of writing'). The bulk of the writing was finished a few weeks before Mishima's ritual suicide, though the final instalment of *The Decay of the Angel* would only be delivered on that last day of his earthly existence, the manuscript marked with the solemn and now notorious date 25 November 1970.

Although rooted in many Western literary traditions, the overall and initial model for *The Sea of Fertility*, and especially its first volume, *Spring Snow*, was a late Heian-period[118] love story from the eleventh century, *The Tale of Hamamatsu* (浜松中納言物語, 'Hamamatsu Chunagon Monogatari').[119] Not only is the Buddhist concept of reincarnation a key thematic motif and structuring device for the narrative, but Mishima's texts would take up rudiments of the plot, including forbidden love affairs, the prophetic power of dreams, and foreign travel in search of both specific revitalized beings and a more general meaning to one's existence.

Important though *Hamamatsu* was to Mishima, more influential in shaping the transcendental and metaphysical backgrounds to *The Sea of Fertility* were two books on Buddhist teachings: Seibun Fukaura's *Outline of Reincarnation* and Yoshifumi Ueda's *The Concept of Karma in Buddhism*. Fukaura elucidated how the theory of yuishiki in the ancient Hossō sect of Buddhism affirms that all existence is subjective, unverifiable, consciousness only, because of the core belief that reality, including

---

118 794–1185.

119 Its authorship is shrouded in some mystery and speculation, though it has traditionally been ascribed to Sugawara no Takasue no musume (菅原孝標女, c.1008 – after 1059), also known as Takasue's Daughter or Lady Sarashina, author of the memoir *Sarashina's Diary* (更級日記, 'Sarashina Nikki').

the objective world and the subjective mind that considers it, are developments of consciousness in line with karma and the karmic kernels in the depths of this consciousness. Accordingly, reincarnation involves not the rebirth of a soul, per se, but psychologies in a continuous process of creation and destruction.

The Sea of Fertility provides Mishima's own version of and variation on this philosophy. It also incorporates his interpretation of Ueda's account that though the world was an illusion fashioned in the depths of consciousness, this illusion was constantly generating its own karmic sources. An infinity of mini reincarnations is continually forming countless illusory worlds and consciousnesses, generating what we think of as time, which is not an autonomous external phenomenon but something produced within each particularized consciousness.

Such profound, arcane, and often impenetrable philosophical and religious concepts frequently make their way into *The Sea of Fertility* – especially part three, *The Temple of Dawn*, with its extended discussions of reincarnation – but their importance to most readers lies in recognizing how Mishima structures his novel and develops his themes of repetition, illusion, and decay. At times there are inconsistencies and discrepancies to his (re) interpretation of Buddhist concepts, especially relating to yuishiki and the existence of souls, but we should always bear in mind that Mishima was a novelist, not a theorist or theologian, and never intended to create a consistent, watertight philosophy.

Just as Shakespeare, writing in the ongoing aftermath of the Reformation, made use of whatever ethical, religious, or political concepts suited his purposes as a dramatist – often, for example, playing Catholic and Protestant ideologies against each other for comic aims – so Mishima employs Buddhist theories in a dynamic, shifting fashion to suit his literary objectives (which were, as we shall see, often acutely critical of Buddhist world views). Certainly a thoroughgoing command of Buddhist metaphysics is not a requirement for either understanding or enjoyment of the tetralogy, though a briefing in some of its basic concepts can assist with some of the more esoteric passages as well as comprehending the overall scope of Mishima's vision.

Although it contains flashbacks and reminiscences to the last years of the Meiji period,[120] Mishima's tetralogy commences in October 1912, during the early months of the Taishō era.[121] It then travels through several stages of tumultuous twentieth-century Japanese history, including the onset of the Shōwa era,[122] the increasing nationalism of the 1930s, the rapture and suffering of the Second World War, and the economic growth / spiritual decay of the post-war state, before closing during the imagined future summer of 1975.

Mishima's is no orthodox multigenerational saga, however, rumbling and grumbling across the years as a family's fortunes decline and fall.[123] With characteristic audacity, and to confer unity upon the great expanse of historical ground the novels cover,

---

120 Named for Mutsuhito, Emperor Meiji, who reigned from 23 October 1868 to 30 July 1912.

121 Named for Yoshihito, Emperor Taishō, who reigned from 30 July 1912 to 25 December 1926.

122 Named for Hirohito, Emperor Shōwa, who reigned from 25 December 1926 to 7 January 1989.

123 Such as Anthony Trollope's Palliser novels (1865–80) and John Galsworthy's *Forsyte Saga* (1906–21).

Mishima made use of a simple device: a pair of contrasting but intertwined narrative threads. First, the seeming reincarnation in each of the four books of a spontaneous, active hero: Kiyoaki. Second, the continued presence throughout of one passive, guarded, and observant character: Honda.

In the mythical catastrophe of *Spring Snow*, amid fading aristocrats and the newly rich, Kiyoaki is a heroic but emotionally tempestuous lover; in *Runaway Horses*, he returns as the rash and impetuous athlete cum political agitator Isao. The third novel, *The Temple of Dawn*, sees him restored as a beautiful though indolent Thai princess, Ying Chan, before, in *The Decay of the Angel*, he resurfaces a final time as the arrogant, ungrateful, and manipulative Tōru. Against this divergent series of apparent reappearances is the persistent presence of Mishima's most fully realized character, Honda, Kiyoaki's friend and foil (who, in his own manifestations as law student, lawyer, and judge, is an obvious seeker of rational truth).

As in a Noh drama, across the span of *The Sea of Fertility*, the novel's hero journeys through different forms (Kiyoaki reappearing as Isao, then Ying Chan, then Tōru), following Buddhist laws of karma and transmigration. But to this Dionysian force, there must be the Apollonian figure of Honda: a constant; searching, questioning, watching, recording. Through the four novels Honda changes, but more subtly, and his role as a vital but impotent observer is brought to a demeaning, ironic end with his arrest as a common peeping Tom. Unlike the youthful reincarnations, all of whom are seemingly preordained to die, in their respective texts, at twenty, Honda lives, grows, and degenerates (morally, physically, spiritually) across the grand arc of the novels. *The Sea of Fertility* is, in many ways, Honda's journey, Honda's tragedy – the tragedy Mishima never wanted for himself: dying an old man, perverted in mind and body. (A fate he dodged by committing seppuku.)

In addition to providing an all-encompassing philosophical framework, this twofold literary strategy – Honda's continuing appearance and the death/reincarnation of youthful heroes – also had the attraction of opposites, a phenomenon which had always appealed to Mishima. The wandering soul could be perpetually young and daring, the ageing passive hero subjected to time's forces and ruinations; one had romance, the other realism. Vitality and energy could be in a constant textual skirmish with weariness and ennui. There were also inherent dialectics at work between mind and body, masculinity and femininity – tensions which preoccupied the author throughout his life. What is more, Kiyoaki and his transmigratory cognates could ultimately embody Mishima's own bursting greed for life, his passion for eternity that mere mortal, physical existence could never quite satisfy (the last thing he ever wrote, a note left on his desk the day he died, was 'human life is limited, but I would like to live forever').

The span of the four *Fertility* novels witnesses a change in the relative prominence given to the active/passive heroes. By the later novels, the strength and vivacity of the dynamic combatant is almost eclipsed by the darkening potency of the passive protagonist – Honda asserting his increasing dominance over the narrative. Lest we assume this represents Mishima's heightened respect for the intellectual, or diminished interest in warrior heroes, the crucial factor remains the *relationship* between the active and passive forces, not merely the apparent eminence of one over the other. Indeed, although Ying Chan and Tōru in *The Temple of Dawn* and *The Decay of the Angel* seem to be outshone by Honda in terms of narrative space and drive, their chilling comparative grip over this increasingly corrupt figure is exceptional – which will have a key role in how we interpret Honda's emptiness in the summer garden that closes the tetralogy.

※

Mishima's tetralogy has an air of fantasy and myth which endures until part two of *The Temple of Dawn*, where a more marked realism takes over, grooming us for the sombre final revelations, in *The Decay of the Angel*, that meaningful dreams and honest desires cannot exist in the fraudulent post-war world of modern Japan (a conclusion which, although bitter and brutal, is a call to actual and emblematic arms).

Before the desolation arrives, imagination, hope, and fancy exert their thrall on the text, especially via Mishima's mythically contrived fixation on traditional Japanese culture and the nation's glorious past. It is a preoccupation with high culture and the grandest aspects of society, attested in the lurid, mythic evocation of the late Meiji aristocracy in *Spring Snow* and the romantic militarist thrusts of the 1930s in *Runaway Horses*. By part one of *The Temple of Dawn*, set in the 1940s, this colour and distinction has shifted to the glamorous palaces and mysterious temples of Bangkok, perhaps an acrimonious indication that the land of the rising sun cannot offer such excitement. When *Temple of Dawn* returns to Japan for its second part (1952), and then for the closing book of the sequence, *The Decay of the Angel* (1970s), it is to sour reality, to a grotesque and pitch-black fantasy, a perverse, immoral, and counterfeit fairy tale.

Closely aligned to the role of the fantastical or mythical, alien or exotic, and a clear suggestion of the way Mishima interrogates the present and the past throughout *The Sea of*

Fertility, is the cycle's obsessive concern with time. Like several other great multivolume novels – but especially Proust's *À la recherche du temps perdu* (1913–27), Mann's *Joseph and His Brothers* (1933–43), and Powell's *A Dance to the Music of Time* (1951–75) – *The Sea of Fertility* is a text consumed by the interplay between a mythical, imaginary, even illusionary time, and modern reality including world history (which the Japanese tetralogy so acutely attaches to). Across Mishima's four texts we march with relentless certainty through the grim realities of the alternately gloomy and expectant twentieth century. And this forbidding century, this artificial expanse of time, is uncompromisingly despotic to all, without prejudice or qualification, crushing everything and everyone in its path – either via war, disease, anarchy, materialism, industrialization, or the menacing proliferation of a concrete ugliness to the landscape.

Although we saw how many of his earlier texts – *The Sound of Waves, The Temple of the Golden Pavilion, The Sailor Who Fell from Grace with the Sea* – engaged with the realities of the Second World War (and other real-world events), there is always the preponderant suggestion that their worlds are timeless, isolated from grey reality via the fantastical, rejuvenating function of islands, sanctuaries, and the sea in each text. But in *The Sea of Fertility* Mishima's preoccupation with exploring the status of personal and universal mythology, and the pestiferous influence of time, takes on a more alarming bleak authenticity since the overarching events of the novel's hinterland are apparently too vast to be ignored, their impact left unheeded.

࿐

In *The Sea of Fertility* we discover that the true arbiter between these worlds of myth and reality is undoubtedly Mishima's active heroes, who must accept the challenging crossing – the twisted, complex quest – between actual and imaginary worlds. In these texts it is a demanding traversal: these active heroes transcend time and space through their transmigratory reappearances, occupying both the real and unreal world via the phenomenon of metempsychosis.

Kiyoaki, the stylish, sophisticated young hero of *Spring Snow*, is nonetheless a wanton being, unbalanced, living only for passion, emotion, and the senses, occasionally fading away only to accelerate again with greater force, shrinking, then blazing without any clear bearing or resolution. His path, and his purpose, begin to coalesce, however, when his complex, hesitant love for the beautiful, blue-blooded Satoko is frustrated by her engagement to a prince of the imperial court. In order to realize his love, Kiyoaki nosedives into one irresponsible and careless act after another, which drives the narrative toward its tragic conclusion – one which all the same opens the cycle to its more potentially optimistic thematic concerns.

Romantic-sexual ardour turns to martial-political passion in *Runaway Horses*, where we rejoin the narrative twenty years later amid the nascent nationalism of the early 1930s. The new hero, Isao, wants for Kiyoaki's elegance but counterbalances this through his zeal in maintaining the purity of his own being and that of Japan, embodying overtly masculine virtues of power, strength, skill, and virility. An athlete who becomes a political patriot determined to restore national pride by overturning the country's desecration by foreign influences and achieving unity with ancient notions of divinity, he is betrayed and meets his own premature end in an act of sacrificial immolation.

In *The Temple of Dawn*, the active hero takes on a less conspicuous role, as the malign influence of the passive protagonist begins to make its presence felt more keenly in the tetralogy. Here the reincarnated soul is a beautiful Thai princess, Ying Chan, an embodiment of sensual pleasure and mystery but one destined, like Isao and Kiyoaki, to die at the age of twenty, her own life thwarted for the ambitions of the tetralogy's broader canvas.

By the fourth and final novel, *The Decay of the Angel*, we not only anticipate the new incarnation of the active hero but, like Honda himself in the text, watch and wait for their journey, their revelation, their demise. Yet the new hero, Tōru, is a less obviously mythical and romanticized figure than Ying Chan, Isao, or Kiyoaki – indeed, in his arrogance and cynical churlishness, he is dangerously close in mental outlook and temperament to Honda. The tangible evidence of each reincarnation, the three moles on the body of each hero, is witnessed on the new form of Tōru, but he is gradually revealed to be the direct opposite of his predecessors, threatening to dislocate the credibility of the previous heroes. He is physically beautiful but increasingly governed by both his intellect and an encroaching sense of manipulative malevolence, the earlier heroes' acts of rapturous unrestraint replaced by premeditated iniquity. The division between active hero and passive protagonist has become precariously narrow, the borders overthrown and polluted. Realism has apparently trumped romance.

❧

In *The Sea of Fertility* the passive protagonist, Honda, is engaged in a pursuit of truth. But his role as a smart and positive, albeit observant and inert, force in the first two novels is darkened as he begins to take centre stage in *The Temple of Dawn* and *The Decay of the Angel*. By falling in love with Ying Chan and then adopting Tōru, Honda is perverting the natural separation of the physical and the intellectual, disrupting the mystical exclusivity of youthful bodily beauty with his ageing and coercive mind.

Unlike the first three youthful heroes (none of whom, we should remember, are entirely pure or blameless), Honda is subjected to the devastating forces of time and corruption, his body becoming old and hideous, his mind distorting into an arena of contamination and perversity. He has always been slightly cynical, quizzically sharp-eyed; but by the second half of *The Temple of Dawn* and *The Decay of the Angel*, he is monstrously tainted – and mirrored in Tōru, the dark, duplicitous new reincarnation of his long-lost friend Kiyoaki. Evil penetrates this world, just as exploitation, sleaze, and venality have corrupted contemporary Japan. There can be no room here for a pure impulsive hero, a wholesome beauty, a physical embodiment of clarity and deed.

Desperately seeking a return to the past, Honda revisits Satoko at the site of the first novel's tragic climax, where she still lives, now an aged and enigmatic, semi-divine figure. But she cannot remember the past; her history is wiped out. It is an amnesia which infects Honda himself as he is left at the cycle's close in the sadness and serenity of the empty temple garden, a horrifically ironic spiritual space without memory or love, blank and abandoned. Yet despite this bleakness, this ruinous debasement of both the active and passive hero, there is room for light and optimism. This is initially denoted in the organic summertime location with which the saga ends, one which causes the reader to reflect positively on the redemptive possibilities within the preceding text.

Honda, a lawyer and judge, is an enquirer into truth, a hunter of certainty and reality. Beyond the relatively mundane, even banal, truths of the legal and judicial worlds, he seeks a more fundamental, even universal, truth which might emancipate him, bestowing a meaning not only upon his own tawdry, sterile, and warped existence but that of the cosmos itself. It is a strenuous and at times cryptic quest, but one of necessity. Just as Mishima's fiction had ironically sought the renewal of Japanese literature through the inclusion of Western literary styles and techniques, so his passive hero is sent out from the vanishing domain of Japan to the wider sphere abroad in search of the means of the nation's rejuvenation.

In the suggestively titled *Temple of Dawn*, Honda travels to the exotic lands of Southeast Asia,[124] where hope for that reinvigoration is to come. He is ostensibly on a dull business trip, so he is not overtly escaping the realm of waste and deterioration, but subtly seeking answers to the questions of *The Sea of Fertility*'s text. Honda is a passive hero, not an egocentric, narcissistic active hero undertaking a rite of passage or spontaneous voyage of discovery. His quest for truth is more understated, indirect, but perhaps reaps a harvest akin to those of the active heroes.

Seeking a truth to restore a fading culture, Honda unwittingly pursues the value of myth, the quiet but potent proof that the insipid world can contain more than that which is observed by intellectual impressions and rational thought. This is the myth that can revivify lives, metamorphosing the humdrum into the colourful and surprising. The tranquil closing desolation in the empty garden is not proof that such a quest was either fruitless or without purpose; on the contrary, it shows that the mission itself

---

124 The 'garden of the world', muses Bloom in James Joyce's *Ulysses* (1922).

was sufficient. It was a mythical quest, however burdened and encroached by anti-mythical reality. The quest, especially in aesthetic terms, is more vital and significant than the elusive end goal.

The Sea of Fertility ends in placid nothingness, with a corrupted figure in an empty garden, a space devoid of myth and pervaded by bleak reality, blunt time, burdened history. Honda has discovered, through both the gloomy revelation that Tōru is not a true reincarnation of Kiyoaki and the amnesiac reappearance of Satoko, that myth is a dangerous, tenuous illusion. The romantic zeal which pervaded the first three books of the tetralogy is shown in the face of grim experience to be a perilous lie. But even this desolate ending to the cycle is not the whole truth.

By the very existence of the text itself, the degeneration of modernity and the monotonous consumerism of the contemporary world are themselves shown to be illusions. The factual reality of the multiple reincarnations might be false, a misapprehension of spiritual enchantment at work in the cosmos. But art authorizes and promotes the existence of deeper truths and profounder certainties, beyond the dingy realities it depicts. Honda ends without memories, without imagination, without life, without myth. But the book in which he fades endures.

The four principal active heroes in *The Sea of Fertility* – Kiyoaki, Isao, Ying Chan, and Tōru – are not only various literary incarnations of their author but take on the responsibilities and possibilities of art, appearing in all its complex and multifaceted guises: sometimes arduous, disagreeable, or severe, then challenging and traumatic; elsewhere welcoming and intoxicating, exquisite, and even hallucinogenic. But beyond these features that marry art and action, the energetic, dynamic protagonists offer, like literature, endless opportunities for renewal and redemption, regeneration and rebirth.

In *The Sea of Fertility*, not only does the metempsychosis device allow Mishima to maintain the presence of a youthful active hero across four books and several decades of time, it also sanctions their metaphorical role as embodiments of art. The emptiness of the memoryless garden which closes the final novel, *The Decay of the Angel*, is starkly beautiful, shimmering with sadness and despondency. Yet, like the bleak beauty which closed *The Sailor Who Fell from Grace with the Sea*, there is enfolded within the texture of the text the underlying suggestion that the act and processes of art, of literary endeavour, can endure, outshine, and surmount the meaninglessness of modernity. Art, the very books that we have been reading, which we can open again and again to read and reread, transcends the austerities of existence.

Written in the second half of the 1960s, as Mishima hurtled, like his active heroes, toward his own premature termination, *The Sea of Fertility* carries an ironic warning in its title. The feature to which it refers is the Mare Fecunditatis, a lifeless expanse of basaltic lava flows on the surface of the moon – that ultimate mythical object – which is neither a sea nor fertile, but a barren wilderness. The author counsels us to be careful in hunting for myths, to be wary of the power of romance and fantasy, history and tradition, for there are mirages and misconceptions threatening to curtail, even extinguish, their potential for meaning, truth, and enrichment.

But Mishima knew, too, that we should never stop looking at the moon.

Chapter Twelve

Spring Snow

THE PRINCESS & THE LEOPARD

The conjoined names of great literary lovers chime down through the centuries: Orpheus and Eurydice, Antony and Cleopatra, Romeo and Juliet, Heathcliff and Catherine, Daisy and Gatsby, Charles and Sebastian, Sally and Clarissa. 'Satoko and Kiyoaki' will be less familiar to many, yet their tragic love story, which forms the basis of the opening volume of *The Sea of Fertility* (1969–71), is as powerful and memorable as any other, offering glimpses into a vanished world but one resonant with timeless human emotion and personal agony.

Spring Snow (春の雪, 'Haru no yuki', 1969) merges Western modes of storytelling with Eastern philosophical ideas and exacting, idiosyncratic Japanese images and metaphors. It employs varied, often apparently conflicting, symbols, traditions, and techniques to create a mosaic of motifs and narrative tensions. It portrays both a transitional, liminal phase of Japanese history and a convincing story of a doomed romance. Yet its mythical atmosphere and the quiet introduction of the refrain of reincarnation is an essential, anti-historical, element of the novel, too, laying down long-term thematic and narrative markers that will take later instalments of *The Sea of Fertility* into complex spatio-temporal arenas.

For Mishima, the themes of time and history, and the aristocratic love story which forms the plot, were crucially interlinked, forming a key element of the novel's central concerns with custom, change, and external intrusion. The construction of an authentic modern romance was beset with problems, Mishima once argued, because the impediments to love that a couple must prevail over no longer existed. The more liberal social, sexual, and moral mores of the (imperially emasculated) post-war period had removed, or at least tempered, many of the traditional obstacles to love and romantic relationships. (Obviously this hadn't stopped contemporary writers finding new hurdles to passion for their novels, though there was certainly some validity to Mishima's outlook.)

Back in the earliest stage of the Taishō period (1912–26), however, when *Spring Snow* is set, many of the traditional problems – actual or illusory – were very much still around. And the gravest taboo of the imperial era was to violate an imperial princess; this constituted the most alarming defamation of the monarch. Betrothed to a royal prince, ranking aristocrat's daughter Satoko is, to all intents and purposes, an imperial princess, making her lover Kiyoaki's transgression against the emperor through their passionate affair not only an act against time and tradition but a genuine experience of true love, perhaps one now accessible only in the past.

Spring Snow can be appreciated as a stand-alone work, floating free from its *Sea of Fertility* siblings in elegiac isolation.

In some ways, its protagonists' tragedy is more absorbing and exquisite when experienced this way, with the redemptive potential of both reincarnation and the multivolume literary form severed just as the young lovers are. Yet Mishima always regarded *Spring Snow* as the first part of a sequence. In the opening novel of the tetralogy, he shows us the dying embers of a fading world resigned to its fate (embodied in the more private catastrophe of Satoko and Kiyoaki), before disclosing to us in subsequent instalments how that world came to be overtaken, transitioning toward the assimilation of alien values and the decay of modernity.

Although circles have no beginning or end, their curve can suggest both direction and orientation. *Spring Snow*, in its poetry and tragedy, insinuates the whole movement and programme of *The Sea of Fertility*, inaugurating not only its characters and plot but the deeper philosophical concerns and metaphysical yearnings which the succeeding novels will explore. When they reach the emptiness and irony of *The Decay of the Angel*'s final words, hundreds of pages later, many readers are compelled to turn straight back to the rich, evocative magic of *Spring Snow*, in all its agony and ecstasy. Here they may experience again its ponds and birds, its balletic, billowing clouds, its scarlet maple leaves and fragile cherry trees, its love letters and illicit rendezvous, its poetry and sadness, its intricately connected psychological and environmental descriptions, which offer the key to so many of the tetralogy's ideas.

The circle, once spun, continues to revolve.

For a series that will explore the boundless, cyclical nature of the cosmos, *The Sea of Fertility* begins in audacious fashion with the discussion of an image fixed in time: a historic photograph. Specifically, it is a picture of a group of soldiers during the Russo-Japanese War,[125] entitled 'Vicinity of the Tokuri Temple: Memorial Service for the War Dead, 26 June 1904'.[126]

The photograph, with its soldiers and trees, initially offers suggestions of life, but, with its wooden cenotaph and as a memorial service for the fallen, it is also pervaded by death, as *Spring Snow* and *The Sea of Fertility* are to be. Moreover, a cenotaph is not only a symbol of death but of isolation, of separation, standing as an emblem of remembrance for soldiers that have died and whose remains are elsewhere, at sea or upon distant battlefields. Though the cenotaph is sequestered, alone, bounded by a swathe of soldiers, we are told how the photographer nonetheless adeptly brings it to the foreground, just as Mishima is able to isolate his individual characters and events from among the swirling mass of history.

As a literary device to open not only a historical novel but a subsequent sequence of novels that will travel through the century, the description of a photograph is inspired, pulling us into another world far removed in time and space. Bathed in a strange half-light, age and sepia ink tinge the picture with an 'atmosphere of infinite poignance' while simultaneously cleansing it of the terror and slaughter of war, purifying the past and ostracizing the present. We are set to enter a complex but controlled world of love and sorrow, with modern Japan prudently remote.

---

125 8 February 1904 – 5 September 1905.

126 The photograph is real and available for the reader to view for themselves on the internet by searching for the image 'Tokuri-ji Memorial 1904'.

Like the photograph, and the narrator's discussion of it, *Spring Snow* itself manages to do two conflicting things at once: it offers a plausible, realistic portrait of a point in Japanese history; but it also flaunts itself as a fairy tale, a storybook romance, interrogating its own authenticity as a historical document. The mystery and beauty of the photograph, and the wider narrative, point both toward the higher truths available in myth, as well as to the inherent problems in reconstructing the past.

The person inspecting the picture is Kiyoaki, two of whose uncles have died in the war the photograph honours and observes. He is the novel's eighteen-year-old hero, introverted and capricious as Hamlet, brooding and solitary as a leopard. We are furnished with flashbacks to his childhood in the last years of the Meiji era (1868–1912), to ostentatious garden shrines for dead relatives and the presence of his overbearing matriarchal grandmother, who lives in imposing isolation, attended by a cohort of maids yet a constant nuisance for the younger generations. We are told of when Kiyoaki acted as an imperial page for a princess, the retelling rich in lyrical, whimsical details of perfume and hair, comportment and demeanour, privilege and self-reproach. The realm we are presented with is opulent, a domain of peers and aristocrats, pavilions and ponds, grand houses with ornamental lakes and striking panoramas, strong men and beautiful women, all of which firmly establishes the fairy-tale atmosphere of the story – something ironically heightened by the actual chronological period in which it occurs. Myth and history are coalescing, the tension between them tangible, dangerous, hostile.

Beauty, like time or history, is shown to be an elusive force. The imperial princess for whom the boy Kiyoaki acts as a page is described in a sensual fashion, Mishima lingering on intimate, even imperfect or unexpected, details of the body – the earlobe, the nape of the neck – and recognizing that it is here, in the hidden minutiae rather than in the charade of cosmetics, perfume, and clothes, that the essence of true beauty resides. A stray hair or slight limp carries more attraction than the artificial constructs of femininity that most men foolishly crave, deluding and disorientating themselves.

Our hero Kiyoaki is shown to be different from and indifferent to these oafs, these graceless hunters of fleshly prizes. Sensitive, sophisticated, he is able to appreciate these features of true beauty, not only noting their value but infusing them with a sense of misfortune and heartbreak, the same tragedy as the transience of youth. Kiyoaki himself is beautiful in a strikingly feminine way: at thirteen he is 'too handsome' and imbued with delicate features that give him an ethereal presence which even (and especially) his own father finds disconcerting.

We are in Tokyo, 1912, shortly after the death of Emperor Meiji, the charismatic and pragmatic monarch who presided over a period of intense modernization and industrialization for Japan, transforming it from a feudal state into a global power, opening it after foreign pressure to international connections following its long seclusion from the community of nations, known as the Sakoku era.[127] Sumptuous, distinctive, everything in *Spring Snow* is a world away from the (for Mishima) empty economic powerhouse of 1960s Japan when it was written, offering an alluring escape from the bleakness of modern reality. Yet occurring as it does on the cusp of a new era, Kiyoaki's sphere is given an irresistible frisson, with the air of change full of both promise and trepidation. (Something contemporaneously occurring in other places around the globe, not least in Edwardian Britain, as

---

127 'Sakoku' literally translates as 'locked country', i.e., 'isolationism'.

countries and empires hurtled toward the cataclysm of the First World War and other twentieth-century turbulence.)

Much of this twin sense of possibility and foreboding is bound up in Kiyoaki's beauty, whose personality is shown to be as otherworldly as his physical appearance. Kiyoaki is a pensive, aloof loner, observant and perceptive, preferring his own company to that of his vulgar schoolmates. Nonetheless, he has one good friend in the stolid and studious Honda, his foil and relief. Honda is sensible where Kiyoaki is impulsive, intellectual where his friend is emotional. They exist like the 'flower and leaf in a single plant', distinct yet bound and peculiarly drawn together, as they will be across the whole grand arc of *The Sea of Fertility*, beyond even Kiyoaki's youthful death at the end of *Spring Snow*.

As these early chapters develop, however, we begin to question just how unalike Honda and Kiyoaki are, how far their differences are merely exaggerated for the mutual benefit of the other. It is an amplification that will have implications both for Kiyoaki's future and his friend's fluctuating personality as Honda begins to dominate the cycle of books, acting as witness to the novels' avowed reincarnations of Kiyoaki's soul, as his own character begins to sour and spoil. In truth, whatever their complex similarities and differences, the friends balance each other because their disparities personify the contradictory nature of contemporary Japan, an era of intense discord and antagonism.

To a degree, Kiyoaki is intended to represent some form of traditional, elegant Japan (which, attached as it is to the past, necessitates his demise at the end of the novel). On the other hand, Honda epitomizes an encroaching, but more rational, westernized consciousness that is in the ascendancy (which, accordingly, can survive and corroborate the future as it progresses). Contrasting with Kiyoaki's melancholic attachment to the past, Honda hopes to become a lawyer, optimistically extolling the belief that, whatever our personal history or social standing, we are all answerable to empirical principles which rise above ephemeral customs. Whatever the phases of history, Honda asserts, there remains a timeless, universal natural law – an Aristotelian and Aquinian tenet which constitutes both a symbolic and literal infiltration of Western ideas into Japanese culture (though there are Eastern counterparts to this view, as we shall see). It is a belief indicative of the incipient modern era which will, in reality, bring so much chaos and destruction.

Honda's father is a magistrate who admires Western philosophy and advocates a logical, judicious legal system, while his mother is a member of a modern women's society. By contrast, Kiyoaki's family are nouveau riche, abrasive and uncouth, coming from humbler origins: in the previous century they had been honoured as samurai, living simply but with grace and dignity. Now they represent the direction Japanese society is taking, toward a more monetized, modernized, and westernized culture, accumulating land, wealth, and an only superficial elegance. Their aristocracy is a facade, a pretence, whereas Kiyoaki's nobility, like his impending love for Satoko, is to be regarded as genuine – though the novel will test the true degree of that decency, both in his personal conduct and when his actions set him against the tradition he is regarded as upholding.

Throughout *Spring Snow* we see Kiyoaki as both a catalyst for the wider decline of tradition and as a staunch protector of its more magnanimous values, a collective/cultural and private/

individual tension that is not only Kiyoaki's tragedy but that of Japan. He, like several subsequent figures in *The Sea of Fertility*, is an active hero consigned to become only a passive vessel within a broader national, then cosmic, enterprise of despair (though the extent of this passivity, and its negative repercussions, remains open to doubt and extensive reinterpretation).

Within his own family Kiyoaki is a black sheep, a toxic elegant thorn in the coarse but freshly soaped hand of his family. He is alienated but exceptional – as romantic heroes need to be – fated to violate the proprieties and expectations of his kinfolk. Having been sent away from home at a young age to learn the manners of a gentleman from an authentic aristocratic family, albeit one on the wane, Kiyoaki is now in effect an orphan, an outsider cumbersomely reassimilated back into a world where he is emotionally, ethically, and intellectually estranged from his parents. Quasi-orphan amid the parvenues, he is doubly false, a bogus progeny in a phoney family, a sham son within a pretentious, dishonest household – but do these twin falsities cancel each other out, making him true?

Kiyoaki's orphan-like status confirms the fairy-tale atmosphere *Spring Snow* emanates. This exquisite but menacing world is further enhanced by memories of the ominous initiation ceremony shown to us early in the narrative. At this rite for his adolescence, known as his 'Otachimachi' or 'divination ritual' and held on 17 August 1909 when he was fifteen, the hitherto hidden moon suddenly appeared to cast its reflection into a basin of water, predicting the boy's future.

Although this was theoretically a good omen, Kiyoaki was immediately thrown into doubt, for contentment is but fleeting, future joy always in debt to the happiness of the past, which can never be recaptured. Like his creator Mishima, for Kiyoaki youth is a time of beauty and fruitfulness, adulthood of ugliness, deceit, and decay; yet even amid the bounties of youth, he is trapped by the certainty of its future corrosion and deterioration. Indeed, it is when this family memory of the initiation ceremony is discussed at their dinner table that mention is made of Satoko's rejection of a marriage offer, part of a sequence of events that will lead inexorably to the novel's tragic denouement. In *Spring Snow*, like all good fairy tales, time and fate, past, present, and future, are intimately, inescapably, interlinked.

Kiyoaki is an idealist, a romantic, even a fantasist, absorbed and controlled by the feeling that the indefinable, electric nature of existence which one feels so overwhelmingly in one's youth is vanishing moment by moment, second by second: 'like a leather bag filled with water, there was a little hole, and it seemed to him that he could hear time leaking from it, drop by drop.' Like many a Mishimian hero, and as his friend Honda will discover in the tetralogy's subsequent novels, especially *The Temple of Dawn*, Kiyoaki yearns for the impossible, to shape the world according to his own tragically imperfected and unfeasible ideals.

That yearning is for a dreadfully, unreasonably, beautiful love – a love that is exclusive, superior, romantic, circumscribed by death in order to maintain its own apparent perfection. It is a selfish mission, a proud pursuit, one that will destroy itself and those around it in the egotistical, greedy energy of its quest. For Kiyoaki, the only valid purpose of life is emotion and commitment to love and beauty. Yet this line of reasoning and its obligation to perilous, even disingenuous, ideals will make the ambition his downfall. His quest is for true beauty in love, and although it is more authentic than the insincere beauty so many pursue, it remains an impossible ideal within the tainted world of reality.

That impossible ideal is, of course, the love between Kiyoaki and Satoko.

૨૬

Throughout his work, Mishima introduces darkness and ugliness to scenes of conventional beauty, especially those familiar from Japanese culture and history, and particularly those involving the juxtaposition of natural and human elements. This is not simply to desecrate tradition or inflict damage upon it; on the contrary, it heightens our awareness of the fragility of those customs and conventions, while also offering a potent illustration of the complex, often conflicting, way in which Mishima observed the world. The pivotal early scene in *Spring Snow* where we first meet Satoko contains one of these repellent, intimidating incursions, an intrusion which serves not only as a simple gloomy premonition but that underlines the 'fairy-tale and fantasy' nature of the narrative, the mythic nudge that corruption and death prowl amid the beauty and brightness of life.

The whole scene is a magnificent set piece of conventional Japanese imagery involving light and water, colours and shadows, as Honda and Kiyoaki go boating on the family's ornamental lake, one warm Sunday afternoon in the autumn of 1912. Sun, sky, and trees combine with the artificial design of the setting, the description of which employs a series of increasingly sinister omens and images, including snapping turtles, iron birds, and dark ripples. Crimson maple leaves abound as symbols of danger, lust, and desire, red flags of warning to match Kiyoaki's progressively more pessimistic thoughts amid the dazzling splendour of the backdrop.

Into this scene come a group of women, including Kiyoaki's mother, a visiting abbess, and Satoko herself, the breathtakingly beautiful twenty-year-old daughter of a count. Initially, Satoko's mystery and beauty are enhanced by the vitality and vibrancy of her richly embroidered blue kimono, which is conspicuous against the more subdued colours of her companions. She is compared to the transparent, translucent sky after sunrise, her exquisite garments intimately connected to images of dawn which, in *Spring Snow*, are a persistent evocation of love and desire. Red maple leaves re-enter the scene, silently offering their warning like persistent musical motifs.

Kiyoaki has known Satoko for most of his life, since hers was the declining noble family who adopted him as a boy (giving their future illicit romance the auxiliary quiver of a quasi-incestuous liaison). Their childhood friendship has curdled, however, into the mutual indifference and submerged feelings of late adolescence and early maturity. At first, Kiyoaki does not recognize Satoko, fantasizing that the nape of her neck reminds him of the princess for whom he once acted as page. But then reality must encroach upon the mythical magic of one's past, and Satoko is revealed as something more apparently mundane, merely an irritation to be met with Kiyoaki's disdain.

Before long the air and tension of the day are broken by the discovery of a dead black dog blocking the waterfall in the garden. Although death has already been a pervasive feature of the text, the way in which it disrupts the largely harmonious beauty of the scene, just as it literally interrupts the melodious flow of the stream (and becomes inescapably linked to the relationship between Satoko and Kiyoaki), bestows it a sinister power. Yet the encounter with the canine's carcass, and its role in the narrative, is not merely an omen of future tragedy but a crucial threshold the active hero Kiyoaki must cross in his pursuit of love. Since his quest for an idealized love is an emotional rather than literal journey, Kiyoaki's movement in the text is fairly static – no setting forth to boldly conquer mountains, monsters, or dwarves – but Mishima is nonetheless keen to include motifs familiar from countless myths and legends which function as representative markers for him to traverse.

The dog is an early test, and one Kiyoaki fails since he is too self-conscious to mention the discovery, too unwilling as well to break the generally happy mood of the party, who themselves are trying to ignore the gruesome finding. It is as if the hero Siegfried has timidly whistled past the dragon on his way through the forest, instead of stopping to fight it. Satoko, however, has none of Kiyoaki's misgivings, plainly pointing the corpse out to the others and upsetting his pride in the process. Dumbfounded by her swiftness of conduct, as well as this apparently unfeminine behaviour, Kiyoaki is intimidated by the elegance and straightforwardness of her actions, compared to his cowardice. It is a trial he fails, but it remains a crucial staging post on his amorous quest – one which, like all good fairy tales, offers revelation even where it does not provide reward.

It becomes clear that Kiyoaki is obsessed by Satoko, and that Satoko loves him, though she is unable to directly express her feelings given the proprieties of her gender and culture. Kiyoaki's reticence is more connected to his own general sense of wounded honour and self-respect as well as his history of being admired for his looks; he instinctively rejects any displays of affection or intimacy (with Satoko, and others). Writing her a disordered, insulting letter, full of personal and broader misogyny, its anger a bid to subdue his increasing emotional torment, Kiyoaki attempts to assert dominance but succeeds only in confusing himself, and the situation, further.

When Satoko is tendered a marriage proposal from an imperial prince, Kiyoaki claims indifference, but the proposal is a key, and perhaps ultimate, threshold he must negotiate in his emotional quest, introducing as it does a fundamental, fateful dynamic into their relationship. Having repeatedly snubbed Satoko himself, he must now regard her, in fairy-tale fashion, as impervious, untouchable, verboten – and the fulfilment of his pursuit of an impossible ideal of love. In Imperial Japan, betrothal to a prince was not merely a matter of private feeling but a sacrament connected to affairs of state. Violation of this contract would be a spiritual as well as political transgression with consequences far beyond individual lives, devastating the families connected with it and potentially creating waves that would become tsunamis through the course of Japanese history.

Dreams play a significant role in *Spring Snow*, as portents and conduits, so it is unsurprising that Kiyoaki experiences one just as he learns about Satoko's engagement. He has a vision of travelling down a dark corridor, with a door at the end securely fastened by a golden padlock: suddenly, with horrific noises like the grinding of giant teeth, it opens, causing a 'metallic rasp [to echo] in his ears.' There is a clear sexual connotation to the dream, with its phallic, yonic, and penetrative imagery, the gleaming padlock Satoko's now forbidden flesh, but the obstruction and its security device are also key to the next stage of Kiyoaki's emotional journey, one where sex and death are intimately entwined. The quest is alluring not simply because of its sexual promise but also due to its attendant morbidity.

Spring Snow, and *The Sea of Fertility* more generally, is a magnificent maze of prophesy, doubling, premonition, and repetition, aspects which inform both its structure and its themes, all enhancing the mythical and metaphysical qualities of the text. Accordingly, as Kiyoaki and Satoko embark on an affair, archetypal folk- and fairy-tale features of the narrative mount. 'The Dream of the Golden Padlock', as we could call it, might be straight out of the Brothers Grimm. Not only is there an explicit and dangerous royal prohibition which must be breached, but, by directing the orphan Kiyoaki to his illicit encounters with his de facto sister Satoko, Honda becomes the hero's devoted and trustworthy helper (joining Hamlet's Horatio, Don Quixote's Sancho Panza, Frodo's Sam). There is also Kiyoaki's tutor and attendant, Iinuma, a bitter, resentful figure, slightly sinister, and a reluctant accomplice in the first stage of his master's forbidden affiliation (the false friend to Honda's faithful one). He himself conducts an illicit liaison, with a maid from Satoko's household, but is dismissed from his post upon its discovery – it being necessary, under the conditions of a fairy tale, to remove him from the action in order to leave the stage clear for the hero and heroine.[128]

There are also the two Thai princes who stay with Kiyoaki and his family while studying in Japan. An exotic double act, they add a further element of colour and mystery to the story,

---

128 A reactionary figure, Iinuma will, in a literary form of rebirth, reappear to play a key role in the next book of the tetralogy, *Runaway Horses*, where he is a prominent right-wing writer whose son, Isao, becomes embroiled in a terrorist plot against the government – and whom Honda believes to be the reincarnation of Kiyoaki.

while also providing eerie auguries of what is to come for the main characters. One of them is in love with the other's sister, and her untimely death – foreshadowed in fairy-tale terms by the loss of the emerald ring she gave her beloved, a ring intimated to have magical, transmigratory properties – compels the princes to return home, again emptying the stage for Kiyoaki and Satoko. Finally, there is Satoko's ageing female maid, Tadeshina (who herself had a forbidden liaison with Satoko's father). Controlling those around her for the benefit of the lovers, she takes on the magical qualities of a fairy godmother or the more menacing characteristics of a witch.

As Kiyoaki's and Satoko's love affair gets underway, the dramatic tension between generic forms reaches a new height. The reality of the relationship, and the two participants' feelings, are shown in an authentic, highly persuasive, and convincing manner, yet with a narrative both pervaded by, and constantly threatening to collapse entirely into, actual fantasy or fairy tale. But then, of course, what love affair does not engender such intoxicating concoctions, mixing reality with illusion, whim, and fancy? The setting of *Spring Snow*, with aristocrats and princes, ornate lakes and carriage rides in the snow, presents an exclusive, dreamlike realm of a bygone era, but the emotions it contains are as contemporary, real – and potentially mundane – as the most perfunctory amorous liaison. It is this reality, as much as the fantasy, which bonds us to Kiyoaki and Satoko, while linking them to other couples from folk and fairy tale, as well as to any other literary lovers who faced their own negotiations with borders and barriers.

For all the fairy-tale and knowingly literary aspects to *Spring Snow*, which borrows from and refers to Western as well as Asian traditions (at times we feel in one of the great nineteenth-century Russian or French novels, especially *Anna Karenina* or *Madame Bovary*), its philosophical attachment to the East is a vital part of not only its deeper meanings but its rich poetic textures. Perhaps nowhere is this more apparent than during the scenes of the summer vacation at Kiyoaki's family villa on the coast in Kamakura, just south of Tokyo, which lie at the literal and symbolic centre of the novel. Here, in both narrative and abstract terms, we are given an extended discussion of the Buddhist concept of ālaya, of which *The Sea of Fertility* generally is a vast exemplification.

Ālaya is a Sanskrit word denoting a storehouse, for within the ālaya were the karmic seeds that contained the effects of all deeds, both good and evil, and which are the origin of the great chain of causation throughout the cosmos. The Japanese word used to render this term is 'kura', and its kanji character (倉) appears in the place name 'Kamakura' (鎌倉), making this city an appropriate location for the metaphysical discussions which enrich the novel and anticipate the succeeding volumes of the cycle.[129]

In Kamakura clouds form a constantly shifting presence in the text, shadowing the fluctuating nature of human life as it journeys through time and the cosmos, reminding us that what we take for granted may soon disappear. The lives of the four young men – Kiyoaki, Honda, and the two Thai princes – on vacation are already swiftly changing, in ways that they are only

---

129 Along with Kyoto and Nara, Kamakura is also one of the ancient capitals of Japan.

vaguely aware of and certainly cannot predict. Above them, the clouds alter and evolve, unfolding their tragic drama, while the sea persists in its own constant process of never-ending change.

Toward the end of the trip, one of the Thai princes learns that his beloved and the sister of the other, the Princess Ying Chan, has died.[130] Plunged into violent grief 'as powerful as a tropical cloudburst', they cannot, being human, accept this universal principle of change, events vacillating and unstable like ballooning summer clouds in the sky. Our instinctive tendency is to attach ourselves to things and people, but in the process we cause suffering since we treat them as if they were fixed and permanent. People live; people die. Lovers meet; lovers part. Clouds merge; clouds dissolve.

On the shore at Kamakura, Kiyoaki, Honda, and the Siamese princes are both literally and symbolically between two worlds, between life and death, light and dark. Trapped on the coasts of time and space, the blue-green sea is shown to be both a jade jewel and a violent void, solid and hollow, a realm of creation and destruction. It can be shallow and playful; it can also be the deep, dense mass of the open ocean. Everything is subject to change and difference – even Buddhism itself, a trans-oceanic philosophy. From its formidable but remote sources in South and Southeast Asia, the teachings which eventually reach the shorelines of Japan are said to be diminished, polished and refined far away from their rougher and more mystical origins (which will become a key narrative and thematic concern of *The Temple of Dawn*).

Kamakura accordingly becomes a crucial threshold for the novel, and the tetralogy at large, for *The Sea of Fertility* is a work

---

130 Ying Chan shares the name of the Thai princess who will infiltrate *The Temple of Dawn*.

about change: in human lives, in the fate of a nation, and in the much vaster span of the cosmos. Not only do the princes hear of Ying Chan's death at Kamakura, but it is here that Kiyoaki's and Satoko's destinies will be irrevocably decided. Honda arranges for Satoko to be smuggled out of Tokyo – ironically but auspiciously via that symbol of American mass production, the Model T Ford – to visit Kiyoaki for a single night of passion in Kamakura. As they make love on the shoreline under the moon, a beached fishing boat looms over them amid their ecstasies, becoming a phantom-like presence, part of a darker world, the monarchy of night, the cosmic ocean of death.

It is suggested that this is the occasion on which Satoko becomes pregnant, a shift in their already transgressive relationship that will make it irreversibly tragic, though it will also consecrate their love's authenticity in a false world. The immense leitmotifs of Mishima's own life and work, love and death are bound together in an unholy but unbreakable union: 'Just beyond the merest flicker of time there boomed a monstrous roar of negation.'[131]

Earlier in the summer, watching Kiyoaki sleeping on the sand, Honda had noticed for the first time the three moles on his friend's side that will become the ominous insignia of reincarnation on the bodies of Kiyoaki's successors in *Runaway Horses*, *The Temple of Dawn*, and *The Decay of the Angel*. As befits their transmigratory function, the moles are linked to the vast voids of sea and sky, since not only does their alignment match that of Orion's Belt in the chasm of the heavens, but initially

---

131 A Liebestod, the imagery and metaphysics carry Buddhist sensibilities, and are also comparable to Richard Wagner's musikdrama *Tristan und Isolde* (1865), a work of art with a considerable debt to Eastern religions and which Mishima had employed as a soundtrack to the film version (1966) of his short story 'Patriotism' (1960).

Honda mistakes them for grains of sand dredged up from the depths of the marine abyss. Physical markers, the moles are also spiritual messengers, cosmic signals.

Shortly after Satoko's visit, the Siamese princes learn of the princess's death, and a week later, Kiyoaki and Honda watch them depart for Thailand aboard a huge cargo-passenger liner from Yokohama Port, the cosmic principle of perpetual change in full operation. Kiyoaki waves goodbye to the princes and to his youth, both now about to vanish beneath the horizon. A few weeks later, in the autumn, Satoko observes that the lovers' own destiny is imminent, advancing with relentless haste: their path, she says, is not a road but a pier, ending 'someplace where the sea begins'. This path can only lead to the void of death. The phantom vessel which loomed over their lovemaking on the beach now seems ready to take them on a journey to their own places of darkness, Satoko's a symbolic one, Kiyoaki's unbearably literal.

So in the end, of course, tragedy comes home. Coerced into an abortion at Osaka, and after an attempt by her parents to force the imperial marriage to go ahead, instead Satoko cuts her hair and relinquishes the world, entering a nunnery, the lair of the abbess with whom we first met the now denuded princess in the early chapters of the book.[132] In February 1914, a fraught Kiyoaki attempts to visit her there, in mounting desperation trying to traverse a further heroic/mythic threshold. But he is denied access,

---

132 In 1965, Mishima made a research pilgrimage to the nunnery attached to the Buddhist temple complex of Enshō-ji, near Nara, an ancient capital of Japan, located some five hundred kilometres west of Tokyo and just to the east of Osaka. This remote convent was to be the ideal setting for the climax of the novel (though Mishima changed it from a Rinzai Zen temple to a Hossō one, to better fit in with his cycle's particular moral and metaphysical panoramas, while also changing its name from Enshō-ji to Gesshū-ji).

eventually contracting an illness due to his repeated exposure in the snow as he traipses from his inn to the convent and back again, an act of rhythmic atonement, contrition, and despair.

Mishima's prose during these passages of Kiyoaki's penance is extraordinary, reaching new pinnacles of beauty and desolation. Kiyoaki's fever worsens as he makes his futile pilgrimages through the landscape, his memories of Satoko and their affair, especially its romantic rickshaw rides in winter, mingling with his experience of the spring snow falling around him. His world becomes ethereal, dreamlike, hypnotic and unreal, the true realm of fairy tale. The snow and clouds, the intermittent pale sun, the bare cherry trees – all seem to merge into one, light and white converging as the atoning Kiyoaki is finally able to purge the darkness and guilt in his soul.

Honda comes looking for him, trying to establish a final meeting with Satoko to save his friend's life, but the abbess refuses any reunion.[133] It is a scene haunted by the ghostly presence of a small wooden box decorated with a picture of a pallid boy chasing a red-and-purple butterfly, the child suggestive of Kiyoaki, the insect the elusive Satoko. The friends leave that night for Tokyo. Even amid death, Kiyoaki's appearance maintains his tragic beauty, his face knotted in pain but still striking, intense suffering instilling it with 'an extraordinary character, carving lines into it that give it the austere dignity of a bronze mask'. The mortally sick Kiyoaki relays to Honda a final dream where he sees his faithful companion again, 'beneath the falls', the nine tumbling stages of the waterfall in his father's garden (which was so prophetically blocked by the dead dog at the beginning of the

---

133 Satoko will return at the very end of the cycle, in a deeply moving and disorientating reappearance.

novel). Two days later, aged twenty, he dies, his tragic destiny fulfilled as he crosses the final heroic threshold: from life into the mystery of death.

It is a severe but exquisite conclusion, the contrition haunting, the guilt, grief, and sense of loss overwhelming, an ending that leaves the stage ideally set for the next instalment of the cycle, with the exhilarating expectation of reincarnation's transcendent power.

The belated and unlawful nature of Kiyoaki's relationship with Satoko corresponds to the mythic hero's psychosexual desire for an impossible love, one that can only occur once the object of his affections becomes truly unavailable. Like *Spring Snow* itself, Kiyoaki and Satoko's love affair is also an interrogation of time and history, one which communicates a number of deeper political and philosophical patterns that both this novel and *The Sea of Fertility* explore, with individual/personal and communal/ national repercussions, as well as the wider cosmic insinuations of the tetralogy.

Such is Kiyoaki's destiny. By challenging both the emperor and the traditions and institutions he represents, Kiyoaki accelerates the deterioration of the nation and its bonding mesh of complex hierarchical structures. The liaison promises to further the decline, in the case of Satoko's, or halt the rise, in the case of Kiyoaki's, of the two very different aristocratic families connected with the scandal of their affair. Kiyoaki's natural family, with its recently acquired money, is more immune to the mud of the disgrace – commerce and industry, in the new century, being more crudely resilient. Satoko's family's older wealth and accumulated grace are a more fragile commodity. (Given that Kiyoaki himself is representative of a certain form of Japanese tradition and grace, there is a tragic irony to his role in perpetrating its own destruction.)

There is nothing ironic, however, when Kiyoaki's actions are viewed through a more personal and psychological, even existential, rather than merely collective and cultural, lens. The relationship only appeals to him when it promises to generate a wretched splendour, tragic beauty being of more interest to him than any conventional form of contentment, which he pessimistically comprehends as bound to be transient in any case. From the outset of our engagement with him, the pardine Kiyoaki has been a fated, nihilistic presence, disconsolate and distrustful, oozing an elegant gloom. And this has not gone unnoticed among his close acquaintances, with Honda recognizing that it was the impossibility of the association with the betrothed Satoko that captivated him, drawing him into its poisonous cosmic vortex.

Marriage, children, grandchildren – a life of conventionality and respectability would have irritated Kiyoaki, scratching against the polished ethics and aesthetics of a mind that observed the world through a dark glass of death and decay. Satoko's engagement to the prince condemned their chances of orthodox love, thus arousing his ardour for the unattainable, unconventional kind he yearned for. Selfishly seeking an impossible love to fulfil his own sense of personal destiny, the leopard Kiyoaki rendered his princess Satoko the innocent victim marred by the lethal claws of his ego.

Paced to perfection, and in full control of its mythical, romantic atmosphere, *Spring Snow* never confuses the melancholic with the mawkish, recognizing the dynamic power and redemptive energy of nostalgia. As his creator knew, Kiyoaki could not, on his own, revive the barren wilderness of contemporary Japan which Mishima lamented. But his life, and death, perhaps provide something more fragile, more fleeting, more elusive – more valuable too. Kiyoaki's idealism and egotism, married to his melancholy, wistfulness, and romanticism, produce an image, and it can only be an image, of a more elegant age, one which, for all its spectral flaws and foibles, exists in affirmative, mythological distinction to the emptiness of modernity that was developing as Japan reasserted itself in the 1950s and '60s. It is a beautiful, helpless attempt to connect with and rejuvenate an earlier, perhaps more passionate and formidable period of Japanese history that Mishima felt had been vaporized into global uniformity.

Though he dies in the final line of *Spring Snow*, Kiyoaki's influence will endure both in the tantalizing prospect of his reincarnation – surely the decisive heroic/mythic trait – in each subsequent novel of *The Sea of Fertility*, and through the energizing effect his life has had upon his friend Honda, with whom we will spend the rest of the cycle. Although never dull, across the span of *Spring Snow* Honda's hitherto more humdrum and scholastic mind has been brightened by the beauty and luminous desire of his friend's impossible quest. Honda has been shown the possibilities of the fertility and abundance of existence, even if he himself will struggle with such vitality and riches when he encounters them, remaining a crucial but impotent figure: probing, observing, chronicling.

In *Spring Snow*, Mishima is a god, resurrecting a vanished world with assurance, skill, and heart-rending grandeur. Yet he does so not only to revitalize the past but to give a context and impetus to the arc and spin of the rest of his tetralogy.

The journey has begun.

Runaway Horses

BARE FEET ON HOT SAND

One of the most enduring literary myths is Hamlet's delay. Any number of moral, political, theatrical, social, sexual, and psychological theories have been given down the centuries (and, indeed, by Hamlet himself) to explain why he hesitates in exacting revenge upon his murderous uncle. The prince of Denmark has been turned, perhaps not entirely unreasonably, into history's archetypal ditherer, the epitome of the overthinker whose actions are weighed down by the brilliance of their own brain (and now the decisive symbol of disaffected youth and gloomy solipsism, inspiration to countless artists and adolescents).

Yet this character is far more practical and combative than we have usually imagined. Once Hamlet has established Claudius's guilt,[134] he immediately[135] tries to kill the king (only to find he has slain his counsellor Polonius instead) before eventually, at the cost of his own life, achieving his retribution. In a delicious, calculated irony, this notoriously cerebral character concludes the drama he intellectually dominates amid physical activity, indeed among the clichés of stage action and Elizabethan revenge theatre: swordfights and poisoned cups. For Shakespeare, Hamlet was the ideal Renaissance prince: resourceful and possessed of a dazzling mind on top of being nimble with a blade – master of wordplay and weapon play.

Mishima found Hamlet fascinating precisely because of this unity between thinking and doing, between the mental and martial arts.[136] After all, Mishima was one of the foremost writers of his generation, dedicated to a life of language and ideas; but he also pursued an array of physical activities – kendo, karate, bodybuilding, and political agitation. Moreover, much of his work, both fiction and non-fiction, blends the two, both in subject matter and style: for all their psychological and philosophical depth, his novels also contain some extraordinarily visceral, sensuous prose. For Mishima, mind and body were two opposing but interconnected means of existence – playing,

---

134 After the staging of *Hamlet*'s play-within-a-play, *The Murder of Gonzago / The Mousetrap*, in III.ii.

135 Hamlet's hesitation in III.iii, when Claudius is at prayer in the chapel, has a direct theological and soteriological foundation: he reasons (III.iii.73–95) that to kill the king at prayer would send him straight to heaven (a Protestant idea), thus thwarting the desired punishment and revenge.

136 As we witness in his dealings with the players visiting Elsinore, Hamlet is also a fine actor, writer, and director, highly skilled – like Mishima – in the multifaceted workings of the theatre. (Cf. *Hamlet*, II.ii.388–405; 476–78; III.ii.1–43.)

performing, wrestling, working together in his life and art. Each was seductive, persistent, creating a vital network.

In *Spring Snow*, the first part of *The Sea of Fertility*, Mishima had refashioned aspects of Hamlet's romantic introspection via his hero Kiyoaki, while distilling the Dane's more rational and scholarly features into his friend Honda (who also acts in a Horatio-like capacity). For the second instalment of the tetralogy, *Runaway Horses* (奔馬, 'Honba', 1969), Honda maintains his brain, while Kiyoaki's apparent reincarnation, Isao, takes on the more glamorous, weapon-wielding, and man-of-action side to Shakespeare's prince. Here Mishima scrutinizes in chilling detail a figure of passionate (and problematic) patriotism who also has eerie echoes of Macbeth, Coriolanus, and Henry V.

Runaway Horses carries a relatively straightforward plot – a young fanatic in 1930s Japan plots to overthrow the establishment but is thwarted and put on trial – yet has a structural complexity and intricate sense of history which belie the surface simplicity of its narrative. It contains extended imbedded texts that, though they can feel a distraction or digression, work as adroit strategic and rhetorical devices. They also deepen the work's emotional textures and poetic communication with the past, both from its own perspective (it was written in the mid-1960s) and our own, when debates over nationalism and patriotism are once again a constant of politics the world over (if ever they went away).

The novel explores the early years of the Shōwa era (1926–1989), with significant glances back to the Meiji period (1868–1912) via the protagonist Isao's increasing obsession with an 1876 insurrection which he seeks to emulate. From here Mishima is able to dissect a range of lifelong preoccupations, including youth versus age, the present versus the past, purity versus corruption, language versus action, reason versus passion, hierarchy versus equality, and Shintoism versus Buddhism, as well as the function of good leadership and the consequences of bad governance.

Runaway Horses maintains the high standard of Mishima's later prose – exhibiting a verbal fluency to match the physical dexterity of its hero – while developing the *Sea of Fertility* cycle in daring, confrontational, and troubling directions, probing the limits and possibilities of a pure and unadulterated Japan, exploring the clash between cultural amalgamation and a sometimes belligerent nostalgia. It is a work that inspires both admiration and a sense of confusion and frustration. After the romantic tragedy of *Spring Snow*, for many readers *Runaway Horses* can be a hard book to love – in its nihilism, in its embrace of death, in its confrontation with (and occasional rewriting of) history, and given the relationship of the hero's alarming anger and extremism with that of the author himself.

Far more than simply a political roman à thèse, however, at the book's centre lies the fascinating dynamic between Honda and Isao, one character attracting us via his capacity for rational thought, for compassion and logic; the other seducing us with his desire, his devotion, his danger – his destructive clarity and concentration. Most human life is a battle between these two competing forces, as we try to balance the Apollonian and Dionysian sides to our nature. We all possess both to varying degrees, and *Runaway Horses* explores this struggle in exhilarating new ways.

The Shinpūren, a radical, xenophobic, and fanatically superstitious organization made up of Shinto extremists and former samurai, were strongly opposed to the westernization and de-feudalization of Japan that had taken place under the Meiji government in the 1870s. Any foreign influence was abhorred: from Christian missionaries and electricity cables to trousers, trains, and Buddhist priests (though Buddhism had, of course, been in Japan since the sixth century AD).[137] They would never walk under telegraph wires, would touch banknotes only with chopsticks, and carried salt with them at all times, in order to perform impromptu purification rituals should they encounter a foreigner or other 'pollutant'. They were also infuriated by the recent loss of many of their class privileges, including the right to bear a sword, along with the income that went with such privileges.

For these extremists the final straw came when word reached them that the emperor was planning an overseas trip. Accordingly, on 24 October 1876, under the leadership of Tomoo Ōtaguro, a Shinto priest, they took part in an uprising in Kumamoto, on the large south-western island of Kyūshū. In what became known as the Shinpūren Rebellion, the agitators launched a surprise attack on the imperial army barracks and succeeded in killing dozens of soldiers and officials before the upheaval was quashed the following morning, with most of the surviving insurgents either being arrested and executed or killing themselves via seppuku.

The Shinpūren Rebellion was far from being an isolated occurrence but was one of many so-called shizoku ('warrior family') uprisings during the early years of the Meiji period as the new emperor opened Japan to the wider world and sought to modernize the country. Indeed, in one form or another such attitudes and disturbances persisted long into the twentieth and

---

137 The first railway service in Japan, between Tokyo and Yokohama, had begun on 12 September 1872.

even twenty-first centuries as nationalists and other right-wing groups strove to maintain Japan's cultural and historical identity (debates over which have often revolved around the status and function of the emperor, an abiding concern for Mishima himself).

One such incident took place on 15 May 1932 (the date giving the event its historical name). Following the London Naval Treaty (1930), which limited the size of global aquatic armed forces, many junior officers sought to overthrow the Japanese government and replace it with a martial leadership. Ties were made with other ultranationalists who similarly pursued a 'Shōwa Restoration' with the intention of reinstating powers to the emperor, abolishing the more liberal policies of the representative Taishō democracy, and even assassinating many significant business leaders (the zaibatsu), whom the rebels regarded as abominable promoters of capitalism.[138]

Bizarrely, the plotters intended to kill not only Prime Minister Tsuyoshi Inukai but English comic actor and filmmaker Charlie Chaplin, who was in Japan as a guest of the premier, in the hope that the murder of a Hollywood movie star would provoke war with the United States and necessitate implementation of the renegades' wider demands. Chaplin, providentially, was watching a sumo wrestling contest at the time and escaped unhurt; Inukai, however, was assassinated, along with several other prominent officials, while grenades were hurled at the Mitsubishi Bank headquarters and several electricity substations were damaged. Their actions complete, the participants simply hailed a taxi and surrendered themselves at the nearest police station.

---

138 Like Mishima, of course, as ferocious opponents of capitalism they were by no means automatically supporters of communism, as has often been mistakenly presumed. If anything, they considered the followers of Marx and Engels far worse.

The fallout was hardly peaceful. At their trial, the insurgents used the platform to proclaim their undying loyalty to the emperor and awakened popular sympathy by demanding governmental and economic reform. Huge public support helped lead to lenient sentences for the accused, destabilizing the already weak rule of law and bolstering the rise of Japanese militarism, ultimately leading to the 26 February Incident (1936), and thence the Second World War.

This is the fundamental backdrop to *Runaway Horses* – its atmosphere, mood, and theme – and in fact Mishima opens his book in the aftermath of the 15 May Incident itself. Set between June 1932 and December the following year, the novel follows Isao, a student at his father's 'Academy of Patriotism', a right-wing institution that imparts traditional Japanese values, rebuffing the modernizing influences of foreign cultures. His father, who happens to be Iinuma, Kiyoaki's tutor from *Spring Snow*, has taught him in the samurai code, and Isao excels in kendo and other martial arts and is highly regarded by his peers because of the honest, unironic purity of his spirit.

A fictional creation but akin to many youthful right-wing reactionaries who crowded 1930s Japan, and further instilled with Mishima's particular ingredients for a great hero of action, Isao is authentically, and exceptionally, dedicated to a life realizing his values. Skilled in physical arts, decorous to authority figures, meticulous in his loyalty to Shinto ritual, Isao is an intense but charismatic figure, a born leader committed to every gesture, every nuance, every word. As the novel progresses, this active hero will instigate a plot to – on 3 December 1932 – depose members of the zaibatsu business conglomerates along with high-flying government figures who he believes have together besmirched the Japanese spirit[139] and betrayed the will of the emperor.

With heavy Mishimian irony, it is Isao's scrupulous obligation toward national customs and traditions that ultimately creates conflict with the more moderate conservative governing classes of Japan – including Iinuma, his own father, and that emblematic patriarch of the nation, the emperor himself, along with various military, legal, political, and corporate leaders. All these self-interested parties have been affected, even infected, by the processes of cooperation, compromise, and concession that decadent modern democracies must undergo. Thus Isao is betrayed by the very organizations he vows to revive and sustain: it transpires that his meticulous principles and standards are too deep-seated, too pure, for modernity, meaning his radical, though reactionary, activities are ordained to end only in frustration, capitulation, or catastrophe.

Captured and imprisoned before the coup can be carried out, Isao is put on trial but essentially exonerated of his crimes, which were at least patriotic, and released (with some assistance from Honda, who resigns as a judge in order to act as Isao's lawyer). Freed but furious, Isao tracks down the financier (at his weekend house on the coast) whom he believes to be the embodiment of modern Japan and executes him. With this symbolic fragment of his much wider aspirations realized, at the very end of *Runaway Horses* Isao then aims to complete the most cherished aspect of his ambitions: carrying out seppuku at

---

139   大和魂 or 'Yamato-damashii'.

the top of a cliff at dawn, paying homage to the sun and looking down upon the sparkling sea.

Unfortunately, in another layer of Mishimian irony, Isao is to be further betrayed, this time by the heavens and by his own efficiency. Although he finds his way to the ocean through rough country, he is too early, and it is still night:

The sun will not rise for some time ... and I can't afford to wait. There is no shining disk climbing upward. There is no noble pine to shelter me. Nor is there a sparkling sea.

He removes the remainder of his clothes and, hearing people pursuing him, thrusts his knife into his body, an excruciating act which creates the internal exploding sun behind his eyes that closes the book. (As with Kiyoaki in *Spring Snow*, Isao dies aged twenty, and in the novel's last line.)

Perhaps this exploding sun is a recompense for the solar disc lingering below the horizon, reimbursement for the denial of that noble pine and sparkling sea. But it is also a reminder that an 'ideal death', like any perfection, can only exist in the imagination. And this, surely, is one of the purposes of literature – especially since *Runaway Horses* is, for many, a fictional preparation for its creator's own imminent self-authored demise.

In dynamic parallel with this story of Isao, *Runaway Horses* reintroduces us to Honda, the law student whom we last saw in 1914 at the end of *Spring Snow* (when his school friend Kiyoaki died of pneumonia and a broken heart) and who will now dominate the remaining narrative of *The Sea of Fertility*, arguably making the tetralogy as much his story as it is those of the active heroes (Kiyoaki, Isao, Ying Chan, Tōru) who (re)join him in each instalment. In the eighteen years since *Spring Snow*, Honda has married and risen in his profession to become a junior associate judge at the Osaka Court of Appeals: 'I represent reason for the nation,' he ponders, a 'height upheld by logic, like a tower formed of steel girders.' As the narrative develops, however, through a series of encounters and semi-tangible signs he comes to believe Isao is the reincarnation of Kiyoaki, something both opposed to and curiously supported by his logical legal mind.

This perception, and the related realization that Isao is careering toward his own catastrophic early demise, form much of the delicate drive of the text, as Honda tries to save Isao from a premature death. Indeed it is this personal tension, even forceful friction, between two distinct characters that prevents *Runaway Horses* from descending to being merely a dry novel of ideas centred around political dogma which, regardless of a fascinating plot (in both senses), might otherwise be somewhat arid and repetitive. The reincarnation motif, too, as well as offering intense spiritual and metaphysical perspectives, also operates as a brilliant literary device, allowing Honda to maintain his friendship across the decades/books while also, in a probing reinterpretation of Wilde's *Dorian Gray*, preserving the textual energy of a youthful active hero.

At the end of *Spring Snow*, in an image of tender beauty, the dying Kiyoaki assured Honda that they would meet again, 'beneath the falls'. Early in the next volume of *The Sea of Fertility*, that promise/premonition suggests itself. Honda has been asked to give an address at a kendo tournament at Ōmiwa Shrine, Sakurai, an ancient sacred structure especially notable because it directly serves a nearby mountain, Mount Miwa, which is said to embody a deity, and is an indication of how many simple early Shinto shrines would have appeared.[140] After lunch, Honda climbs Miwa before descending to wash in the nearby Sanko Falls, where he notices many of the kendoists are already bathing in acts of ritual purification.

Their number includes the promising young athlete the chief priest had earlier pointed out: Isao, whose flawless grace and virile energy had captivated the competition (which Mishima describes with both the rousing excitement of a devoted fan and the cool insight of a practising expert). Closely inspecting the waterfalls in his capacity as a passive observer, which will continue throughout the cycle with severe personal consequences, Honda notices Isao has a line of three moles on his side, just as Kiyoaki did. He recalls his friend's parting words and is cast, like the reader, into a maze of memories and possibilities.

The novel, which hitherto slowly and simply unfolded before us like a flower welcoming the dawn, suddenly snaps into extraordinary life, pulling the fraught tragedy of *Spring Snow* into its orbit. Whatever our rational or logical doubts about the significance of Isao's moles, which Honda shares, as readers we are swept up in the literary prospect of Kiyoaki's rebirth even if we do not subscribe to the metaphysical one. Whether we were entranced or repelled by the lithe athlete who has been on show, with his furious talent and agile ferocity, we are now intrigued by his every move and utterance, as a possible return of the romantic hero we have grieved.

---

140 Most later Shinto shrines exist to specifically house ('enshrine') one or more kami, the deities of Shintoism.

Honda, and the novel, is at pains to ensure that Kiyoaki and Isao are shown to be both distinct and the same: distinct in order to represent different aspects of Japan, heroism, and Mishima's personality; the same so that they can connect the themes and events of *The Sea of Fertility*'s volumes across time, both operating as fiery, impulsive active heroes. So we have the waterfall and the telltale trio of moles, as well as the correct number of years since Kiyoaki's death and Isao's birth, along with particular occurrences that correspond to details in Kiyoaki's dream diary. But then we also have the crucial differences: Kiyoaki's refined grace, and its embodiment of an ancient, classical Japan, which diverges from the purity and ferocity of Isao, with their direct connections to martial pre-Meiji Japan, a world of samurai warriors and ritualized customs.

After a sleepless night listening to the frogs outside his hotel and half hallucinating about Kiyoaki, Honda attends the Saigusa Festival at Isagawa Shrine, Nara, the details of which – the light and lilies, drink and dancing – are all lovingly laid out in Mishima's scrupulous prose. Amid the throng and bustle, Honda meets Isao and his father, Iinuma, who is ageing terribly, beset by decades of distress, misfortune, and a choleric commitment to his causes as a right-wing personality. The more studious, reserved tutor of *Spring Snow* is now a talkative bore, a garrulous drag – Nigel Farage in a kimono – and Honda is lost in thoughts that Kiyoaki is here with him among the festive crowds. Reality and dream blur, like sea and sky at the horizon, and Honda, arch-protector of law and logic, starts to quake at the personal – and universal – implications if the reincarnation proves real.

Despite a heap of work he has to undertake that evening, the normally fastidious Honda rather rashly invites Isao and his father to dinner (one of the first signs that the composed, level-headed judge is falling under the thrall of Kiyoaki's posthumous influence, an obsession that will dominate his life). The meal is an opportunity to explore some details of the lost decades between *Spring Snow* and *Runaway Horses*, and various regrets and recriminations are expressed before, at the end, Isao lends Honda a copy of his favourite reading material: a pamphlet by Yamao Tsunanori called *The League of the Divine Wind*.

After the guests have left, and once again ignoring the pile of legal papers he needs to attend to, Honda sits down to read the booklet – as do we, for immediately *Runaway Horses* dissolves into a new text, the embedded book-within-a-book that is *The League of the Divine Wind*, a laudatory fiction about the ultranationalist samurai insurgents who struck the army in Kumamoto in October 1876, in the so-called Shinpūren Rebellion. Mishima does not short-change us here, for chapter nine is some fifty pages long and represents one-eighth of the entire novel.

Burdened by jingoistic creeds and sometimes tiresome rhetoric, this protracted text has caused consternation since its inception. It is an extended interpolation, an imitation of various apologetic texts, and its language replicates political propaganda down the ages, full of unnecessary redundancies which undermine, rather than enhance, the writing as a work of literature: narrative duplications; repeated points of view; two-dimensional characters; a crude, black-and-white perspective of complex issues; a certain circularity of direction. Although it is hardly difficult to follow, it can be tiresome to read, since we not only miss the lithe elegance of Mishima's usual prose but wonder how necessary it is for us to be so consumed by this journey into the past.

Its purpose can seem rather curious at first, since on the one hand Mishima is clearly parodying propaganda and poor writing, yet on the other he wants us to at least be convinced by elements of the story so that we will believe how inspired his hero, Isao, has been by the text. Although peculiar over the wider course of the novel, this delicate tension tends to work, since it deepens the texture of the book and our interest in Isao himself, while directly showcasing the world(s) Mishima's work is confronting. Even allowing for the parodic/propagandistic nature of the text, we are mystically transported into the realm of early Meiji Japan: a double chronological framing, since *The League of the Divine Wind*'s parent novel *Runaway Horses* is itself a work of historical fiction written from the perspective of the mid-1960s.

Although we might scoff at the relative literary poverty of *The League of the Divine Wind*, ridiculing its naivety and artlessness, its function in *Runaway Horses* is perhaps even more subtle than merely furnishing the historical background. Just as Honda has been distracted by it from his legal work, to an extent the embedded text diverts us from Isao, whose developing persona is gradually revealed to us. By sneering at *The League of the Divine Wind* we are sidetracked from the sinister young man and his extreme points of view; these, by comparison, will seem much more coherent. From chapter ten on, we are to become increasingly absorbed by Isao and his ideology, so the pre-emptive imposition of the latter's cruder version in chapter nine automatically allows Isao's exacting belief system to (rather disingenuously) appear more refined, more reasoned, more sound.

It is a technique which certainly won't work on all readers, but it does have an intriguingly mollifying effect on how we perceive Isao, appeasing many reflexive disapprovals of the character (though, it has to be said, the *League of the Divine Wind* chapter is still probably slightly too long). By offering a linguistically cruder version of Isao's beliefs before they emerge in the surface narrative, Mishima's embedded text works to deceptively moderate elements of his hero's beliefs as they appear, a form of textual shock treatment, prejudicing the reader more favourably toward the more equivocal and obstruse Isao. The long implanted chapter is a deliberate, defensive contrast, intended to spotlight the subtleties, opacities, and intricacies of the rest of the novel. The reality, of course, is that *The League of the Divine Wind* represents a direct ideological spur for Isao, who forms a rebel faction he designates Shōwa Divine Wind and strives to emulate his Meiji forebears.

Almost immediately after the *League of the Divine Wind* chapter, Mishima inserts another pre-emptive embedded text, which serves to both strategically anticipate and rhetorically represent many of the reader's own concerns about the hero's extreme ideology, paradoxically working to push us toward the protagonist's outlook. Having read the book, Honda writes Isao a long letter, split into two basic sections. First, he outlines his own experiences, including some references to Kiyoaki, and warns the young man about undertaking any heedless actions, about the treacherous allure of romantic fantasy and myth out of touch with contemporary reality. Second, after confessing a degree of admiration for the patriotic heroes, Honda delineates several criticisms of *The League of the Divine Wind*, pointing out absurdities and inconsistencies within the text. Although we may be fond of Honda by now, he is necessarily an unheroic establishment figure, and his words begin to grate, sounding like the chastisement of a schoolmaster, or the condescending rebukes of a magistrate in sentencing.

The author of *Lolita* (1955) undertook a similar literary technique. By having the absurdly entitled psychologist 'John

Ray, Jr., PhD'[141] narrate a false foreword to Humbert's memoirs, with its pompous appeal to parents, social workers, and educators to bring up 'a better generation in a safer world', Nabokov parodically predicts many readers' own moral concerns with the book in their hands. This subtly pushes those same readers into Humbert's embrace: as discerning, independently minded students, scholars, and bookworms, we do not like to be told what to think or feel. Moreover, Dr Ray's simplistic analysis seems crude, invalid, unconvincing, his psychological explanations rudimentary and unsophisticated. We distrust him and are automatically impelled toward the perilous, alluring first-person narration of the rogue Humbert. It is a high-risk strategy, not least given the novel's subject matter – child abuse and sexual assault – but one which works effectively in the long run while also heightening our affection and concern for Lolita herself as Humbert's victim.

In *The Sea of Fertility*, although Honda's character will darken in the final two novels of the tetralogy, *The Temple of Dawn* and *The Decay of the Angel*, the figure of *Spring Snow* and *Runaway Horses* is an essentially upright, if sometimes intentionally lacklustre, one. He is, after all, a court judge. As we have said, he is an observer, a chronicler, a witness to history, a role we often partake in ourselves, as consumers of the text. And, to a degree, we want to share his moderate, safe, reasonable point of view. But, as readers, we also yearn to identify with the hero, to experience and empathize with their world, their character, their beliefs, even and especially if it is a disturbing domain obsessed with death and sacrifice. By reprimanding this same hero with

---

141 A JR/JR replication which anticipates the sinister doubling poetry of the narrator's name: Humbert Humbert.

a shrewdly interpolated epistolary text, Mishima again gently nudges us into fellow feeling with his protagonist.

At the very least, through the strategically embedded texts of *The League of the Divine Wind* and Honda's letter, Mishima anticipates many of the criticisms *Runaway Horses* was likely to receive.[142] These literary grafts operate tactically not only within their own narratives but as peculiar external safety valves, desensitizing and manipulating readers, while also potentially depressurizing critical reproaches before they have even had occasion to be made.

Isao, of course, does not take kindly to Honda's none-too-subtle rebuke, and he is understandably puzzled as to why such a comparative stranger would take the trouble to write to him in this way – for he knows nothing of Honda's belief in Kiyoaki's possible reincarnation. Just as we, the reader, are likely to have been cajoled into more sympathy for Isao than we might hitherto have had, in response to the letter, the hero now coaxes himself into formulating a plan to emulate those compatriots depicted in *The League of the Divine Wind*.

The judge's good intentions have spectacularly backfired, and he will now be set in tension against Isao, whose sombre pursuit of an early death will begin to transform the equable and optimistic Honda into a much darker, more cynical figure, tormented by the futility and desolation of the world.

---

142 A third embedded text also exists in the court transcripts which are produced during Isao's trial toward the end of the book. They have the effect of generating both authenticity and artificiality, and are a surely intentionally imposed disorientation between reality and imagination, history and myth, which the novel as a whole explores.

Runaway Horses is the most overtly political novel of the *Sea of Fertility* cycle and, indeed, of Mishima's entire output (even allowing for the satirically political narrative of *After the Banquet*). Like his short stories from the 1960s, 'Patriotism' and 'Voices of the Fallen Heroes', of which *Runaway Horses* is in part an extended retelling, this novel is an encounter with the past, an engagement with history, perhaps even a deliberate attempt to evade, elude, and surpass it via the freedom of fiction. All three works to some extent rewrite the past, exploring history in a dynamic, potentially even disingenuous, fashion, though attempting to retrieve it for a nobler purpose, and each employs the theme of youthful sacrifice as a powerful statement about not only national but personal loss.[143]

'Patriotism' (1961) tells of the ritual suicide of a young army officer and his wife resulting from the 1936 attempted coup d'état known as the 26 February Incident. Though based on the story of a real-life couple, 'Patriotism' is a contemporary romantic myth, frequently associating the characters with divine figures, and penned in an elaborate, almost baroque style that recalls much of Mishima's earlier work. It closely links graphic sexuality with violence and a quasi-religious sense of sacrifice (as we remarked above, it can be no surprise that when he came to

---

143 An additional short story, 'Execution of Love' (1960), published anonymously in *Adonis*, a magazine aimed at gay men, tells of a graphic double suicide between a good-looking but malicious adolescent and his naive but sexually repressed schoolteacher. For decades, the author's estate denied this extraordinary little piece of sadistic erotica was by Mishima, though they were forced to back down when the story's handwritten manuscript surfaced in the mid-1990s.

direct a film version, the author chose the claustrophobic ardour of Wagner's *Tristan und Isolde* as the soundtrack).[144]

In terms of sex and death, 'Patriotism' puts the erotic imagery of seppuku on pornographic display: like writing, disembowelment is a form of ejaculation, blood joining ink and semen, plus sweat and tears, as fluid expressions of our common humanity. Although sex is an act of intimacy and affection, as well as an undertaking of personal communication, again like writing, it is also a functional bodily activity, a grand leveller, reducing all humans to the same basic parts and processes, just as they are in death. Sex and death remove individuality – something to be equated, too, with both authenticity and religion. This spiritual aspect of 'Patriotism' is part of a Mishimian trinity of sexuality, death, and divinity but is further significant in terms of the wider post-war spiritual malaise the author explored in his work.

An elegy for the war dead and a short story of exquisite imagery, 'Voices of the Fallen Heroes' (1966) maintains Mishima's obsessive enthralment to themes of youthful sacrifice and treachery. It describes a form of Shinto seance which calls forth the spirits of kamikaze pilots of the Second World War: they admonish Emperor Hirohito for renouncing his divine status and grieve for Japan's contemporary decline. Reproaching the emperor, as Mishima would do at the end of his own life, was a complex, immensely painful activity since it involved rebuking the figure one worshipped as a deity, making the apparent betrayal all the more penetrating and paradoxical (and ignoring the empathy with his people the emperor could now possess, de-deified but now more closely and compassionately human).

---

144 For himself, Mishima was never quite sure what to make of his story, claiming it contained both 'the best and worst features' of his writing.

The tragedy of the young couple in 'Patriotism', and the fallen heroes of 'Voices', was the betrayal of their religious faith in the emperor – since it was the sovereign himself who furiously quashed the 1936 uprising and later surrendered to the Americans in August 1945 (something Mishima never forgot hearing on the radio). It is a classic Mishimian trope: the predicament of one who places absolute faith in something, only to then be castigated or scorned (as Isao experiences for himself).

Troubling but unforgettable texts, 'Patriotism' and 'Voices' lay clear groundwork for *Runaway Horses*, exploring a number of Mishima's persistent themes and, crucially, showing the intimate, often ironic and enigmatic, connections between them: sex, death, sacrifice, devotion, and betrayal. In *Runaway Horses*, although Isao is denied the sun and sparkling sea he yearns for at the moment of his death, and is betrayed by almost everyone and everything he believes in, he is able to fulfil his desire to kill someone (the financier Kurahara) in the apparent name of the emperor.

The extremity of Isao's views is held in check, in both narrative and literary terms, by the presence of the sharp-eyed Honda – who also assists the hero at this trial – and by Mishima's historical foregrounding of 1930s Japan (or, at least, his version of the period). The author was keen, especially in this second volume of a cycle intended to cover the sweep of Japanese history in the twentieth century, to show the reader in precise detail the way the country had declined from the gentle exquisiteness depicted in *Spring Snow*. (Which was something of a romantic myth itself, offering less a portrait of the late Meiji / early Taishō years than one closer to the elegance and mystique of the classical Heian period, when Chinese influences were on the wane and a more mature national culture emerged.)

In *Runaway Horses* we witness not only the particulars of Isao's romanticized, often irrational, realm of the armed forces, the emperor, and such surrounding traditional paraphernalia, but the oppressive reality of amoral politicians, crooked bankers, dodgy lawyers, and craven military officers.

Isao's strength, his purity, his exuberance are conveyed throughout *Runaway Horses*: from the extended display of his expertise with the sword at the kendo tournament early in the novel to his precisely implemented seppuku at its close.[145] Bookending and repeating his commitment and prowess in this way is rather contrived and might become wearisome were in not for the fine prose Mishima employs to exhibit his hero's talents. Moreover this hero is himself not unaware of the idealized nature of his personality and mission, recognizing at one point that not only is there something romantic to his pursuit, but that it is almost part of a romantic fiction, and he a character within it.

Indeed, for all the rich and absorbing detail of 1930s Japan that Mishima is keen to embrace in *Runaway Horses*, making it a truly historical novel, there is also an important sense that it is nothing of the sort, but a yarn, a fable, an adventure that even flirts with mirroring that much-maligned internal text, *The League of the Divine Wind*. It is the tension between the status of *Runaway Horses* as a realistic historical novel and a romantic myth that generates much of its interest as a work of art, as a complex literary apparatus for exploring the events and personalities of mid-century Japan.

Although Isao is a romantic, an idealist (as well as a xenophobe in his extreme patriotism), his witness of the corruption and

---

145 In kendo, the shinai players use is meant to represent a Japanese sword (katana) and is composed of four bamboo slats bound together by leather.

contamination of contemporary Japan is hardly all fantasy or myth. As part of its course of modernization, Japan, like any other country, had had to forego much of its past as well as accept the often dirty reality of modernity. As Isao frequently points out, this included the kind of literal contamination via industrial chemical pollution as well as alterations to language, etiquette, political covenants, business transactions, social structures, family customs, and any number of large and small changes that, depending on one's point of view, were to be welcomed or rejected. In *Runaway Horses*, such alarm and denunciations can, on occasion, diminish the book as a literary novel, shifting it dangerously near to either a Japanese history textbook or a political tract, though Mishima is usually astute enough to know when to hold back or move on.

If such ideological aspects of the novel can be exasperating for many readers, this is perhaps only if we approach them as blinkered attitudes to politics and history. Mishima himself, in his life and his art, was highly westernized and enjoyed the fruits of modernity like anyone else, while also deploring changes when it suited him to do so. Such was his own duplicity and double standard. But if we appreciate the text as a rich survey of a period of time, and as an intense prose portrait of a zealous hero, allowing for the contradictions and complexities such figures will always present, then we can surely take more from it as a literary achievement, as a resonant exploration of the anxieties and influences of modernity.

Passionate, ferocious, and deeply problematic – containing homicide, suicide, and frankly terrorist activities – Isao's self-romanticized mission has, at least, a certain gallant, external, theoretically altruistic quality to it, especially compared to Kiyoaki's hyper-obsessive personal quest involving Satoko. Isao is, after all, attempting to restore and revive a country he loves and believes is being destroyed. However misguided he might be, his intentions, especially when affirming his commitment to its rituals and traditions, carry a nobility that go some way, especially in literary terms, toward redeeming him.

In contrast to both Kiyosaki and Isao, Honda's keen sense of logic and reason, though often under attack in *Runaway Horses*, tends to maintain its equilibrium, allowing him to usually remain the passive, poised, and perceptive observer of events, the cautious intermediary between realism and romance, arbitrating their extremes. It is this which sanctions him to be the foil to Isao's passion, just as he had been to Kiyoaki's, a tension which helps propel both *Spring Snow* and its successor forward.

Aside from a passive/active, rational/irrational, realist/romantic series of divisions between Isao and Honda, there is also a significant spiritual or metaphysical divide, namely between Isao's fanatical adherence to the indigenous faith of Japan, Shintoism, and Honda's fascination with, if not strict observance of, the imported religion of Buddhism. The rendering of Japan's native religion in *Runaway Horses* is perhaps a romanticized version for literary purposes, ornamenting its commitment to ceremony and ritual – though, of course, its hero is obsessively, and necessarily, devoted to ritual as an aspect of his psyche and mission. Moreover, there can be no denying that ceremony and ritual are key features of the faith, as are its notion of purification in order to achieve a divine nature and its denial of any provisional concepts involving a potential hereafter. Action, crucially, touches this world and no other (though occasional mythological references to the way dead human spirits assist the living and restless avenging life forces point to some moderate post-mortem beliefs).

The key tenet of Buddhism, so far as *The Sea of Fertility* is concerned, involves the transmigration of souls – which themselves are, in the end, nothing at all. This instils Buddhism with an inherent passive melancholy and desolation that is almost part of the DNA of the faith.[146] It is this passivity of suffering, along with what they perceive as its almost narcissistic, vainglorious sense of grief, which enrages Isao and many of his mentors, declaring the Buddha a fool that teaches 'a philosophy of evil that reduces everything to nihilism'. Isao the active hero cannot abide the seemingly inert, sullen, and submissive acceptance of Buddhism, which is, like capitalism, a foreign introduction draining the vigorous strength and spirit of the Japanese people, turning them into a decadent, docile, and blindly acquiescent society, while making its rituals and traditions merely a tourist's spectacle.[147]

---

146 Though one, some Buddhists might counter, that is also its basis for overcoming anguish and moving into an acceptance of transience and liberation from a clinging material existence toward enlightenment.

147 Eventually, of course, by the end of *The Decay of the Angel*, Honda will relinquish any trust in reincarnation, succumbing to a recognition of ultimate emptiness, though not before the processes and implications of rebirth are comprehensively explored in *The Temple of Dawn*, parts of which are set in South and Southeast Asia, wellspring of Buddhism. Toward the end of *Runaway Horses*, Honda overhears Isao call out vaguely in his sleep: 'Far to the south. Very hot … in the rose sunshine of a southern land…' thereby anticipating the next reincarnation.

For all these crucial differences between Isao and Honda, within Honda himself is a developing internal pressure, which operates as a further driving force of the tetralogy. We witnessed it first in *Spring Snow*, as we observed how Kiyoaki had a subtle though profound revitalizing effect on Honda, radiating life into his friend's more routine and academic mind. For it is Honda's transformation across the cycle of novels that remains one of Mishima's most fascinating and enduring accomplishments. The active heroes need to remain relatively unchanging characters; but Honda must shift and progress through the volumes as we travel through his life as through the Japanese century.

In *Runaway Horses* the cautious, scholarly Honda is gradually pulled into Isao's precarious orbit by the intensity of the hero's vision and personality, and then when acting as his legal representation – literally resigning his status as an impartial judge – but also as he begins to more intensely believe in Kiyoaki's reincarnation (something Isao himself is never made aware of). Despite the influence Kiyoaki had on the Honda of *Spring Snow*, he has remained fairly normal: the law student has since married and established a fine career. But the passive spectator, and intermittent accomplice, of the earlier novel is now one increasingly engaged in his own mission, his own dangerous, and potentially destructive, quest for truth (even engaging in archetypally 'heroic' activities, such as the climbing of a mountain, which he does just before witnessing Isao bathing under the waterfall).

To an extent, it is not simply Kiyoaki who has been reborn, but Honda, too, awakened to a life beyond the routinely rational, the prosaically logical. Dreams, imagination, reveries – even delusions – are revealed to him as radiant possibilities that enliven existence, even if they are states of being he instinctively fears. We might recall Mishima, once a law student in the dreary world of the post-war Ministry of Finance, resigned to a life of dutiful compliance and bureaucratic monotony before the ferocity and exhilaration of his night-time writing overpowered him and he quit.

Honda's transformation is appropriately more subtle and ambiguous, quietly evolving, the passive intellectual slowly altered by life and the people around him. In *Runaway Horses*, Honda tries to persuade Isao against his reckless quest but can only be a passive adviser. A more tangible, active participation comes when he defends Isao at his trial, his logical legal mind coming to the aid of the irrational hero. Yet this itself becomes a betrayal of the very person he is trying to save, thwarting Isao's sombre pursuit of both an idealized oblivion and a grand and daring youthful death honouring his country and his sovereign. When Isao reclaims some form of courageous farewell with his seppuku, Honda is rendered void, futile, pointless – a state of mind that will, across the final two books, gradually infect and warp him into a state of corrosive passive nihilism.

Runaway Horses is a complex, challenging, and sometimes paradoxical work, the romantic fervour of *Spring Snow* yielding to the thorny and more provocative problems of political passion. It pulls in many directions, developing the verbal, moral, and philosophical sonorities of *The Sea of Fertility* in remarkable and often surprising new ways – like other great works of art, asking more questions than it answers. It is a study of dishonesty and duplicity, of self-interest and villainy, of corruption and change, a protest against modernity and the tyranny of time. Yet *Runaway Horses* is also an extraordinary presentation of Mishima's most ardently held convictions, a demonstration of his unquenchable belief in the power of heroism and the potential of heroes – seducing and repelling us, earning our admiration even as they alarm us.

Chapter Fourteen

The Temple of Dawn

REMEMBRANCE OF THINGS FUTURE

Wat Arun Ratchawararam Ratchawaramahawihan, the 'Temple of Dawn', is a Buddhist temple located on the west bank of the Chao Phraya River in Bangkok, its name derived from the Hindu god Aruna, who was often personified as the rays of the rising sun. Surrounded by four smaller spires, a huge, phallic prang, or pagoda, juts into the sky, symbolizing levels of existence and encrusted with countless colourful ornaments, mostly made from porcelain and marine gastropod carapaces, *Mauritia mauritania*.[148]

Despite its name, the Temple of Dawn is best viewed in the early evening, from the river, the soft glow of twilight creating a dazzling spectacle that lasts only a short time and which is,

---

148 Many of them originated as ballast on the boats that brought trade from China – a wonderful example of the commercial being repurposed for the spiritual.

accordingly, regarded as a reminder of earthly transience. The building can feel eternal, a permanent presence on the river, but, like everything else, is temporary, one day to turn to dust. It is an exquisite but terrifying sight, ostentatious but graceful, both sublimely simple and intricately multifaceted. And what the Temple of Dawn achieves in stone and sea snail shells, Mishima achieves in the words of his eponymous novel: *The Temple of Dawn* (暁の寺, 'Akatsuki no tera', 1970) is imposing yet vibrantly decorated, a work of dazzling design and detail encompassing profound concepts – an elegant construction with cosmic implications.

In one important sense, *The Sea of Fertility* quartet ends with Isao's suicide at the close of *Runaway Horses*: this was the heroic death its author idealized and then, in rather less romantic circumstances, carried out for himself in November 1970. Everything from now on is, accordingly, posthumous, and ominously, surreally so, as we encounter Mishima's increasingly twisted vision of old and middle age. In *The Temple of Dawn*, and then *The Decay of the Angel*, Honda takes centre stage and gradually warps from the generally calm, reasonable being we have got to know – loyal friend, respectable judge, and lawyer – into a progressively perverse, irrational, and agitated creature: sexually furtive, spiritually anxious, intellectually illogical. Some warning signs have been present in the previous two novels, of course, but Honda now plunges into Mishima's own darkest nightmare for himself: a dirty old man, a voyeur, ugly in mind and body, trapped in the corruptions of terrestrial existence. And we, the reader, become as deviant as Honda, spying on the phantom old age of Yukio Mishima through the peephole of literature.

With knowing irony, in *The Temple of Dawn* all this debasement and despondency takes place either amid the flamboyant wealth of Honda's materially luxurious retirement, with its swimming pool, cypresses, and views of Mount Fuji, or far from Japan in the spiritually luxurious, verdant lands of India and Thailand, as Honda chases meaning. His life in the twentieth century, like that of his country, has been beset by destruction and death, especially youthful death, in addition to its experience of social and economic advancement. In this novel the personal and universal repercussions of these dynamics congregate in a work of moral and metaphysical anxiety, with extended sections on Buddhist and Hindu philosophies which can make the text at times much more dense than we find elsewhere in this writer's work. Mishima's lucidity often disappears for long stretches – though the passages not only are fascinating in themselves and for their connection to the themes of both this volume and the wider tetralogy but are an important indication of Honda's own impenetrability, his private perplexity and rampant internal demons.

Materially rich but spiritually, and increasingly ethically, bankrupt, Honda is a fascinating invention, a Wotan-like figure becoming ever more entangled by his own obsessions and disappointments. In the first part of *The Temple of Dawn*, we see him still noble, still valuable, embedded both literally and emotionally in the opulent lands of South and Southeast Asia, but more and more preoccupied by his own past, particularly the deaths of Kiyoaki and Isao, and its significance for both his present and his future. As we will discover, this search for meaning will not only consume Honda but corrode him, his spiritual, sexual, and material worlds fusing in a climactic scene of devastating Mishimian irony.

The storylines of *Spring Snow* and *Runaway Horses* each occur over about eighteen months and are set in Japan; *The Temple of Dawn* not only whisks us to Thailand and to India, too, but broadens its chronology, comprising two parts, set first in 1941–45 and then in 1952 (with a brief, post-scriptural, final chapter in 1967). Despite the greater breadth of these temporal and topographical horizons, *The Temple of Dawn* is a narrative that can, on occasion, seem static as it spins its philosophical threads. Yet these very concepts, and the manner in which Mishima presents them to us, entrenched within both his narrative and the soul of his protagonist Honda, also take the novel into spatio-temporal realms far beyond the grisly confines of the twentieth century. They launch it into the spiritual stratosphere, past-present-future colliding and coalescing, and making the reincarnation theme not simply a plot device but an abiding concern, a governing need, an unsettling necessity.

The Temple of Dawn is one of Mishima's most challenging novels, an exquisitely shaped if often opaque labyrinth of pleasure and pain, desire and disenchantment. Initially, like *Spring Snow* and *Runaway Horses*, *The Temple of Dawn* shimmers in a haze of hypnotic intrigue, revelling in fantasy and the past, before turning in its second part toward a more realistic disposition, as the tetralogy prepares to catch up with the timeline of its own creation in *The Decay of the Angel*.

Grim reality and the present day are fast approaching.

After the intense textual claustrophobia of *Spring Snow* and *Runaway Horses*, with their psychological and geographical internalizations, the short but ineluctably expansive opening line to *The Temple of Dawn* reads like a breath of literary fresh air:

It was the rainy season in Bangkok.

Immediately, and perhaps with some surprise, we are carried far from the confines of Japan and Japanese history toward another world. More than just glamorous locales and passages of exotic narrative colour, the overseas sections of *The Temple of Dawn* are a crucial deep dive into cultures materially and spiritually different from modern Japan. They help expose and convict what Mishima disparaged as the vacuum of his contemporary homeland, which is set to dominate the second half of this novel and the entirety of the next, *The Decay of the Angel*. Here the writer could witness and record societies living more (apparently) authentic lives compared to the 'counterfeit' ones of westernized modernity – places that offered the world, in its blind pursuit of relentless technologization and commercialism, the possibility of spiritual redemption and meaning.

In the autumn of 1967, Mishima travelled to India, Thailand, and Laos – mainly to research key atmospheric and religious details for *The Temple of Dawn*, but also to avoid the endless annual frenzy of media speculation about the Nobel Prize that plagued him every October. Mishima was deeply moved by India, relishing its commotion and variety, as well as what he regarded as its dogged refusal to accept westernization and embrace its spirituality (though he was not entirely blind to its terrible poverty). Green and purple parrots, holy white cows, amber saris, crimson turbans, even the flies – all were part of the colour, buzz, and bustle that created a complete picture of life at any given moment, and which seemed a million miles from the sterility and emptiness of modern Japan. Mumbai, Aurangabad, Jaipur, Agra, New Delhi, Varanasi, and Kolkata were on his Indian itinerary, with the cave-bound temples of Aurangabad a highlight, along with the goat sacrifices of Kolkata, the Pink City of Jaipur, and Agra's Taj Mahal.

It was the rituals and setting of Varanasi (formerly Benares), however, that proved to be the most inspiring of the trip, especially the stone steps, or ghats, along the Ganges where people rested, bathed, and were cremated. The public open-air funeral pyres were unlike anything Mishima had seen before: a man obsessed by death, face to face with an astonishingly stark exhibition of mortality and its associated rites of purification and renewal. Death, here, immediately reduced the complex human experience with all its intricate anxieties and grandiose concerns into the humility and modesty of the five (Hindu) elements – earth, water, fire, air, and ether – before initiating the world-wandering and transmigration of the soul (the ambitious, binding theme of Mishima's tetralogy).

So moved was the novelist by the sights of pilgrimage and mourning on the Ganges – the earnest ablutions; the smouldering corpses – that he returned to witness them a second time, something he compels his protagonist Honda do in *The Temple of Dawn* (and with a graphic intensity that probably exceeded the tourist-tamed spectacles his creator had observed: skulls, Honda ponders, are particularly hard to burn). The scenes on this sacred river, so galvanizing and unsettling, will return in tawdry, tragicomic fashion at the end of the novel amid the trappings of modernity, as Honda's sumptuous villa goes up in flames after a house party.

From India, Mishima moved on to Bangkok, where research continued. Of particular interest was the city's Rosette Palace, whose interiors feature so exquisitely in *The Temple of Dawn*, especially in those crucial parts regarding the next reincarnation of Kiyoaki: the Thai Princess Ying Chan. Although it was usually fairly easy to arrange a visit, during Mishima's trip the palace had been commandeered by the Thai army as a command post for hunting communists and was strictly off limits to civilians. After several unsuccessful attempts to secure an appointment, Mishima was beginning to annoy the authorities. In his frustration, he did something extraordinarily dangerous: parting a section of the fuchsia bougainvillea, he peeked through the hedge at the palace grounds. At any moment he might have been shot on sight by the guards. It was a risky business for his art.[149]

At the time, Mishima's brother, Chiyuki, was working at the Japanese embassy in Vientiane, so an additional trip to Laos was added to the schedule. Chiyuki managed to wrangle a brief audience for his famous brother with no less than King Savang Vatthana (1907–1978), who lived modestly in Luang Prabang some three hundred kilometres north of the capital. What was intended to be a short meeting lasted almost an hour, since the monarch and the writer discovered they shared a mutual interest in Proust (an auspicious connection, given Mishima's own ongoing experiments with time and memory in *The Sea of Fertility*). After the appointment, the two brothers returned to Vientiane together on an American military plane, which flew with its rear ramp left open, exposing the magnificent forests below. Chiyuki was terrified; Mishima claimed it one of the most thrilling experiences of his life.

For a time Mishima was disappointed he hadn't set the Thai parts of *The Temple of Dawn* in Laos, such was his new-found love for the country. He found the people relaxed (despite the

---

149 It is likely Mishima had been able to view the palace's interiors during an earlier visit to the city. The level of detail in his text certainly suggests first-hand knowledge – though it may, of course, be purely the product of book-based research and his imagination.

constant threat of war) and the flora and fauna a revelation. The turquoise lizards and emerald vipers in his brother's garden were especially fascinating: he would watch them with all the wide-eyed absorption of a child or zoologist. Enchanting, too, were the dragon fruits, papayas, and bananas simply growing on trees – existing spontaneously in a fertile paradise rather than stacked in an antiseptic, impersonal Tokyo supermarket. Mishima would pick and eat them, savouring the bounty, before settling down for an afternoon nap amid the luxuriant vegetation.

At the commencement of *The Temple of Dawn*, Honda – now aged forty-seven – arrives in Bangkok in order to conduct a legal case. It is 1941; the menace and promise of war hangs in the air. Honda retains his unflappable exterior, but inside he is becoming increasingly erratic and nihilistic in his outlook. Mishima treats us to an extensive extended tour of the great City of Angels on the Chao Phraya River, including details of the royal family and its history, as well as Thailand's particular branch of (Hinayana) Buddhism. To Honda, the elaborate beauty of the architecture, indeed the whole atmosphere of the city, seems to exude an extravagant sense of anti-rationalism, evading any systematic organization.

It is the ideal place for Honda's search for meaning to begin. During his stay he ponders meeting again the two Thai princes with whom he was at school (in *Spring Snow*), but they are away in Switzerland. Hishikawa, Honda's smug, somewhat pretentious translator and guide, suggests it might be possible to meet another member of the family. One of the princes has an apparently unbalanced seven-year-old daughter named Ying Chan, named after the fiancée who died during *Spring Snow*, who claims to be the reincarnation of a Japanese boy. This 'poor little mad princess' is the despair of her family and is kept virtually as a prisoner in the Rosette Palace.

Hishikawa comments complacently that her name, meaning 'moonlight', is appropriate for a lunatic, but Honda is intrigued. He indirectly recalls Isao's words, spoken as he slept just before his death at the end of *Runaway Horses*: 'Far to the south. Very hot … in the rose sunshine of a southern land…' With him, too, Honda has brought Kiyoaki's dream diary, part of which mentions Siam, a palace, a garden, peacocks, a golden crown, and the 'lovely face of a small girl'. The threads and signals from the tetralogy's previous instalments lead to only one place: Honda's hope for another cosmic restoration of his childhood friend.

In keeping with the by and large dreamlike quality of the setting, amid the heat, rain, and temples of Thailand, at the Rosette Palace Honda meets the princess. Their encounter seems to be the consequence of supernatural or divine forces coming together, for Ying Chan claims that she is neither mad nor Thai but Japanese and that she died eight years before (Isao committed his seppuku in 1933). She also appears preternaturally aware of the date of Kiyoaki's death in 1914, along with numerous other details of his and Isao's lives. It is an entirely surreal and fantastical scene, probably the strangest of all four books of *The Sea of Fertility*, perhaps of everything Mishima wrote. Deliberately and transparently bizarre, it is brilliantly paced, mixing peculiarity and an ominous sense of dread with the magic of a fairy tale, dream and illusion ebbing and flowing in Honda's mind as in our own.

The princess invites Honda for a second meeting two days later at the Bang Pa In Palace in the jungles north of Bangkok, this time thankfully without the tiresome accompaniment of Hishikawa – who claims reincarnation a fraud and that the only mystery in human life lies in the arts. Moreover, without the prosaic interference of translation, the princess's words can now simply be music. The day is recounted in intense, exquisite detail, full of both intellectual and aesthetic pleasure, as we witness water buffalo, green snakes, golden spires, and the charming interactions between the world-weary lawyer and the innocent princess. Guided by the child's 'tiny, damp fist', they visit the palace's Chinese villa, French arbour, Arabian tower, Renaissance garden, and floating pavilion. These are tender scenes, among the most delightful Mishima ever wrote, the childless, analytical Honda feeling the presence of the daughter he never had.

Now and then, Honda contemplates the vast realms of time and space the little girl must be experiencing, if she is Kiyoaki's reincarnation, simultaneously seeing in multiple dimensions, staring into the deep abyss of the cosmos. Honda himself feels empowered, as if he is standing at the centre of time, spacious and free, an expanse created by the princess's happiness, but one with the serried ranks of countless black pillars, 'transmigrated shades lurking breathlessly as though in a game of hide-and-seek.' When the child raises her arms at one point, Honda tries to spot the telltale trio of moles that might offer proof of her status but cannot see them – though he chalks it up to the texture of her skin rather than seeing it as a definitive refutation.

Given the frightening, voyeuristic obsession Honda will develop with the older Ying Chan in part two of *The Temple of Dawn*, it is important we experience these touching scenes for all their innocence (even if there must be an inescapable impression of catastrophe hanging over them). Indeed, the episodes with Ying Chan are extraordinary: a mixture of the metaphysical with the demonstrably real – poetic philosophizing flirts with charming minutiae concerning the flesh-and-blood world (at one point, the little girl even goes, as little girls must, to the bathroom).

Honda himself is aware of the curious union of the two realms. He relishes the way he pursues Kiyoaki/Isao in a physical, substantial, coldly intellectual fashion (like a 'jungle beast stalking its prey with drooling fangs'), which is intimately linked to the abstract, ontological joy he will feel knowing they have been reborn. It is a quest bestowing emotion, excitement, and aesthetics once again on a drab life, just as it did in *Spring Snow* and *Runaway Horses* – a mundane business trip suddenly enfolded not only in the material magic of palaces and princesses, but in the metaphysical magic of reincarnation.

Although he does not yet have the tangible 'proof' of the moles that will substantiate Ying Chan as the third link in the chain of reincarnation, a mystical, numinous love for the young princess has already been kindled in Honda the logical lawyer. This love guides him to embark on a prolonged spiritual journey, to holy sites of Buddhism and Hinduism, which will intensify his quest for a deeper meaning to his life – but which will also nearly destroy him.

His lawsuit in Thailand complete, Honda travels to India (funded in gratitude by the firm that had hired him as their legal representation). He relishes arranging his journey all around India, planning to travel only via slow-moving steam trains in order to properly experience the country. He is attracted to the prospect of the unknown: just as Kiyoaki and Isao had before them, Ying Chan has awakened the active spirit in the passive man.

The trip synthesizes nightmare and dream, phantasy and reality, spiritual enquiry and material witness. In Kolkata he watches a headless goat kick back its legs, its open neck spraying his youthful executioner with blood – here the transcendent and the grubby are intermingled, amalgamated, holiness and corruption bound together, where in contemporary Japan they are kept fixedly apart. In Varanasi he walks narrow streets, observes a psychic, glimpses lepers, notices flies assembling on the wounds of deformed creatures. Watching the funeral pyres on the Ganges, he sees a burning body bend over as if the man were merely turning in his sleep; the sound of boiling travels across the water, and he sees a strong man with a bamboo stick breaking the skulls that are left after the fires. The sound of their cracking echoes off the walls of the nearby temples.

It is all painstakingly described in macabre detail, yet in truth there is nothing sinister or sad about any of it: 'What seemed heartlessness was actually pure joy. Not only were the *saṃsāra*[150] and reincarnation basic ... but they were actually accepted as part of nature.' With this, Honda experiences a profound, if somewhat intellectual and analytical, epiphany: karma is a fundamental and entirely natural phenomenon akin to fruit on a tree or rice in a paddy field, a witness to the universal truths available in the world should we seek them.

At Ajanta, Honda beholds twin waterfalls, one running between rocks, the other plunging like a silver twine, both echoing from the mountains that surround him. He is caught

---

150 The Sanskrit word for 'wandering' as well as 'world', referring to the cyclical changes associated with death, transmigration, reincarnation, and karma. Curiously, it is possible the word and its meanings contributed to the naming of the main character of Franz Kafka's most famous story, *The Metamorphosis* ('Die Verwandlung', 1915): Gregor Samsa.

amid a frenzy of colour and life. Green trees, scarlet flowers, and yellow butterflies gather about the falls, the water generating a shimmering iridescent light and rainbows hanging in the mist. Honda recalls the words of his dying friend Kiyoaki, who spoke of meeting again under the falls. It is a scene of intense poetic mystery and emotional connection, almost a farewell to the fantasy and fairy-tale aspects of *The Sea of Fertility*, which will now begin to shift to the more matter-of-fact, realistic world of wartime and post-war Japan.

Having returned to Bangkok, amid tedious dealings with Japanese businessmen that Mishima describes with satirical mischief, Honda pays a last visit to Ying Chan. The little princess becomes hysterical when she learns, via a bumbling mistake from the translator Hishikawa, that she cannot accompany Honda back to Japan, and the scene rends our hearts as much as hers. After Honda returns home to Japan in December 1941, war breaks out with the Americans, and he spends most of the global conflict, which occupies the rest of part one of the book, ignoring the hostilities, isolating himself from the world. (Though he does meet Tadeshina, Satoko's former maid from *Spring Snow*, by chance toward the end of the war, an eerie, gossamer thread to the past.) He plunges into a study of karma and other intense religious and philosophical concepts, many of which link with his experiences in South and Southeast Asia and connect, too, with musings on concepts from ancient Greece and Rome (especially those of Heraclitus and Pythagoras) as well as more modern European philosophers (Vico and Nietzsche).

It is a challenging part of the novel, whose ideas we will return to, a section understandably skimmed or passed over by many readers, even though the verbal-emotional textures on display offer insights into the crisis Honda is experiencing. When he comes out the other side, in part two of the novel, the war will be over but the world will begin to slip through his fingers. The search for meaning will now be an obsessive chase, a fanatical pursuit. Fantasy still exists in part two of *The Temple of Dawn*, but it is of a Stygian, malign kind, a gruesome folk or fairy tale. It is horrifically real, as Honda pursues his proof of Ying Chan's reincarnation alongside and entwined with his growing lust for her (both of which, of course, centre upon her body).

In part two of *The Temple of Dawn*, the mood changes; it will continue in this despondent state for most of the remainder of the tetralogy as it staggers toward its sombre conclusion and final revelations. No more exotic, enigmatic faraway lands, no more youthful warriors, not even the melodramatic cushion of war. It is 1952; Japan is beginning its post-war miracle, though the air is curiously full of a sense of downfall and deterioration, failure and fatigue. Honda is fifty-eight, ageing, jaded – but rich: an old legal case has been redeemed by a change to Japan's new Constitution of 1947, netting him a fortune. With the proceeds he has purchased a country villa overlooking Mount Fuji.

What might be a comfortable, dignified maturity is nothing of the sort. Honda encloses himself with a gallery of grotesques, a grisly set who represent Mishima's indictment of contemporary Japan. There is an affluent but cynical lesbian, Keiko, and her dissolute nephew; a lewd, ageing writer specializing in German literature who obsesses about a sadomasochistic fantasy world he has invented called 'the Land of the Pomegranate'; a poet, Tsubakihara, with ghoulish, prurient tendencies that will mirror

Honda's own. Some decaying aristocrats make up the numbers (as does Honda's wife, Rié). Ying Chan is now eighteen and a student in Japan, as her father was in *Spring Snow*.

Honda again enters into a quest for knowledge, pursuing confirmation of the reincarnation of Kiyoaki. This time, however, his pursuit takes on a more desperate and repulsive edge, fuelled as much by lust and envy as any meaningful desire to encounter again his long-lost friend. Honda is turning from the passive hero of the earlier books into a dangerously active villain, albeit one still inertly observing, pulling the strings in sinister silence out of sight. In his new house, Honda has installed a peephole between his study and a guest bedroom; he uses it to spy on the sexual activities of his guests. There is something especially nasty about seeing the calm and resolute Honda reduced to this, his compulsive, even neurotic desires curdling into behaviour of the most degenerate sort.

He meets with Ying Chan for lunch, returning to her the emerald ring which was lost by the Thai boys in *Spring Snow* but which has now turned up in an antique shop – a miraculous reappearance that is one of the glimmering embers of fantasy and fairy tale that are from now on almost entirely absent from *The Sea of Fertility*. We are offered lingering memories of the past: returning home from his lunch with Ying Chan, Honda finds Isao's decrepit father, Iinuma, loitering at his house like a rat. After a sob story about a failed suicide attempt, Honda gives him a wad of money to be rid of him, an act which, while on the surface generous, strikes us as hostile, uncharitable, that of a rich man paying to forget selected portions of the past.

Some of the past he cannot ignore, however, and the question of Kiyoaki's/Isao's reincarnation continues to obsess him. During a house party he conspires with Keiko to have her playboy nephew seduce the princess so that he can witness the three moles on her torso through the spyhole. The plan fails, however, and Ying Chan flees to the arms of Keiko next door. Unbowed, and with increasing absurdity as we watch a once distinguished and honourable man turn into an obsessive lunatic, Honda comes up with another ludicrous plan to see the moles. He will construct a swimming pool at his house, host a pool party, and observe the moles on Ying Chan's bikini'd body this way.

Here the spiritual, sexual, and material aspects of Honda's life come together: his lust for Ying Chan's flesh, his longing to see the telltale moles on that body, the financial resources that will allow him to achieve it – all three collide in a hot mess of tragicomic futility. Were it not for the compelling dexterity of Mishima's prose, it might collapse into a shambolic circus, but he holds it together as the novel surges toward its shattering denouement. Unable to see the moles when Ying Chan is in her bathing costume, he puts her that night with Keiko in the guest room and observes them making love. Finally he observes the three extremely small marks on her body ('like Pleiades in the dusky sky of her brown skin that resembled the dying evening glow') which identify her as the apparently authentic reincarnation of Kiyoaki and Isao.

His gratification with this visual testimony is short-lived: that night, while smoking in bed, another guest – the fanatical sadomasochist writer – falls asleep, and Honda's villa burns to the ground. The writer, along with the ghoulish poet Tsubakihara, with whom he was in bed, are killed, but everyone else survives. The princess returns to Thailand, and for a long time Honda believes he has saved Ying Chan from the karmic fate that befell Kiyoaki and Isao: dying at twenty. But fifteen years later, in 1967, he learns by chance from her twin sister that the young princess died at the appointed age from the bite of a cobra (those colourful snakes which Honda, and Mishima before him, witnessed in Thailand now taking on a more ominous, prophetic edge).

ꝏ

As with Kiyoaki in *Spring Snow* and Isao in *Runaway Horses*, Ying Chan dies in the final line of *The Temple of Dawn*, but time is now stretched, scrambled, creaking and wobbling as its relentless linear flow through history is disrupted. In part this is in keeping with the tangled sense of doubt and decline the cycle is now taking on, but it also reinforces the spatio-temporal concepts Mishima is exploring. By having Ying Chan die at a curious distance in time and space, the philosophical realm of the novel broadens to match many of its internal discussions regarding transmigration. Her death is swiftly reported to us in the text as it leaps ahead fifteen years before glancing back across those same years. This demise occupies a dual time, occurring both in the present and the past, so that between 1952 and 1967 the princess is both dead and alive – Schrödinger's aristocrat – with all the dizzying sensations and implications this implies. But by confirming her death at twenty, Mishima is able to maintain the illusion, going into the final novel, that she *is* the reincarnation, since it turns out she in fact died at the same age as Kiyoaki and Isao (with the three moles, the other substantiation of her transmigratory status).

Many commentators have asked why the author did not have Ying Chan die in the fire at the end of *The Temple of Dawn*, perhaps while she made love to Keiko, surely a suitably climactic and dramatic end to match those of Kiyoaki and Isao. Mishima is more subtle than this, however – and more alert to his thematic anxieties concerning time which, as we have seen, play with ambiguity and uncertainty, deepening his sense of the picture, and texture, of reality. A death in the fire at twenty would confirm her reincarnated status; by forcing Honda into a fifteen-year limbo, Mishima further destabilizes the logical lawyer, leaving him in a position of heightened despair. (It is also crucial that the house fire is merely a symbolic event for Honda, reminding him, as we shall see, of the funeral pyres of the Ganges. For Ying Chan herself to die in the fire, rather than a couple of perverted house guests, would surely be too much for him.)

There is a further strength to setting Ying Chan's death outside the main timeline of the novel – one which enhances her own selfhood, which is much less apparent than that of her fellow active heroes Kiyoaki and Isao. Ying Chan's dying convulsions from the snakebite, reported to us in the brief final chapter, unnervingly echo her orgasmic convulsions in bed with Keiko, witnessed through the peephole before the fire. Through these spasms of ecstasy and suffering, Eros and Thanatos exist in an eerie union. Together they give this relatively subdued active hero a thrilling posthumous power, asserting her sexuality both as a positive thing in itself and a defiance of the lurid inclinations of the spy and pervert Honda.

The complex status of her death, occurring both in the present and the past, as well as the inordinate amount of time it takes Honda to confirm her three moles, mean that, although Ying Chan is an apparently genuine reincarnation of the two heroes of action, Kiyoaki and Isao, this authenticity feels less secure, her cosmic ancestry more uncertain. This is also apparent in the much more minor role she plays in the text, contrasted to the huge, governing positions assumed by Kiyoaki and Isao in their novels. Ying Chan's beauty and sensuality are powerful, attracting Honda and others, and she is capable of great impulsiveness and presence, yet her exoticism triggers disintegration rather than fecundity.

In her sexual union with Keiko, Ying Chan is able to proclaim herself against the controlling influence of masculine demands, while also frustrating Honda's increasingly abhorrent machinations. Honda believes that he is in love with Ying Chan, but his true motivation mixes carnal covetousness for younger flesh and a desire to control both the individual hero and the cosmic forces bound up in her status as a reincarnation of Kiyoaki and Isao. After being passively influenced by the compelling natures of the first two links in the chain, impressed by the spontaneity and impulse of Kiyoaki and Isao, seeing the possibility for a more dynamic world than his colourless existence has offered, Honda seeks to possess Ying Chan both to satisfy his lusts and to become a part of the instinctive, resourceful worlds he witnessed in Kiyoaki and Isao, perhaps even rising above them to become a witness to cosmic change.

While allowing Ying Chan her own autonomy as an active hero, Mishima refuses Honda this realization. He is granted confirmation of her status via the moles, and then belatedly via her death aged twenty, but he is deprived of the participation in a world of exhilaration and vigorous dynamism that characterizes active heroes. Passive to the end, he is not even allowed to witness the moles directly but must fulfil his pursuit for confirmation via a repugnant little pornographic device – the peephole – denied active participation into spontaneous sensuality not only by his gender but his passivity, malice, and absurdity.

Hitherto an emblem of equanimity and judgement, in his middle age Honda has become engrossed by an intense sexual perversion. He is not the first man, or woman, to have a midlife crisis or hanker after younger bodies; but Honda's crisis is confounded by his quest for meaning and certainty, especially regarding reincarnation and transmigration. This is not to excuse his behaviour, which is revolting, but to comprehend its degradation within the context of *The Sea of Fertility*'s metaphysics and Honda's descent into the empty garden at the close of *The Decay of the Angel*, with all its implications for Mishima's dark view of the world, in both political and philosophical terms.

Spying on young couples canoodling in public parks, spying on his own copulating house guests: we are now compelled to judge for ourselves the man who judged others. Honda's past experiences may justify, or at least rationalize, some of his actions: they are part of his need to confirm the existence of the moles (a flimsy excuse for voyeurism likely to be dismissed by any judge, including himself). Yet all Honda's nauseating deeds appear as his clumsy, vulgar attempts to extricate himself from his docile status and endless ennui, ironically by supercharging that passivity to become the ultimate inert onlooker: a peeping Tom. (It is easy to compare him to the thirteen-year-old protagonist of *The Sailor Who Fell from Grace with the Sea*, but where Noboru is a child impatiently exploring his own identity and sexuality when he spies on his mother's lovemaking, Honda is an adult, fully aware of his behaviour and its consequences.)

Honda is passionate, like the Kiyoaki of *Spring Snow*, but in an ugly, awkward fashion, since his ardour is not genuine or vibrant but decadent and deceitful. He is not gripped by youthful forces; he is bored by his retirement, debauched by his lifestyle, no longer tied to the routines or demands of his work. His sexuality is both literally impotent (he remains childless throughout the tetralogy) as well as figuratively empty and worthless, symptomatic of the wider society in which he is a part and which Mishima sought to condemn.

Furtive, stealthy, duplicitous, Honda has become one of the snakes that slither their way through the text of *The Temple of Dawn* – and which for Mishima were a symbol of Western corruption – so that, in some dark fashion, he is able to assert a manner of malign control over Ying Chan at the moment of her death, the cobra/venom a form of phallus/ejaculation. But if he has, it is only a passive, metaphorical assertion, and Ying Chan retains her own energy through her active denial of Honda and in her conscious coupling with Keiko.

Much of the iniquity and depravity of Honda's sexual perversion derives from his creator's own fears of becoming just the man he wrote on the page. Keen to maintain his body's outward appearance via fanatical bodybuilding, Mishima knew he was in a losing battle against the consequences of time. The idea of lusting after young flesh while housed in what he considered an ugly old body was abhorrent to Mishima (and is a partial, though only partial, explanation of his suicide at forty-five). Where Nabokov's engagement with corrupt sexuality in *Lolita* (1955) was a gruelling exercise in creativity, Humbert Humbert being about as far as possible from the contented married man Nabokov was, the detailed descriptions of Honda's voyeurism seem to come from a more unequivocal line of inventiveness: Honda represents Mishima's imaginative leap into his own frightening future.[151]

---

151 Nabokov always claimed *Lolita* was the hardest of his books to write, given both the desolation of the subject matter and the extreme moral and sexual distance between himself and his narrator.

If Isao in *Runaway Horses* is Mishima's idealized dream of himself as a youthful heroic warrior, physically self-controlled and ideologically pure, the Honda of part two of *The Temple of Dawn*, and thence *The Decay of the Angel*, is Mishima's fantastical nightmare, his disconcerting *Portrait of the Artist as a Dirty Old Man*. Here we witness a profound aspect of Mishima's psychosexuality, one which he feared, fought against, and ultimately defeated through his own self-annihilation. All the bodybuilding and artfully posed pictures in the world (such as Mishima's near-naked 1968 recreation of Saint Sebastian's martyrdom) couldn't, for the author, prevent either inevitable bodily fragmentation or mental degeneration into sexual aberration. The detail and intensity of the sex scenes in *The Temple of Dawn* are extraordinary, full of a writer's pleasure with the pen, yet they also carry an impression of despondency and dejection, of agitated melancholy and reticent rage. 'Human life is limited,' wrote Mishima the day he died, 'but I want to live forever.'

Both Honda and Mishima are wounded – carnality, desire, and self-loathing locked in a fierce embrace hurtling toward unavoidable self-destruction. Their very beings are mutilated, impaired, torn open and apart by the apparent contradictions they perceive between age and youth. To long for youthful flesh is to long for the past, to long for time to operate against its remorseless linearity. Our bodies decay, our minds yearn for the majesty and release of eternity. It is a fracture, a fissure in the fabric of existence. In Honda it generates his perversion and the ennui of his later years, entombed within the prison of the physical world, able only to observe, powerlessly and passively, from the periphery, trapped behind doors and walls, or the trees of a public park.

In Mishima the existential cleft spawned both his self-destruction and, be it thanked, *The Sea of Fertility*.

❦

In India, Honda became enthralled by the 'consciousness only' doctrine found in the yuishiki theory of Mahāyāna Buddhism – something neither he nor Mishima could fully subscribe to as a way of life, only as a fractional, transient aspect of ethical, intellectual, and metaphysical enquiry. (We can learn from Buddhism but do not have to 'believe' it.)

According to this concept, if we perceive ourselves less as a substance and more in flux and fluidity, like a waterfall that is anointed by the seeds which contain the dynamic energies of the cosmos, many of the mechanical problems of transmigration (which have bothered the rational Honda) fall away. Rather than being a fundamental, personal constituent disseminated from past to future, what we consider our 'self' is in fact a ubiquitous trace that infuses reality, like the scent of perfume. Past, present, and future do not exist; everything is merely a vast flow of consciousness, permeated with the kernels of karmic intrusion and disruption, as things are constantly created and destroyed. Transmigration is not the literal exchange of a being ('Kiyoaki'; 'Isao') across time, for this is a simplistic, somewhat naive conception; rather, it is merely a minor reflection of the ongoing condition of the universe's being.

Watching the funeral pyres on the Ganges, Honda realizes how the burning of the bodies returns people to their seed-like status, so the destructive power of the fires is also a creative, liberating force. This connects not only to the scorching happiness

Isao experienced as he committed seppuku at the end of *Runaway Horses*, the sun blazing behind his eyelids, but to the fire at the end of *The Temple of Dawn* – which destroys Honda's house but develops his heart and mind toward the wider manoeuvrings of the cosmos: 'All triviality had turned to ash and nothing but the most essential was important.'

Creation and obliteration are here shown to be two opposite but equal features of the ongoing process through which we become aware of reality (of which Buddhism, for Mishima, is an echo, a hope, not a universal truth). The universe is simply the endless flow of one state to another; nothing, neither time nor being, is autonomous, only an immense, noiseless, exquisite nothingness. This is the true nature of existence, as Honda will discover in the tranquil emptiness of the temple garden at the end of *The Decay of the Angel*, which, although on the surface dark and pessimistic, is perhaps nearer to the sanguine truth. So while Mishima, and *The Sea of Fertility*, derive many of their insights and philosophical arguments from Buddhism, both are clear never to endorse the Buddhist world view as such. Indeed, more often than not they actively repudiate it as a decadent 'Western' contamination or misleading folly, including, as we will see in the next chapter, the very concept of reincarnation itself.

Kiyoaki, Isao, and Ying Chan are to be regarded as part of one continual process – it was only from Honda's disconnected, passive position as an eyewitness that they, and their moles, appeared as separate yet interconnected manifestations. Although Honda is himself a part of the ongoing progression of existence, as an observer, a chronicler – and by implication a writer, like Mishima – he represents a requisite facet of the method by which the universe is discovered. The onlooker who is prepared to stand at a distance from the world, determined to witness the fact that they are disconnected from it, is quietly heroic.

As a sexual voyeur, Honda is despicable; but as an observer more generally he is a crucial figure. Through witness Honda enables unity, gives it meaning, since the world must be dismantled in order to be examined before it can be reassembled. Existence requires someone to differentiate and evaluate the world, someone able to recognize their role as both poor player and supreme spectator – and the spectator sees more of the game, even as they silently yearn to be a participant too.

Honda is immensely privileged to witness and scrutinize the world, despite the fact that he must be subject to the frustrations and annoyances this inevitably brings – which are made manifest through his sexual perversions. A superb literary invention, he does not fit the category of hero, anti-hero, or villain. Instead, he exists in a strange no man's land between them: ambiguous, anomalous, a disconsolate liminal space of opinion and inspection, not involvement. He is ambushed in a purgatorial maze, for although Honda has intellectually grasped some of the truths offered by the cosmos, emotionally he is unwilling to accept the denial of his being they represent.

It is an insolent, defiant attitude which anticipates the dark poetry and gloomy magic to come in *The Decay of the Angel*.

Chapter Fifteen

The Decay of the Angel
THE EMPTY COSMOS

There are many famous final lines in literature, and dazzling last words can define or redefine one's experience of a work, even making or breaking a book. They can leave you bewildered, enraptured, or enraged – hungry for more or sated and satisfied. *Ulysses* (1922) ends with Molly Bloom's radiantly orgasmic affirmation of life and love – 'and yes I said yes I will Yes.' (with its capitalized final 'Yes' and decisive full stop). *The Great Gatsby* (1925) closes by condensing the hollow nightmare of the American dream into fourteen memorable, mysterious words: 'So we beat on, boats against the current, borne back ceaselessly into the past.' The iconic folk horror of Shirley Jackson's short story 'The Lottery' (1948) concludes with a line that leaves it up to the reader to imagine the full terror of the sickening mob violence to be enacted: '"It isn't fair, it isn't right," Mrs Hutchinson screamed, and then they were upon her.'

Mishima's vast sojourn through the Japanese twentieth century ends with lines of eerie serenity and pessimistic tranquillity which prove to be both satisfying and deeply unsettling.

> There was no other sound. The garden was empty. He had come, thought Honda, to a place that had no memories, nothing.
> The noontide sun of summer flowed over the still garden.

It is an entirely unromantic, unheroic ending, as far from the fairy-tale nostalgia of *Spring Snow* or the audacious theatrics of *Runaway Horses* as is possible in time, place, and mood, situating *The Sea of Fertility*, and the reader, in a closing position of unnerving strangeness and doubt. The age of heroes is over; the age of blank, hollow reality and uncertainty is at hand.

In the last novel of the tetralogy we visit the void of old age, the arrogance of youth and the decadence of modernity. Accordingly, *The Decay of the Angel* (天人五衰, 'Tennin Gosui', 1971[152]) is a dark book, not only in itself but in the way it casts a retrospective shadow over the previous three parts of Mishima's final work. It binds together many of the foregoing characters and themes, while also determining that their spectacles of degeneration and deterioration were all part of a mirage of fixed, meaningless reality, a nothingness at the centre of both human life and the wider cosmos, in which we find ourselves confused, disorientated, and alone. Fables, heroes, and traditions are to be

---

152 Literally, 'Five Death Omens of Heavenly Beings', referring to the indication of angelic decay in Buddhist culture which Mishima's novel will map onto the character Tōru. Consequently, the original title directly alerts Japanese readers to anticipate and assess these five signs in the text.

replaced by the barren wilderness of contemporary truth, with its memoryless sterility, its vacuity.

The garden that closes *The Decay of the Angel* is a place of repudiation and abjuration, anti-myth and anti-romance, a forbidding materiality described in elegantly poetic prose, seducing and spurning us. We have arrived at a final place of our own making, forged by our own avarice and delusion. In this closing book, even (and especially) the tetralogy's binding motif of reincarnation, which has been both a plot device to emphasize continuity and a mystic symbol shunning the decay of reality, is – after mounting doubts – finally revealed to be if not an outright lie, then an illusion. And yet by exposing one form of illusion, Mishima is able to unmask and condemn another, more potent, one, revealing the wasteland of modernity for what it is and consequently urging a return to a more meaningful age, to more eloquent and significant traditions (embodied in Kiyoaki and Isao).

We shouldn't fool ourselves with reincarnation, Mishima argues, but neither should we deceive ourselves with empty greed and materialism. Honda's obsessive delusion of metempsychosis is connected to both his and Japan's wider aberrations and mistakes, misapprehensions which have created contemporary insincerity: the modern world is one giant delusion, a falsehood of hollow, disingenuous happiness. Across the span of his tetralogy, Mishima exposes, then convicts the twentieth century, imploring us to abandon its fantasies, deceits, and betrayals – even if this also means embracing a certain mythologization of Japan and Japanese history.

Like another vast mythic-national tetralogy, Richard Wagner's *Der Ring des Nibelungen* (1876), *The Sea of Fertility* is a complex work that perhaps inevitably encompasses, even welcomes, inconsistencies within its gigantic artistic, sociopolitical, and philosophical scope. To an extent, these works' internal contradictions and discrepancies mirror those of their creators, but their artistic/intellectual oversights at least are surely aspects we should acclaim and accept rather than try to solve or eliminate.

For all *The Sea of Fertility*'s difficulty and incongruity, its stark and uncompromising conclusion, there remains something cautiously optimistic about the ending to Mishima's final work, just as there is to the dusky final part of Wagner's *Ring*, *Götterdämmerung*. Amid the emptiness and obliteration, not only does *The Sea of Fertility* offer a subtle rallying cry for renewal, but it shows how literature can be the means for that regeneration. Mishima might have ultimately asserted action over words, but these disturbing novels persist as instruments for rejuvenation. They observe the mysteries, minutiae, and ambiguities of art and existence, bearing witness to the moral, metaphysical, and aesthetic problems that both inhibit and enhance our lives.

The cosmos might be empty, might be ugly, might be flawed. But art endures, imperfectly perfect, urging us on.

*

Although the last words to *Ulysses* are Molly Bloom's 'and yes I said yes I will Yes.', there is an additional – biographical and illuminating – postscript which follows in the text: 'Trieste-Zürich-Paris, 1914–1921'. Europe was ripping itself apart, but James Joyce, exiled from Ireland and trekking across the continent to steer clear of the bombs and generalized belligerence, was knocking together one of the most compassionate and civilized artistic visions in the history of humanity.

Likewise, *The Decay of the Angel*, a potentially pessimistic work in contrast to Joyce's unalloyed comedic hopefulness, ends not with 'the noontide sun of summer flowed over the still garden' but with a poignant addendum to the manuscript:

November 25, 1970.   *The Sea of Fertility*
                    THE END

And yet, for all the particular, precise dating of its manuscript, for all its reality and the contemporary, even future, nature of its setting, the last volume of *The Sea of Fertility* is anti-time, against time, outside time.[153] It is an ideal, and appropriate, closing Mishimian paradox which highlights both his yearning for a mythical past and his condemnation of an insincere present. By showing how modernity has invalidated the past – making myth and memories nothing – *The Decay of the Angel* invites the reader to escape time.

On the day that he wrote that conclusive 'FINIS' beneath the final words of his final book, Mishima killed himself. It was an act contrary to time but one he had long anticipated: as he bellowed his last sermon from the balcony of the Self-Defense Force headquarters in Tokyo, he kept checking his watch while repeating the word 'waited' again and again in his speech. His final act before the seppuku itself, before the cold blade entered his warm flesh, was to remove this watch, extricating himself from time, transcending it in the name of a romanticized, ideal emperor. That afternoon, as the shock of his death was announced, wider public time stood still: TV bulletins were interrupted, civic

---

153 *The Decay of the Angel* ends in the summer of 1975, some five years after Mishima's death.

events postponed, readers and non-readers alike astonished and aghast. It was a long way from the young man who had received a silver watch from the emperor on the day he graduated top of his class from high school – arguably the event at which his career and reputation began, entering time.

The popular, and all too often scholarly, obsession with Mishima's (admittedly flamboyant and conspicuous) death has tended to overshadow engagement with his achievements as a master of both literary performance and the Japanese language. Yet the manner of his demise helps elucidate the meaning of *The Sea of Fertility*, and vice versa (even if neither can be restricted to any such convenient juxtaposition). Mishima's suicide on 25 November 1970 spoke to and aroused something unsettling in the consciousness of Japanese society and identity, something which arguably resonates to this day and is witnessed in the alarmingly divided opinions his life and works generate – whether in the press, in political debate, on social media, or around the family dinner table. *The Sea of Fertility* asks 'Who am I?' not only on the lips of Honda but in the mouths of the Japanese people themselves. And many have not liked the answer to that question, especially when it came in the form of Mishima's bleak critique of modernity, of a country sold to the 'uncouth' Americans in spirit and commerce, a land of litter, loneliness, and languidity.

The arc of *The Sea of Fertility* flaunted the deterioration of Japanese society through the twentieth century: in the decay of the once noble but increasingly disgraced Honda, Mishima symbolically reproached his country for betraying its heritage, for sacrificing its traditions and integrity for cheap profit. Accordingly, the emasculation of the emperor which harassed Mishima so much was both a literal grievance and an emblematic accusation of broader betrayal, an indictment of false, empty progress. The writer presented the Japanese with a problem they knew only too well: no one, apart from some unhinged extremists, wanted a return to a feudal/imperial world of aeons ago – but few desired a complete dismissal of the past and its traditions either.

More than this, Mishima's ritualized death alerted the Japanese to a resurgence (if it had ever gone away) of the militarism that had led to catastrophic global conflict and of the strange traditions that lingered beneath the surface of a thriving modern economy, a thrusting decadent society. Mishima's death, and art, might be extreme, but did it not contain an element of truth about the material prosperity and spiritual poverty of the present day? Japan was hardly alone in either its commercialism or guilt (Germany and Britain, among others, have felt the complex burden of their fascist and imperial pasts), but the explosive nature of its most famous writer's death occurred at a delicate moment, embarrassing and destabilizing the country's diplomatic return to the world stage. Mishima's death, and his work, required either some decisive introspection or vehement condemnation (where it perhaps solicited both).

To this day, in Japan and abroad, to venture a declaration in favour of Mishima's work is, for many, to risk aligning oneself with his pathology, his politics, his apparent privileging of the elite, his dark and dangerous diagnosis of a broken, empty world. While it is true that an affinity for his art need not entail any sympathy for his sociopolitical or historical outlook, it is also true that Mishima's complexity and peculiarities in life have eclipsed his complexity and peculiarities in art. There are vital connections between the two, though we should be cautious in aligning them too straightforwardly.

No writer's life can be entirely separate from their art, but we need to locate more in Mishima, especially in *The Sea of*

Fertility, than simply the advocacy of a right-wing conservatism, a yearning for the past and obliteration of the present. Mishima is an erudite and multifaceted writer, just as *The Sea of Fertility* is an erudite and multifaceted work of art, and his anxieties and obsessions tend to be timeless human apprehensions which concern us all, whether we are Japanese or not, existing in the present, the past – or an as yet unimagined future.

Doubt is a perpetual feature of *The Sea of Fertility*. Throughout the text, we experience qualms and misgivings, reservations and uncertainties – whether concerning motive or character, experience or incident, theme or meaning. Mishima's text breeds suspicion and scepticism as we track the sweep of Honda's life across the twentieth century, following his youthful idealism and commitment to rationality and logic before his deterioration into perversity, disgrace, and emptiness, into a gradual realization of the nothingness at the heart of all existence. Eventually, in *The Decay of the Angel*, doubt comes to dominate his life, curdling into distrust and an extreme negativity as we, the reader, are led to query the veracity of much of the text ourselves, questioning not only its reality but its deeper imports.

With the appearance in *The Decay of the Angel* of Tōru, doubts increase, proliferating like pests while simultaneously coercing dark truths out of the text. The ostensible third reincarnation of *Spring Snow*'s Kiyoaki (following *Runaway Horse*'s Isao and *The Temple of Dawn*'s Ying Chan), the new character is suitably spotted with the three moles, gives the impression of being about the right age, and appears sanctioned by the remarkable physical splendour and good looks that solemnized the trio of earlier, ardent heroes. Yet from the outset, matters of timing and bodily beauty act as subterfuges to the pursuit.

This fresh hero seems the shadowy opposite of Kiyoaki, Isao, and Ying Chan, a malign figure governed by an unsympathetic intellect, exchanging their passions for shrugs of premeditated malevolence or indifference. Like Kiyoaki, Tōru has erotic tendencies, but his are icy and discourteous, apathetic, far from the sensual fixations of *Spring Snow*. Like Isao, Tōru will be given to violence, but his is a cold and calculated violence rather than the instinctive, impulsive passions that roused the hero of *Runaway Horses*. Like Ying Chan, Tōru is physically striking, but his callous, detached beauty carries none of Ying Chan's honest, simple sensuality. And there is a further difference: Tōru does not die at twenty (though he comes close).

We first meet him, unobtrusively, in the opening chapter to *The Decay of the Angel*, a short but superb blend of poetic philosophical musing with shrewd characterization and subtly prophetic plotting. We open with a powerful image of the ocean, so often in Mishima a symbol of being, and there follows a fragmented, uneven meditation, describing phantom, obscure ships and the sea in a fog of longing, mist, and misapprehension. For several pages we are carried through a domain of constantly fluctuating sea- and skyscapes: overcast or sunlit, blustery or serene. It is a disorientating beginning, at once everything and nothing: elusive, vague, unnerving, tantalizing in spite of the confusion, soothing despite the unease. We don't know who is scanning the sea and sky, or why. Then, at the close of this brief opening chapter, we are told of Tōru, a mysterious figure whose job it is to watch the sea and its ships.

The ocean Tōru so meticulously observes is an endless, nameless nothingness which summons 'all the evil in nature' and exists as an 'absolute anarchy' suggesting the absurdity and emptiness at the heart of existence. From the outset, the dark metaphysics of *The Decay of the Angel* are thus established; they will continue throughout until Honda is similarly submerged by an immense cosmic nothingness in the temple garden. Passion, pain, logic, laughter – everything in human life is part of the same nothingness and meaninglessness. Past and future carry no meaning; there is only the now, everything collapsed into a formless unity like the depths of the ocean, whose surface ferocity and commotion are just that: superficial, ephemeral storms, as nothing compared to the vast and unfathomable abyss beneath.

Crucially, in order to link the characters, the text cuts away for a chapter to Honda, now widowed, in his late seventies, who walks the dirty, dilapidated coastline near where Tōru works. The images of decline and detritus stack up: 'a great litter of garbage lay scoured by the sea winds. Empty Coca-Cola bottles, food cans, paint cans, non-perishable plastic bags, detergent boxes, bricks, bones.' There is nothing exotic or magical about this setting: it is gloomy, moody, unsightly, forsaken and forlorn. We are in the early summer of 1970 – almost ready to head into the posthumous future of Mishima's own timeline – and this is utterly contemporary Japan, a polluted wasteland of literal and metaphorical debris. In *The Decay of the Angel*, Mishima reveals *The Sea of Fertility* as a work now operating against myth, where truth-seeking ends in disenchantment and romance exists only as an ironic distinction to decline and corrosion.

The title of Mishima's final book, of course, hints at the hostile thematic concerns of the novel, as well as its Buddhist and literary connections. 'The Decay of the Angel' refers to both the 'Five Death Omens of Heavenly Beings' in Buddhist culture and – to those familiar with classical Japanese theatre – to the Noh drama *Hagoromo* (*'Robe of Feathers'*). In this widely performed ancient play, which echoes the swan maiden motif familiar from global folklore, an angel comes to earth and loses her magical feather mantle without which she cannot return to paradise (after she carelessly hangs it on a branch, it is taken from her by a fisherman). Eventually, after she is compelled to dance, it is restored to her, and she can joyfully ascend to the heavens once again. Mishima employs this eerie, ethereal drama not to suggest that there really are angels and other mystical forces at work in the world but to accentuate what contemporary Japan, with its material obsessions, has lost.

Early on in *Decay*, Honda journeys to the coppice where the mythical *Hagoromo* is said to have been set.[154] But he encounters no fairy-tale idyll. Instead, he finds yet more pollution and deterioration, empty commercialism and rampant decay. Beauty exists only in reading or dreaming, dreams which mirror the delusions of waking life where we imagine a world uncontaminated by the litter of memory as well as the garbage of modernity. Soon after seeing the now ugly pine grove, Honda dreams of a purer one, populated not only by angels but Kiyoaki, Isao, and Ying Chan, a dream which leads to a depressing awareness of reality and the insinuation of future sorrow (including both Honda's

---

154 Miho no Matsubara, Shizuoka, a seven-kilometre-long sandy seashore lined by pine trees with Mount Fuji looming in the background, memorably represented in Utagawa Hiroshige's woodblock series *Thirty-Six Views of Mount Fuji* (1858 version). In 1915, it was designated one of the 'Three New Views of Japan', in 1922 chosen as a National Place of Scenic Beauty, and in 2013 added to UNESCO's World Heritage List.

humiliation for voyeurism in a public park and the empty garden that will close the novel). All is barren, corrupt, corroded.

During a discussion of *Hagoromo* with Keiko (the lesbian from *The Temple of Dawn* who slept with Ying Chan while Honda peeped, now a close friend and travelling companion after his wife's death), Honda relates how the fisherman who discovered the angel saw how she exhibited the five signs of decay familiar from Buddhist discourse. This will have devastating significance for the moral and metaphysical outcome of *The Sea of Fertility*. Literary sources vary, Honda says, including a number of greater and lesser signs, but there is overall agreement on a quintet of major symptoms:

    i.   Its crown of flowers fades
    ii. Its clothes become soiled by sweat
   iii. It produces a putrid odour
   iv. It becomes enveloped in darkness
    v. It remains in one place and loses its joy

Such signs will come and go throughout the novel, appearing as indications not only of the profound connection between Honda and Tōru but as signals of their parallel deterioration, as well as the wider corrosion of Japan.

In *Spring Snow, Runaway Horses,* and *The Temple of Dawn*, the reincarnation motif has generated three active heroes – Kiyoaki, Isao, and Ying Chan – who serve as foils to the passive, rational Honda (though he has begun to lose those characteristics by the third novel, as he attempts to play a part in the aura of the active/ physical). For the final part of *The Sea of Fertility*, Mishima needed to maintain the illusion of rebirth and hope, while simultaneously accelerating the process of decline and decay. Thus, although the fourth hero is tentatively shown as connected to the earlier three, he is also their opaque inverse and a fitting figure to represent the fraudulent desert of modernity. Moreover, Tōru and Honda himself are alarmingly alike. Although physically different – Honda is a desiccated, ugly old man; Tōru a beautiful sixteen-year-old – both are curious, degenerative concoctions of the active and passive; both influence and observe, scrutinize and engineer, watch and manipulate. Both will end up mutually tormenting the other.

After their discussion of *Hagoromo* and the angels, Keiko and Honda encounter Tōru in his watchtower or signal station, the old man immediately realizing that this boy bears a significance, a consequence, a correlation to himself. Though they carry surface differences, something deeper attaches them: a momentous and appalling malevolence, linked to their reciprocal deterioration and binding them together like a mirror and its reflection. Honda's body is obviously in a shrivelled state; Tōru's is youthful and fit but nonetheless displays alarmingly evocative emblems of an angel's decay. When first Keiko and Honda meet Tōru, he has withered flowers in his hair, a gift from his only apparent friend (an unhinged girl named Kinué who is profoundly ugly yet, in a bizarre reversal of body dysmorphic disorder, believes herself to be astoundingly beautiful, constantly harassed by admiring men). Trapped in his little watchtower, Tōru sweats copiously, while remaining in this one location to eat, sleep, and work.

All this suggests to the ageing Honda that there is something significant about this isolated young man, that he carries an importance for his own destiny and lonely quests for meaning. He does and he will, but in ways that will convey only emptiness and disappointment. Honda's mistake is to spot the three moles on Tōru's side and to automatically, inevitably, conclude that this boy must be the next rebirth of his long-lost friend Kiyoaki. To secure his own fantasy, Honda makes the hasty decision to adopt this orphan and raise him as his own offspring. Honda thus embraces Tōru as his son and heir, but expects him, as the reincarnation, to die at twenty, allowing the passive father a vicious, manipulative control over an active hero, savouring his knowledge, apparently superior to that of the oblivious boy – watching and waiting as Tōru's predestined fate approaches. Thus Tōru's story begins as a form of fairy tale, not unlike the first three novels of the tetralogy, but it does so only in order to dwindle sadistically into a nightmare reality.[155]

Tōru himself, while parallel to Honda and fundamentally unlike Kiyoaki, Isao, and Ying Chan, also insinuates nostalgic but ultimately upsetting connections with earlier Mishimian heroes – more authentically romantic figures like the eponymous mariner Ryuji in *The Sailor Who Fell from Grace with the Sea*, or the fisherman Shinji in *The Sound of Waves*. Like them, Tōru is young, handsome, and associated with the sea, but Ryuji's ocean is one of sensation and nomadic drifting, of exotic ports and mysterious women, while Shinji's coastal marine is a spectacular unified potency of nature, environment, flora, and fauna working

---

155 In *Götterdämmerung*, the fourth and final part of Wagner's *Der Ring des Nibelungen*, itself a form of distorted, perverted fairy tale, the villainous manipulator Hagen sits waiting for his evil plans to come to fruition: 'Here I sit on guard, watching the house' (I.ii). Hagen's music, like that associated with the ring which gives Wagner's tetralogy its name, is a corrosive, destructive force, eating its way into the fabric of the score.

as one. Tōru's sea is a vast nothingness that is also a mechanical, marketable product, a place of commerce and communication, dry messages and cold logic. The fantasy, imagination, and enjoyment of *Sailor* and *Sound* are here banished by the ugly stains of oil, the obnoxious contaminations of industry. Although sailing and fishing are jobs, they carry a sense of play and freedom which have been replaced by the confinements of Tōru's bland, entirely unheroic work.

Like Honda, Tōru watches – coldly, passively, accurately, realistically. But where this passive nature might have led to a fascinating change across the novel as he discarded his lassitude and assumed a more heroic disposition, in fact it is a passivity which lingers untouched, unbothered, before simply becoming malicious and rancorous, sadistically emulating the calculating and unscrupulous spirit of Honda. Upon his adoption and transition to bigger and better things, as Honda mentors the boy in Western thoughts and manners, Tōru's personality develops into a parodic distortion of the lonely boy in the watchtower. There is delectable irony at work as Tōru, groomed as a devious experiment, begins to exploit and control any and all of those around him, including Honda himself. The manipulator becomes the manipulatee in a dark dance of mutual manoeuvring.

Tōru's repayment of Honda's lavish material and educational gifts is a magnificently prolonged eruption of hatred and resentment. He annexes and takes charge of Honda's home, humiliating the old judge and physically intimidating him. He dishonours and demeans his fiancée to circumvent a marriage his adoptive father has prearranged, while moving his deranged chum, Kinué, into Honda's home. He is lewd and lascivious, and when the pathetic Honda is caught as a peeping Tom in a public park, Tōru schemes to have his benefactor pronounced senile so that he can access the old man's pile of cash. And all the time, Honda waits on the other side of this abuse, watching the clock tick down to Tōru's twentieth birthday, when, accordingly, the boy will die – if he is indeed made of the same matter as the other heroes.

Gloriously aloof, Tōru does not partake in the lives of those he manipulates. He is empty, devoid of life- and love-giving energy, preferring to remain detached like his younger self watching ships at sea. He observes, scrutinizes, but only for cold, meaningless ends – even Honda's voyeurism, while futile, at least has an erotic exhilaration to go with it. But while he seems to be beating Honda at his own game, Tōru has not counted on learning the truth behind this sport.

When Tōru discovers from Keiko the real reason he was adopted (as part of Honda's quest for truth regarding the reincarnation and to assert himself as an arch-conspirator over an active hero), it sends him into a tumult of desolation and despair. Realizing there is, in fact, nothing special about him at all, he takes poison – industrial wood alcohol – but rather than dying suffers the ultimate ironic and Dantean punishment for an observer/voyeur: he is blinded. A man whose professional occupation involved watching, and then whose later life concerned the vigilant manipulation of others, has experienced the greatest tragic, if vindicated, fate. This would-be custodian and keeper now needs looking after. It is a drab and dreary downfall for Tōru, one that anticipates the empty garden at the end of the novel, which the text now begins to grope toward.

While Isao was dazzled by an explosive inner light at the moment of his self-willed death, he remained able to comprehend the sea via the eye of his romantic identity; Tōru can now never again glimpse the sea, that potent emblem of being and the romantic symbol that gave him something captivating amid his monotonous employment and frigid intellectualism. Becoming entirely passive and dependent, Tōru is compelled into a liaison with the increasingly bizarre Kinué, and he gradually exhibits further signs of the decaying angel outlined above.

As someone who cannot see her own ugliness, observing herself and the world via an atrociously distorted lens, Kinué makes for an unpleasantly ideal companion to the sightless, decaying Tōru. And all this is exhibited with a horrific credibility: Mishima makes Tōru's grotesque alteration materialize with a reality that makes for some grim reading – especially when Kinué scatters flowers over her inert companion and swathes him in a grubby robe. We are light years from the ordered, well-turned-out meticulousness of Kiyoaki or Isao (and Mishima is doubtless having a slight dig at lax attitudes among contemporary youth in matters of dress and personal grooming).

For all the irresistible dreadfulness of Tōru's demise, it is Honda upon whom our interest lies as *The Sea of Fertility* moves toward its own termination. With tantalizing timing, Tōru's blinding occurs just before his twentieth birthday – that is, just before the time passes for his status as the reincarnation to be confirmed. Where there was doubt (and delay) as to the exact age of Ying Chan's death, here there is nothing but the relentless cold tramp of the clock. Mishima's text is ruthlessly callous and unsympathetic, 20 March coming and going with an airy indifference: 'He showed no sign of dying.' For Tōru, it is simply another day in darkness, as he begins to learn Braille and listens to records; for Honda, it is 'proof' of the falsehood of the reincarnations, and soon after, his own body begins to exhibit signs of decay, with severe stomach pains and awareness of a tumour. Honda and Tōru, those symbols and embodiments of decay, are both falling apart.

Readers of *The Sea of Fertility* have often been disappointed, unconvinced, or confused by Tōru, but they have often perhaps misunderstood his role in both the novel and wider cycle. Mishima's tetralogy is not a surface-led work concerning a single soul revisited over several lifetimes but a profound exploration of the nothingness lying at the heart of the incurable disease of (modern) existence. It charts not the Kiyoaki / Isao / Ying Chan / Tōru reincarnation trajectory – which, it turns out, is no trajectory at all but a series of coincidences and/or projections – but the psychological and spiritual journey of Honda, the only character to appear in all four books.

What we experience as we read the constituent novels of *The Sea of Fertility* is not a detached, impartial view of historical time and event but a reflection of Honda's cognitive, moral, and emotional processes. This is not to suggest that the reincarnations/heroes were made up but rather that their connection to objectivity is less significant than their relationship with Honda's subjective world. Mishima meticulously constructs and dismantles the myths of fantasy and hope, which find their fullest realization in the folkloric tradition of reincarnation, an illusion which serves only to shield us from the harsh truth about the emptiness of the cosmos (but which should propel us toward more meaningful values and experiences).

Those with only a casual acquaintance with *The Sea of Fertility* have often supposed that it endorses a Buddhist world view, especially with regards to reincarnation. Yet Honda's (and Mishima's) fascination with the philosophical and metaphysical tenets of the faith only goes so far, setting them up only to pull them to pieces. In part this is because of Mishima's assertion that Buddhism and reincarnation were imports alien to Japanese culture, systems of belief which tainted and polluted the country, just like certain economic or industrial endeavours had, and which were a manifestation of decadence which exerted a negative sway on the authenticity of the Japanese spirit. Reincarnation is synthetic, false, insincere, a lazy means through which Honda et al. attempt to locate order and continuity in a cosmos that is in fact hectic, anarchic, inconsequential, and essentially impenetrable.

At least to some extent, Honda has successfully controlled Tōru – though much of this rather hollow triumph has been down to Tōru's despair and self-isolation. Moreover, this very victory undermines his quest for cosmic truth since the young man's endurance beyond his twentieth birthday fatally destabilizes the legitimacy of the reincarnation(s). Honda's logical mind cannot stay still when faced with the likelihood that the whole sequence of regenerations was untrue. His tumour prompts him to further seek the truth at a place of origin and return, of source and homecoming: the temple where *Spring Snow* ended and where Satoko, Kiyoaki's lover, has spent her life ever since, renouncing the world to become a nun (and now the monastery's abbess).

It is one of Mishima's great ironic surprises that in this, his final work, he positions Honda exactly in the steps of the earlier, and active, hero Kiyoaki. That earlier quest, for a radiant, youthful love, is here replaced by the aged, gasping paces of an old man looking to find meaning to not only his whole life but that of the wider universe. Resolved to shadow his friend Kiyoaki's footsteps on the day of his death six decades before as he waited outside the temple for Satoko, Honda travels alone to this temple and struggles up the long mountain road. It is an unaffectedly, honourably heroic pursuit, perhaps the most genuinely courageous and intrepid of all Honda's journeys, as he places himself not only in great physical suffering but, given his health and the hot weather, mortal danger.

Mishima gives us the scene over a number of agonizing pages but in prose of delicate economy and grace. We seem to feel every step Honda takes, every wheezing breath and drop of sweat, as he moves slowly up the road. The doubts of the tetralogy reimpose themselves as both Honda and reader question whether he will make it to his destination (never mind what might occur when he gets there). It is an excruciating but exquisite journey, thick with sensations in sight, sound, and smell: pine trees, the endless sky, the heat of summer, the odours of the body and the air.

As he makes his lonely, unbearable way to the temple on this purgatorial pilgrimage, Honda himself starts to show some signs of the decay of the angel. He notices that the path ahead is draped in dark shadows, made by the trees but seeming to come from another source entirely; he observes shrunken flowers along the roadside, all portentously and menacingly dry; sweat comes through his shirt, soaking his back and jacket, producing a fetid smell. A white butterfly seems to lead him on his journey yet stays low to the ground, appearing pulled by the weight of existence, like the decaying angel's wings, unable to convey it from earth back into heaven.

By journey's end, doubt and fear set in again as Honda becomes reluctant to enter the temple and meet with Satoko after so many decades. Stepping inside, however, he is consumed by a sense of harmony and tranquillity, inviting expectation that this pursuit will end in a victory. As in all good myths, Honda has come to a holy place to seek the guidance of a blessed religious figure who will reveal to him the truth. But this is Mishima, late

Mishima – *very late* Mishima – and such an idealistically, even whimsically, gratifying ending will not be forthcoming. Myths and fairy tales are over, and reality is at hand. Honda finally meets with Satoko: she has grown older but not deteriorated; become purified rather than decayed. She seems to represent an alternative to Honda's decline – all flesh will age, but one's perspective on, one's attitude toward, existence will determine how far one appears sanctified or desecrated.

Over the course of the long arc of *The Sea of Fertility*, Honda has aged considerably in mind and body, as he has rummaged for signs that death leads not to everlasting oblivion and annihilation but to something more, that the fundamental quintessence or substance of being, one's spirit or soul, lives on, somehow reborn in another form to live again. His is an understandable anxiety that most humans face when confronted by their own mortality, and explains why so many turn to religion. All Honda's life has been a quest to extend his reach beyond the boundedness of his unsatisfactory existence on earth. Life and being, for Honda, are rendered meaningless without their eternal renewal. Having lived out her life cloistered in the same place, as Honda travelled the world and engaged in all manner of restless, fruitless activities, Satoko appears unconcerned with the truth about the afterlife and reincarnation. She is stoic, composed, unable (or unwilling) to even recall the person (Kiyoaki) who for Honda might offer evidence of the processes of rebirth.

During their discussion, she insists she never knew anyone called Kiyoaki – and, moreover, insinuates that he never existed. Honda now has to grapple with doubts concerning his own being, his own memories, his own life, even the history of Japan in the twentieth century. Satoko's 'amnesia' regarding Kiyoaki might be just that: the result of faulty memories in old age; it might simply be a rebuke to the friend of the lover who caused her so much shame and ruined her life. It might also be the truth, a dizzying denial that any of the foregoing pages conveyed any truth in reality (which, as fiction, of course they have not).

The 'truth' regarding Satoko's memory, such as the word can carry meaning amid so many layers of doubt and distrust, is probably best seen as a combination of different features of each interpretation. Yet its real power comes when it is connected to the lines which follow, when her visitor is in the temple garden: 'There was no other sound. The garden was empty. He had come, thought Honda, to a place that had no memories, nothing.' Satoko is not claiming that Kiyoaki never existed or that she cannot evoke or remember him but that, in the grand scheme of things, it doesn't matter. There is no past or future, only an eternal now of nothingness and emptiness, an unfathomable abyss of being. To recollect Kiyoaki is as absurd as predicting whether it will rain or shine in a year's time.

After leaving Satoko's presence, Honda had walked to the temple garden wondering if he himself was merely an illusion – a contemplation familiar to those who question the nature of reality. Seeing the summer clouds ranging 'their dizzying shoulders over the green hills', he arrives in the 'bright, quiet' garden realizing that there are 'no memories, nothing', that ultimately his existence is empty and meaningless. Bleak as the outlook might seem, it also brings peace, and the whole brief closing scene is suffused with an enigmatic air of tranquillity and acceptance. Honda seems finally to accede and acknowledge his own finitude, even if that prospect entails an absence of meaning and a parade of nothingness. He can now avoid the confusing, distracting false promises of myth and hope, ethereal dreams and uncanny deceptions. He aspired toward heaven and eternity but now accepts his place on the earth, a decayed angel in the still garden under the noontide sun.

Amid the exquisitely strange serenity of the garden, Mishima's beatifically economical prose exerts an extraordinary power. We discover a man, and realize that the cycle of novels which revolved around him are not about the truth of reincarnation. They explore a man who refused to accept that our lives are all we have, who could not believe that our brief earthly span is the entirety of existence. Honda, the man who could be so pitilessly, coldly logical, in fact burned with a searing passion for existence, desperate that it would not end with his own death. Honda is human, weak, full of misdirected, illogical hope and what is often called sin. He lacks certain kinds of courage and discipline, but his boldness in searching for truth and meaning surely earns our respect, even our gratitude, at the same time as we denounce him for his iniquities.

The emptiness of the garden at the close of *The Sea of Fertility* might imply unequivocal judgement upon the man who acted in such malevolent ways – manipulating others, controlling acquaintances, spying on strangers. But Mishima is not interested in moral condemnation when the stakes are as high as the meaning and nature of existence. He knew how close to Honda he himself was, how difficult it was to live a life that seems to lack courage, that merely envied and admired those outside themselves, like Kiyoaki or Isao, who acted out their convictions, devoting their lives to their ideals. Mishima feared becoming even more like Honda as he aged, and chose to celebrate and endorse his active heroes with an act of violence that, for a moment, made him one of them – writing his own meticulous, difficult poetry in his own hot crimson blood.

But where does the ending of *The Sea of Fertility*, with its serene desolation and apparent confirmation of the meaninglessness of existence, leave the reader? With words. With art. With beauty. Although he was less formally innovative or stylistically experimental than many of his peers, Mishima's legacy in language and literature prevails: in its radiance, in its poignancy, and in its collective powers of communication. His final writing was, in many respects, a return to simplicity, to universality, and to the kind of frugal tragic valour which he had long striven for, pushing words to mimic the tense, taut bodies and actions of his heroes (both inside and outside his work).

With its majestic, elegant cadences, formal airs, and sense of cultivated refinement, the language of *The Sea of Fertility* tends to operate against the zealous characters, peculiar circumstances, and dark themes of its own narrative. This is one of the great and familiar paradoxes of Mishima's art, one which helps illuminate the power and persistence of his prose. It has ensured that, whatever occurred outside his pages, his writing has endured and will continue to speak to all those that seek aesthetic and intellectual nourishment amid the blank insignificance of an empty cosmos.

After all, as he sits in the temple garden, Honda finds exquisite beauty as well as nothingness.

Annotated Bibliography

Persona: A Biography of Yukio Mishima
Naoki Inose
(Expanded adaptation and translation, Hiroaki Sato)

A vast and encyclopaedic tome. Naoki Inose's original biography has an especially detailed survey of the bureaucratic and political aspects of Japanese history as they are connected with Mishima; Hiroaki Sato's English version adapts and expands a number of areas in Mishima's life, particularly those relating to his literary, theatrical, and ideological theories and activities, as well as his pursuit of numerous sports and martial activities, the author-translator elegantly bringing the two together. Although at times the translation can be a little awkward, on the whole this is an invaluable book: exhaustive in its detail and rich with insights into Mishima's life and work.

Yukio Mishima
Damian Flanagan

In his refreshing, at times even quite radical, reappraisal of Mishima's life and work, Flanagan writes with style and conviction about the problems and paradoxes at the centre of both. Flanagan has done a special service for those keen to get away from the overly familiar portrayals of Mishima the right-wing patriot, discovering instead the more complex, philosophical figure behind the nationalist facade. He also devotes considerable time to disentangling the fact and fiction within Mishima's memoirs, in so doing allowing a shrewder analysis of his evolution as a writer. A relatively short but very welcome addition to contemporary Mishima studies.

Mishima: A Biography
John Nathan

A persuasive and frequently perceptive biography from the man Mishima often considered his 'official' English translator, Nathan's book is both an absorbing, shrewd portrait of Mishima the man and a useful study of many of his works.

The Life and Death of Yukio Mishima
Henry Scott Stokes

A more personal biography from a British journalist who lived for a long time in Japan, knew Mishima well, and often made controversial statements surrounding Japanese history (especially events such as the Nanjing Massacre). Scott Stokes is helpfully honest in expressing his frustrations at the contradictions within his subject, though he can, on occasion, also be a little fussy and fastidious in his desire to convey his (undoubted) insights into both Japan and Mishima. A valuable book but one to be read with caution, *The Life and Death of Yukio Mishima* offers a number of powerful, if subjective, perspectives, not least from one of the few non-Japanese able to gain close access to Mishima.

Escape from the Wasteland: Romanticism and Realism in the Fiction of Mishima Yukio & Oe Kenzaburo
Susan J. Napier

An exceptionally good academic study of Mishima and Ōe, exploring their similarities and differences and the way their work investigates the recurrent emptiness and pain of contemporary Japanese life. Napier not only maintains a high degree of scholarship throughout but writes beautifully, and her book is full of articulate readings and elegant insights. Unafraid to delve deeply into the complex nexus of sex and violence at the heart of these writers' works, this is a revitalizing, invigorating, and essential part of Japanese literary studies.

Five Modern Japanese Novelists
Donald Keene

A wonderful scholarly introduction to contemporary Japanese literature, as well as a fascinating chronicle of the author's own lifelong love affair with Japan, Keene's work is full of precious insights and valuable perspectives on not only Mishima but Tanizaki, Kawabata, Abe, and Shiba, along with the wider cultural contexts of their writing.

Mishima, Aesthetic Terrorist: An Intellectual Portrait
Andrew Rankin

In his powerful, often thought-provoking academic book which explores the radical nature of Mishima's life and art, Rankin is especially good at exploring the deep realms of Mishima's Japanese essays in order to connect them with the more well-done fictional works. At times the book is a little pugnacious and repetitive, but the evaluations are often worthwhile.

Deadly Dialectics: Sex, Violence and Nihilism in the World of Yukio Mishima
Roy Starrs

A brilliant academic study of the intellectual background to Mishima's fiction, with particular insights into the way Mishima engaged with European philosophical novels (Goethe, Dostoyevsky, Thomas Mann). Pleasingly written and full of astute, judicious understanding of its complex subject.

Mishima: A Vision of the Void
Marguerite Yourcenar

This famous, pioneering book is a landmark in non-Japanese engagement with Mishima. Although some of it feels a little dated, and a lot of the prose is rather ostentatious and at times obscure, it offers a number of precious insights into Mishima and his work.

Mishima's Sword: Travels in Search of a Samurai Legend
Christopher Ross

At the quirkier end of things, a personal travelogue-type book: a writer sets out for Japan to discover some of the people, places, and ideas behind Mishima's suicide (as well as the location of the antique sword which beheaded him). A charming, often quite funny, mixture of memoir, travel writing, and philosophical pondering, it is a hodgepodge of engaging perspectives – a bento box of treasures.

Acknowledgements

I would first like to thank a number of Japanese friends and colleagues whose bonds (and assistance with the rigours of the Japanese language!) have meant so much to me over the years, not least in the conception and production of this book: Aki Nishikawa, Naoki Yasuda, Chisato Kusunoki, Hiromi Matsuda, Hana Kobayashi, Sachiko Tanaka, Aiko Watanabe, Aiko Nakamura, and Kenji Matsumoto. I would also like to thank my dear friends Theresa and Irfan Tayabali for their many kindnesses over the years, from our time in Japan together to this day.

Furthermore, I would like to express my gratitude to the staff and curators of the National Institute of Japanese Literature, Tokyo; the Mishima Yukio Literary Museum, Yamanakako; the Japanese Embassy, London; and the British Embassy Tokyo for their kind and prompt assistance on a number of matters, especially as this book was going to press.

My editor, Elyse Lyon, has – once again – been a model of tolerance, endurance, diligence, and brilliance, seeing what I cannot and always knowing what I am trying to say. Any errors are, of course, my own.

My wife's perspicacity and patience have been, as ever, absolutely essential to my work: thank you again, darling, for your endless love and support during the writing and revising of this tricky book. My life could not be lived without you.

I would also like to thank the great people, places, and institutions of Hiroshima, which made my years in Japan so enjoyable and illuminating. Hiroshima is famous around the world for a terrible moment in human history, yet the city's nobility, energy, and charm in the aftermath of this horror have never ceased to astonish and inspire me.

Finally I would like to thank Steven Lally. Steve is a brilliant writer for movies and the small screen, but he is also a very dear friend. This book is dedicated to you, Steve – in admiration, with all my love, and in immeasurable appreciation for the many kindnesses you've given me over the years.

About the Author

Dr David Vernon is a writer and academic. He studied at Trinity College, University of Oxford, before teaching language and literature in China and Japan. After returning to Europe, he completed his doctorate on Shakespeare's tragicomedies in Berlin and taught English literature for many years in London. He has written extensively on classical music and literature, and his first five books, *Disturbing the Universe: Wagner's Musikdrama*, *Beauty and Sadness: Mahler's 11 Symphonies*, *Ada to Zembla: The Novels of Vladimir Nabokov*, *Beethoven: The String Quartets*, and *Sun Forest Lake: The Symphonies & Tone Poems of Jean Sibelius*, were published to critical acclaim. He lives in the Highlands of Scotland.

www.ingramcontent.com/pod-product-compliance
Lightning Source LLC
Chambersburg PA
CBHW050611170726
48283CB00001B/202